THE DARK ROAD

Ma Jian was born in Qingdao, China in 1953. He is the author of *Stick Out Your Tongue*, which in 1987 led to the permanent banning of his books in China, *Red Dust*, winner of the Thomas Cook Travel Book Award 2002, *The Noodle Maker*, and *Beijing Coma* which narrated the Tiananmen Square protests of 1989.

While writing *The Dark Road*, Ma Jian travelled through the backwaters of central and southern China. Posing as an official reporter, he visited family planning offices and hospitals where forced abortions and sterilisations are carried out. He later adopted the guise of an itinerant worker and lived among fugitives of the One Child Policy who scrape a living on the Yangtze River and the vast waste sites of Guangdong Province.

Flora Drew has translated five works by Ma Jian into English. She studied Chinese at the School of Oriental and African Studies and worked in television and film. She lives in west London with Ma Jian and their four children.

MA JIAN

The Dark Road

TRANSLATED FROM THE CHINESE BY
Flora Drew

VINTAGE BOOKS
London

Published by Vintage 2014

2 4 6 8 10 9 7 5 3 1

Copyright © Ma Jian 2013
Translation copyright © Flora Drew 2013

Ma Jian has asserted his right under the Copyright, Designs
and Patents Act 1988 to be identified as the author of this work

First published in Great Britain in 2013 by
Chatto & Windus

Vintage
Random House, 20 Vauxhall Bridge Road,
London SW1V 2SA

www.vintage-books.co.uk

Addresses for companies within The Random House Group Limited
can be found at: www.randomhouse.co.uk/offices.htm

The Random House Group Limited Reg. No. 954009

A CIP catalogue record for this book
is available from the British Library

ISBN 9780099572268

The Random House Group Limited supports the Forest Stewardship
Council® (FSC®), the leading international forest-certification
organisation. Our books carrying the FSC label are printed on FSC®-
certified paper. FSC is the only forest-certification scheme supported
by the leading environmental organisations, including Greenpeace.
Our paper procurement policy can be found at:
www.randomhouse.co.uk/environment

Typeset in 10.25/15.5 pt Fresco by
Palimpsest Book Production Ltd, Falkirk, Stirlingshire

Printed and bound by CPI Group (UK) Ltd, Croydon, CR0 4YY

For Flora

The Dark Road

KEYWORDS: *sterilised, dugout, breast milk, family planning squad, date tree, longevity locket, Nuwa Cave.*

The infant spirit sees Mother sitting on the edge of her bed, her hands clutching her swollen belly, her legs trembling with fear . . .

Meili rests her hands on her pregnant belly and feels the fetus's heartbeat thud like a watch beneath a pillow. The heavy banging on the compound gate grows louder, the dim light bulb hanging from the ceiling sways. The family planning officers have come to get me, she says to herself. She raises her feet from the basin of warm water in which they've been soaking, hides under her quilt and waits for the gate to be forced open.

This afternoon, as warm sunlight was melting the last patches of snow on the maize bundles in the yard, their neighbour Fang was laying out sesame seeds to dry, her three-week-old baby suckling at her breast, when suddenly four family planning officers stormed in and dragged her off to be sterilised. Fang kicked and howled like a sow being towed to the slaughterhouse. The glutinous rice she'd left soaking in a basin on the ground in preparation for dumplings was overturned, and two mongrel ducks scuttled over to peck at the grains. Eventually they managed to tie her hands together and force her into the open back of their truck. Her white vest was ripped by then, and her shoulders smeared with blood that had fallen from the shaven-headed officer's nose when she'd kicked him in the face. He was crouching at her feet now, binding her flailing legs with rope and firmly securing her to the metal bars. Trapped from the waist down, Fang leaned over the side and shouted: 'I damn the eight generations of your ancestors! Have you forgotten that every one of you was nursed by your mother as a child? And now you dare tear a baby from its mother's breast? May your families produce no sons for nine generations! . . .' Meili climbed over the wall and scooped Fang's baby into her arms, and pleaded with a uniformed officer to let Fang go. 'If she's sterilised, her milk will run dry. At least wait until her baby's three months old.'

'Keep out of this!' he replied, rubbing his cold red hands together. 'Haven't you read the public notice? If a woman is found to be pregnant without authorisation, every household within one hundred metres of her home will be punished. You should have reported her to the authorities before the child was born. As her next-door neighbour, you'll be fined at least a thousand yuan.'

Meili didn't recognise the officers, and presumed they'd been drafted in from neighbouring counties. Had she not been afraid that they'd notice her pregnant bulge, she would have run to Fang with a blanket and wrapped it over her shoulders. Instead, she stood rooted to the spot and watched the truck trundle away, Fang jolting up and down at the back, breast milk dripping from her exposed red nipples.

The banging at the gate pauses then starts again. 'It's me – Kongzi!' she hears her husband cry out. 'Open up!' Remembering at last that a couple of hours ago she wedged a spade firmly against the gate so that it couldn't be opened from the outside, she runs out into the yard and lets him in.

Kongzi staggers into the house, his hair wild and his gaze distracted, and paces restlessly about the room. He's just returned from a Party meeting. 'The squad of family planning officers that arrived yesterday has been sent from Hexi Town. The village Party office isn't large enough for their purposes, so they've commandeered a classroom in the school and are doing the abortions and sterilisations there. This crackdown will be merciless.'

'What are we going to do?' Meili says with fear in her eyes.

'I don't know. The officers were clear: any pregnant woman who doesn't have a birth permit will be given an immediate abortion and a 10,000-yuan fine.'

'Ten thousand yuan? We couldn't raise that even if we sold our house. Thank goodness we bought that fake birth permit last month.'

'It won't fool them,' Kongzi says, taking off his glasses and rubbing his face. 'They're examining the permits closely this time, checking for fakes.'

'How many women did they round up today?' Meili asks, feeling a wave of nausea.

'Well, there were ten tied up outside the Party office. The school caretaker saw his wife among them, and tried to rescue her. But the family planning officers struck his head with a hammer, took him to the school and locked him up in the kitchen. The old seamstress who lives on Locust Tree Lane tried to hide her pregnant daughter from the squad, and got beaten to death.'

'They killed her?' Meili gasps. She strokes her swollen belly and watches Kongzi move around the room, the outer corners of her eyes slanting upwards like outstretched wings. He's throwing his hands about and groaning. She's never seen him in such a disturbed state. Abruptly, he slumps down beside her, knocking over the basin of water by her feet. A dark puddle spreads over the concrete floor. Small feathers gather on the surface, resembling flimsy boats on a lake. 'Why didn't you clear the basin away?' Kongzi says, jumping to his feet. 'Look, my shoes are all wet now.'

'I was keeping the water for you. Come on. Sit down again.' Meili fetches the thermos flask, pours more warm water into the basin, then kneels down, takes off Kongzi's shoes and washes his dirty feet. After drying them in a towel, she mops up the mess on the floor.

'Classes have been suspended,' he says. 'I doubt whether many pupils would have turned up anyway. Some have already been sent to stay with relatives in other counties until the crackdown is over.'

'Will you still get your salary?'

'Huh! I haven't received proper payment for three months. The education bureau was only giving a measly hundred yuan a week, but now it can't even pay me that. Last week all I got was a small can of diesel and a pad of writing paper. And the county authorities have the nerve to say that this crackdown against family planning violators has been launched to raise money for village schools! Well, you can be sure that our school won't be receiving any cash.'

Meili looks over to the right and sees her daughter, Nannan, crouched in the corner near a muddled pile of shoes, staring at the wet floor. 'What are you doing there, Nannan?' she says. 'Go back to bed.'

Nannan raises her sleepy eyes to Kongzi. 'Me want to pee, Daddy.'

'Go and do it yourself. You're two years old now. You shouldn't be afraid of the dark any more.'

Nannan moves grumpily to the front door but can't turn the handle. Meili pushes it down for her and swings the door open. A cold draught blows in and makes the skin of her belly tighten.

Kongzi shivers and lights a cigarette. On the wall behind him is a huge mosaic mural of green mountains and blue rivers which his friend, a renowned local artist called Old Cao, created for him after Kongzi built this house three years ago. Last year, Old Cao moved to a town fifty kilometres away to live with his son and daughter-in-law, a low-level cadre, in a luxurious apartment block for government employees. On Kongzi's left, beside the entrance to the kitchen, hangs a scroll of the Confucian text for children, *The Three Character Classic*, and a framed photograph of Kongzi and Meili, standing in Tiananmen Square during their honeymoon in Beijing. On his right is the doorway that leads to Nannan's room where, under the bags of fertiliser and pig feed beneath the bed, lies the secret dugout Kongzi made for Meili to hide in once her pregnancy can no longer be concealed.

'Old Huan, the district family planning chief, was at the meeting,' Kongzi continues, after taking a deep drag from his cigarette. 'He said it's a countywide crackdown. Every high official has been mobilised. The squad officers are under pressure to meet targets. Tomorrow, they want to insert IUDs into every woman in the village who's had one child.'

'I won't let them put one of those metal coils inside me! Yan said hers causes her so much pain, she can't bend over in the fields.'

'Yes, and if they did insert one, it might lead to a miscarriage. So, stay indoors tomorrow. If the family planning officers turn up, convince

4

them that you're not pregnant, then flash the birth permit at them and say you don't need an IUD because you've been authorised to try for a second child. My father's still well regarded by the Party, so with any luck, they'll let you off.'

'But my bulge is definitely noticeable now. And when I was walking through the village yesterday, I had a bout of morning sickness and vomited in the lane. Kong Dufa's wife passed me and gave me a suspicious glance.' Meili shines a torch on Nannan, who is still outside, squatting beside the low wall that runs between their house and the home of Kongzi's parents.

'You idiot! What if she's reported you to the police? They pay a hundred yuan for public tip-offs now.' Seeing Nannan walk in and sidle up to him, he says, 'Off to bed now, or you'll catch cold.'

'My bottom did big pee, Daddy,' she says, treading over a bundle of cables. 'Me thirsty.'

Kongzi looks away and flings his hands in the air. 'Abortions, sterilisations, IUDs! What has this country come to? Confucius said that of the three desertions of filial duty, leaving no male heirs is the worst. Now, two thousand years later, I, his seventy-sixth generation male descendant, am forbidden to perform my sacred duty to bring his seventy-seventh generation male descendant into the world.'

'I don't want to be dragged to the school tomorrow,' Meili says. 'I'll hide in the dugout.'

'The rabbit breeder in Ma Village hid in her secret dugout for two months, but the family planning officers found her yesterday. They pulled her out, took her off to be sterilised and confiscated her three hundred rabbits.'

Meili feels a sickening, rotten taste fill her mouth and her nose, and wonders if it comes from the darkness outside or from the depths of her own body.

'Look, Daddy, my tummy can go big too!' Nannan says, lifting her jumper and sticking her belly out.

'Bed! Now!' Father shouts.

Nannan bursts into tears and rushes into Mother's arms. 'Me hate that daddy,' she cries. 'Me want different one!'

Mother carries Nannan to her bed, tucks the quilt around her and brushes out her thin plaits.

Travelling in reverse motion, the infant spirit has retraced Mother and Father's journey, floating upstream along the watery landscapes down which they drifted for nine years. Now, it has finally reached its place of origin. This is the rightful home of Mother's second child, whom the infant spirit was assigned to inhabit until it achieved a successful birth.

Only scenes that took place in the darkness are now clearly visible to the infant spirit. It sees shadows tremble, as though stirred by the wind, and hears echoes from the past drift through the now window-less and roofless house, and linger near a patch of mosaic still stuck to a crumbling wall. The yard is pitch black, and empty, apart from a date tree which lies bent over the ground, a few leafless branches rising from its trunk . . . Father said that when he found out that Mother was pregnant for the second time, he planted a date tree in the yard to ensure the child would be a son, and buried a longevity locket in the soil beneath to grant the child a safe birth. Mother said that before the date sapling was planted, she took it to Nuwa Cave and rubbed it across the sacred crevice so that, in years to come, all her children would be born under the tree and receive Goddess Nuwa's blessing. Father also mentioned that in the secret dugout under Nannan's bed there is a red lacquer chest containing an ancient edition of Confucius's *Analects* and a bound volume of the Kong family register. The red chest is still there, buried now under the smashed bed and the thick rubble of a bulldozed wall. Piercing black eyes of mice glint through the weeds and broken roof tiles above.

In the lane behind, a willow tree rises from a mound of singed cobs like a graceful fairy frozen mid-dance. Further away, beyond a red compound wall, are two small osmanthus trees and the public road that leads out of the village.

KEYWORDS: *IUD, Fucking Communists, flames, fallopian tubes, Kong the Second Son, class enemy.*

Distraught residents of the village sit crammed on Meili and Kongzi's bed, on the sofa opposite and on the floor. Almost every one of them is, like Kongzi, a member of the Kong clan, direct descendants of the most celebrated Kong: Confucius. Meili is perched on the end of the bed, her hands carefully crossed over her belly. She suspects that Kongzi's parents have guessed that she's pregnant. His father is sitting by the headrest, shooting furtive glances at her as he sucks on his cigarette. He was village head for twenty years, and although he retired recently, he still commands respect, which explains why so many villagers have gathered here tonight to vent their anger.

Kong Qing, a former artillery soldier, is slumped in the corner, weeping and cursing, a bloodstained bandage wrapped around his head. 'Fucking Communists,' he cries, 'depriving me of my son. My branch of the family has been extinguished . . .' When the family planning squad came banging on his gate yesterday, he and his wife, who was heavily pregnant with their third child, escaped through a secret tunnel and fled to the tall reeds near the reservoir. In the evening, his father took them food, unaware that the police were trailing him. He quacked like a duck – their usual secret signal – and as soon as Kong Qing and his wife emerged from the reeds they were pounced upon by the police. The wife was dragged to the school, where family planning officers strapped her to a wooden desk and injected two shots into her abdomen. The aborted fetus is now lying at Kong Qing's feet in a plastic basin. It has its father's flat nose and small eyes. Scraps of congealed amniotic fluid are still stuck to its black hair.

'Former Village Head, you must stand up for us,' says Kong Zhaobo, a prominent member of the clan who attended high school in Hexi and now owns the only motorbike in the village. 'Filial piety demands that we produce sons and grandsons. The male lines must continue. We can't let the Party sever them.'

'And anyway, the authorities said that we peasants can have a second child if our first one is a girl,' says a man nicknamed Clubfoot, who is sitting by the television clutching his walking stick. 'So why are they bunging IUDs in women who've only had one child? If this carries on, we'll become a village where the children have no brothers or sisters, uncles or aunts. What kind of future is that?' Clubfoot is always searching for ways to make money. Last year he bought a desktop computer, surfed the internet and informed everyone that a fortune could be made rearing a breed of wild duck that lays golden-yolked eggs. His house stands on the site of an ancestral temple to Confucius which was built by Kongzi's grandfather and demolished in the Cultural Revolution.

A frail, spindly woman, whose third daughter, Xiang, Kongzi once taught, speaks up. 'The family planning squad came to our house today and demanded a 10,000-yuan back payment for Xiang's illegal birth. She's twelve years old now, for God's sake! I told them we didn't have any cash on us, but they searched our house, and found the two thousand yuan my eldest daughter sent us after slaving in a Shenzhen factory for a year. They took the cash, our bags of rice, our pots and pans, even our kitchen clock, and they want us to pay them the rest of the money by the end of the week.'

'And you know where all that money will go?' Clubfoot says, rubbing the handle of his walking stick. 'Straight into the mouths of the corrupt bureaucrats in Hexi Town. Have you seen the new District Party head-quarters they've built themselves? It's vast. As grandiose as Tiananmen Gate. And after they've guzzled our money, they come to murder our babies. Well, this time, we can't let them get away with it. We must fight back!'

'No, that would be madness,' says Kongzi's father, stubbing out his cigarette and smoothing back his white hair. 'The road out of the village has been blocked and a police boat is patrolling the reservoir. We're trapped. If we put up a fight, they'll crush us.'

'The squad officers have the names of the one hundred women of childbearing age in the village,' says Kong Wen, chair of the village family planning team. 'We had to send them the list last week. Forty of the women will be subjected to an IUD insertion, and the sixty who have two or more children will be sterilised.' Kong Wen worked in a Guangzhou clothing factory for three years, sewing zips into trousers. Almost every woman in the village is now wearing a pair of the Lee jeans she brought back with her. When she was informed that this crackdown was imminent, she gave her pregnant sister a letter of introduction stamped with an official seal and told her to escape to Beijing. As a result, she's been given the minor role of record keeper during this crackdown, and once it's over will probably be sacked.

Yuanyuan pushes her way into the house, reeking of rotten cabbage. She's eight months pregnant. Her home doesn't have a dugout, so she's been hiding in her neighbour's vegetable hut. Squeezing down next to Meili, she announces: 'I've just seen a woman halfway up a tree. She's out of her mind! Refuses to come down. She says her baby's up in the branches.' Yuanyuan went to Guangzhou with Kong Wen and found a job in an Apple computer factory, where she plans to return after the birth of her child. She looks at her now and says, 'You sucked up to the cadres when you came back here, hoping they'd make you village head. Well, are you happy now, helping them kill our babies? We're women of Nuwa, descended from Goddess Nuwa, who created the Chinese people from the yellow soil of this plain. And now the government wants to stop *us* having children! Are they trying to eliminate the Chinese race?' Yuanyuan is the only woman in the village to own a pair of knee-high leather boots. Meili longs for the day when she too can own a pair.

The villagers in the yard who've been unable to squeeze into the house poke their heads through the open windows. 'Even dogs have the right to bark before they're slaughtered!' one of them calls out. 'Kongzi: why don't you take the lead and speak out on our behalf?'

9

'Yes, Kongzi!' Kong Zhaobo agrees, running his hand along the turtleneck of his black sweater. 'You're eloquent and well read, and you've always had a rebellious streak.' Kongzi's defiant nature was recognised at the age of nine. When the entire school sang *'Lin Biao and Confucius are scoundrels'*, Kongzi dared change the words to *'Confucius was a gentleman and a sage'*, and was taken to the district police station. Thanks to his father's back-door connections, he was released the next day, on condition that he sing the song correctly one hundred times. Kongzi's real name is Kong Lingming, but after his courageous expression of support for his ancestor, everyone began to call him Kongzi – Confucius's more common name. Sometimes they call him Kong Lao-er, meaning Kong the Second Son, the derogatory nickname given to the sage during the Cultural Revolution, or just Lao-er for short, which also means 'dick'. As he grew up, his interest in his ancestor deepened, and he became the village authority on the sage's life and works.

'You've studied Sunzi's *Art of War*,' says Kong Dufa, a po-faced Party member who is married to the village accountant. 'Just choose one of the thirty-six strategies and write out a plan.'

Kongzi raises his palms. 'No, no, I may be a teacher, but I have no formal training. I'm just a simple peasant, a farmer who's read a few books. I can't come up with any ideas . . .'

Desperate to prevent him from becoming involved in a political protest, Meili throws Kongzi a meaningful look. He fails to notice. So, to attract his attention, she leans over to Nannan, who's curled up in the lap of Kongzi's mother, and gives her a sharp pinch.

'Ouch!' Nannan shrieks. 'A mouse bit me, Grandma.'

'Shh, little one,' Kongzi's mother says, rubbing Nannan's arm. 'Here, have a malt sweet.'

'No, me want chocolate.' Nannan hates the way malt sweets stick to her teeth. Villagers traditionally offer them to the hearth god at Spring Festival to make sure that when he meets the Lord of Heaven he'll be unable to open his mouth and utter any inauspicious words.

'I've heard peasants have poured into Hexi Town to protest against the crackdown,' says Li Peisong. 'They've stormed the Family Planning

Commission and smashed all the computers and water dispensers. We should sneak out of the village tonight and go and join them.' During the Cultural Revolution, Li Peisong was head of the village revolutionary committee and in 1966 was sent to Shandong Province to help Red Guards destroy the Temple of Confucius in the sage's native town of Qufu. While swept up in the revolutionary fervour, he changed his name to Miekong - 'Obliterate Confucius'. But by 1974, when the Campaign against Lin Biao and Criticise Confucius was in full swing, he'd undergone a change of heart. Not only did he fail to denounce Confucius at public meetings, he changed his name back to Li Peisong and married a member of the Kong clan. They now have two sons. The second son, Little Fatty, is two years old, but they still haven't paid off the fine for his unauthorised birth.

'What's a water dispenser?' asks Scarface, a man whose forehead is badly disfigured by a childhood burn. He is destitute, and can only pay for the education of his three daughters with beans adulterated with sand.

'You know - those large plastic canisters that cadres have in their offices, filled with mineral water that's supposed to cure a hundred illnesses. It works out at one mao a cup!' This burly man, Kong Guo, went to Wuhan last year to work on a construction site but was arrested for not having the necessary temporary urban residence permit, fined two thousand yuan and escorted back to the village by the police.

'So, they're just drinking all our money away,' says a mild, gentle man who cycles around the village every morning collecting eggs to sell in the county market. His fists are resting on the metal table, tightly clenched.

A dishevelled peasant called Wang Wu stands up, unable to contain his rage any longer. 'They wanted twenty thousand yuan for the illegal births of my two younger daughters. I told them I don't have enough money even to buy seeds. So they tied one end of a metal cable to the central eave of my house, the other half to their tractor. When the tractor reversed my entire roof came off. Where do those bastards expect us to live now?'

Suddenly, loud clanging thuds can be heard, the front gate swings open, and district policemen sweep inside followed by members of the family planning squad. The women in the house scurry into the kitchen and the men rush outside. Before Wang Wu gets a chance to launch into a tirade he's bashed to the ground. Kongzi's father steps onto a bamboo stool and shouts, 'No fighting. No violence!'

Clutching the plastic basin containing his aborted son, Kong Qing yells, 'Fascist slaughterers! I'll have my revenge! A life for a life!'

Old Huan, director of the Hexi Family Planning Commission, steps out from behind the policemen. 'I warn you, Li Peisong,' he says, jabbing his finger aggressively. 'If by tonight you haven't paid the remaining nine thousand yuan for Little Fatty's birth, we'll confiscate your stove, pans and wok, and pull down your house!'

Kong Guo elbows his way to the front and butts in, 'Go ahead! If you tear our houses down, we'll just come and move in with you.'

The policemen head for Kongzi's front door, shouting, 'Yuanyuan was seen entering this compound. We must search the house.'

'Step inside and I'll kill you!' Kongzi yells, waving a kitchen cleaver, unrecognisable when compared to the teacher in the grey nylon suit who walks to school every morning with his black briefcase. This is not his first experience of protest, however. In 1989, he travelled to Beijing to visit the man he still calls Teacher Zhou – a former urban youth who was sent to Kong Village in the Cultural Revolution and taught Kongzi in the village school. Together, he and Teacher Zhou marched through the streets of Beijing with the student protesters, waving banners and shouting slogans in support of democracy and freedom. The County Public Security Bureau has kept a detailed file of the subversive activities he engaged in during his month in the capital.

In the yard, which is only half laid with concrete, the crowd grows agitated. Villagers begin to push and shove, knocking into the date tree sapling that's propped up with bamboo sticks. Children and barking dogs climb onto a mound of broken bricks in the corner to escape the crush.

District Party Secretary Qian, the most senior member of the squad, emerges from the crowd, accompanied by a hired thug, and shouts,

'Kongzi, as a Party member, you have a duty to assist the squad with its efforts. If you don't behave, we'll fling you behind bars.'

'Don't you dare threaten my son, Mr Qian,' Kongzi's father says with quiet authority, dropping his cigarette stub and grinding it into the ground with his heel. 'Get out of this yard.'

Kongzi goes to stand beside his father. 'Yes, this is my home!' he says. 'A Kong family home, and in here, the Kongs make the decisions. I've committed no crime. So, get out, and take your rotten minions with you!'

'You want to start a fight, then?' says the shaven-headed officer who arrested Fang two days ago. 'We'll bury you alive.' He throws the hired thug a glance, signalling for him to give Kongzi a beating.

But before he has a chance to strike, Kong Qing, who's standing behind him, raises his basin in the air and, shouting 'Fuck you!' at the top of his voice, thrashes it down onto his head. Immediately the villagers grab bricks and shovels and attack the officers and policemen. The children perched on the compound walls hurl stones at Secretary Qian's back. Inside the house, Kongzi's mother crouches with the other women in the kitchen, holding Nannan tightly in her arms, while Meili cowers in the corner of the bed, pressing the folded quilt close to her belly, her eyes squeezed shut.

Kongzi runs back inside to help Yuanyuan into the dugout, then grabs a spade, charges out again and strikes Old Huan on the shoulder. Dusty and beaten, Wang Wu swings a hoe at a policeman's chest shouting, 'May your home lie in ruins too.' The shaven-headed officer grasps his arm and twists it up behind his back but is then struck in the ribs with a shovel. In a sudden rush of courage, the spindly mother of Xiang pounces on a policeman and sinks her teeth into his shoulder. The burly Kong Guo grabs an officer in an armlock and wrestles him to the ground, shouting, 'Fuck your mother, you crooked bastard.' Finding themselves outnumbered and overpowered, the panicked intruders flee. Kong Zhaobo and Li Peisong see Old Huan sprawled in a corner moaning, so they pick him up and fling him out onto the lane as well.

'Bolt the gate, Meili!' Kongzi's mother says, once everyone has left. Meili opens her eyes at last, takes her torch and ventures outside. The red-and-gold Spring Festival couplets which she hung on either side of the door have been ripped to shreds. The date tree sapling has been knocked right over and Kong Qing's aborted son lies trampled on the ground. As a piercing gunshot explodes in the distance, she quickly bolts the gate, then wedges a spade against it and runs back into the house.

In the lanes outside, angry villagers pour out of their houses with hoes and spades and march to the school, Kongzi and his pupils leading the way holding rocks and sticks. When they reach the school's compound walls, the policemen guarding the gates raise their batons and lash out at them.

'Run, Teacher Kong!' the children shout. The marchers scatter in panic. Little Fatty tries to keep up with his father Li Peisong, clutching the corner of his jacket, but is knocked over by the fleeing crowd, pulling his father down with him. Another procession of angry villagers emerges from a lane to the north, holding the old seamstress's corpse in the air and shouting, 'Every murder must be avenged!' and 'Give us back our property!' Enraged by the sight of the corpse, Kongzi and his pupils turn round and attack the policemen at the gates. Young boys stuff a bundle of straw under a police car and toss lit matches onto it, while Clubfoot chases a police dog away with his walking stick. The women who've been locked in the school kitchen bash their way out into the playground, throw chairs at the family planning officers, then run off to grab bags of rice and fertilisers that were confiscated from their homes. The police sergeant fires another gunshot and the women drop the bags and retreat. Outside in the lane, the police car becomes shrouded in black smoke then, with a deafening bang, explodes into a ball of fire. The young boys light torches from the flames and toss them over the compound wall into the playground. 'That man's from the District Family Planning Commission!' a voice shouts. 'Chase him! Kill him! . . .'

The infant spirit sees once more that February night nine years ago when Kong Village became a battlefield. Mother has come out to look for Father. She's wearing a white down jacket. The north wind is whipping up her hair. When a gunshot rings out, she drops to her

knees and shrinks into a tight ball, shivering with fear and cold . . . A man in a sergeant's uniform switches on a megaphone and shouts: 'Villagers! If China's excessive population growth isn't curbed, the whole of society will suffer. Our nation won't be able to achieve sustainable economic development and take its rightful place in the world. Deng Xiaoping has commanded us to take effective measures to ensure the birth rate is brought down. An enemy of the family planning policies is an enemy of the state. A class enemy. The masses must not allow themselves to be manipulated by a small band of troublemakers. The grain and furniture we've confiscated is now state property. Do not touch them . . .' Blazing torches fly into the playground, lighting up piles of doors, aluminium window frames and wooden rafters expropriated from the demolished houses. Below a locust tree further away, flames begin to rise from a heap of confiscated wardrobes, bookcases, fridges, enamel basins and trussed pigs. A cluster of ducks and chickens scurry off to a dark corner, frightened by the noise, while the family planning officers dart about, trying frantically to put out the flames. Outside in the lane, an angry mob swing their hoes and spades at a white slogan painted on the compound wall which reads: SEVER THE FALLOPIAN TUBES OF POVERTY; INSERT THE IUDS OF PROSPERITY. A crack opens which grows larger and larger until the whole wall tumbles down. Fearing for their lives, the family planning officers run to a ladder and escape over the back compound wall.

Mother stands by the gates and watches villagers surge into the playground and search through the piles, pulling out their spades, basins or chairs. Holding a kitchen clock close to her chest, a frail, spindly woman wanders through the crowd shouting, 'Xiang, Xiang, where are you?' Two boys in army caps waving long sticks herd a flock of mongrel ducks over the rubble of the fallen wall and off into a dark lane. Unable to find Father, Mother hurries home. Still gripping her electric torch, she runs down the treeless lanes that are illuminated by the fires' orange glow. In a corner buffeted by the north wind lies a swept-up heap of snow scattered with dog faeces and the red shells of firecrackers that were detonated at Spring Festival.

KEYWORDS: *birth permit, Dark Water River, family planning office, prop-aganda van, Sky Beyond the Sky, subversive slogans.*

Just as dawn is beginning to break, Kongzi creeps back into the house, collapses on the bed and pulls off his grimy glasses. 'The county authorities are sending a thousand riot police to the village and a truckload of Alsatian dogs. We must escape at once.'

'Where to?' Meili says. 'Why don't we just hide in the dugout?'

'No, Kong Guo knows about it. He's been arrested, and is bound to give us away.'

'Why are you wearing that black armband?' She has only just managed to doze off, and her eyes are heavy with sleep.

'The police beat two villagers to death last night. We were so outraged, we hitched rides to Hexi and joined the protests outside the Party headquarters. There were thirty thousand peasants surrounding it. Can you imagine? They'd come from villages all over the county to protest against the crackdown. The police cordon was four-men thick, but we still managed to set light to the building. The Family Planning Commission nearby had already burnt to a cinder. If the One Child Policy isn't repealed soon, there's going to be a revolution.'

'Is that blood on your hands?' asks Meili nervously.

'No, red paint. I wrote some slogans on the wall. If you weren't pregnant, I would have gone to the county police station today and tried to rescue Kong Guo and the others.'

'Subversive slogans? Are you mad?' Meili runs her fingers through the tangles of her hair which still smell of the musty quilt.

'All I wrote was: "Bring Down the County Party Secretary and Execute the County Chief". I didn't dare write "Bring Down the Communist Party".'

'Trying to show off your talent for calligraphy again! How could you be so stupid? You could get five years in jail for that.'

'They won't be able to pin it on me. The whole county is in revolt. But we must leave today, or the baby won't survive. The officers are prowling the village with bloodshot eyes, carrying out abortions in broad daylight. I've just been told about Yuanyuan. She left our dugout last night and went to hide near the reservoir, but the family planning officers hunted her down. They pushed her against the bank, pinned her arms down with their knees and injected her belly with disinfectant . . . My parents have guessed that you're pregnant. They would want us to leave. Did Nannan sleep at their house last night? Well, we can collect her on our way, then. Let's pack our bags. We'll return once the baby's born. Hurry! We'll need our residence permits, the birth permits, our marriage certificate, cash . . .'

'But where shall we go? To your brother in Wuhan or your sister in Tibet?' Kongzi's older brother works for a construction team in Wuhan and his younger sister runs a souvenir shop outside a monastery in Lhasa.

'No, we'll go to Dark Water River, sail down to the Yangtze and stay with my cousin in Sanxia. The town's being pulled down to make way for the Three Gorges Dam project. The place is in chaos, so the family planning policies won't be strictly enforced. We'll be safe there. Quick, get our things ready.' He feels behind the wooden cabinet and pulls out a large hemp sack.

There's still no scent of spring shoots in the cold February air. The young poplars growing in the roadside ditch seem like railings driven deep into the earth. The icy breeze blowing down the concrete road to Hexi raises no dust, but when a truck or bus drives by, the shreds of plastic bags littering the ground fly up and swirl about.

A passing cyclist stops to tell them that a police checkpoint has been set up on the road ahead.

Kongzi has pulled his blue cap low over his face. His glasses steam up when he exhales. His right hand is thrust into his trouser pocket, gripping Meili's forged birth permit.

Squinting into the distance, he sees a police car approach with a red light flashing on its roof. He jumps into the ditch, taking Meili with him, and they crouch on all fours until the car has passed.

'What did you put in there?' Kongzi asks, glaring at the huge sack Meili has brought.

'Not much. Just a few clothes, two flannels, a bar of soap, Nannan's shoes and pencils—'

'Nannan! Oh God, we forgot to pick her up. I must go back to my parents and fetch her. You wait for me here.'

'While you're about it, pop back to our house and get my address book, and my sewing patterns in the top drawer of the cabinet, and your woollen long johns as well . . .' In her clean white down jacket and red scarf Meili looks like a tour guide, not an illegal mother on the run.

After Kongzi climbs back onto the road and disappears into the village, Meili feels a spasm of morning sickness. She leans over, retches and, like a cat, covers the vomit with soil. Then she cautiously rises to her feet and looks around. On the snow-covered field to her left she sees the grave of one of Kongzi's distant relatives. Only a few paper petals remain on the bamboo wreath that was laid during the Festival of the Dead. Behind it, dry stalks arch down onto the snow like strands of black hair on a man's white scalp.

On the other side of the road is a fodder-processing plant. The huge white slogan – RATHER TEN NEW GRAVES THAN ONE NEW COT – which Kongzi was commissioned to paint last year is still visible on the red compound wall. The two osmanthus trees in front are smaller than the one in her parents' garden in Nuwa Village, but they produce beautiful white blossom in spring. She picked a few branches last May and arranged them in a green bottle with some bamboo leaves, and they stayed fresh for two weeks.

So, I'll be leaving Kong Village now, Hexi Town, Nuwa County, she says to herself. Apart from their brief honeymoon in Beijing, Meili has never travelled more than ten kilometres from her place of birth. On television, she's seen images of southern Nuwa, with its forested mountains and prosperous towns where the men dress like high-level cadres and women like hotel receptionists, but she has no idea what lies beyond the county's southern border. There's no need to worry, though. Kongzi will lead the way. As long as they can find a safe place for the baby to be born, everything will be fine and she'll make sure she never falls pregnant again.

In the distance, she can just about make out the two-storey building where she and Kongzi first met. Teacher Zhou came down from Beijing to build it and named it the Sky Beyond the Sky Hotel. Four years ago, Meili travelled from Nuwa Village for an interview, and soon became not only a room attendant but the wife of Kongzi, who was working as hotel manager at the time. She remembers Teacher Zhou turning up with a busload of tourists from a distant town who were dressed even more smartly than the people of southern Nuwa. On the first evening, the guests swam in the pond, and two of the women dared strip down to their underwear . . . She notices smoke rise from a village on a hill to the east and wonders whether its residents have set fire to their family planning office as well.

Looking to the north again, her gaze follows a line of telegraph poles that become shorter and shorter until they vanish into the ground. Beyond them, Nuwa Mountain stretches along the horizon. At its foot is Nuwa Village, where Meili's parents still live. Meili knows she is a mother now only because three years ago she climbed to Nuwa Cave and rubbed the sacred crevice of Goddess Nuwa. A few days later she fell pregnant with Nannan. After Nannan was born, Kongzi said that their next child must be a boy. When he found out that she was pregnant again, he paid a Taoist priest to write an ancient spell on a piece of paper, which he then placed inside a longevity locket and buried beneath the date sapling, saying, 'This is where the seventy-seventh generation male descendant of Confucius will be born.'

A propaganda van draws near. From the large loudspeaker strapped to its roof a voice blares out: 'The County Family Planning Commission has dispatched officers to our village. This morning they will visit every household to fit women of childbearing age with an intrauterine device, and to provide information on reproductive health and fertility management . . .' A truck follows closely behind, its open back packed with pregnant women whose legs are tightly bound with rope. Meili spots an old friend from primary school among them and looks away. A minute later comes the purple minibus which Kongzi's cousin Shan uses to deliver materials to local factories and ferry villagers to the county town to sell their vegetables and eggs. His fares are half the price of the public buses, so his service is very popular. Meili clambers back onto the road and waves him down. The minibus stops briefly, drives on, then reverses and screeches to a halt. Justice Wang, the corpulent president of the Hexi law court, steps out followed by two policemen who seize Meili by the arms. 'Let go of me!' she shouts, kicking at the door as they try to shove her inside. 'I have a birth permit! I'm allowed to fall pregnant so I don't need an IUD!'

'The family planning officers will want to check whether you've conceived yet, then,' says the taller of the two policemen.

'He's my husband's cousin,' Meili says, pointing at the driver. 'Shan, tell them I'm not pregnant!'

'She can't be pregnant, Justice Wang,' says Shan, hunching his shoulders against the cold. 'She had a daughter two years ago and had an IUD inserted straight after the birth.'

'Well, the officers will need to confirm that the IUD's still in place,' the other policeman says. 'Now, get inside.'

Suddenly Kongzi reappears, with Nannan following behind him. 'Let go of my wife or I'll set fire to the minibus!' he shouts, flicking his lighter and holding the flame to a cotton shirt he's pulled from his sack. 'You can't go around arresting people for no reason. Have you no knowledge of the law?'

Shan sticks his head out of the window. 'Don't set fire to my minibus, cousin,' he implores, the wind blowing his fringe right back.

'Me want to pee, Daddy,' Nannan whines, tugging at Kongzi's trousers. The red quilted jacket she's wearing is three sizes too big and almost reaches her ankles. 'Do it yourself in that ditch,' Kongzi snaps.

'Family planning efforts aren't bound by the law,' the tall policeman says, switching on his electric baton and staring at the blue sparks dancing over the tip.

'Bloody traitor,' Kongzi snarls, eyeing Shan coldly.

'Meili flagged me down,' Shan replies, his face colouring. 'I wouldn't have stopped otherwise. The Hexi family planning squad has commandeered every vehicle in the county. They're paying us sixty yuan a day.'

'We'll let her go for the time being,' Justice Wang says, then he turns his fiery gaze to Kongzi. 'As for you, Kong Lingming – if you attempt to obstruct our efforts again, I'll slam you in jail, and not even your revered ancestor will be able to save you then.'

The three uniformed men climb back into the minibus. As it drives off, children who've run out from the village hurl clods of earth at its windows, and a scruffy yellow dog chases after it until it disappears from sight.

Seconds later, a man called Scarface marches onto the road, one hand waving a kitchen cleaver and the other gripping a rope which is tied to the wrists of his three crying daughters. Kongzi tries to stand in his way, dodging his swinging cleaver. The two elder girls are his pupils.

'Out of my way!' Scarface shouts, the burn mark on his forehead turning bright red. 'I'm taking my three daughters to the County Chief. Let him tell me which one is surplus, and I'll kill her there and then, right in front of him.' His youngest daughter is only three years old. Noticing that her shoes have fallen off, her older sisters stoop down and try to pick her up with their bound hands.

Nannan crawls out of the ditch. As Meili crouches down to hug her, her face suddenly creases with alarm. 'Oh God, Kongzi, I've wet myself. I'll have to go home and get changed.'

On a cold night, nine years ago, following a failed morning escape, Father leads Mother and Nannan out of Kong Village and across the snowy fields to the banks of Dark Water River. Here, they board a small boat and, leaving whirlpools and diesel smoke in their wake, head south in search of a safe place for their second child to be born. The infant spirit drifts away from them and continues along Dark Water River, following it upstream all the way to its sacred source in Nuwa Cave.

KEYWORDS: *seasickness, testicles, tangled string, crimson lipstick, boiled frogs, custody centre.*

The pitch-black Yangtze River lies supine along the base of the steep limestone gorge, curving round the sinuous banks. The passenger boat moves over the water, leaving a trail of white foam which stretches hopelessly into the distance. Juddering violently, the diesel engine spews out fumes that fill each corner of the boat then leak into the night sky. Most of the passengers have come out onto the top rear deck to escape the stench of vomit and excrement in the cabins below. Meili is squashed against the railings, next to a woman wearing crimson lipstick who comes from a town only ten kilometres from Nuwa Village. When she came onto the deck and saw how ill Meili looked, she gave her a seasickness pill. She's travelling to Fengjie, a town downriver where she works in a hair salon. She tells Meili that the river towns along this stretch of the Yangtze are being torn down before the dam is complete and the valley flooded, so demolition work is easy to find. She confides that her husband has just had a vasectomy. 'Three days after he was snipped, the wounds became infected and now his testicles are the size of carrots. He spends all day drinking liquor, moaning about the agonising pain, saying he wishes he could murder the family planning officers who botched the operation.' The woman is smoking a cigarette. When she speaks, her white teeth sparkle.

'Men hate the idea of losing their manhood,' Meili says. 'You should press the Family Planning Commission for compensation.' She has grown used to this woman's high-pitched voice, and is now staring at the gold ring on her finger, wondering whether it's real or gold-plated.

Meili has a wedding ring as well, but she keeps it inside her bag as since she fell pregnant her fingers have swollen and it no longer fits.

'He did demand compensation, but they gave him only 1,200 yuan – not enough to pay for even a week of hospital treatment. We asked for a copy of the follow-up examination report, but they refused to give it to us in case we lodged an official complaint. We tried to sue them, but the district judge told us that family planning authorities are above the law. If we took our case to Beijing, we'd be arrested for "illegal petitioning".'

Meili pulls a bunch of bananas from her bag and offers one to the woman. Kongzi is lying fast asleep at her feet, a whiff of alcohol rising from his mouth. A few minutes ago, he stirred from his drunken slumber and bellowed a line from Confucius's *Analects*: 'If my path comes to an end, I will board a raft and drift towards the sea . . .' A group of migrant workers are crouched beside him gulping down bottles of beer.

'No, no, I'm not hungry,' the woman says, taking a banana nevertheless. Meili breaks one off for herself, tosses the peel overboard and watches it disappear into the white waves that cut through the centre of the black river. 'I have an eighty-year-old mother at home to support, and a two-year-old child as well,' the woman says. 'The wages I bring back to them vanish in a day.'

Meili shifts Nannan's head further down her lap, wriggles her numb toes, then stares at the woman's careworn face and contemplates her own predicament. I'm only twenty, she says to herself. I won't let myself age as badly as her. I'll get a job, earn some money and buy myself a nice dress and leather shoes. Kongzi once said that my toes are the most attractive part of my body, and since then, I've kept them covered. But one day I'll buy some elegant leather sandals and paint my toenails red . . .

'Come on, tell me – you're pregnant, aren't you?' the woman says. 'You're on the run from family planning officers.'

'How did you guess? Yes, I'm over three months gone. Nuwa County is clamping down on family planning violators. We would've been allowed to have a second child when our daughter is five, but I've fallen pregnant sooner by mistake.'

'You want a son, don't you? To continue the family line.'

'My husband is a Kong, so of course he wants a son. He keeps quoting that line from the *Analects* that goes, "Of the three desertions of filial duty, leaving no male heirs is the worst," or something like that.'

'How did you avoid getting fitted with a coil? Your family must have a lot of influence. I bet you're the only woman in this boat who doesn't have an IUD inside her.'

'No, my parents are ordinary peasants. My father works in a coal mine now, and my mother looks after the fields. But my husband's father is a war hero and a former village head, so he was able to pull a few strings.'

'He must be a teacher, your husband – quoting from the classics like that. Just look how thick his glasses are!'

Meili smooths her hair back and smiles. 'Yes. Everyone in the village calls him Kongzi, after the great sage. Our neighbours often ask him to choose names for their children or write rhyming couplets to hang outside their doors.' The two women stare down at Kongzi, who is now flat on his back, snoring loudly.

'If we edged our way over there, we'd be able to see the television in the viewing lounge,' the woman says, pointing behind her with her chin. Then, looking over at the migrant workers swigging beer, she murmurs a Cantonese song: '*As the night grows darker, I drink myself into a daze. Softly you approach my broken heart. Be careful what you say, because as everyone knows, I'm a woman who's easily hurt . . .*' The boat approaches a bend in the river and the engine's growl deepens.

'You speak Cantonese, then? Have you been to Guangzhou?' Meili knows the song. She sang it at her interview at the Sky Beyond the Sky Hotel, and impressed Teacher Zhou so much that he gave her the job on the spot.

'Yes, I've been to Guangzhou a couple of times. You need to speak Cantonese to find a job there, especially in the hair salons. But the men in Guangzhou are loaded. I can earn more in a day there than I do in a year back home. You could make a fortune there. Such smooth skin, delicate features, long neck. What man could resist you? I'd move there myself, but it's too far away. I have to go home every week to give money to my family and see my child. If it were up to me, I'd never go back to that damn village.'

'I'd much prefer to be at home. The thought of travel frightens me.' Meili remembers seeing Yuanyuan hobbling back from the school the day they left. Her mother-in-law was beside her, one hand supporting her round the waist and the other gripping the aborted fetus by the arm. Yuanyuan went into labour as soon as she was strapped to the school desk, but by the time the baby was born the disinfectant had already killed it. The family planning officer dropped the dead baby into a plastic bucket, but it was so big it toppled out. It lay sprawled on the ground for hours. No one bothered to pick it up. When her mother-in-law came to fetch her, she scooped it up from the floor and refused to let go of it.

'My village is surrounded by beautiful mountains,' says the woman wearing crimson lipstick. 'The soil is so fertile, anything will grow. But the family planning officers make life there unbearable. They grab women in the middle of the night. They took me once and locked me up in an army office for nine days. I was with nineteen women and children, in a room that was just twelve metres square. We didn't even have space to lie down. There was a four-year-old girl there who they'd taken hostage to force her mother to return from Shanghai. One poor woman had just had an abortion and was still bleeding. But on her second night, Officer Zheng and his colleague pulled her out into the corridor and raped her.'

'It wasn't so bad in our village – the officers demolished a few houses and made arrests, but they never raped anyone,' Meili says, afraid to talk openly about the true nature of the brutal crackdown. She glances over to the migrant workers beside her. The boiled frogs they're eating remind her of tiny fetuses.

'I detest that Officer Zheng,' the woman continues. 'I fell pregnant again last year. He promised he'd make sure I could keep the child, but I still ended up being dragged to the clinic for an abortion. He's the reason I left the village. The filthy bastard!'

'Did you tell your husband about it?' Meili asks, suspecting that the officer forced her to sleep with him.

'What for? He wouldn't have had the balls to beat him up – he would've just beaten me instead. Take my advice: never rely on a husband for your happiness. The government persecute men, then men persecute their wives in return. And what do the wives do? If they have a child, they slap it to let off steam. If not, they drown themselves or swallow bottles of pesticide.'

Meili thinks of the women who leave the village to find work in the south and return a year later, laden with cash. Yuanyuan told her that women who can't find jobs in factories work as prostitutes in hair salons. Meili doesn't dare ask the woman whether she sleeps with men for money, but remembers her saying she could earn a year's salary in a day, so presumes that she must.

The conversation unsettles Meili and brings to her mind the time a man almost tricked her into sleeping with him when she was fifteen. She looks into the night sky and suddenly becomes aware of the infant spirit animating her fetus, making it quiver and sink lower in her womb. Hunching her shoulders and squeezing her thighs together, she whispers, 'Don't be afraid, little one. Just stay where you are.'

That night, Mother looks into the darkness, as though wanting to converse with the infant spirit. Moonlight falls on the narrow bridge of her nose. Her mouth appears to be smiling. A woman wearing crimson lipstick is saying to her, 'Take care in train stations, town squares, hotels. Agents prowl those places. If they see a women they suspect of being illegally pregnant, they pounce on her and drag her to a clinic for an abortion. They're paid fifty yuan for each woman they bring in. And be especially careful in the big cities. Peasants aren't welcome there. The authorities think we give foreign tourists a bad impression, so they round us up, lock us in custody centres and charge us an "urban beautification tax", which is really just a fine for entering the city. The only way to avoid arrest is to live on the water.'

'What do you mean, live on the water?' Mother stares out at the wide river. She can see no land, no people, only flowing water, and this seems to bring her comfort.

'Have you no idea how dangerous this country is? If you're unlucky enough to have been born with a cunt, you'll be monitored wherever

you go. Men control our vaginas; the state controls our wombs. You can try to lock up your body, but the government still owns the key. That's just women's fate.' The woman's eyes start to redden.

'Do you mean that people who live on the river don't get their residence permits checked?' Mother asks.

'Yes, because every day they're in a different place. They become part of the floating population. In Guangdong they're called the "egg families" because they live on boats that look like half eggshells and float from one town to the next.'

Meili thinks of her childhood on the banks of Dark Water River. Every day she'd watch boats moor at the jetty and offload cargos of bricks, tiles and lime. Sometimes a motorboat would draw up, and peasants in festive clothes would disembark and set off on pilgrimage to Nuwa Mountain. She never liked going near the river, especially after she learned that it flowed from Nuwa Cave and bestowed fertility on any woman who touched it.

The woman wearing crimson lipstick looks Meili in the eye. 'There's one place in China where you can live in complete freedom, though: Heaven Township. It's in Guangdong Province. I worked there for a while. No one checks how many children you have. And it's almost impossible to fall pregnant there.'

'Not if you have a husband like mine!' says Meili, thinking of how Kongzi insists on making love to her every night, leaving her feeling like a heap of tangled string.

'No, the town's air contains chemicals which kill men's sperm. The newspapers call it pollution, but I wouldn't go that far. The air has a slight tang to it, that's all.'

'Heaven Township, you say – where is it, exactly?' Meili asks excitedly, as though hearing of a promised land, then glances down at Kongzi to check that he's still asleep.

'It's near Foshan in the Pearl River Delta, just an hour from Guangzhou. It used to be a small village, but it has tripled in size in the last five years. It has a large lake in the middle called Womb Lake, and its streets are piled with mountains of foreign televisions and telephones, and electronic devices you never see in the countryside.

The machines are brought in by the truckload. You work sitting by the lake, watching television, and get paid eight hundred yuan a week, with free food and lodging. There are children scampering about everywhere. No one comes to check your birth permits, or drag you off to a clinic for an IUD insertion.'

'But you said it's impossible to fall pregnant there, so how come there are so many children?' Meili asks, tucking her hair inside the hood of her down jacket and wiping the snot from Nannan's nose.

'You have to inhale a lot of those chemicals before they can take effect. They're called dioxins, apparently. The family planning officers there are very relaxed, because they know that however hard a man tries, he's unlikely to get his wife pregnant.'

'What a wonderful place it sounds!' Meili feels wide awake now. She imagines herself sitting on a stool beside the lake, scrubbing vegetables, watching her children paddle in the shallow water, and seeing Kongzi return from teaching at the local school, wearing a suit and tie and gold-rimmed glasses.

'It's full of workshops that dismantle the electronic goods. It's a Special Economic Zone now, like Shenzhen. But to reach it, you must travel through many large cities. If the police catch you, you'll be slammed in a custody centre and booted back home.'

Meili pictures herself in Heaven Township again, sitting in a safe and peaceful yard, knitting quietly while inhaling deep breaths of the chemicals that prevent women conceiving. She doesn't know how long it will take to travel from the fertile mountains of Nuwa to the sterile fields of Heaven Township, but at least she now has a sense of where happiness lies.

She closes her eyes and sees her mother's jabbering mouth always admonishing her for wasting food, and her father's cowardly soot-engrained face. She's heard that after people work in the mines for a while, even their lungs turn black. Her brother is a coward, too. As a child, he was always too scared to go outside alone when he needed to piss in the night. Although Meili had to leave school when she was eight to help her grandmother in the fields, she still dreams of leading a modern life. She may be registered as a peasant, but she will do everything in her power to ensure that her children go to university and find work in a city. She is not untalented. She has perfect pitch, and learned the art of funeral wailing from her grandmother. At the Sky Beyond the Sky Hotel, she'd sing 'On the Fields of Hope' every night, finishing on a high C that would receive rapturous applause. Even before she married, she was determined to achieve happiness and success, and avoid the monotonous peasant existence her parents have led. At another bend in the river, the boat's engine splutters noisily. Nannan rouses from her sleep, crawls back onto Meili's lap, rests her head on the hemp sack and returns to her dream.

When dawn breaks, Meili wakes from her doze and sees Nannan's face bathed in the early rays of sun and the reflected glow from her red quilted jacket. The mosquitoes that buzzed noisily all night have left small bites on Nannan's neck, but her face is as smooth and unblemished as an egg. Meili's own dream slowly dissipates as the boat continues downstream. All she retains of it is a vague sensation of swimming as freely as a fish through the deep waters of Womb Lake.

KEYWORDS: *river towns, stray dog, contraband, happiness, spring earth, civilisation, toes.*

'Why we leaving boat, Daddy?' Nannan asks, waddling up to him.

Kongzi lifts her up with one arm and joins other passengers, laden with bags, across a rickety boat and onto the steps of the wharf. Following closely behind, Meili scans the crowd nervously, trying to hold back another wave of nausea. Instinctively she places her hands over her belly, feeling like a woman she saw in a television drama who concealed contraband drugs inside her body. The red backpack she has filled with biscuits, milk powder and dried sausages drags on her shoulders as she climbs the wharf's one hundred stone steps, dodging out of the way of travellers who are scrambling down to catch the boat.

At the top of the wharf, Kongzi cranes his neck back to take a look at the town clinging to the side of the steep mountain, the black plastic bag swung over his shoulder scraping the ground. 'So this is Sanxia,' he says. 'In a few months, the water level will rise 150 metres, and all of the old town will be flooded. Look, they're pulling it down now, and will move everyone into those newer buildings higher up the slope.'

The air is thick with charcoal smoke and the scent of boiled corn-cobs. A stream of people jostles past. 'Looking for a hotel?' a man calls out. 'See that barge down there? You can get a bed in it for just five yuan a night. You won't find cheaper accommodation in the whole county.'

'Should we trust him?' Meili whispers to Kongzi, folding her arms over her belly, convinced that everyone is staring at it, especially the men wearing blue caps. 'That man over there looks like a policeman. He might try to drag us to a custody centre.'

'No, he looks like a tax collector to me,' replies Kongzi. 'And only large cities have custody centres. Sanxia is smaller than Hexi. Look, that department store is only two storeys high, and there are hardly any cars about. So stop worrying.'

A young man on a motorbike passes them, then looks back and shouts to Kongzi, 'Hey, my friend! Five yuan a ride. How about it? I'll take all three of you.'

Kongzi shakes his head. 'Dad, me want motorbike!' Nannan cries as it speeds away. 'Me want sit on motorbike!'

'We'll walk,' Kongzi says, setting off down the dirt road.

'You horrid!' Nannan says in a huff. 'Me hate you.'

Kongzi doesn't understand how I feel, Meili says to herself. If the police arrest us, I'm the one who will be punished. The condemned fetus is hidden in *my* belly.

They pass houses and billboards smothered in dust then, further along, the gloomy skeletons of gutted and abandoned buildings. Wooden beams, floor tiles, glass panes and revolving chairs have tumbled onto the dirt road. The rows of ancient houses clinging to the steep slopes above appear to have subsided into a layered heap.

'Look at all those houses squashed together up there,' says Meili. 'None of them have doors. How do people get inside?'

'Don't you know? In river towns, all the windows face the river, and the doors are at the back,' says Kongzi. They come to a pathway of stone steps that leads endlessly up the mountain. Kongzi takes Nannan's hand and begins to climb.

'So many steps,' Meili says, struggling up behind, sweating and puffing. 'How high are we going? What if I faint and fall down? Kongzi, will your cousin still remember you?'

'Of course. We ran through the village together as kids, stealing peanuts and dates from the neighbours' yards. We grew up eating from the same cob of corn!'

'Daddy, you got your energy?' Nannan says, lifting her sweaty face

31

to his, her ponytail skewed to one side. Her red quilted jacket is far too hot for this town.

'No, I left it at home,' Kongzi says, knowing she wants him to carry her.

'Me tired. Carry me.'

'I told you, I haven't brought my energy,' he says, squeezing her hand. 'Keep climbing. Don't look up.'

Halfway up they reach a narrow lane. Kongzi leads them to the left and stops outside a dark entrance. Rows of rusty letter boxes are nailed to the cement walls inside. Some have been smashed open, others are stuffed with flyers offering to buy unwanted television sets.

'Look at that slogan on the wall,' says Meili, still catching her breath.

Kongzi turns to the crumbling wall and reads out loud: '"After the first child: an IUD. After the second child: sterilisation. Pregnant with a third or a fourth? Then the fetus will be killed, killed, killed!" Don't worry. That's an old one. Look, the paint is flaking off. Yes, this is definitely the right place. Here's his letter box. Flat 121.' He dumps his plastic bag on the ground and opens the door to the communal stairwell.

'Daddy, careful, big bad wolf in there,' Nannan whispers.

'I'll wait here with Nannan,' Meili says. As he disappears, a smell of boiled mutton blows out from the stairwell and makes her stomach churn. She falls to her knees and vomits. Nannan jumps back in disgust.

'Quick: cover it with some of that rubbish,' Meili tells her, pointing to the dusty newspapers and orange peel in the corner.

Kongzi returns a few minutes later. 'He's not there. The woman in the flat next door said he moved to another town two months ago.'

'I need to pee,' Meili says in a panic.

'You can't do it here – we're not in the countryside any more. Let's go back down to the wharf and find you a toilet.'

So they pick up their bags, tramp back down the steep steps and book into the stationary barge hotel.

At night, the newly built apartment blocks jutting from the mountain top resemble featureless planks of wood. A few have lights on, but most are still dark.

'Look at that block up there: it must be twelve storeys high,' Meili says. 'If the top windows were opened, birds could fly straight in.' Now that Nannan is asleep, she and Kongzi have come out to sit on the barge's open deck. The hotel is mostly occupied by migrant workers. The cabins reek of mould and the toilets are so squalid no one dares to use them.

Kongzi wraps his down jacket over his shoulders and looks out at the river. 'What a fine view! It reminds me of that Tang Dynasty poem: "In spring the river swells to the height of the sea. / The bright moon lifts from the surface of the water and rises with the tide."' He takes a drag on his cigarette then exhales slowly, clouding his thick glasses.

'I'd like to go up one of those blocks and see the view from the top,' Meili says, still staring at the lights twinkling on the mountain.

'What a philistine you are! How can you look at apartment blocks when we have the eternal Yangtze to gaze upon? Our greatest poet, Li Bai, sailed down this river a thousand years ago and immortalised it in his verse. The Yangtze is our nation's artery of life. It's by these banks that the Chinese people first settled and cultivated the arts of civilisation.'

'You think I haven't heard of Li Bai? "I bid farewell to Baidi Town in the rosy clouds of dawn. / By nightfall, I'll be back in Jiangling, a thousand miles away. / On both sides of the gorge, apes cry unceasingly. / My light raft has already passed through ten thousand mountain folds."' Meili smiles proudly, then, as she always does when Kongzi accuses her of being uncultured, says, 'I can't be too much of a philistine, or you wouldn't have married me, would you?'

'I taught you that poem,' says Kongzi, his white teeth gleaming in his thin, dark face.

'Nonsense! I learned it at primary school.'

Kongzi takes another long drag. 'What a crime it is to destroy this beautiful ancient town!' he says, and after a long sigh recites: '"Against the river's jade waters, the birds appear whiter. / Against the blue mountains, the flowers appear aflame. / Yet another spring ends. / How many more will pass before I can return home?"' Then taking Meili's hand, which she's been keeping warm in the sleeve of his down jacket, he says, 'I'd love to hear the "Fishing Boat Lullaby" now. It's an ancient zither song. Do you know the words?'

'Stop testing me,' she says, stuffing her hand back into his sleeve. 'You know I only like pop songs.'

'Well, sing "In the Village Lives a Girl Called Xiao Fang", then.'

'No, we've left the village behind. I want to sing songs from the city. Listen to this one: . . . *You say you're mine, but still I'm not happy. What is love? What is pain? I don't know any more . . .* **Before she reaches the end of the chorus, Mother looks up, takes off Father's glasses and says, 'Kongzi, promise me that once this baby is born, you and I will get sterilised. I don't want to go through this again.'**

'Only if the baby's a boy. I have a duty to my ancestors to carry on the family line. Huh! Since time began, the Chinese people have been able to procreate in freedom. Just my damn luck to be born in an age of birth control!'

'But I'm your wife – you have a duty to protect me,' Mother says, resting her head on Father's shoulder. 'It would be reckless to have a third.'

'What is a wife for if not to produce sons? Besides, now we're here, you've no need to worry. The family planning officers of Sanxia leave boat people alone. The hotel didn't even ask to see our marriage certificate when we booked in. It's full of fugitives like us. We're safe.'

'Why are you so obsessed with having a son? It's so feudal! Don't you know that men and women are equal now?'

'My brother has no sons, so it's my responsibility to continue the family line. Our daughters will join their husbands' family when they marry, and their names won't be recorded in the Kong register. So they serve no purpose to us.'

'Still clinging to those outmoded Confucian beliefs! I warn you, the modern world will leave you behind.'

'Huh! Just a few days on the road and already you've become worldly-wise! Don't forget, you left school at eight while I graduated at sixteen, so I'll always be cleverer than you.'

'Stop being so patronising. We're both fugitives now. Let's see how far your male chauvinism gets you here.'

'Oh God! I've just remembered. I left our Kong family register in the dugout.'

'Was it wrapped in newspaper, on top of that old edition of the *Analects*?'

'Yes. It dates back to Emperor Qianlong's reign. It's the twenty-second volume in the series, and proves that I'm a seventy-sixth generation descendant of Confucius in the direct patrilineal line.'

'Look how you gloat at being his successor!' Mother says, pinching his ear.

'Well, Confucius had to wander through the country like a stray dog after he was banished from the State of Lu. So I'm happy to become a stray dog as well for a while, as long as I have you, my little bitch, to keep me company!'

'You rascal!' says Mother, running her hand further up Father's sleeve to pinch his chest. In the darkness surrounding them, all that can be perceived is their laughter and warm breath. Someone wanders out on deck to have a smoke. Another figure leans out of a porthole to drop an empty orange crate into the river.

'We've been away two weeks now,' says Meili, nuzzling her face against his jacket. 'I still haven't dared write to my mother. What are we going to live on now?'

'Don't worry. I signed up to join the demolition team. They pay thirty yuan a day. So we can stay here until our son is born. In a year's time, I'll have saved enough money to pay the fine for his illegal birth, and we can all go home.' He slides his hand up onto Meili's breast. She feels her face grow warm. He hasn't touched her for days.

'It frightens me to think how little we have now,' she says.

'Yes, we're starting from scratch, but we'll soon have everything settled.'

'I mean, I feel empty, cut off . . . You won't leave me, will you?'

'Never. Let me feel our baby.' Kongzi lifts Meili's jumper, undoes the lower buttons of her shirt and places both hands on her belly.

'What if it's a girl?' she says, her heart thumping.

'Well, she won't be recorded in the family register with the boys of her generation who've been assigned "Righteousness" as the first character of their name.'

'Never mind, let's call her "Happiness" then.'

'Yes, that's good. And we can still add "Righteousness" to the name when we register her with the government.'

'You really think we'll be able to get this baby officially registered?'

'Absolutely! Once it's born, I won't rest until I've made enough money to pay the fine . . .'

'Your hands are freezing. Let's go back to the cabin.' As soon as Meili pushes Kongzi's hands off her belly, he slides them between her thighs.

'Don't touch me there, it hurts . . .' she says, sensing herself losing control.

'It hurts? Let me make you feel better then . . .'

Meili feels her blood vessels prickle as though filled with scuttling spiders. She stretches out and lets the waves of pleasure sweep through her . . . 'Don't press on my belly. Keep going, keep going . . .' Her thighs tremble against the metal bench; inside her leather shoes her ten toes clench.

With his hand still inside her, Kongzi puts a cigarette to his mouth and lights up.

'Put that out!' Meili says, tugging his hand out of her and wiping his middle finger on her sleeve.

A cruise boat sails past, a Viennese waltz pouring from loudspeakers on its rear deck. The breeze blowing across the river smells of spring earth and new growth.

'As long as we stay together, I don't care how many children we have. I just want us to be happy.'

'Didn't I make you happy just now?'

'Be serious for a minute! If you loved me, you wouldn't want to put me in danger. But it's strange: the river does feel safer than the land . . .'

The infant spirit notices that there are fewer people walking along the bank now. The lights shining near the wharf sink the distant buildings into a deeper darkness.

KEYWORDS: *cruise ship, wawa soup, kitten-heeled shoes, Three Gorges Resettlement Programme, boat puller, two dragons, bulldozer.*

The May sunlight gleams over the Yangtze, soaking up the river mist and spreading it about the deck. As the damp seeps into Meili's skin, she feels her body soften and warm blood course through her veins into her unborn child and its infant spirit. In a relaxed stupor, it extends a leg. Don't kick so hard, Meili whispers. She's leaning on the deck railing wearing a white shirt and a long flowery skirt. When the breeze drops, her skirt becomes still. She's finished washing Kongzi's dirty work clothes and has hung them out to dry. Whether you're a boy or a girl, you're my flesh and blood and I'll make sure you have a good life, she whispers, stroking her belly. You'll go to university, then find a job in a tall building. Every morning, you'll take a lift to your office on the top floor.

Kongzi's white vest and her white bra flap in the wind. Meili sees a tall cruise ship glide slowly upstream like a floating skyscraper. Against the blue sky, the tourists on the front deck resemble party balloons tethered to the white railings. They turn their cameras to her. One man smiles broadly and waves. Meili raises her hand, about to wave back, but feels her face redden and quickly lowers her head. Inside her womb, the fetus squirms like a fish in a net. A foreigner, she says to herself, regretting her uncouth appearance. Kongzi told her that foreign men travel to China with the sole intention of sleeping with Chinese girls.

The ship's large wake rocks the boats and barges moored at the bank. Meili stares at the white clouds sliding across the blue-green water, and the spray hovering above the wake's splashing waves. Time seems to slow down. She looks up at the river town and through the corner of her eye sees the cruise ship slip away. Beyond it, where the river becomes enclosed by two bulging precipices, a small raft appears to sway towards a place beyond river and sky.

What am I doing, lazing in the sun like an old woman? she says to herself, then remembers that this morning she must go into town to buy mosquito coils and fresh vegetables. It's her third wedding anniversary today. Kongzi has given her a pair of kitten-heeled shoes as a present, and she's eager to try them out. They've been away for almost three months now, and this evening she wants the three of them to enjoy a celebratory meal. Although the barge hotel is foul-smelling and shabby, there's a television in the meeting room, which Nannan is happy to watch for hours, so the days go pleasantly by. Meili also wants to phone her brother, who's working in a coal mine with her father fifty kilometres from Nuwa, and tell him to go home and assure her mother that all is well. As it's the second week of May, he'll need to spray the sesame plants with insecticide. Her grandmother is eighty years old and too frail to help in the fields.

'Me want jump in river, Mummy!' Nannan cries, rushing out onto the deck and stepping onto the lower railing. 'Me want see King Crab's palace.'

'Get down!' Meili cries. 'That palace only exists in the television – it's not real.'

'It is real! Me saw it. It has ice cream and big bed.' Nannan is wearing a long green dress, and has her hair in two small bunches.

'Come on, let's go and buy some vegetables,' says Meili. She pulls a pair of socks over her nylon tights, steps into her kitten-heeled shoes, grabs Nannan's hand and leads her across the gangplank. As soon as her feet tread onto the bank, her muscles tense with apprehension. 'Remember, if anyone asks you whether your mum is pregnant, just shake your head. Do you hear me? Don't babble a load of nonsense like you usually do, or the family planning officers will give you a nasty injection.' Meili thinks of her primary-school friend Rongrong who was the prettiest girl in the class. Two years ago, she went to hide up in a mountain hut to give birth to an unauthorised child, but when her baby boy was just two weeks old, three family planning officers tracked her down and gang-raped her. She only narrowly escaped with her life, and still has to take herbal medicine for the pelvic disease she contracted.

'Shh!' Nannan says, pointing to Meili's mouth. 'Give me hot hat!'

Meili pulls a yellow sun hat from her bag and claps it on Nannan's head.

'Hurray!' Nannan cries. 'Let's go!'

They ascend the steep stairs to the old town and stroll through the street market. The air reeks of fish. Everyone is shouting. Meili sees dozens of silver carp writhing in the shallow water of a polystyrene box, waiting to be pulled out, slit open and gutted. Bright green mustard tubers and pungent-smelling preserved sprouts lie scattered on the wooden counter above. The stallholder reaches into a large bucket and pulls out the black, mottled tail of a giant salamander. 'Fancy this wawa fish? I caught it today. It makes wonderful fish stew. Just the thing for pregnant women.'

Fish stew would be nice, Meili thinks to herself. A bit of garlic to bring out the flavour. But that creature would cost at least eight yuan. Too expensive. She remembers the wedding feast she attended last Spring Festival. The steamed fish were still alive when they were served to the guests. Displayed on the centre of each table were two roast chickens, the male mounted on the female, mimicking the position the married couple would adopt later that night. She hasn't been able to eat chicken since.

'I want wawa fish, Mum,' Nannan says, looking down at the wriggling black tail.

'No, it smells bad,' says Meili, staring at the guts, fish scales, spinach leaves and noodles trampled onto the ground. She goes to a fruit stall, buys a jin of oranges, peels one and puts a segment in Nannan's mouth. Nannan wrinkles her nose and says, 'Too sour! Me no want orange. Me want wawa. If me eat wawa me be wawa too.'

'Come on, lady, buy this one,' another fish seller says, walking over with a large bucket. 'Wawa nourishes the yin and fortifies the yang.

It's a nationally protected species, unique to the Yangtze River. We're only able to catch them now because of the chaos caused by the dam project. Usually, you'd never get a chance to taste one.' He leans into the bucket and pulls out a slippery beast that is twice the size of the wawa at the other stall. Its arms and legs flailing wildly, it opens its wide mouth and takes a gulp of air.

'Why called wawa fish, Mummy?'

'Because when it mates, it cries "wa-wa", just like a baby.'

'Why it called fish? It no look like fish.'

'It just is. Don't touch it. It's very expensive.' Meili remembers reading that women are given wawa soup during their one-month postpartum confinement to restore their energy and encourage lactation. 'All right, I'll buy it,' she says. But as she digs into her bag for her purse she looks up and sees the words RATHER RIVERS OF BLOOD THAN ONE MORE UNAUTHORISED CHILD sprayed in red paint onto a wall that is splattered with chicken shit and blood. Struck with panic, she abandons the purchase, grabs Nannan's hand and runs away down a side lane, turns left into another and stops outside a row of half-demolished buildings. 'Why your face red, Mummy?' asks Nannan.

'I'm hot, that's all.' Meili pulls off Nannan's yellow hat and fans her face with it. Her new kitten-heeled shoes are covered in dust.

The deserted lane is littered with broken bricks and refuse. An old man passes through the ruins behind, dragging a bundle of flattened cardboard boxes. Nannan climbs a heap of rubbish and picks up a plastic duck.

'Drop it, it's filthy!' Meili shouts. She thinks of their house in Kong Village. Before Spring Festival this year, she and Kongzi painted the front door and window frames dark red and began re-cementing the yard. She'd wanted to plant an osmanthus tree beside the date tree so that when she opened the windows next spring the house would be filled with its fragrance.

'Me wash it,' says Nannan, smiling at the dirty plastic duck. On the broken window frames and doors behind her is an empty can of almond juice and some smouldering charcoal briquettes.

They walk down another lane, climbing over toppled telegraph poles. The segments of wall on either side are still pasted with flyers advertising the services of lock-breakers and door-menders. On a broken bulletin board next to an abandoned shop is a list of women of child-bearing age drawn up by the local residents' committee. Around the next corner they find themselves in a large demolition site from which there appears to be no way out.

'Mum, that dog poo is dead,' Nannan says, pointing to two dry turds.

Meili takes Nannan's hand and enters a roofless building which was once a restaurant. On one of the greasy walls are a photograph of a roast duck on a white platter and a laminated menu featuring Sliced Beef in Hot Chilli Oil and Fish Poached in Pickle Broth.

Meili has lost all sense of direction. She climbs over the rubble and heads downhill, searching for a path. As long as she makes her way down to the river, she'll be able to find her way back to the barge hotel.

'Me can't walk, Mum,' says Nannan, her floppy sun hat slipping off her hot head.

Meili squeezes her hand and leads her across the shattered tiles and bricks. In the distance she sees a red car speeding past. Assuming it's driving along a proper road, she walks in that direction, and soon comes to an ancient brick house that's in the process of being torn down.

A large crowd has gathered to watch. A bulldozer is ramming into the remains of the ground floor. Workers with hammers are pounding the compound walls. The owner of the house bellows a curse, picks up a wooden bed leg and charges at a man dressed in the uniform of a judicial cadre. But before he can strike, three policemen jump on him and throw him to the ground. The cadre shouts, 'If you continue to put up a fight, you'll be charged not only with endangering state security but with political crimes as well, and will get three years in jail.'

'I'm just a simple boat puller,' the man shouts back, his face contorted with rage. 'I can't read or write. What would I know about politics?'

'We have all the evidence we need. We found the business card of a Hong Kong journalist in your drawer, so we can have you for "resisting the Three Gorges Dam Resettlement Programme" and "divulging state secrets to foreigners".'

'What state secrets do you imagine I know? I warn you, if you upset it enough, even a timid rabbit will bite! I'll take this to the higher authorities. Just wait and see!' He's kicking his legs wildly now, as the policemen press his face onto the floorboards and twist his arms behind his back.

An old man in a straw hat, presumably the owner's father, scrapes some loose plaster from a wall into a paper bag then holds it close to his chest.

An elderly woman beside him wraps her arms tightly around a wooden chair and sobs: 'The Japanese bombers didn't manage to flatten our house in 1941. Who would have thought that you Communists would end up destroying it!'

Two demolition workers pick up the old woman and carry her to the pigsty, her arms still clutching the chair. Meili wonders whether this is the demolition team Kongzi belongs to. The team manager has a limp. He hobbles over to the owner and shouts angrily: 'I warn you, if you petition the higher authorities we'll bury you alive. We offered you land to build a new house on, a weekly allowance, but you turned it all down. You dare resist the edicts from the Party Central Committee?'

'The land you offered was in the mountains, a hundred kilometres away,' the owner says. 'What would I do there? I've spent my life working on that river.' He looks down over the compound wall. Although the view of the sky and river is intersected by tall emerald peaks, one can still sense the sweeping expanse beyond – the warmth of the sunlight on the boats and barges, the coolness at the base of the gorge, the giddiness one feels when disembarking onto the river-banks.

'Shut up and go, and take your parents with you,' the team leader yells to the man. 'There's no need to worry about your future. The authorities are going to pay boat pullers like you to tug rafts up a tributary as a spectacle for foreign tourists.' He then knocks off an elm door lintel carved with two dragons leaping through turbulent waves. After a brief glance at the intricate design, he stamps on it, breaking it in two. The two children squatting on a sofa cushion behind him look younger than Nannan.

Spluttering clouds of diesel fumes, the bulldozer knocks over the last section of wall, then trundles back and forth across the rubble, until all that remains of the house is a flat expanse of crushed wood, glass and brick. The old woman is cowering behind the toilet hut now, a finger in each ear. The heady fragrance of the lilac tree beside her scatters onto the ground.

Meili feels the fetus give a sharp kick and tug its umbilical cord. Afraid that someone might notice the juddering of her belly, she turns away and runs, forgetting for a moment Nannan, who was crouched at her feet playing idly with the dirty plastic duck.

KEYWORDS: *glossy magazine, peach blossom, azure, barge hotel, deep-fried meatballs, black children.*

After dusk has fallen the crowds and buildings disappear and the riverside becomes tranquil. Scraps of polystyrene criss-cross the dark green river like flecks on an antique mirror, making one forget the watery world that extends a hundred metres below the surface. A song drifts from a cassette player on a nearby boat: '*I give you my love, but you always refuse it. Did my words sadden you that much? . . .*'

At this moment, Meili feels happy, as though every part of her body were connected, from her toenails to the hairs on her scalp. A sense of contentment, long dormant, stirs within her. She knows that to remain happy, love is not enough: one must make a living, strive to accomplish something, find a sense of purpose. When she realised that Kongzi's only aim in life was to impregnate her again and again until she produced a son, she feared that her road to happiness would be blocked for ever. But now she is confident that as long as she pursues goals of her own, however unachievable they may be, a happy life will be possible.

Only a few lights are still twinkling in the old town. Soon the mountains will merge into the dark sky, and everything will become quiet. Meili remembers opening a glossy magazine and seeing a fashion spread featuring a woman walking barefoot on a beach, her white dress fluttering in the wind. Not daring to let her gaze fall too long on the exposed legs and cleavage, she leafed through the other pages, mesmerised by the vibrant scarves and jewellery. She'd never seen such vivid colours before. As a child, she'd always loved the soft hues of the countryside: the dark greens and light greens, the pale yellow of celery shoots, the tender pink of peach blossom, the milky white of osmanthus blooms and the rusty orange of the wild chrysanthemums that grow at the margins of fields. But the colours in the magazine seemed to come from another world. She didn't know where this world was, but sensed that its colours were infused with joy. She used to loathe blue. It was the colour she had to look up at every day when she worked on the fields. But the azure of the sea in the magazine transfixed her. If coffins were painted such a heavenly blue, she thought to herself, one could lie down inside one without fear. She was sitting in the garden of the Sky Beyond the Sky Hotel at the time, facing the setting sun. The magazine had been left behind by a guest from a distant city.

The cabin is filled with the smell of someone's fish and red turnip soup, and the deep-fried meatballs Kongzi bought at a stall near the wharf. The meatballs will be delicious once they're reheated: crisp on the outside, with a soft, piping-hot interior. She can almost taste them in her mouth now. Kongzi is kneeling by the kerosene stove, tossing chopped spring onions into the wok.

'Have a glass of Addled Immortal with us, Mr Kong,' calls out one of the four men who live in the cabin next door and work for the same demolition team as Kongzi. On the dirty wall behind them is a pin-up of a Chinese model with peroxide hair.

'No, you carry on without me,' Kongzi replies, dropping the meatballs into the sizzling spring onions. His greasy hair is thick with dust. The only clean thing on his body is the sweat running down his face.

As Meili gets up to fetch some bowls, she feels the blood rush to her head. The fetus kicks her low in the abdomen, making her lose balance. She has to remind herself that this isn't their kitchen back at home. There is no table to lean on. They have left the village and are now living on a barge hotel.

'Why not have a shower before we eat?' she says to Kongzi. After he grabs a towel and wanders off, she sits down and hums along to the song playing on the distant cassette player. Closing her eyes, she imagines herself onstage belting out the ballad wearing an elegant silk

45

gown. But soon two men on the deck below start arguing over a stolen leg of ham, a child cackles in the corridor and a soap opera's theme tune booms from the television in the meeting room. Annoyed by the din, she wraps a rag around her hands and carries the stove onto the deck. The air is fresher outside, although smells of rust and mould from the cabins leak out now and then.

'I know there's no family planning squad here,' Meili says to Kongzi when he returns from his shower, 'but I still feel nervous, living on this boat like outcasts.'

'You've no need to,' Kongzi says, sitting down, bare-chested, beside the cardboard box they use as a table. 'We've been in Sanxia almost four months, and haven't been approached by one family planning cadre. Your hormones are making you overly anxious.'

'Have you called home recently?' she asks, slipping her shoes off and rubbing her bare feet on the metal deck.

'Not since last month. Father said the whole of Nuwa County is under martial law. Riot police have been stationed in every village. He told me not to phone them again until the baby's born. I don't know why he's so nervous. The county authorities would never turn on a war hero like him. The school's summer term has started. Kong Dufa has taken over my post.'

'That po-faced bore – what does he know about teaching?' Meili says testily, whisking a mosquito from her face. 'If only we'd waited five years before having a second child. Look at all the sacrifices we've had to make to bring little Happiness into the world. When is this going to end?' She sits on a stool, bending her legs behind her so that her knees don't press into her large belly.

'Don't worry – we'll go home as soon as martial law is lifted,' Kongzi says, trying to sound confident.

'The baby is due in three months, but this town is a demolition site – it doesn't even have a hospital. I think I'm developing a fever. You must buy me some Yellow Ox pills tomorrow to bring it down.' Meili feels stifled by the darkness surrounding her, and wishes something stimulating could break the atmosphere. She looks over to the boat near the wharf which has been converted into a video parlour. Three coloured light bulbs are flashing above its entrance. It screens martial arts films during the day and porn movies at night. Kongzi sneaked off to watch one a few nights ago without telling her. When he returned to the cabin afterwards he made love to her like an animal.

'I'll find a hospital for you when the time comes, I promise,' he says to her. 'I earn ten times more as a demolition worker than I did as a teacher. Once I've saved enough money, we'll buy ourselves a boat. Many local fishermen are planning to leave town before the valley is flooded. I met one who's moving to Guangzhou. He owns a fishing boat that's worth ten thousand yuan, but he said he'll sell it to me for just three thousand. Once we have a boat of our own, we'll be free. We won't need residence permits. If the police try to arrest us, we'll start the engine and escape. And if we don't manage to find a hospital in time, you can have the baby on our boat.'

'Yes, at least a boat would give us somewhere to hide. How much money have we got now? Last night I dreamed that little Happiness left my belly and flew into the sky. It was terrifying.'

As night falls, the infant spirit can see Mother and Father sitting at the cardboard box eating dinner. Nannan has come out from the meeting room. She's walking along the deck, or skipping – it's hard to tell.

'You keep talking about the fetus having a spirit,' Father says. 'That's why you had the dream. We have one thousand yuan now. In two more months, we'll have enough to buy the boat.'

'I know you don't believe in ghosts, Kongzi, but I'm convinced the fetus has a spirit. I saw it the moment I became pregnant. It often speaks to me. Why do you think babies cry when they're born? It's because the infant spirits that have been assigned to their bodies don't want to go through another incarnation. They want to break free and fly away.'

Nannan grips Mother's hand. 'I want nice food, Mum.'

'What kind of food?' says Mother, her belly jutting out as she sits up straight.

'That!' says Nannan, pointing to the deep-fried fish being eaten by the four bare-chested workers who, in the soft light cast from the lamp behind them, resemble four smooth eggs. At the bow, a few

47

men are leaning against the railing having a smoke. Other figures are sitting or lying down in clusters on the still-warm metal deck.

'Try this meatball,' Mother says to Nannan. 'I sprinkled some magic powder on it just for you. And here's a tomato. You like tomatoes.'

'Me want fish,' says Nannan, stamping her feet. 'Me want *that* fish!'

'Don't be so rude!' Mother whispers, slapping her bottom. 'It's their fish, not yours.'

Nannan frowns and tries to hold back her sobs. 'You bad mummy,' she splutters. 'You no wear glasses, so you bad mummy.'

'Come and sit down here by the mosquito coil,' Mother says, pulling Nannan close to her. 'Remember what I told you? If anyone asks you how old you are, you must say you're five years old. Don't tell them you're only two and a half. Do you hear? If you do, I'll have to spank you again.' She watches Nannan crawl onto Father's lap. 'You're too soft on her, Kongzi,' Mother says. 'If she blabs out our secrets, the authorities will arrest me, and our family will be finished.'

'Stop worrying,' says Father, lighting a cigarette. 'Nannan's a good girl. She won't blab.'

'Oh, what are we going to do? This baby will never get a residence permit. It will be one of those "Black Children" who are born without permission and banned from getting free schooling and medical treatment. When it grows up, it won't even be able to marry, and it'll curse us for condemning it to a life as an outcast.'

'Me not black children!' says Nannan, punching Mother's thigh. 'You bad mummy.' She kicks a leg in the air, sending her flip-flop flying across the deck.

'I'm sure that in a couple of years Nuwa County will have calmed down,' says Father, lifting a meatball with his chopsticks. 'Then we can go home and do our best to get little Happiness registered.'

'Stop kicking my bladder, little one!' Mother says, glancing down at her belly. 'I'm sick of having to go to the toilet every five minutes.'

'Do me kick you when me inside you, Mum?' asks Nannan, wiping a scrap of meatball from her hot face.

'No, you didn't have as much strength as this one,' Mother says, then mutters to Father: 'Nannan's getting so naughty. She threw your lighter into the river this morning.' A speedboat passes, churning up waves that tip the barge to the side. Mother puts her hands over the bowls on the cardboard box to stop them falling off.

'Me no throw lighter away!' Nannan protests, wrinkling her nose. 'Baby Crab wanted lighter, so I borrowed it him.'

'Look – see how she thinks she can get away with everything!' Mother says, wiping the sweat from her face with the corner of her shirt. A damp breeze lifts her skirt and Father's cigarette smoke into the air. Flies encrusting the remains of the food flutter up briefly then settle back down again. The long dank barge, crammed with male guests, floats beside the bank like the corpse of an old woman, its lower half soaking in cool water, its upper half still swollen from the intense heat of the day. As the night air cools, the metal decks and wood-panelled cabins contract, letting out creaks and groans.

'Stop kicking, will you, and allow me to finish my dinner in peace!' Mother says, rubbing her belly and expelling a loud fart.

KEYWORDS: *bamboo bird cage, the wise in water, housewife, safe refuge, wild duck, floating happiness.*

It's an old fishing boat, about five metres long, with a bow and stern wide enough for two people to sit side by side. The cabin at the centre has a bitumen-coated canopy attached to a bamboo and metal frame. Although you have to crouch down to enter it, once you're inside it feels like a proper room, almost the size of a double bed. Plastic sheets can be lowered over the front and back openings to block out the wind and rain. Meili has become fond of this new home. She likes the washing lines strung between the canopy and the bow, and the bamboo birdcage attached to the side of the boat. The only problem is her constant fear that Nannan might fall overboard. When Meili stepped onto the boat for the first time, she immediately tripped and fell, landing hard on her swollen belly. The thought of Nannan falling into the river makes her twitch with alarm.

'Slow down, Kongzi!' Meili calls out. 'We've gone far enough. Let's turn round and go back to our mooring.' She's sitting in the cabin with her arms around Nannan. This is the first trip they've made on their new boat. Meili can't swim, so as soon as Kongzi accelerates, her body becomes rigid with fear.

A giant, shark-like fish swims past, its long snout and crenulated spine rising above the water.

'What's that strange creature?' asks Meili.

'A Chinese sturgeon,' Kongzi replies. 'It's the oldest vertebrate in the world. The government has granted it Class One Protection. They hatch in the upper reaches of the Yangtze then swim down to the sea.

Ten years later, they swim back against the river's flow to spawn in their place of origin.'

'Class One Protection for fish, indeed! What about us humans? When will *we* be able to return to our place of origin?' Meili grasps the bottle of lemonade Nannan is drinking and takes a quick sip.

'The Yangtze has become so polluted, there are only a few hundred sturgeon left. And when the dam is finished, their migration route will be completely cut off. They're doomed to extinction.' Kongzi watches the sturgeon sink below the surface. As he slows the boat down, Meili crawls to the bow. The breeze moving through the blazing summer heat feels cool and refreshing. Grassy embankments, mud houses and mandarin trees slip by on both sides. Her fears seem to blow away. Closing her eyes, she imagines soaring over the golden waters like a wild goose, the river mist in her face, seeing the boats and barges behind her form dark silhouettes against the low sun and the Yangtze stretch into the distance, dissolving finally between two cliff faces into a haze of water and sky.

She begins to sense that drifting down the river could offer her a new way of life, a floating happiness. She feels free and at peace.

Kongzi notices a barge approach and bites his lower lip nervously. He's never driven a boat before, and is afraid of colliding. In a fluster, he decelerates too quickly and the engine stalls. Once the barge has passed, he pulls the start cord again, adjusts the throttle and the boat sets off once more. Eager to regain face, he slows the boat, throws it in reverse then artfully turns it in a circle. Looking both surprised and proud, he glances back at Meili and says, 'As my great ancestor Confucius once remarked: "The benevolent find joy in mountains, the wise in water." How right he was! When he left home after offending the Duke of Lu, he wandered from state to state for thirteen years, an exile in his own country. Now two thousand years later, I'm also on the run, but unlike him, I'm not free to travel across the land, so all I can do is drift down the Yangtze.'

At noon, before Nannan has woken from her morning nap, Meili goes to the tiny galley area in the stern, lights the kerosene stove and puts a pan of water on to boil. Beside her is a mound of spinach leaves she cleaned earlier. Whenever she needs to wash vegetables or clothes, she simply leans overboard and scoops up a bucket of water. Thrilled to have a place of their own at last, she has already scrubbed the boat from stern to bow, torn off the mouldy bitumen canopy and replaced it with new tarpaulin. Now when they sleep in the cabin at night, they're no longer disturbed by a musty smell of rot. Meili has also tied a rope from Nannan's waist to the cabin frame, short enough to prevent her leaning overboard to dip her hands in the water. But Meili can't stop the boat rocking. Although she feels more free on the water than she did on the land, she knows it will take time for her to become used to this fluid substance that adapts its form to the contours of the earth and exists in constant flux. The river is a moving landscape which flows in directions she can't always determine.

After becoming pregnant with Happiness, the earth no longer felt solid underfoot. Not even their house or the dugout Kongzi created beneath Nannan's bed could provide a safe refuge. The land belongs to the government. Whether it's rented or borrowed, every patch of soil in this country is controlled by the state; no citizen can own a single grain. If she'd stayed planted in the village like a maize stalk waiting to be trampled on, she too might have had her belly injected with disinfectant like Yuanyuan, or been bundled into a cart a few weeks after childbirth like her neighbour Fang, milk leaking from her bare breasts. Ever since they left the village, her muscles have clenched with fear as soon as her feet touch the ground. Although the barge hotel was on the river, it was in effect an extension of the town. But this wavering fishing boat has liberated her. She will learn to drive it and survive on the little they possess. She told Kongzi that in Guangdong Province there's a place called Heaven Township where people can have as many children as they wish, making sure, of course, not to tell him that its polluted air renders men sterile. Kongzi said that this was just the kind of enlightened place where Happiness should be born.

'Cooking lunch?' Meili calls out to the pregnant woman in the houseboat moored a few metres away. 'It smells good.'

The woman is sitting at the bow, her toes like chicken claws gripping the edge of the boat. She and her husband already have a baby, and two daughters who are old enough to go into Sanxia and buy provisions on their own. Meili glanced at the baby when the woman held it over the river to defecate, and saw that it was a girl. The woman's boat is twice the size of Meili's. It has a tall control room and a shorter cabin behind with a bitumen-coated felt roof held down with bricks. When the boat is stacked with polystyrene panels the husband hauls to construction sites, it looks like a sparkling iceberg. While he's away on a trip, the woman and her daughters often wander around the wharf, hawking home-made snacks, shaking plastic bags of eggs boiled in tea, spiced tofu and marinated broad beans below the windows of buses waiting to board the ferry.

'It's imported Thai rice,' the woman calls back to Meili. 'I bought it in the supermarket. What are you having?'

'Fried celery and some reheated chicken soup.'

'You shouldn't drink hot liquids in the middle of the day,' says the woman, hoisting up a bundle of garlic shoots she's been soaking in the river. 'And with a belly that size, you should move more slowly around the boat.'

'Let those soak a little longer if you want to wash off the chemicals. I planted half a field of garlic shoots last year and had to spray pesticides on them twice a week to keep the insects away.'

'No need – I'm going to boil them for ten minutes. The river water may look clean, but it's riddled with threadworm.'

Meili grimaces. They've been drinking boiled river water since they moved onto the boat. 'But the water's safe to drink, surely, if you boil it?' she asks.

'No, not at this time of year! You should fetch your drinking water from the barge hotel's washroom. Go at lunchtime when no one's about. Or give the man at the diesel station a couple of mao and he'll let you fill your bucket at his tap. You can drink river water in the winter, but in the summer, it's infested with germs and parasites.'

'How come your stove doesn't give off smoke?' Meili asks, looking at the broad beans the woman has laid out to dry on the deck.

'It's a gas stove. Cost me a hundred yuan. Come and have a look at it, if you want.'

Meili fetches her hooked bamboo pole.

'Always turn off your stove before you disembark,' the woman says, her eyes beady as a cormorant's. 'If it topples over, your boat will burn to a cinder.'

Meili extends her pole, drags the woman's boat towards hers then ties them together with rope.

'The current is strong,' the woman says. 'Your boat will break free with a knot like that.' She loosens Meili's knot and reties it. 'This is a bowline knot. It won't slip.'

'I should learn how to do that,' says Meili, gripping her canopy. She glances into the woman's spacious cabin, and inhales the fragrant smell of rice wafting from the pot on the gas stove.

After checking that Nannan is still asleep, Meili steps over onto the woman's boat and squats on the cabin's vinyl-covered floor. 'What a great stove!' she says, and looks at the clothes and hats hanging neatly on the wall next to a glossy calendar with a photograph of a woman in a long silver dress.

'You should buy one. One canister will last you a whole week. And another tip: when a large vessel approaches head on, slow down and turn towards the bank so the waves hit you at right angles, or your boat will capsize. Ha! I could tell from the way you were gripping your canopy just now that you haven't been on the river long. Is that your daughter sleeping in the cabin? Make sure she stays inside when the boat is moving, or she might fall overboard.'

'You're right. We only bought the boat a week ago. I haven't got used to the constant movement. I feel as though I'm rocking on a swing the whole time. You have a television and an electric fan, I see. What luxury.'

'We've lived on this boat for ten years. I still get seasick, though. Summers are tolerable, but in winter, if you don't have an electric heater it's as cold as the grave. Before the frost sets in, tell your husband to buy a mini generator and a heater or you'll freeze to death.'

'What do you use for a toilet?' asks Meili, watching an army of weevils scuttle across the scorching deck and fall into the river.

'When we're anchored here, I just do it on the bank.' Then she crawls to the bow and lifts a square panel from the deck. 'And when we're sailing, I can do it straight into the river!'

'You're family planning fugitives too, aren't you?' Meili says, seeing the baby strapped to the woman's back focus her triangular eyes on her. 'What's your name, little one?' she asks, realising suddenly that other people's children are of little interest to her.

'She's called Little Third. A third girl. What bad luck! This one in my belly will be my last. I'm fed up with this drifting life. I want to live in a brick house with a front door I can lock, a wardrobe to store my clothes in, a big fridge to keep all my food fresh and a comfortable armchair I can sit on.'

'But this boat is so much better than ours. It has everything you could need.'

'The river may be nice to look at, but I don't want to spend my life on it. I have parents back home. Fallen leaves must return to their roots, as the saying goes. Besides, this vagrant life is not good for men. My husband seldom sleeps here at night.'

'Yes, like crops in the fields we all need roots to survive.' Meili feels her belly expand. She wants to lie on her side and breathe deeply. Little Third peeps over her mother's shoulder again and smiles. She has two upper and two lower teeth. Meili pretends not to see her.

'I've seen your husband on the boat in the evenings,' the woman says, 'sitting out on the deck smoking while you cook supper. How lucky you are!' Then she turns to the bank and shouts to her two older daughters, 'Come and have your lunch, girls.' They're standing on a field of cabbages near an abandoned barge that's being used as a chicken hutch. A rooster digging at the muddy bank spots a cabbage leaf out of the corner of its eye and scuttles over to it.

'But your husband has done so well, setting up his cargo business,' Meili says. 'Mine just works on a demolition site. He used to be a teacher, though. Men – if you don't keep them on a tight rein, their eyes are bound to wander.' She glances into her boat and sees Nannan is still asleep. Her sweat-soaked hair is stuck to her face, and below her rucked-up skirt insects are crawling over her chubby thighs.

'He's grown tired of me,' the woman says, snapping the garlic shoots in half. 'You know what they say: the song of the wild duck in the fields always sounds more melodious than the clucking of the hen at home.' Her T-shirt has large damp patches over her breasts.

Meili watches the woman move about the deck – sallow cheeks, lined forehead, hunched, twig-like frame – and imagines how a man would feel lying on top of her at night. She thinks how, in ten years, she will be thirty and by then she too may have three or four children. The thought terrifies her. Whatever happens, she won't confine herself to the role of housewife like this woman. Once Happiness is born, she will find a job, train as a beautician and dress her children in the finest clothes. The woman's elder daughters jump aboard and the boat tips to the side. Their faces are grimy and their bare feet covered in mud.

'I'll leave you to have lunch,' Meili says, stepping back onto her boat and unfastening the rope. 'It's time for my daughter to wake up.'

The noon sun scorches the tarpaulin canopy and the wooden deck at the bow and stern. Even the shade inside the cabin is swelteringly hot. Meili wants to sail downriver to pick up a breeze, but isn't confident using the outboard motor yet. Kongzi has said he'd like to pick up some work hauling cargo, but doesn't know who to approach. There are thirty or so families living in the houseboats moored here. Most of the men work in factories or on demolition sites; only a few have managed to make a living transporting goods. When the men return at dusk, they come laden with vegetables, deep-fried dough sticks and packets of instant noodles, and the wharf area becomes filled with the smell of chemical flavourings and the squealing and cursing of children.

KEYWORDS: *watermelon, dirt poor, purple lines, osmanthus branches, blush, porn movie, I love you.*

Sitting outside the cabin with his knees drawn up to his chest, Kongzi looks into the night sky and recites a Tang poem: '"Beside my bed, bright moonlight sparkles on the ground like frost. / I raise my head and gaze at the moon, then lower it and think of home . . ." Look how golden the moon is tonight. No wonder it's inspired so much beautiful poetry.'

Meili remains silent, queasy from the heavy rocking of the boat. Every evening at this time, as mosquitoes start to swarm above the banks, they sail to the middle of the river to hide from the police patrol boat, and the waves are always much stronger here. Last night, Kongzi came home late, so Meili sailed herself and Nannan into the moon's reflection which spanned almost the entire breadth of the river. When they reached the middle, she dropped anchor and watched the splintering moonlight on the water's surface quiver and embrace, just as she and Kongzi did the night they first kissed behind the Sky Beyond the Sky Hotel. Although it was a squat concrete building with faded paint, its neat brick paths, circular doorways, trimmed lawns and white fences brought an air of the city to Kong Village. That night four years ago, when the moon hung high overhead, Kongzi pressed her against a tree, kissed her on the lips, then pulled her knickers off.

Meili brushes mosquitoes from Nannan's sleeping face and looks out into the darkness. She remembers how sometimes when she stepped outside at night back in Kong Village their yard would look frozen, silver, dead. Now, she can see the same eerie and sombre light falling on a distant bend of the river.

'What's troubling you?' Kongzi asks her as she walks out onto the deck. 'Relax. Just look out at this wide-open space. It's strange – I knew nothing about boats before, but now I feel I belong on the river. Life is so much better here than it was in the village.' He's lying across the bow, his head propped up on a folded jacket, swigging from a bottle of beer. He's just had a dip, and his wet underpants are clinging to his skin. Meili and Nannan haven't learned to swim yet, but are confident enough to wade about at the edge of the river, wearing inflatable rings. This afternoon, Meili floated in the river until sunset, enjoying feeling the water wash the sweat from her skin and her body become weightless. She could tell that Happiness was comfortable as well as it swirled around her womb, trailing its hands through her amniotic fluid.

'How soon you're ready to forget your own home!' Meili says, rinsing Kongzi's muddy sandals in the river then placing them neatly outside the cabin. 'Kong Village is beautiful, too. Dark Water River is almost as broad as the Yangtze, and the reservoir is larger than any lake I've seen here.' In her mouth she can still taste the sweet watermelon they ate a few minutes ago.

'Confucius said, "The noble man embraces virtue while the petty man thinks only of his home,"' Kongzi replies defensively. When he's not wearing his thick glasses, his features seem to protrude more. His hands and face are covered in plasters. For the past week his team has been demolishing Sanxia's Cultural Centre. He's brought back many books and magazines he rescued from the shelves.

'Last year, when I suggested we should leave Nannan with my mother and go south to find work, you said: No, we can't leave home because Confucius said, "While your parents are alive do not travel afar." You're always contradicting yourself.'

Kongzi gets up and drives the boat back to the bank. Above the wharf, a single light bulb shines down on three bare-chested men who are leaning on a green billiard table smoking cigarettes. 'You know very well that if we returned to the village now, we'd be finished,' he says. He manoeuvres the boat into its mooring then sits down and takes another gulp of beer. 'Half of these houseboats are occupied by family planning fugitives like us. We're safe. The authorities won't bother us. Next week I'll find you a midwife.'

'There's no need. That pregnant woman who has three daughters told me she's attended many births, and has offered to help me when my time comes . . . Stop drinking that cheap beer. If it's fake, you're going to get very sick.' She turns down the radio Kongzi salvaged from the Cultural Centre, then leans over to scratch the mosquito bites covering his legs. 'If we had a fridge, we'd be able to save the rest of the watermelon for tomorrow,' she sighs.

'As soon as I get my next wage, I'll buy a mini generator and an electric heater,' Kongzi says, proud that he's now able to provide for his family. Yesterday, he bought four ducks and put them in the bamboo cage. This dilapidated boat has offered them the possibility of a better future.

'No, let's buy a television first. It's so quiet here at night, I can hear every thought passing through my head.' Meili lies down on her back next to Kongzi and stares at her bulge. 'What if it's a girl?' she says. 'I warn you, I won't get pregnant a third time.' Feeling her circulation become restricted, she turns onto her side and rests her swollen feet on Kongzi's legs.

'If it's a girl, we'll keep her. Then, when I've made enough money, we'll buy a bigger boat, with two cabins, sail downriver and try again for a boy. No one will be able to stop us.'

'You really think so? The land is controlled by the land police and the rivers by the river police. We can never escape the government's claws.' A smell of duck shit wafts up from the cage below and she wrinkles her nose in disgust.

'The river police only collect navigation fees and check licences. They don't deal with family planning crimes.'

'But we can't live like this for ever. Your parents need us. They shouldn't be having to chase pigs around the yard and rake up chicken shit at their age.' Under the bamboo stool beside her is a bag containing a towel, two muslin cloths, and a tiny vest and pair of shorts, ready for Happiness's arrival. Knowing that she'll be preoccupied after the birth, she has already made the small quilt Happiness will need in the winter. She'd like to light a candle now and begin sewing a baby jacket, but fears it might attract more mosquitoes.

'All I miss about the village is the school,' Kongzi says. 'I miss standing in front of my class and delivering a lesson. My throat is dry from lack of use.'

Meili feels a pang of sympathy for him. To protect their family, he's had to give up his vocation. Scratching his bitten calves with her toes, she says, 'Let me sing you a song to cheer you up, then. *Darling husband, we shared our home and the household expenses, trod the same floorboards, slept in the same bed. My head next to yours on the pillow – how happy I was! Now, alone under my single sheet, I roll to the left and weep, then roll to the right and sigh . . .*'

'Don't sing me a funeral lament!' Kongzi says, flicking his cigarette stub into the river. 'It'll bring us bad luck. Besides, your grandmother's songs belong to the past.'

'It's supposed to be bad luck to bring a woman on board a boat, so why not throw me into the river if you're so superstitious!' Meili's grandmother is a small, fragile woman whose forehead is pockmarked from childhood measles. When she was thirteen, and Nuwa County was gripped by famine, her destitute parents sold her for just half a bag of rice and a bamboo lute to the aged caretaker of Nuwa Temple. A year later, the old man married her. He taught her traditional opera and let her sing at every temple ceremony. At twenty, she learned the art of funeral wailing from a singer called Old Lady Wu, and became so proficient that her fame spread throughout the county. Meili remembers watching her stand before crowds of grievers wearing a turban of white mourning cloth, and unleash agonised high-pitched laments with tears streaming down her face. It was considered a mark of prestige for a family to have her sing at a wake. 'The songs my grandmother taught me are beautiful,' Meili says to Kongzi. 'Her voice has cracked, so I'm the only one in my family who can sing them now. All right, if you don't want a funeral song, here's a Deng Lijun ballad instead: *If I forget him, I'll lose my way. I'll sink into misery . . .*' When she finishes the ballad, she rolls onto her back again, bends her knees and waves a fan over her face. 'I blush with shame when I have to tell people you work on a demolition site. When you were a teacher, I could hold my head up high.'

'It wasn't such a great job. The salary was pitiful.'

'But I was the wife of a teacher. I had status. I didn't care how much you earned.'

'Before we married you said you'd love me even if I were dirt poor. I was manager of the Sky Beyond the Sky Hotel at the time. Is that what impressed you?'

'That miserable job? Ha! One day, I'll set up my own business and show you what a real manager is. I never did understand why Teacher Zhou closed the hotel in the end.'

'He couldn't attract enough people. I advised him to start breeding crabs in the hotel pond to make some money on the side, but he said if we did, the guests wouldn't be able to swim in it.'

They fall silent. The only sound they can hear is the rumble of trucks on a distant mountain road, transporting cement to the construction site of the Three Gorges Dam.

'I do still love you, Kongzi,' Meili says at last. 'But when you changed my name from "Beautiful and Pretty" to "Beautiful Dawn" you promised that our marriage would be the beginning of a wonderful new life.'

'You regret me changing your name? But it's so much more poetic. I promise you, Meili, a beautiful dawn is waiting for us.'

'I never imagined that being pregnant could be so terrifying. Last night I dreamed that the baby had become frozen solid. I put it under a light bulb to warm it up, then I was afraid someone might see it, so I wrapped it in toilet paper and hid it in a drawer. I walked away and forgot all about it, and when I next opened the drawer I discovered it had suffocated to death.' Meili's eyes fill with tears.

'Don't cry, my dear wife. Everything will be all right. I give you my word: if this one's a boy, we won't try for a third. Let me feel your belly. My goodness. It's so large now. So hard.'

'I'm sure the baby is bigger than Nannan was at this stage. Stronger, too. Look at all the purple lines around my tummy button. Let's not have a third, even if Happiness is a girl. We need to get on with our lives.' Kongzi slides his hand down between her legs and she slaps it hard with the tip of her fan. 'Don't touch me! I'm boiling.'

When Kongzi came back late last night he confessed that he'd been to see a porn movie in the video parlour boat docked near the wharf. He said he couldn't help himself because she hadn't let him touch her for weeks. Meili knows that those films feature men and women making love in the nude. She'd always considered Kongzi to be a respectable man, and the knowledge that he'd watched porn movies in a grubby video parlour lowered him in her estimation.

'All right, my turn to sing a song, then,' Kongzi says, sitting up and tossing the fly-encrusted remains of the watermelon into the river. '*In the village, is a girl called Xiao Fang. She's pretty and kind, has big dark eyes and wears her hair in bunches*—'

'Agh! So out of tune . . .' Meili groans. Sensing he wants to make love to her, she pulls the peony-printed sheet over her thighs and tries to change the mood. 'You must phone home tomorrow, Kongzi. Find out what the situation is.'

'I told you, my father asked me not to get in touch until the baby's born. All right, I'll phone them, if you insist, but if the line is tapped and the police track us down, don't blame me.' He pinches her arm playfully.

Meili hunches her shoulders and crosses her legs. 'Just make sure you don't tell them we're in Sanxia,' she says. In the breeze blowing across her face she can smell the scent of the osmanthus branches she put on the canopy. The smell always transports her back to her parents' house and her grandmother, who planted an osmanthus tree in the garden the day Meili was born. She remembers how her grandmother always likes to rub the blossom between her fingers and dab the scent behind her ears.

'So black and smooth,' Kongzi says, stroking Meili's hair that glistens like the skin of an eel.

'At least it's easy for me to wash my hair on this boat,' she says, tucking a stray lock behind her ear. Every morning, she leans overboard and dunks her head in the river.

'And such slender legs,' Kongzi continues, running his hand up to her thighs.

'Careful of the money!' Meili gasps, and quickly presses the sachet of cash she sewed into the lining of her knickers to check that it's still there. As he strokes her thigh she feels her face begin to flush. 'If I weren't pregnant, I'd have a slender waist as well,' she whispers, nuzzling her head into the nape of his neck.

'You're beautiful from top to toe, but your best part is . . . here.' He leans down and pulls her knickers off.

'Can't you even say "I love you" first? Since you watched that porn movie, you think you can just ram yourself inside me and tell me to moan.' She cranes her neck round to check that Nannan is still asleep in the cabin, then closes her eyes and waits for Kongzi to repeat what he did last night.

'No, my darling wife, all I want is to make you happy,' he whispers into her ear. 'That's why I work so hard every day. I want to give our family a better life.' Then he mounts her belly and pushes himself inside her.

'No!' Meili cries, knocking him off. 'You know I black out when you go on top.' She rolls onto her side, letting her belly rest on the deck, then reaches for an inflatable safety ring and wedges it under her head. Kongzi puts his arm around her and enters her from behind. Their breaths smell of the fried fishwort they ate for breakfast. Meili's forehead and cleavage perspire and the blue veins on her belly pulsate. A stench of dead fish rises through the cracks in the wooden deck. The boat rocks from side to side as Kongzi moves in and out of her. A sense of well-being spreads through her soft ample body. 'Careful of my belly. Gently, gently . . .' Her head pressed against the bow, she raises her hips and clenches her thighs. With a loud groan, Kongzi releases a river of sperm into her and sinks back down onto the deck.

Suddenly Meili sees the infant spirit flit before her eyes, laughing inanely. Waking from her daze, she pushes Kongzi back. 'Get out of me,' she cries. 'I don't want to give birth to a dead child.'

'Stop worrying! Everything will be fine. We're living on the river now. We're free! Look at the beautiful view . . . "The distant shadow of the lonely sail vanishes into a blue-green void. / All that can be seen is the Yangtze River flowing to the edge of the sky."' He fumbles for his matches and lights another cigarette.

'I just saw the infant spirit again,' says Meili, still catching her breath. The moon has become hidden behind clouds and the scent of osmanthus in the air seems to be flowing from her skin.

'You were dizzy. Your mind must have been playing tricks on you. I always follow Confucius's advice: respect the gods and the spirits of the dead, but keep your distance from them.'

'But I saw the spirit. It flickered right in front of me like a candle flame, then drifted to my belly button and vanished. It must have returned to Happiness's body.' She sits up and brushes off the insects that have settled on her bump. Then she looks out at the river glimmering in the darkness and sees a white polystyrene lunch box float by. A few days ago, she saw a dead baby with thick black hair float by just as slowly. As it passed, children climbed onto a rocky outcrop and prodded it with long twigs.

'Happiness is punching me again,' she says. 'Look, you can see its little fists poking out! It wants me to give birth to it on the river so it can float to the sea and travel the world. It won't be long now. Just another week or two.'

Kongzi puts his hand on hers and exhales a cloud of smoke. Inside the cabin, Nannan coughs in her sleep. Meili looks up at the broken town. The ancient houses at the base of the mountain are flattened now, while the jagged edges of the unfinished structures above seem like the ramparts of a ruined city. On this single mountainside the past, present and future appear to have merged. Meili senses that her own future is hovering in the air above her, swirling about like the millions of sperm that are now entering her cervix.

She lies back, rests her head on Kongzi's thigh, then wipes her damp forehead and says, 'Here, give me a puff of your cigarette.'

KEYWORDS: *soldering iron, family planning violators, stationary hands, imported oxytocin, miscellaneous expenses, dewy eyes.*

At the end of a long day, looking grief-stricken and dusty, Kongzi shuffles across a raft moored close to the bank, steps onto the boat and collapses into the cabin.

'So you got through?' asks Meili. When she sees the look of despair in his eyes her heart sinks. 'What's the matter? What's happened?'

'Our house has been torn down. They bulldozed it, just like I bull-doze those buildings up there every day. They didn't leave so much as a window frame.' He digs into his large pocket and pulls out a small plastic doll with long yellow hair and a red dress which he found on the demolition site. He taps the dust off its face and hands it to Nannan.

'They've demolished our house? What about the walnut wardrobe where I kept my photographs and my grandmother's bamboo lute?'

Kongzi lights a cigarette and presses it to his lips. A dragonfly that settled on the side of the boat darts into the air.

'And your parents?' Meili asks. She sees the ducks she let out to swim a few moments ago head for the shore, and wishes she could return them to their cage.

'Their house wasn't touched, thank goodness. I phoned Kong Zhaobo as well. He said the family planning squad destroyed the homes of nine families who refused to pay the fines. Li Peisong managed to pay off the remaining nine thousand yuan for Little Fatty's birth, so he was allowed to keep his house. Of the forty-three villagers who were arrested, nine have been released and the rest are still waiting to be sentenced.'

65

Nannan kisses the plastic doll and presses it close to her chest. 'What's her name, Daddy?'

'Unlucky,' Kongzi replies. He lies on his side on the bamboo mat, next to Nannan's half-eaten banana, a pair of Meili's knickers and the dirty vest he's just pulled off.

'Is she real, Daddy? I like her yellow hair. I want wash her face.'

'But why did they bulldoze *our* house?' asks Meili. 'They had no idea I was pregnant. Perhaps the police were monitoring the line when you phoned your father last month.' Turning to Nannan, she says, 'Let me wash that doll before you play with it.' The cabin is suffocatingly hot. Unable to bend down over her pregnant belly, Meili picks up Kongzi's vest with her toes, folds it and places it on the stool. Then she goes outside, turns her back to the setting sun and inhales deeply. The scorching breeze blows against her sweat-soaked dress. 'At least the Kong Village police won't be able to track us down to this place,' she says. 'Not from a phone call.'

'Probably not. But I've heard that the authorities here are sending police to check the documents of every migrant worker in the county. Our team manager told us to make sure our papers are in order.'

'Let's sail downriver, then. If the inspectors find me, that'll be it.'

Meili looks over to the bank and notices some men stepping off a van. Then a white boat approaches and a fat officer standing at the bow shouts out to her: 'Hey, you with the big belly! Do you have a birth permit for that? Where are you from?'

Panic-struck, Meili stoops down into the cabin and says, 'Kongzi, quick! Start the engine. They've come to arrest us.'

Kongzi scrambles to the stern and grasps the steering wheel, but before he manages to pull the start cord, three men from the van jump aboard and yank his arms behind his back. As swiftly and quietly as she can, Meili crawls to the starboard and lowers herself into the river.

'Get back on the boat!' one of the men shouts at her.

'I'm just having a . . . w-wash,' she stutters. She's up to her shoulders in water, quaking with fear.

'There's no point trying to hide your belly from us. We can still see it through the water. Get back on board and show us your birth permit.'

'She's not pregnant – she's just plump,' Kongzi says, the colour draining from his face.

'We'll need to take her to the clinic to confirm that.' As the man speaks, the white boat draws closer and is hooked to theirs. The fat officer at the bow takes a swig from his can of Coke then says to Meili, 'Get out of the water! We're from the County Family Planning Commission, and we've come to round up every woman in Sanxia who's pregnant without permission.' The silver buckle of his belt glints in the sun.

Kongzi pulls Nannan out of the cabin and says, 'It's my wife's first pregnancy. This girl here belongs to our neighbours.'

'I'm your girl, Daddy, not neighbour girl,' Nannan splutters, bursting into tears. 'I not blabbing nonsense. Mummy, Mummy . . .'

The fat man eyes Kongzi sternly. 'If we take the girl away with us, will you still claim she's not yours?'

A man in black sunglasses steps aboard. 'Any woman pregnant without authorisation is both violating the family planning laws and endangering the economic development of our nation,' he says. 'You think you can turn up here and breed as you wish? This is the Three Gorges Dam Project Special Economic Zone, don't you know?'

'If you cooperate with us, you won't have to pay the fine,' another man says. 'But if you resist, we'll get your village Party Secretary to arrest every member of your family.'

'We're peasants, with rural residence permits, and our daughter here is already five years old, so my wife's entitled to have a second child,' Kongzi says.

'Five years old, you say?' says the man in sunglasses. 'Three, more like. And who knows how many more children you've got hidden away.'

'My wife's eight months pregnant. Don't take her to the clinic, I beg you. I'll pay the fine right now.' Standing stripped to the waist among the men in white shirts, Kongzi appears feeble and submissive.

The fat man drops his empty can into the river. 'We've been ordered to terminate every illegal pregnancy we discover. If we let any woman off, our salaries will be docked.'

The word 'terminate' throws Kongzi into a fury. 'Have you no

67

humanity?' he shouts. 'You want to kill our unborn child? Have you forgotten that you too once lay in your mother's womb?'

A female officer steps forward. 'Humanity?' she sneers. 'If your baby turns out to be a girl, you'll throw her into the river, so don't talk to me about humanity! You migrant workers travel around the country, dumping baby girls as you go. You're the ones who have no shame! You think we wanted to come here and deal with you squalid boat people? No, the higher authorities sent us here because of all the filth that's been washing up downstream.'

Meili remembers the dead baby she saw floating past the other day, and suspects that this is what the woman is referring to. She wishes she could sink into the water and swim away.

'Enough talk!' barks the man in sunglasses. 'Take her to the van!' Four men reach down, tug Meili out of the river and drag her ashore. When she tries to resist, an officer kicks her in the belly. She yells in agony and feels her limbs go limp. After they shove her inside the van, she looks through the back window and sees Kongzi knock an officer overboard with a wooden oar, then two men push him onto the deck and force him into handcuffs. As the van drives off, she hears Nannan weeping inside the cabin.

The van trundles up through the flattened old town. Each bump on the road makes her aching belly throb. She screams to be let out, punches the window and bangs her head on the glass. The officer beside her grasps hold of her wrists. The van slowly climbs the mountain along a road flanked with new buildings, then turns down a dirt track and comes to a stop.

Meili can smell a stench of blood which reminds her of Nannan's birth, but this time fills her with dread. She's pulled to the entrance of the concrete building but refuses to go in. She knows that this is where they want to rip Happiness from her. But the men push her inside, drag her to an operating room and close the door. A woman in a white uniform looks up from a desk. Meili runs over to her and pulls the woman's hair. The woman digs her nails into Meili's hands and shouts, 'Quick, call Dr Gang!' Two men yank Meili's arms behind her back. Forgetting about her belly, she kicks at everything in sight:

the men, the woman in white, the air, the stainless-steel surgical table, the walls. Another man tugs her back by the hair. Then the door opens and Dr Gang walks in with a syringe. 'Hold her left arm out for me,' he commands. Meili manages to wrench her arms free, but is quickly punched in the small of her back. Startled by the jolt, Happiness pokes a clenched fist through her belly. The woman in white kneels down and grips Meili's legs. From behind, a man locks his arm around Meili's waist and another man pulls her left arm out, holds it straight and says, 'You can inject her now, Doctor.'

Dr Gang lifts the syringe and stabs the needle into Meili's upper arm. Meili sees the bulb dangling in front of her and the light filtering through cracks in the steel door begin to splinter and blur.

'Where were you off to when I passed you in the corridor this morning?' she hears the woman say.

'To the latrines. The wawa I bought yesterday gave me the runs.'

'Tell your wife that wawas must be soaked in boiling water and scraped clean before they're cooked . . . Right, I think she's under now. Lift her onto the table . . .'

The infant spirit watches Mother being tied to the steel surgical table all those years ago, her hands bound in plastic and hemp ropes, her pale, exposed bulge resembling a pig on a butcher's table.

A man in a white coat rubs his nose, then plucks Mother's knicker elastic and watches her flinch. 'Give her another shot, to be safe,' he says.

'Don't kill my baby, don't touch my —' Mother splutters, white foam bubbling from her mouth. But the man slides his hands beneath Mother's bottom and pulls off her knickers. 'Hooligan!' Mother weeps. 'If my baby dies, its spirit will haunt you for eternity.' She tries to spit the foam covering her mouth onto his face, but it rises only slightly then falls back on her lips.

The man begins to prod Mother's belly.

'Don't do it, I beg you . . .' she moans. 'Let me keep this child. I won't have another, I promise . . . It's a Chinese citizen. It has a right to live . . .'

The man is handed a second syringe with a much longer needle. He inserts the tip into Mother's belly and pushes it all the way in.

'Stop, stop! Don't hurt my baby . . .'

The infant spirit observes its first incarnation writhe and squirm as the long needle enters its head. When the cold astringent liquid is released into the brain, the spirit sees the cells shiver and contract, and the fetus flail about in the amniotic fluid, pounding Mother's warm uterine walls, then gradually grow weaker and weaker until all that moves is its quivering spine.

'Is this what your mothers brought you into the world for?' Mother cries out to the men. 'To kill babies? Well, you'd better kill me too, while you're about it . . .'

'Good work, Dr Gang!' the woman says. 'You must have been studying me on the sly.'

'It was much simpler than this morning's one. Look, when you press the belly here you can see the head clearly. It was easy to hit the target.'

Ignoring her moans and handling her as roughly as they would a corpse, the doctors part Meili's legs, slide a speculum into her vagina, mop up the discharge, then, when the mouth of the cervix is visible, insert a prostaglandin suppository. Meili tries to scream but can produce only a soft sigh. She tries to roll onto her side but, apart from her neck, nothing will move. 'Forgive me, Happiness,' she whispers. 'I couldn't protect you. I'd kill myself if I could, so that we could die together, but my hands and feet are bound . . .' She lifts her head, squeezes her eyes to expel her tears and stares at her belly. A sharp pain shoots through her womb, spreads to her lower back and flows to every part of her body.

'Goddess Nuwa, Mother of Humanity, rescue me!' Mother wails. 'Oh, Father of Darkness—'

'What a fine voice you have,' the man says coldly. 'Your cries won't change anything, though. We've seen it all in this room: vomit, faeces, blood, urine, screaming tantrums. But however much the women curse and resist, they must all surrender their babies to us in the end. You think you can defy the state? Don't waste your breath.'

'When we tied you to this table there were two of you, but when you get off there'll be just one,' a male nurse in a blue hat tells her softly.

'Devils! Animals!' Meili moans. She tries to cross her legs to close her cervix, but all she can feel is her toes clench slightly. The hot air in the room smells of deep-fried sausage. **'May you die without sons or grandsons! May your family lines perish!'** Mother cries, drenched in sweat, her lips the colour of frozen meat.

'If you want to leave this room alive, you'd better shut up!' the male nurse says, taking off his blue hat and fanning his face with it.

'Yes, if you don't keep quiet, you'll be responsible for any medical accident that might happen in this room,' says the woman. **'Your womb belongs to the state. Getting pregnant without authorisation is against the law. Argue your case with the government, if you want. Go to America – see what they say. China's population control policy has the full support of the United Nations. Do you understand, you ignorant peasant?'**

'Doctors have a duty to rescue the dying and heal the wounded, but you—'

'We're professional surgeons. We had well-paid hospital jobs. You think we wanted to come here and operate on you lot? For the measly bonus they give us?'

'If you don't like this job, I'll tell the director to transfer you back home,' says the woman. The men behind her chuckle.

The blood-engorged walls of Meili's womb begin to soften and the cervix is prised apart. She watches blood trickle down her thigh towards the fingers of her left hand, then sees the trickle become a stream which runs along the table's incline and falls onto the floor.

'This imported oxytocin seems to take effect much faster. Look, the membranes have already broken.'

The woman walks round and takes a look. 'What thick black hair it has! Let's use the forceps.'

Meili senses what feels like a hot soldering iron enter her body. When she hears the sound of ripping flesh, in her mind she sees the baby's eyes, ears, throat.

'Mother, help me!' she howls through every strand of her hair. 'Don't come out, my child. Don't come out into this evil world. Stay inside me and we can go to our deaths together . . .' But the forceps continue to press around the baby and yank it from her flesh.

Hearing the baby cry, Meili lifts her head, desperate to catch a glimpse of it.

'It's still alive, the stubborn little thing,' Dr Gang says, holding Happiness by the neck. 'What shall we do with it?' Happiness kicks its little legs about just as it did in the womb. Meili looks at the space between its legs. It's a boy. She tries with her eyes to reach out to him, but soon all she can see is the colour red.

'Strangle it,' the woman says. 'We'll register it as a stillbirth. Don't wipe its face. Illegal babies aren't entitled to have their mucus removed. Squeeze the neck here. That's right. Keep squeezing. That's it . . .'

When Happiness's body turns stiff, Dr Gang drops it into a plastic bag as though it were a criminal who's just been dragged from an execution ground.

Meili cranes her neck, straining to catch another glimpse of her son. 'Your mother heard you cry three times, my child. I heard you. Come back to me soon in your next incarnation and I'll give you my milk to drink . . .' She looks up at the doctors, and with no strength left in her voice mutters: 'Murderers, murderers . . .'

'I'm going to miss the afternoon boat and won't get home until ten. I bet my son will sneak off to that damn internet cafe . . . Wen, fill this basin with water.'

'They've just done the woman next door as well. Whose name shall I put on the abortion certificate?'

'Guo Ni, the wife of the Road Bureau chief. She gave birth to a second son yesterday. The chief gave the clinic twenty thousand yuan this morning, so we'll all receive a good bonus this month.'

'It's not your son you should be worrying about, Dr Su. I heard your husband visits the sauna house every night on his way home from work. Won't be long before he finds himself a "second wife".'

'You want to break up our marriage? No chance!'

'You don't believe me?' says Dr Gang, pulling off his bloodstained surgical gloves. 'Just wait and see.' He sits on a plastic chair, dangles a sandal from his toes and puts a cigarette in his mouth.

'Stop stirring things up. And go outside if you want to smoke.'

The electric fan overhead circulates the smell of stale blood through the room. Meili's placenta flops onto the metal table like a wet, purple sock.

The woman in white coils the remains of the umbilical cord around her gloved hand and puts the placenta inside a second plastic bag.

'That placenta looks nice and plump.'

'Well, you can't have it. The Party Secretary has already reserved it . . .'

Meili feels as though she's floating on water. Her thoughts become foggy and vague. Like the severed neck of a duck, the hole between her legs drips with dark blood.

When she returns to consciousness, the bulb is still shining and the electric fan still whirring. She remembers the image of Kongzi being forced onto the deck and handcuffed. The girl on night duty is curled up on the desk, fast asleep. Empty intravenous bags hang from a nail next to a clock with stationary hands. The room smells like rotten fish. Suddenly aware that she's lying on the surgical table naked from the waist down, she lifts her limp hands to shield herself and discovers the ropes have been removed. She tries to sit up but can't summon the energy. Her womb feels utterly empty. A jolt of pain shoots through her lower abdomen. Her legs are still leaden and numb. From a radio further down the corridor, a man's voice sings, '*I've just met a beautiful woman with soft arms and dewy eyes . . .*'

The girl gets off the desk and rubs her eyes. 'You've woken up, then,' she says to Meili. 'Here – once you've signed this form and paid the bill, you can leave.' She takes Meili's pillow and pulls off the case. Meili's left arm is so swollen from the injection that she can't bend it. 'This bag is for you, too,' the girl says. 'There's a free bottle of mineral water inside, four packs of condoms and a contraceptive handbook. Now, please get off the table. I need to wash it.'

After carefully shifting her legs to the side, Meili leans on the girl and lowers her feet to the ground, but as soon as she puts weight on them, her knees buckle. She collapses back onto the table and pulls her dress over her belly. The girl mops up the blood and amniotic fluid that has dripped onto the floor then helps Meili put on her knickers. Meili rolls onto her side, looks down and sees Happiness lying in the plastic bag below. His tiny corpse reminds her of the chickens she used to buy freshly plucked and slaughtered from the village market. He's floating in a shallow pool of fetal and maternal blood, his eyes and mouth wide open.

'Yes, that's your baby,' the girl says, glancing down. 'If you want me to get rid of it, you'll have to sign the form and settle the bill.'

'He's my son. I want to take him with me.'

Suddenly the door swings open and Kongzi charges in, pushing back the officer escorting him. When he sees the blood on Meili's legs he explodes with rage. 'Fucking bastard! May your family line perish! You bastard, you fucking bastard—'

'Swear at me again and I'll strangle you,' the officer barks.

The girl hands Kongzi the bill. 'It's all itemised,' she says. 'Two hundred and ten yuan for the intrauterine injection, 160 for the anaesthetic, 190 for miscellaneous expenses – which is the fee for disposing of the corpse – then there's laundry, labour. It comes to a total of 775 yuan. The usual fee for an eighth-month termination is 1,400 yuan, so you've been given a 50 per cent discount. I'd pay up and leave, if I were you. If you haven't gone by midnight, you'll be charged an extra thirty yuan for the room. You can take the form home and fill it out later. Just sign here, agreeing that you, Comrade so-and-so, willingly consented to terminate the pregnancy in accordance with state guidelines, and in so doing have made a glorious contribution to China's population control efforts.'

'You've killed our baby,' Kongzi says, red with anger. 'And now you want us to give you money and sign forms?'

'Forget about the form if you want,' says the officer, 'but next time the Family Planning Commission arrests you, you'll be sorry.'

'Let's pay the money and leave, Kongzi,' Meili says, leaning down and picking up the plastic bag with both hands.

'You can't take the baby with you,' the officer says. 'It's against the rules. Throw it in the bin. What do you want a dead baby for, anyway?'

'We have a right to take our child away,' Kongzi says. He takes a wad of cash from his trouser pocket, hands it to the girl and signs the form.

'I warn you,' says the officer. 'We're in the Three Gorges Epidemic Prevention Zone. If you dare bury that baby anywhere around here, you'll be arrested and fined.'

'Arrest me then, arrest me!' Kongzi shouts. Two security guards appear, seize Kongzi by the arms and fling him out onto the street. Clutching the plastic bag, Meili carefully dismounts the table and hobbles out of the room, leaning against the walls for support. As soon as she leaves the main entrance, she crumples to her knees. Kongzi rushes over and pulls her up.

'Get lost now, you vagrant scum!' the officer shouts as they walk away.

A man on a motorbike pulls up and says, 'Five yuan a trip. I'll take you anywhere. Are you coming?'

Kongzi tries to help Meili onto the back seat. 'I can't get on,' she cries. The blood clots clogging her vagina have begun to harden, and she's terrified she'll haemorrhage if she opens her legs. Gently, Kongzi lifts her left leg and moves it over the back seat. Squealing softly, Meili lowers herself onto the seat. Her face turns deathly white. 'Does it hurt?' Kongzi asks, sitting down behind her and wrapping his arms around her waist. 'No, no,' she hisses through her teeth. 'Let's go back to the boat.' She closes her eyes and rests her head on the driver's back. 'Did you leave Nannan alone?' she asks Kongzi. 'What if she's fallen overboard?' The motorbike drives down the broken mountain road. No matter how hard Meili is jolted, her hand remains fiercely clamped around the plastic bag on her lap.

KEYWORDS: *newly hatched carp, water heaven, red dress, frozen blood, funeral song.*

Kongzi stares at an object floating down the river, wondering whether it's a dead fish, a piece of straw or a chopstick. He's turned off the ignition and allowed the boat to be dragged downstream by the current. Grassy embankments and scatterings of mud houses slide swiftly by. The side winds nudging the boat off course smell of the factory effluent flowing into the river from large waste pipes.

Meili is lying on her front on the side deck, staring at the passing hills and bamboo forests, her left leg trailing in the water. The deep still river is as blue and transparent as the sky. Nannan splashes some water onto Meili's head and cries, 'Look, Mum! You have flowers on your hair!' Then she ties a piece of string around her plastic doll and lets it trail in the water as well. The doll's red dress fans out like a pool of blood. Meili closes her eyes and hears her grandmother wailing a funeral song: *'My darling child, like a newly hatched carp that leaps from its pond for the first time only to fall into the jaws of a cat, you have entered the netherworld before your first tooth has appeared. The mother and father you've left behind weep in misery . . .'* Meili grew up listening to her grandmother's grief-stricken wails. They planted inside her a seed which has grown into a tree that supports her spine, pelvis, ribs and every fibre of her flesh. She wants to sing a line from the lament, but all she can do is cry: 'Mother, Mother, oh Mother . . .' She puts her arms around Nannan and, unable to cry out, breaks into sobs, her back rising and falling, rising and falling, like a rag tumbling over a wave.

'Your face has too much crying, Mummy,' Nannan says, edging

away. Against the green shorts she's wearing, her tanned legs look as dark as soy sauce.

A long time later, Kongzi puts on his black vest, steers towards the middle of the river and drops anchor. Then he picks up the plastic bag containing Happiness's corpse, places a brick inside and ties the top with string.

'Wait!' Meili says. She opens her cloth bag and takes out the little hat, vest and pair of shorts she knitted for Happiness. 'Put these inside too,' she says to Kongzi, handing them to him.

'Why my brother dead, Mummy?' Nannan asks, pressing her small hand on Meili's sunken belly.

'The bad people took him out before he was ready,' Meili answers. She thinks of the anxiety and nightmares she's endured since their flight from Kong Village, and realises that in this country there is not one roof under which she can live in safety. In the past, she ignored Kongzi whenever he described the horrors of the Tiananmen Massacre, the Cultural Revolution, the Campaign against Lin Biao and Confucius. Only now does she fully understand that, in the eyes of the Communist Party, she is but a criminal whom they can torture as they please, a woman who doesn't even have the right to be a mother to her unborn child.

'But I not want him dead, Mummy,' Nannan cries, pointing to the plastic bag. 'I want him moving. You said you give me brother.'

Against the pallor of her face, Meili's lips are the colour of dark plums. After returning to the boat, she slept for two entire days, still leaking clots of blood. In her sleep, she could hear Nannan crying out to her and feel Kongzi place fresh wads of paper inside her knickers or pieces of banana into her mouth. When she woke, she saw blood on her dress, on the bamboo mat, and even under Nannan's fingernails.

A swarm of flies crouch on the canopy like a squad of family planning officials.

In the twilight, a sand-dredging vessel sails past, leaving a trail of gleaming foam that makes the surrounding water appear wetter and heavier.

'I finished,' Nannan says, lifting her bare bottom in the air and peering down into her potty.

Mother wipes Nannan's bottom and hugs her tightly. 'Your brother had a sad fate, Nannan. He must go to heaven now. Say goodbye to him.' Her eyes are two narrow slits between lids red and swollen from crying.

'But heaven in the sky. Why you put brother in water heaven? He can swim? He going swim to Sea Dragon's palace?'

'No, your brother just wants to have a long sleep,' Mother says. 'Kongzi, put Happiness into the river.'

Mother flops onto her stomach again and lies on the deck with her long hair over her eyes, her swollen left arm outstretched towards the bow. Two ducks stick their heads out of the bamboo cage below and stare at the darkening water and sky. 'Wait,' Mother calls out. 'Drive back to the bank and pick some osmanthus.'

The infant spirit can hear the sounds from that evening, but can't see the images clearly as the sky is not yet pitch black. The river is calm. All that can be heard is the dull thud of the propeller churning through the water. After a short absence, Father returns to the boat holding three branches of osmanthus. He drives the boat back to the middle of the river, threads the branches through the string knot of the plastic bag then gently lowers the bag into the water. The infant spirit plummets to the riverbed and watches the bag descend.

'Look at that leaf, Mummy,' Nannan says. 'It swimming.'

Once the water burial is finished, Kongzi sails back to the bank and drops anchor. 'Let's spend the night here,' he says, crouching down and staring out at the smooth surface of the river.

The night thickens and the river turns black. Happiness and the osmanthus flowers have vanished. The flies have gone. In the candle-light, Meili sees Nannan's doll floating in the river, one arm outstretched. After soaking in the water all day, its red dress has turned the colour of frozen blood, and its eyes a more intense blue. Its yellow hair streams and scatters around the shiny plastic face.

Meili feels milk begin to leak from her breasts. She leans over the side of the boat and squeezes it out. Drip, drip, drip . . . The river opens its mouth and swallows.

KEYWORDS: *sand island, National Day, forced abortion, blood clot, potassium permanganate.*

Before nightfall, Kongzi anchors the boat near a jetty that juts out over the river beneath a municipal rubbish dump. Other ramshackle boats and barges are tethered nearby, each one crammed with scavenged plastic crates, sofa cushions and lampshades. Chickens, ducks and children are scampering over the muddy shore while above them foragers pick their way over the dump's broken bricks and tiles. The buildings on the hill behind are festooned with National Day celebration banners and flags. It looks like a sizeable county town.

Meili sees a woman in the next boat washing spinach, and reminds Kongzi that they've run out of rice.

'I'll go up to the town and buy some,' he says. 'And I'll buy some soap as well, so you can wash in the river this evening.' Kongzi hasn't earned any money since he paid the abortion fee, and only has fifty yuan left.

'No, I don't want to wash.' Meili still can't bring herself to touch the river in which Happiness is buried. Her body is filthy and covered in insect bites, but at least the swelling on her left arm has subsided, and she can now bend it again.

'I want play with them, Daddy,' Nannan says, pointing to some children in a cabbage field who are poking a flock of chickens with bamboo sticks. The ducks in the cage on the side of the boat ruffle their wings, desperate to be let out onto the river.

Kongzi ties the boat to a broken slab of concrete, picks Nannan up into his arms and crosses the dump, heading for the town.

Meili turns round and sees a long sand island in the middle of the river. A jumble of houseboats, as dilapidated as theirs, lie anchored by the shore. Children are playing hide-and-seek among the bushes and babies are lying asleep on car tyres. Colourful laundry hangs from cables strung between trees, giving the place a homely air. She can tell at a glance that the islanders are fellow family planning fugitives and, suspecting that they club together to bribe local officials into leaving them alone, thinks it might be safer if they joined them. She wouldn't want to stay long, though. Once they've crossed Guangxi Province, they'll reach Guangdong, and be able to make their way to Heaven Township. For the first time since her abortion, she allows her hand to touch her hollow belly. A taste as foul as rotting vermin rises into her mouth. She senses that death is lurking somewhere deep within her, cold and implacable. Her abdomen cramps as another blood clot is expelled from her womb. She remembers her friend Rongrong's sallow face wince as she swallowed the bitter herbal medicine for her pelvic disease, and feels frightened and far from home.

At night, the river is tranquil, apart from the occasional dog bark or squealing of a baby. The roar that flows from the distant motorway makes the trees tremble but doesn't stir the boats. Meili rests her head on a baby mattress she found on the dump and hugs a hot-water bottle, her breasts beneath her white shirt drooping to either side. The kerosene lamp casts an orange light over her neck and face. 'Let's moor by the sand island for a few days, Kongzi,' she says. 'This river is so broad and winding I've lost track of where we are.'

'We've left the Yangtze and have followed the Gui River into Guangxi Province. This town is called Xijiang. Guangdong is just over there in the east. All right, let's stay here and rest for a while. I can pick up some work and we can search the dump for things to sell. The shops here aren't expensive. Peanut oil is four yuan a bottle, and rice is just 3.2 yuan a jin. Diesel and kerosene are quite reasonable too.'

Although Meili can eat now, she still suffers bouts of acute abdominal pain. 'The days are like water,' she says to Kongzi. 'They stretch out before me but I can't hold them in my hands.' Before supper, Kongzi poured some boiled water into a basin for her. She scrubbed her hands and face with soap and, for the first time since the abortion, washed between her legs as well then disinfected the area with potassium permanganate.

'You mustn't give way to despair,' Kongzi says to her. 'We'll have another child. We won't give up.' He opens the bottle of rice wine he bought at a stall near the motorway and pours himself a glass. A white cruise ship passes in the distance, a red flag tied to the mast. A couple on the back deck stand locked in an embrace beneath a loudspeaker blaring out 'Ode to our Motherland': *Our beloved nation is rich and powerful. Signs of prosperity are all around us . . .*

'Why don't we just go home and hand ourselves over to the authorities?' Meili says. 'If we show them the abortion certificate, perhaps they'll drop the fine. Life here is no safer than anywhere else. I've had enough . . .'

'The certificate wasn't stamped, so it's not valid . . . Oh, it's all my fault. We should have left Sanxia as soon as we bought the boat. Rivers are our country's arteries. As long as we keep following them, we'll eventually reach the heart – a mystical haven where we can live in peace.'

'You think we'll find anywhere more mystical than Nuwa Cave? As soon as I placed my hand on it, I fell pregnant with Nannan. Women from Nuwa aren't destined to have sons. You'd better accept our fate.' Happiness's asphyxiated face suddenly flashes before her eyes. She leans over and extinguishes the lamp. 'Besides, I can't go through another illegal pregnancy and forced abortion. Do you want to see me die?'

'Of course not. You're my wife. But we have a right to try again for a son.' Kongzi slaps his arm, trying to swat a mosquito. Then he stares into the darkness, at the mosquito's fluttering wings, perhaps, or a remembered image of Happiness's corpse.

'We have no rights, you stubborn fool! Only the state can decide whether I have another child or not. Pull the curtains down. I'm cold.' As the darkness thickens around her, Meili feels her heartbeat slow down and her hearing become more acute.

Kongzi takes a last drag from his cigarette and says, 'The bloody

Communists have destroyed Confucius's legacy. Benevolence, right-eousness, propriety, wisdom – all the values he upheld have gone. If a panda gets pregnant, the entire nation celebrates. But if a woman gets pregnant she's treated like a criminal. What kind of country is this?' He tosses his stub into the river then sits silently, his eyes darting about. When it becomes too dark to see a thing, he lowers his head and lets out a guttural cry of misery. 'My son, my son! Make your way back to us. "Summer wildfires cannot destroy the grass, For in spring, soft winds will restore it to life . . ." I cannot believe that in this immense country there is no space for my male descendant.'

Kongzi's brother, three years his senior, also has one daughter, but didn't register her in Kong Village in case they had a second child before she turned five. But a fellow villager who worked on his construction team in Wuhan reported him to the village police, so now neither his daughter nor any second child they might have will be granted a resi-dence permit. Kongzi and his brother look almost identical. The brother left home ten years ago to work in Wuhan, and when he returned every Spring Festival with bundles of cash, Kongzi, the poorly paid school teacher, always felt inferior. The village school had so little money that parents had to buy the children's desks and Kongzi had to provide his own. His brother paid for their wedding, spending five thousand yuan on a banquet for eighty guests and entertainment provided by the local song-and-dance troupe. He doesn't enjoy conversation or reading books. When he returns to the village, he sits in front of the television all day, chain-smoking. Kongzi would love to talk to him now, but knows that if he mentioned the family's need to produce a male heir, he'd be met with a blank silence. Kongzi is still convinced that only a son will bring him happiness. If his brother fails to produce one, the responsibility to continue the family line will fall on him. His brother's wife is almost forty, so time is running out. Kongzi hasn't dared phone his father and tell him that Meili was subjected to a forced abortion, and that the baby was a boy. Nor has he dared tell Meili that after they fled the village, his father was arrested and locked up for a week, and that because Meili didn't turn up for her mandatory IUD insertion, his mother was forcefully fitted with one instead.

Nannan rouses from her sleep, kicks off her blanket and crawls blindly onto Kongzi's lap.

'Go back to your mat, Nannan,' Kongzi says, pushing her away.

'I frightened of Sea Dragon – he hiding here,' Nannan says, pointing to her head. Before she went to sleep, Kongzi told her a story about a fairy called Flower Girl who was imprisoned by the Sea Dragon and rescued by the Bodhisattva of Mercy.

'Don't be silly,' Kongzi replies. 'The Sea Dragon died a long time ago.'

'You said after my brother dead, he wake up again.'

'Come and sleep next to me,' Meili says. She pulls her down onto her mattress. The boat rocks from side to side. 'Didn't you hear me, Kongzi? Lower the curtains – I'm shivering. Now go back to sleep, Nannan.'

'I like sleeping next to daddies, not mummies,' Nannan says, rolling back towards Kongzi who's lying on a folded blanket, his head resting on three magazines.

'The nights are so cold now,' Meili says, tucking a jumper around Nannan. 'If we don't withdraw some cash from the bank tomorrow and buy a generator and an electric heater, Nannan will come down with a terrible illness. We can't live like animals any longer.'

KEYWORDS: *deep-fried dough stick, sperm, mandatory sterilisation, shiny leather shoes, scorched poultry.*

Meili is woken by distant voices shouting, 'There's a man in the town who's threatening to leap from a five-storey building. Quick, everyone, go and have a look!' As Meili sits up, a stream of Kongzi's sperm leaks out from her and runs down her thigh. Grimacing with anger and disgust, she pulls some tissues from a box and stuffs them inside her knickers. That bloody condom must have split last night, she says to herself. If I fall pregnant, I'll become an enemy of the Party again. During the eight months since the abortion she has fended off Kongzi, but last night she relented, and let him push his way inside her.

Kongzi rolls over and says, 'If you're going over to take a look, buy me a deep-fried dough stick. I'm starving.'

'Why would I want to watch a stranger jump to his death?' Meili says. 'I'm not far off from jumping into the river myself. You want a dough stick? What about those noodles left over from yesterday?' Kongzi's cigarette smoke rises straight into her nose. She stands up and coughs.

They've set up home on the sand island. Meili has reared almost thirty ducks, and Kongzi has bought two egg-laying hens and a rooster which he keeps in the bamboo cage. When he isn't hauling cargos of smuggled or fake goods, he scours the town and rubbish dump for junk he can sell. There are twelve other families living on the island, most of them fellow family planning fugitives.

Meili dips a flannel into the river and rubs it over her face and body, flinching from the cold. Their neighbours Xixi and Chen are about to sail over to the town. They were the first family to arrive on the island. Last year, the river police pulled down all the shacks, but the islanders soon built themselves new ones with tarpaulin and wooden planks scavenged from the dump. A strong sense of community has formed among the families. Everyone rears chickens and ducks, so the air is always filled with the scent of roast meat.

'Want a lift, Meili?' Chen calls out. Meili says yes, but quickly changes her mind. 'No, if a big crowd has gathered to watch the man jump, the town will be swarming with police. I don't want to get dragged off to a family planning clinic and have some stranger push an IUD inside me.' Meili has developed a fear of crowds, and has only visited the town three times.

'Stop worrying,' Kongzi says. 'I told you, the head of the County Family Planning Commission is a reasonable man. We wouldn't be allowed to stay on this island otherwise. You go into town, and take Nannan with you.' Kongzi picks up lots of local information from other scavengers on the rubbish dump. Last week, he was told that a professor from Guangxi University was giving a lecture on Neo-Confucianism and Modernity at the County Cultural Palace, which he made a special effort to attend.

'No, I won't take Nannan,' Meili says, stepping onto Xixi and Chen's boat. 'There might be child snatchers in the crowd.'

'But those gangs only snatch boys,' Kongzi says.

'I don't care. You look after her.'

Once the boat pulls away, Kongzi wades into the river and feeds yesterday's leftover noodles to the chickens in the cage.

Up in the centre of town, after walking past the covered market and newly built Eastern Sauna House, Meili sees a large crowd staring up at a construction worker who's threatening to jump from the top of a half-finished office block. When he waves his hands about he reminds her of an old school friend who now works for the governor of Nuwa County. Anxious to escape the crowd, she skirts its perimeter and enters a wide, empty street. In the clear morning light, the family planning banners strung overhead appear even larger. One side of the street has been recently covered with cement; the other side remains potted with holes. She walks on, following smells of dough sticks and fried dumplings which lead her to a small food stall outside a restaurant with blue-glass windows.

Meili buys three dough sticks. Unable to resist, she opens the newspaper wrapping straight away and bites into one. Delicious. She sits on the restaurant's concrete step and reads the slogan daubed on the opposite wall: ANY PERSON FOUND TO HAVE EVADED MANDATORY STERILISATION WILL BE ARRESTED AND FINED. For the first time since the abortion, she is able to read this familiar slogan without her stomach knotting with fear.

She studies the blank expressions of the people passing by on their way to work, and feels frustrated. She too would like to stroll to work every day wearing a smart dress, shiny leather shoes, holding a handbag containing a hairbrush and make-up. But peasants are banned from entering tall office buildings which are warmed in winter and cooled in summer, and where staff are paid high salaries for sitting at their desks all day. Although Meili was born into a peasant family, she longs to live like the rich women in television dramas who own air-conditioned flats and air-conditioned cars and never have to set foot in a field. Once she has joined their ranks, she too will dress herself in a tailored suit, paint her nails red, fasten elegant sandals to her feet and stride into an air-conditioned jet or the carpeted foyer of a luxury hotel. She may be inadequately educated, but she has confidence and determination. She is able, after all, to perform a song in public having heard it only twice. She still dreams of becoming a pop star, and of travelling the country singing ballads in satin ball gowns. Before she married, she and six friends from Nuwa Village formed a group called the Nuwa International Arts Troupe, and toured local coal mines and rural markets, performing pop songs and belly dances. But she quit after a week when the manager of one village hall told her that unless the girls danced naked on the stage, no one would pay money for tickets. She's always believed that women should be respectable and modest. Since marrying Kongzi, she has dedicated herself to their family and endured their poverty without complaint. But she feels now that the time has come to pull herself together, find a job and start earning some money. Even if they never manage to live in a city, she must at least make sure that they can build themselves a new house back in Kong Village equipped with all the latest electronic appliances.

She walks back past the five-storey block from which the construction worker is still threatening to jump. The crowd has swollen. A man who's set up a makeshift stall shouts through a megaphone: 'For the best viewing experience, buy one of my telescopes and folding stools!' People impatient to get to work cry out: 'Hurry up and jump, will you? We can't wait around all day.' Without glancing up, Meili pushes her way through the crowd, managing to reach the covered market with the two remaining dough sticks intact. The smell of scorched poultry in the air is familiar to her. Since she got married, she has always been the one to slaughter the chickens, pluck them, then scorch the soft down from their skin. Glancing around at the busy stalls of the market, she thinks to herself, perhaps I could set up business here too. At least it's sheltered from the elements.

She turns to a stallholder and asks, 'How much are the ducks today, sister?'

'Three yuan a jin, and an extra yuan if you want it killed, plucked and gutted.'

'I can pluck. Are you looking for assistants?' Meili's already contemplating selling their flock of ducks to raise money to rent a space and buy stock.

'No, that guy over there is, though,' the stallholder replies, raising her eyebrows in the direction of a tall skinny man who's standing beside a fish stall.

Meili approaches him and asks for a job. He fixes his large, protruding eyes on her and says: 'I need someone who can gut and scale. I pay one jiao a fish. If you want to see how it's done, sit here and watch.'

Meili pulls over a wooden crate, sits down on it, and sees on the wall opposite her a notice that says: MILK POWDER WARNING ISSUED BY THE MUNICIPAL HYGIENE DEPARTMENT. TO SAFEGUARD INFANT HEALTH AND PREVENT DAMAGE TO THE WIDER POPULATION, A BAN HAS BEEN PLACED ON INFERIOR-QUALITY MILK POWDER . . . She remembers

Kongzi mentioning that he delivered a cargo of counterfeit milk powder to some businessman who'd bought them wholesale for three yuan a bag and was planning to sell them on the streets at triple the price. At the time, she reasoned with herself that whether the powder was fake or genuine, it would at least provide more nourishment than the rice gruel most peasant women feed their babies. Infant formula is always in demand. She is sure that if she opened a stall selling baby products in this market she could make a good profit.

After watching the fishmonger gut and scale for several hours, Meili realises that Kongzi must be hungry for the dough stick and is probably wondering what has taken her so long. She goes out into the sunlight and runs downhill. The June sun is scorching the dust on the pavement and the clumps of withered weeds growing along the kerbs. A hot wind chases her all the way to the river. She wades into the water, panting for breath, and scans the distant sand island, but sees no sign of Kongzi or their boat. Then, turning to her right, she spots their boat emerge from a huddle of rafts tethered to the jetty. The rooster stretches its head out of the cage and stares at her. Wiping the sweat from her face, she waves to Kongzi who's standing behind the wheel wearing a vest and shorts and muddy flip-flops.

He helps her onto the boat with the bamboo pole, frowning disgruntledly. 'What took you so long?' he barks.

Nannan's dress is sopping wet. She sticks her leg out, points her bare toes and says, 'Dad said I can't dance, Mummy!'

'I was in the market, learning how to gut fish,' Meili tells Kongzi. Sensing his disapproval of her independent attitude, she quickly changes the subject. 'So, did that man jump in the end?'

'I thought that's what you went to see. No, no. He didn't jump. The police dragged him away an hour ago. I withdrew a hundred yuan from the bank. There was no problem. It's not connected to our branch in Hubei Province. We still have a thousand yuan left in our account.'

Nannan hugs Meili's thigh. 'Mum, our rooster called Red. His long chin called Little Worm. Dad called Snake in Glasses. You called Big Eyes. You like my names?'

'We need a stable income, Kongzi. I want a job. I want to work, even if it's just on a market stall.' Meili sits at the bow, her damp forehead and shoulders glistening in the sun.

'Mum, this pee or sweat?' Nannan asks, stroking Meili's perspiring thigh.

'So what do you plan to do?' Kongzi sneers. 'Sell fish?'

'I'm a capable woman. You said yourself: I can do anything I put my mind to.'

'Mum, my pee look like orange juice, but I no eat orange today.'

KEYWORDS: *shelter, happy birthday, wanton activities, Empress Yang Guifei, condom, red-fried lion heads.*

As soon as the rooster crows at dawn, Meili gets dressed, crawls out of the shelter and checks that their boat is still anchored by the shore. A boat was stolen from the island a few days ago, so she and Kongzi have taken turns to sleep in theirs, but last night they both forgot. They've lived on the sand island for a year now, and although they haven't made much money, life has taken a turn for the better. Kongzi has bought himself a pair of gold-rimmed spectacles, a gas stove, an electric fan and a tricycle cart which he uses to make local deliveries. He's attached an extension lead from the mini generator on the boat, so the shelter has electricity as well. Meili's bought a watch, a small black-and-white television and a singing cloth doll for Nannan. Although their shelter is a humble affair cobbled together from old doors and decking, it has a chipboard bed Kongzi made which is covered with foam cushions, so at least their nights are comfortable.

Through the bamboo trees and willows on the opposite bank, Meili can see the outline of the town. The illuminated signs of the Eastern Sauna House, still shining at dawn, suggest the wanton activities of the previous night. A junk-laden truck is driving towards the rubbish dump. Once the dump has encroached ten more metres into the river, the Xijiang authorities will cover it with cement and erect a statue of the Tang Dynasty beauty, Empress Yang Guifei, who they claim was born in this town. The central government has urged authorities around the country to develop tourism by erecting monuments and statues honouring local icons. Here in Xijiang, the authorities have already built a mock Tang Dynasty temple on a mound where they claim Empress Yang Guifei was buried, dug a Yang Guifei Well from which they say the beautiful empress once drank, and at the summit of a nearby hill have built a Yang Guifei Pavilion with a dressing table where they claim she sat and combed her long hair. They've also granted protection to the house of a hitherto unknown revolutionary martyr, and charge admission fees priced at ten yuan. Within three years, they hope the county will become Guangxi Province's main tourist destination.

Meili no longer works at the fish stall. She took over a spice stall from a woman who left to have a baby, then, once she'd saved enough money, she bribed the market manager into letting her open a stall of her own. She's also wheedled the job of cleaning the market at night, and is able to scavenge from the discarded produce enough food to feed her family and sell to the islanders as well. Kongzi likes to clean the fish heads, tripe, pig skin and giblets she brings back, then stew them for hours with eight-spice powder to eat as a snack with his beer. Meili has persuaded him to grow vegetables which other stalls don't stock. Discovering that Time Square, a large paved area built hurriedly to impress visiting leaders, is deserted both day and night, he removed a few of the concrete paving stones and planted spring onions in the soil underneath. After checking the patch daily for two weeks without encountering a soul, he lifted some stones under an ornate street lamp that has never been lit, and planted spinach, chives and tomatoes. At the beginning of autumn, when everyone likes to eat hotpot flavoured with fresh greens, he started growing crown daisy leaves for Meili's stall, which have proved very popular. Last month he printed three hundred yellow flyers offering free home delivery of Meili's produce, and distributed them around the market. Meili has realised that, when choices are limited, happiness can only be achieved by striking out on new paths, and that while they wait to set off for Heaven Township, this river town can provide them with sufficient opportunities for a successful life.

She fetches the wok from the shelter and starts preparing breakfast, heating up the fermented rice congee she bought yesterday, adding two raw eggs and a few osmanthus flowers. As she stirs the bubbling mixture, she turns her back to Kongzi and slips two contraceptive pills into her mouth. Although she's checked the dates and is confident that she wasn't ovulating the last time they made love, she doesn't want to take any chances. She has also secretly decided to have an IUD fitted. She's fed up with Kongzi refusing to wear a condom, and having to wash out her vagina with soap and water as soon as he falls into a post-coital sleep. She couldn't endure a second forced abortion. She wants to work hard and make enough money to be able to treat herself now and then. She especially deserves a treat today: it's her birthday. She's decided that after she finishes at the market, she and Kongzi will have an evening out in the town.

At dusk, after she's packed up her stall, Kongzi arrives in his tricycle cart, having left Nannan with Chen and Xixi. Meili jumps cheerfully onto the back of the cart. As he pedals off, she picks up some yellow flyers lying at her feet and tosses them into the air, then she unties her cotton scarf and holds it up, letting it trail behind her in the breeze. The street widens as they head for the town centre. They pass rows of drab grey buildings, a merry-go-round with brightly painted wooden horses, rabbits and tigers, then the tall red edifice of the County Cultural Palace, where kung fu movies and foreign films are shown. Meili has already chosen what to order at the restaurant tonight: steamed silver carp, red-fried 'lion head' meatballs and hot-sour soup – dishes she can't easily cook on the island. So when the food is brought to the table, she's able to remain composed, taking small delicate mouthfuls, while Kongzi wolfs the food down with embarrassing haste. It's not the food itself that Meili appreciates most, it's the joy of sitting in comfort in a clean restaurant, with waitresses purring, 'Red-fried lion heads, madam, I hope you enjoy them,' as they lower the dish onto the table. How wonderful to be treated with respect, to be able to pay others to do the cooking and washing-up. As long as she continues to work hard, she'll be able to sit at cloth-covered restaurant tables like these several times a year. When Kongzi raises his glass and wishes her a happy birthday, she feels transported back to her honeymoon.

'We must celebrate your birthday like this as well, next month,' she says. She's already decided to buy Kongzi a CD player and a CD featuring his favourite song, the 'Fishing Boat Lullaby'. For a moment, she forgets that they're vagrants, illegal fugitives who don't own a house, a table or even a proper bed. She forgets that she has a daughter back on the sand island, and is even uncertain how old she has turned today. As a child, the only difference between her birthday and any other day was that there would be a few more noodles in her bowl. When she was fifteen, her father gave her a nylon fleece jacket when he returned home for Spring Festival, three months after her birthday. Although she and Kongzi ate at a restaurant during their honeymoon in Beijing – Teacher Zhou took them to a famous Beijing Duck emporium – Meili was so shy during the meal, she never once lifted her eyes from her plate. So, this is the first birthday she has celebrated properly. Swept up in the excitement, she helps Kongzi finish a whole bottle of rice wine. Only when he raises his last cup and makes a toast to their future son does she finally wake from her happy daze and see the infant spirit flit before her eyes once more.

KEYWORDS: *balloons, uterine walls, work permit, vegetables, vaginal speculum.*

As Kongzi boards the ferry holding a bag of rape seeds he plans to sow in Time Square, Meili asks Xixi to look after Nannan for the morning and prepares to go into town. She's determined to prevent the infant spirit re-entering her womb, the fleshy prison in which it would be doomed to await another execution.

Standing at the edge of the river brushing her teeth, she watches Kongzi disembark on the other side. The colourful rags and plastic bags caught in the trees above him remind her of the balloons that were hung above their front door on their wedding day. It suddenly occurs to her that this view is unfamiliar. The river level must have fallen, exposing the rubbish-festooned trees. In the bright morning sun, the rags and plastic bags sparkle like jewels. The river has dropped and the days are getting colder. Meili remembers Kongzi say that they should start trying for a baby before winter sets in, so that by the time her bump shows it can be concealed under thick jumpers. He ejaculated twice last night onto the entrance gate of her state-owned womb. Get on with it, she tells herself. No time to waste.

The street is dusty and scattered with broken bricks. Workers with greasy hair push past her. When she catches sight of the forbidding sign of the Family Planning Centre, she hesitates. Installing a security device at the entrance of her womb would enrage Kongzi, but the thought of falling pregnant again and being bound to the surgical table of an abortion room fills her with greater dread. Happiness's motionless face flashes through her mind.

She walks in and goes to the reception. 'Comrade, I want an internal examination and an IUD insertion,' she says to the young nurse sitting behind the counter.

The nurse's eyes narrow. 'I'll need your identity card, marriage certificate and migrant workers' fertility record.'

Meili's mouth goes dry. 'I only have an identity card and an abortion certificate,' she replies. The nurse gives her invoices for a forty-yuan pelvic examination and a fifteen-yuan disposable vaginal speculum, then takes her to the Family Planning Management Room at the end of the corridor and hands her a married woman's gynaecological and fertility assessment report form.

A female doctor wearing a white face mask palpates and prods Meili's breasts and abdomen, then tells her to lie on the bed and let her legs flop apart. The nurse tears open a sachet, pulls out a plastic speculum the shape of a duck's head, inserts the device's cold beak into Meili's vagina and opens it. A smell of disinfectant wafts into Meili's body.

'You say you just have one, three-year-old child, but it's clear you've given birth much more recently,' the doctor says, shining a torch onto Meili's cervix. Then she turns to the nurse and says, 'Write: smooth, no cervical erosion or polyps.'

'Yes, look – you can tell these red nipples have just been sucked,' the nurse says, resting her pen in her mouth and squeezing Meili's left breast.

'There's no milk in there!' Meili says. 'I have no baby, I promise, just one daughter who'll be four next month. I had an abortion last year. Why would I lie to you? I came here to have an IUD inserted because I don't want to fall pregnant again.' Meili is embarrassed by the redness of her nipples. It's Kongzi's fault: he insists on sucking them every night as he drops off to sleep.

'Why didn't you have one fitted after your first child?' asks the doctor, glancing at Meili's abortion certificate. 'And what does your husband do?' She clearly assumes that Meili is a hair-salon prostitute.

'He's a boatman, and grows some vegetables on the side,' Meili answers, feeling ashamed of Kongzi's diminished status. She winces with pain as the speculum continues to stretch open her cervix.

'All right, we'll give her an IUD,' the doctor says, pulling on rubber gloves. 'You're lucky the director isn't here today. If he were, we'd have to take you straight up to the third floor and get you sterilised.'

'But women are only supposed to be sterilised after their second child, and I only have one.' Meili looks at the door, unconsciously preparing for an escape.

'How do we know how many children you have? You said you were at the end of your cycle, but look how much blood there is on your sanitary towel. Are your periods usually so heavy? When did this one start?'

'Ten days ago. They're very irregular.' She wonders whether the doctor has seen traces of Kongzi's sperm inside her. A wad of surgical gauze is pushed into her vagina and twirled around. She grits her teeth and squeezes her eyes shut. Beads of sweat run down her face.

A cold pair of forceps yanks Meili's cervix forward, then a long needle is inserted into her womb, extracted and measured against a selection of IUDs.

'I suggest this oval one,' the nurse says to Meili. 'It's a domestic product, and only costs eighty yuan. The Sino-foreign joint venture ones cost two hundred. Go for the cheaper one. With the procedure fee, it will come to 180 yuan.'

'Oh no! I don't have that much money on me,' Meili says, wishing she could close her legs. 'I thought the IUD would be free.'

'It's only free for local residents,' the nurse replies.

'Exactly how much money have you got?' the doctor asks brusquely.

'Check my pockets,' Meili says, pointing to her trousers.

The nurse pulls out the cash from the pockets and counts it. 'Only a hundred yuan,' she says. 'Are you sure this is all you've got on you?'

'Haven't I seen you in the market?' the doctor says. 'Do you run a stall there?'

'Yes. I sell vegetables, herbs and pickles. Look out for me next time you go. All my produce is free from pesticides.' Meili's lease on the stall will soon expire, and the market's manager has informed her that since she doesn't have an official work permit it can't be renewed.

'Well, we'll do it for a hundred yuan then. I hope you appreciate our leniency. Bring me the oval one, nurse.' The doctor picks up the IUD with long blunt tweezers, opens the speculum even wider and slides the device inside. As her warm uterine walls tighten around the cold metal object, Meili stares at the two red gulls painted on the wall above the radiator.

The nurse hands Meili an appointment form. 'You'll have a follow-up examination three months from now, to check that the IUD hasn't fallen out or been deliberately removed,' she says. 'Any woman who attempts to take out their IUD, even if it's causing them pain, will be fined five hundred yuan.'

'You may suffer cramps, nausea and light bleeding, but these side effects are usually only temporary,' the doctor says, removing her face mask and revealing her brightly painted lips.

The nurse continues to fill in the examination report. 'Did you say her vaginal ridges have flattened out?' she asks, glancing up at the doctor.

Meili watches the bloodstained speculum being tossed into the bin and hears her cervix release a last thread of air before closing its entrance gate.

KEYWORDS: *willow branches, dead chick, chicken wings, cotton fluffer, Three Nos, ox in a yoke.*

'Come and join us, everyone. It's my daughter's birthday. Let me fill your glasses so we can drink to her health!' Kongzi is sitting on a broken, legless office chair he found on the rubbish dump and has tied to a tree trunk with rope. The battery-operated strip light he bought today is suspended from branches overhead, lighting up the plates of food set out on wooden crates.

'Thank you, Master Kong,' says Dai, a gentle man with large bulbous eyes and a deeply lined forehead. 'Me and Yiping are simple peasants. It's an honour for us to share a drink with a schoolteacher! A toast to your daughter, Master Kong!' Dai grits his teeth and forces himself to down the drink in one. He and Yiping are from Purple Mountain in Jiangsu Province. They moved to the sand island six weeks ago, and have built a shelter under the trees just behind. Meili came across them over in the town. Dai was wandering through the streets with a pole on his shoulders, a bucket of clothes and pans on one end and a cotton fluffer for quilt-making on the other. Yiping, half his height and heavily pregnant, was waddling behind him holding their two daughters by the hand. Meili approached them and advised them to move to the island to avoid being arrested by family planning officers.

A skinny, bald man called Bo lifts his glass and says, 'Drink, drink!' his scalp and bony shoulders gleaming under the strip light. His fingernails are black and broken from scavenging the rubbish dump. He and his wife have three daughters and a four-month-old son.

Kongzi has fried some chicken wings and Meili has made a salad of wild wood ear fungus. Smells of garlic and sesame oil drift from the men's faces as they tuck into the food. A gaggle of children run up, grab some chicken wings, then go to chase each other along the river's edge. Chen arrives in his boat, tethers it to a rock and climbs the sandy beach. 'So you still manage to remember birthdays on this island!' he says to Kongzi, clapping his hands. 'Ha! We haven't remembered our kids' birthdays for years.' He puts a bag of deep-fried meatballs onto the wooden crate. When he laughs, exposing his black and yellow teeth, he looks like a monkey.

'My daughter and I both have birthdays in November, so I never forget hers, and we always end up celebrating them together,' Kongzi replies.

Meili and the women are sitting beside them on cardboard boxes, eating rice and braised tofu. The smell of the duck stew simmering on the gas stove outside the shelter makes the breeze feel a little less cold.

'Have some more, Xixi,' Meili says, tapping the bowl of tofu with her chopsticks. 'You're eating for two, now. And try some of this liver. It's full of vitamins.'

'Thank you, thank you,' Xixi says, buttoning up her angora jerkin and rubbing her small bump. She turns to Yiping and asks, 'So, when's your one plopping out?'

'Not for another four months. But look, my belly's already so big I can't see my legs any more. Dai said our padded quilts are too hot for this town. He wants us to go into the mountains and see if we can sell them there.' Yiping is sitting cross-legged on a mat. With her large belly bulging from her tiny frame, she looks like a sweet potato freshly pulled from the ground.

'Wait until your baby's born before you leave,' says Bo's wife, a scruffy woman called Juru. 'You can give birth in the backstreet clinic behind the Family Planning Centre. The midwife only charges three hundred yuan.' Juru pulls out her breast from under her shirt and stuffs it into her baby's mouth. When Meili visited her shelter she was shocked by the sodden, mouldy straw on the ground, and advised Juru, for the sake of her baby's health, to replace it more frequently.

'Yes, if you set off now, the authorities might arrest you and give you a forced abortion,' Meili says. 'Dai should forget about selling quilts and try to find work on the rubbish dump. I'm thinking of buying a hundred more ducks and building a large pen on the beach. I reckon I could make ten thousand yuan a year from a flock that size.' Meili feels that now that she no longer has to worry about falling pregnant, she can concentrate on building a comfortable life for themselves here.

'Admit it – you've had an IUD fitted, haven't you?' Yiping says in the thick mountain accent Meili finds hard to understand.

'No, no,' Meili replies, glancing nervously at Kongzi. 'I considered it, but then realised that if I wanted another child I'd have to bribe a nurse a hundred yuan to remove it.'

'I'm so stupid,' Yiping laughs. 'All I'm good for is making babies. First time I saw a condom, I didn't know what it was. I thought it might be a piece of tripe, so I plopped it into a soup and ate it!'

'I wouldn't dare let anyone put an IUD inside me,' says Xixi. 'A neighbour back in our village tried to remove one from his wife. He stuck his hand inside her and groped around for hours, but couldn't find it. In the end, he got so frustrated he exploded her womb.' Xixi cringes at the memory, then spits a shard of chicken bone onto the ground.

'Exploded it?' Meili says, her mind returning to the dead face of Happiness.

'Yes, he bunged a firecracker up her vagina and set light to it,' Xixi says, crossing her legs and wriggling her toes.

'Men get so obsessed with carrying on the family line, they lose all reason!' Meili says, glancing at Kongzi again. He's banging his fist angrily now, shouting: 'Those fucking officials, turning up here and bombarding us with bloody condoms.' Two days ago, officers from the County Family Planning Commission came to the island to hand out floating population fertility registration forms and bags of condoms printed with photographs of movie stars.

'Hope you didn't swear at them like that when they came,' Chen says, then licks his teeth. 'When my brother was locked up in a detention centre last year for entering a city without permission, he swore at an official, and they cut half his tongue off.'

'I've been detained for vagrancy as well,' Bo says, scratching his bald scalp. 'If you have money and connections, they let you out after twenty-four hours. But I had nothing. They forced me to labour in the fields for two months, and beat me viciously every day. By the time I was let out, I was skin and bone.'

'So, what documents do you need to avoid arrest?' Dai asks, brushing some white cotton fluff from his jumper.

'Identity card, health certificate, temporary urban residence permit, temporary work permit, birth permit, marriage licence . . .' Kongzi says, rattling off the list. 'But even if you have them all, if you are in a big town or city and you look like a peasant, they'll still arrest you. And once you're in handcuffs, they'll squeeze as much money from you as they can.'

'They call us the "Three Nos": no documents, no homes, no income,' says Bo. 'When our son's a bit older, I'll go and work on a building site. Start living a normal life.' Bo is in his late forties. A rumour has circulated the island that he spent time in jail for abducting his neighbour's wife and selling her to a widower in the countryside.

'No, what they really call us is "blind vagrants", aimless drifters,' says Chen, a foolish smile spreading across his face. The Western suit he's wearing is thin and torn. He's making good money now, hauling cargos of oranges up the river several times a week.

'To think that it's now a crime for us to live in our own country!' Kongzi cries out, his face red from alcohol. 'Where do they expect us to go?'

'Keep your voice down - you're not in a classroom now,' Meili says. She looks over towards the town. An old warehouse behind the rubbish dump has been renovated and turned into the Earthly Paradise Nightclub. Its bright neon lights outshine the ones of the Eastern Sauna House above. People walk past and gaze up in wonder. A motorbike stops outside the entrance, and a smartly dressed couple climb off the back seat and become engulfed by children selling roses and chewing gum. Nearer the jetty, a crowd is wandering aimlessly outside a second-hand stall which is lit by a bright bulb. Meili suddenly remembers the CD player she bought from the stall and gave to Kongzi for his birthday. She rushes into the tent, brings out the CD of the 'Fishing Boat Lullaby' she also bought him, slides it into the CD player and turns the volume up. The melancholy notes of the zither ripple out like water. She closes her eyes and pictures fishing boats moving through an empty night, their sails gleaming above cresting waves. As plucked notes quiver, rise and fade, she imagines the sun setting in the west, waves lapping against a riverbank, willow branches softly swaying, a heron soaring into the sky. Slowly, the willows, waves, sails, river and sky turn the same brilliant gold, then the light fades and darkens. In a brief moment of silence, she remembers lying on the deck of their boat, wailing a funeral song for Happiness as the infant spirit flickered above her. After a final dissonant strain resolves into a sad chord, Kongzi raises his head to the moon and sighs, 'Ah, can you feel yourself dissolve into the landscape? It's just like the poem: "Scoop water from the river and the moon is in your hands. / Pick blossom from a tree and its perfume infuses your clothes." Thank you, Meili, for my wonderful presents. I will treasure them.'

'Yes, it's a beautiful song,' Chen says. Everyone else remains silent and begins to help themselves to more food.

As they're surrounded by water on all sides, at dusk the air becomes cool – especially now in winter – and the island feels more spacious.

'How much grain do you feed your ducks every day?' Juru asks Meili, picking a piece of straw from her jacket. Seeing the children come running up waving branches in the air, she shields her bowl and shouts, 'Careful not to kick sand into the food!'

'Here, one for each of you,' Meili says, handing a meatball to each child.

'Rub your hands on your trousers first, you grubby girl!' Juru says to her daughter. 'Look, they're covered in mud.'

Nannan wanders out from behind a tree and watches the children scurry into the bushes.

'Don't tread in the poo!' Chen calls out to them.

'I wish people wouldn't shit in those bushes,' Meili says, staring pointedly at Juru. 'When there's no wind blowing, the island stinks to high heaven. You asked how much we feed the ducks? We only have twenty-three left now. We give each bird a cup of grain a day, or two cups if they're laying eggs.' She sees Nannan pick up a tiny dead chick and says, 'Drop it!'

'Why is it dead, Mum?' Nannan asks, studying its face closely.

'It got sick, probably.'

'Why it wants to leave its mummy and daddy?'

'Huh, always asking questions! Come here and have another meatball!'

'I'm full up,' Nannan says, frowning. 'My tummy's tired.'

'Why not bury the little creature in the ground to keep it warm?' Meili says, and looks down at the ducks in the small pen Kongzi wove from branches and twigs. Nannan puts the chick down next to the stove and presses it into the sand with her foot.

'You're lucky to be able to have fresh eggs every day – my ducks seem to have stopped laying,' Xixi says, taking a fried pickle from the plate Juru is passing round.

'I've heard you're not producing enough breast milk, Juru,' Meili says. 'You should give your baby a formula top-up before you put him down to sleep.' The baby is sucking Juru's left nipple now, his little nose and hands red from the cold.

'The formula they sell at the market is fake,' Juru says. 'It's just ground rice and sugar. No protein.'

'I would've been lucky to have been fed rice and sugar at his age!' Meili says. 'Come on, let's taste the duck soup. Pass me your bowls.'

'"Condemned to the same life of wretched vagrancy, / At our first encounter, we laugh like old friends . . ."' Kongzi intones, his gold spectacles glinting under the strip light. 'So, who wrote that poem? If you can't answer, you must drink a shot!'

'We're peasants,' Bo protests. 'What do we know about poetry?' Bo never washes when he returns from the rubbish dump. As soon as any alcohol reaches his stomach, a smell of rot rises from his skin.

'How about a game of rhyming couplets, Kongzi?' says Dai, tossing his stub on the ground. 'Let's fill our glasses and have a go.'

'No, play with him first,' Kongzi says, pointing to Chen with his chin.

'All right,' Dai says, raising his glass to Chen. 'You and me, then. If you can't complete the couplet, you must empty your glass in one gulp. Here goes: Men who drift down the river . . .'

Chen pauses for a moment then blurts: 'End up getting stabbed in the liver . . .'

Dai rolls his bulbous eyes. 'Stabbed in the liver? When have any of us been stabbed in the liver?'

'Help me out, someone!' Chen whines.

'No, I'm afraid you've lost, my friend. Drink up!'

The infant spirit sees that these lives have now vanished from the island. All that remains is a smell of darkness and wisps of Mother's breath blowing from the bushes that have grown over the sandy beach. The reflections of the town's neon lights stretch right across the river into the reeds below. Mother and Father's plastic bag is still hanging from a branch. Inside it are some yellow flyers, a pocket mirror, three condoms, a stick of cinnamon, some star anise and a mouldy stub of ginger. Sounds from the evening return once more.

'Come on, Master Kong. My turn to challenge you.'

'All right. I'm ready.'

'A man who doesn't drink . . .'

'Lives a life more tedious than you could think.'

'A man who doesn't smoke . . .'

'Lives more miserably than an ox in a yoke.'

Father's efforts receive loud applause. 'What a scholar! It's clear you're a chip off Old Confucius's block. Such learning! Come, Master Kong, let's fill our glasses again and have another go . . .'

KEYWORDS: *inferior breed, Mount Yang Guifei, merry-go-round, trampoline, bandages.*

Last month, after two days of torrential rain, the sand island flooded. Some families retreated to their boats, others moved over to the opposite bank and built temporary huts near the rubbish dump. When the floodwaters receded, they all returned to the island and rebuilt their shelters. At Spring Festival, Kongzi wrote rhyming couplets for every family to hang outside their doors. Bo and Juru didn't have a door, so they hung their couplet – IN THIS GOLDEN AGE, EVERY FAMILY WILL PROSPER / IN THIS NEW YEAR, EVERY HOUSEHOLD WILL REJOICE – from the branches of a nearby tree.

Kongzi has released the ducks back onto the island. He lets them forage under the trees for water weeds, fish and slugs left behind by the flood, so only has to give them a full meal – usually a cabbage and cornmeal gruel – after he returns them to their pen at dusk. The pale brown hens scuttling about in the sunlight are squealing like children running home from school. Meili's favourite bird is the large white drake that is double the size of the female ducks. Since she was forbidden to renew her lease on the market stall, she has spent most of her time on the island, looking after the birds. Every morning, she collects five or six luminous eggs from the cardboard boxes in which the egg-laying ducks roost.

Kongzi bought a hundred little ducklings yesterday for just two hundred yuan. Meili suspects that at such a cheap price they must be an inferior breed. She tears a cardboard box into pieces, scatters them over the beach and ladles boiled rice onto each one.

'Get up now, it's lunchtime!' she calls out to Kongzi, watching the yellow ducklings wander off towards a bush littered with plastic bags. It's noon already, but Kongzi is still fast asleep, his legs draped over his blanket and peony-printed sheet. The new shelter he built from scavenged tarpaulin, wooden planks, tiles and old doors is finally, after many repairs, waterproof. It's taller than their last one, and wider than the cabin of their boat, so the three of them are able to sleep quite comfortably. On the inside of the door Meili has nailed a coat rail, and on the outside a kitchen rack in which she keeps ladles, spatulas, chopsticks, spoons, and bottles of soy sauce and vinegar. Next to the pile of shoes beside the entrance is a coil of rubber hose which Kongzi found on the rubbish dump. He was going to take it to Time Square to water his plants, but last week the police discovered his vegetable patches and destroyed them, so it's useless to him now.

'Help me up, Meili!' Kongzi shouts.

Meili peeps inside the shelter and sees Kongzi's penis sticking up under the sheet.

'No, my hands are dirty,' Meili says.

Kongzi reaches up, pulls Meili down and presses her hands onto his penis. Reluctantly, she begins to rub it, peering out through a crack in the door at a duck stretching its neck in the sunlight. She glances down at the erection in her hands and feels a warm jolt between her legs. Kongzi squeezes her nipple. Her face flushes. 'You lecherous pest,' she says. 'Can't you wait until tonight?'

'Don't stop,' Kongzi moans, trying to tug her trousers off. 'Sit on me, will you?'

The zip of her trousers breaks. She pushes him away and says, 'Let me go for a pee, then we can do it in the cabin.'

Once she's lying flat on the heart-shaped sheet inside the cabin of their boat, Kongzi thrusts his penis into her, swivels it about for a while like an oar in a fulcrum, and ejaculates. Meili's stomach cramps. His sperm is inside me now, she says to herself. Never mind. The IUD will kill them. She breathes a sigh of relief and crosses her legs.

'This time, I'm sure I've planted a son inside you,' Kongzi says. He ejaculates almost every day now, hoping desperately that one of his seeds will sprout.

'The ducks have finished their lunch,' Meili says, pulling her trousers back on. 'I must spray some water on them.'

'With what?' he asks, scratching the mosquito bites on his arms.

'My mouth. I heard the other day that if you spray them after a feed, it encourages them to preen their feathers. They need to rub themselves every day. It makes them feel good.'

Kongzi sniggers quietly.

'Oh, don't be so vulgar! What's happened to you? I preferred you when you were a schoolteacher and wore a clean suit and a shirt buttoned to the top.'

'One must adapt to changing circumstances. I'm not a teacher any more, I'm a family planning fugitive.'

'Well, I won't let my standards drop. From now on, we must brush our teeth every day. Just look at yours – they're as brown as rust. When you next go into town, buy three toothbrushes and a tube of Black Sister toothpaste – the advert said it protects against gum disease. And buy some roundworm tablets for Nannan as well. She's always hungry these days. She probably has ringworm too. Have you seen that red patch on her leg? You can go to the pharmacy after you sell the eggs tomorrow.'

Meili climbs out of the boat and walks to the shelter. A few seconds later, Nannan comes running up searching for something to eat. She stumbles over a ladle and wok lid and bumps into the stove, overturning a pan of boiling gruel straight onto her bare foot. She yells in agony. Meili steps over the pan and scoops her into her arms. Kongzi scrambles up the beach and stares at the large red blister already covering Nannan's foot and ankle. Meili douses the blister with soy sauce and says, 'This is serious. We must take her straight to hospital.'

Kongzi carries Nannan to the boat, shouting out to the other islanders, asking if anyone can lend him some cash. Meili runs after him. 'No, stay here, Meili,' he says. 'If you come to the hospital, they'll put an IUD inside you.'

She watches Kongzi sail Nannan across the river, carry her onto the jetty and disappear into the town. She imagines him carrying her along the road that leads to the hospital. First, they'll pass the pleasure pond where she took Nannan last month, and watched her pedalling cheerfully in a small plastic boat, her lips and hands blue from the cold, while on a trampoline behind, two girls stared into space, munching sunflower seeds. After the pond, they'll pass the Empress Yang Guifei Roast Chicken Store, with platters of burnished birds displayed in the front window, then a poky shop cluttered with crates of instant noodles and beer. The smell of roast chicken will follow them to the end of the road, all the way to the hospital forecourt. The entrance lies behind a cluster of large ornamental rocks and a large poster advertising cosmetic surgery. The thought of entering the hospital doors makes Meili sick with fear. To distract her mind, she boils up some water in which she'll dunk their clothes and sheets to kill the bedbugs that have infested their shelter.

A few hours later, Kongzi returns. Nannan is still sobbing, her left foot now wrapped in bandages. 'Mum, take the hurt away,' she cries. 'It hurts, it hurts!' Meili squeezes Nannan's little hand and bursts into tears. 'Good girl,' she says. 'I'll buy you some instant noodles tomorrow, and a chocolate monkey. I promise.' At this moment, Meili suddenly realises she's a mother, and that her body is still connected to Nannan. She can feel the burns on Nannan's feet as though they were singed into her own skin. She'll make sure she never comes to harm again. Nannan curls up on Meili's lap, as hot and limp as a boiled duck.

'I had to pay two hundred yuan,' Kongzi says, slumping into his legless chair, 'just for a few bandages.'

As the sky darkens and the air grows damper, ducks leave the bushes and waddle to the feeding bowls. The feathers they leave on the branches quiver in the cold breeze.

Dai's two daughters wander up and tell Kongzi that their father wants to have a drink with him.

'Tell him I can't tonight. Nannan's hurt herself.' Kongzi seldom refuses an invitation to join his neighbours for a drink. Many families have come and gone since they arrived, but their firmest friends are still here. The children spend their days playing together, and the families often eat together at night.

'The ducks seem to be suffering from cramps,' Meili says to Kongzi, carrying Nannan into the shelter. 'We'd better not let them wade in the river.'

The infant spirit watches Father squat down and tune the radio to a different station. A nasal voice whines: 'Today, prosperity is within everyone's reach. If you want to turn your dreams into reality, make sure you catch the next edition of *The Road to Wealth* . . .'

'A man in the waiting room tipped me off about a good job,' Father tells Mother. 'It pays seventy yuan a day, lunch included. I'd be painting the jagged mountain behind the town. The authorities have renamed it Mount Yang Guifei. They've closed the quarry and are getting workers to paint the exposed rock face green, in time for a visit next month from the Provincial Tourism Department.'

'I could do that,' Mother says, lying down in the shelter, squeezing a flea that's jumped onto her blue cotton trousers. 'You could stay here and look after Nannan and the ducks.'

'No, the spray paint is toxic. It can render women infertile. Two workers passed out from the fumes today. I saw them being carried into the hospital on stretchers.'

'If they want to hide the quarry scar, why don't they just plant some trees in front of it?' Mother asks, pulling down the door curtain to block the draughts.

'It would take too long. They need it to look presentable before the officials arrive.'

'This island was clean after the flood. But now there's so much shit about, it's becoming infested with mosquitoes again. The Hygiene Department is bound to clamp down on us. I'm fed up with Bo and Juru shitting in the bushes. Why can't they just dig a hole like everyone else? When the wind blows from the west, the smell is revolting. It's time we left. I've asked around and found out that Heaven Township isn't far from Foshan Mountain. Let's pack up and sail south.'

'You're not talking about Heaven Township again, are you?' says Father, scratching a bite on his neck. 'I won't leave this island until you get pregnant. We've been trying for six months and still nothing's happened.'

'Empress Yang Guifei didn't have any children, did she? It must be something in the water.'

'Mum, I bury the dead chick in the sand, so why it hasn't wake up yet?' Nannan asks. Backlit by the kerosene lamp, her face looks as dark as her hair.

'It's having a long sleep,' says Mother, stroking Nannan's bandaged foot.

'Tell Daddy to pull it out,' Nannan says, her eyes two pools of light in the darkness.

'I can't pull it out, Nannan,' Father says, resting his head on his bent knees.

'Mum, flowers don't have eyes, so why do they die?'

'Because flowers are too pretty for this world.'

'Daddy said I'm pretty, so I'm going to die soon too?'

Father frowns. 'Stupid girl, you can't even write your own name yet. What do you know about death?'

'Huh! You're a naughty daddy. I want a different daddy. I hit your neck. See, my dolly is very angry.'

'Don't lose your temper with her, Kongzi,' Mother whispers. 'Look, Nannan. Your toes are exactly the same shape as mine. Let me clip your nails.'

'What does lose temper mean, Daddy?'

'It means to get angry,' Father says, his tone softening. 'Yes, I can tell your doll's angry – her black hair has turned yellow and her brown eyes have turned blue.'

'Daddy, you trick me. The chick isn't sleeping. You sold it to a man, and the man is going to eat it for supper. Tell me the truth.'

'No, I didn't sell it, Nannan. Perhaps your little chick woke up and flew into the sky.' Father switches on his torch and opens a copy of *Confucius and Neo-Confucianism*.

'The chick is not in the sky and not in the trees . . .' Nannan says, holding back her sobs. 'Mum, Daddy said I came out your bottom. So I must be very smelly.'

'No, no, you aren't smelly,' Mother says. 'After you came out, you drank my milk every day, so now you smell milky and sweet.' Then, glancing back at Father, she says: 'I can't believe she's four already. The years fly by so fast, we never get a moment to stop and enjoy ourselves.'

'Yes, time has flashed by. If you fall pregnant now, Nannan will be five by the time you give birth, so the baby will be legal.'

'After today's accident, I just want to concentrate on Nannan. Tomorrow I'll take her into town for a ride on the merry-go-round, then I'll go to the market and see if I can rent another stall.'

KEYWORDS: *Yin forces, silkworm pupae, hunted animal, duck shit, bamboo mat, army tanks.*

In the dark hour before dawn, Meili wakes with a start and feels as though she's trapped inside a coffin. Last night, as she was falling asleep, Kongzi whispered into her ear, '"Autumn shadows linger. / The frost is delayed. / Lotus leaves withering on the pond / listen to the patter of rain,"' then climbed on top of her. Rain is rattling on the shelter's roof, sounding like dried beans dropping into a metal bowl. Gusts of wind sweep water from the trees and send it crashing onto the tarpaulin in heavy sheets. Meili closes her eyes and waits for the storm to reach its peak. As lightning flashes through the black sky and thunder shakes the ground, Kongzi rolls on top of her again. 'Be kind . . . to me . . . Kongzi,' she mumbles. 'I don't want to . . . fall pregnant . . .' Her hands linked behind his neck, she holds onto him, tighter and tighter, until her body is so compressed and her lungs so empty, she feels she is drowning. She opens her mouth and gasps for air. The alcohol on Kongzi's breath makes her stomach turn, but she can't escape it. She senses herself sinking into the ground as his jolting body weighs down on her. 'It's pouring outside. I must . . . bring in those pickles . . . I left to dry on the hutch.' Desperately she tries to push him off.

To avoid having intercourse with him every night, Meili often goes to sleep on the boat with Nannan. She's terrified of falling pregnant, of the government cutting out from her a piece of flesh as warm as her own, of having to conceal inside her body a contraband object which would grower larger and more visible by the day. She left Kong

Village to find freedom, but if she falls pregnant again she knows she will become a hunted animal once more.

After the rooster in the bamboo cage greets the dawn, smaller birds begin to sing in the willows and insects fly out from the reeds. Meili feels a stream of sperm leak out from between her thighs. Am I already done for? she wonders to herself. Her period is three weeks late, and she suspects that her IUD might have fallen out.

She sits up and looks at the imprint of the bamboo mat on Kongzi's forehead. He's grown so familiar to her, he almost looks like a stranger. She wants to shout, 'I'm pregnant! Are you happy now?' but stops herself just in time. If she is pregnant, she wonders whether she could induce a miscarriage by lifting heavy objects or encouraging Kongzi to make love to her more aggressively than usual. She crawls outside and puts on a T-shirt. Her breasts feel heavy and tender and she can detect a sour taste in her mouth. Yes, I have all the symptoms. As her bare feet press into the sand, images from the past flit through her mind. She sees the winter morning she first set eyes on Kongzi, walking up to her wearing a yellow down jacket like a promise of a golden future. The first time he asked to meet her in the woods, her legs trembled with fear. She and Kongzi crouched in the dark shade of a tree beside a group of gravestones. He gave her some peanuts and said he'd invite her to a film in the county town and take her out for a meal. He told her a friend of his had opened a Sichuan restaurant on the ground floor of the County Cultural Centre which served beef poached in hot chilli oil and Chongqing hotpot. She remembers the photograph of Kongzi as a child, standing next to Teacher Zhou with a big smile on his face. She knows that Kongzi was Teacher Zhou's favourite pupil, and that in 1989, when he went to stay with him in Beijing, they joined the democracy protests and, on 4 June, stood at a street corner arm in arm and watched the army tanks enter the capital. Now she is Kongzi's wife. For his sake, she left the village designated on her residence permit and the comfort of their tiled-roofed house. She'd dreamed that if she worked hard, she could open a shop one day and buy a modern apartment in a county town with a flushing toilet and hot shower, like the one owned by Cao Niuniu, the son of Kongzi's artist friend, Old Cao. She still believes that as long as she avoids another pregnancy, she'll be able to live a good life one day, and stroll along supermarket aisles wearing nylon tights and high-heeled shoes.

She peeps back into the shelter. Nannan sits up and says, 'I want to cuddle Daddy.'

'No, you'll wake him up,' Meili replies.

'I want to tell him I not going wake him up, then!' Nannan says, leaning over to hug Kongzi's head. Meili puts a second jumper on Nannan, then shuts the door and goes down to the beach. Hugging herself against the cold, she watches the rising sun stain the horizon red and pour its soft light over the river, the banks and the distant bridge. Once more, she feels an urge to tell Kongzi that she's pregnant, just to see the look of joy on his face. Then she considers keeping quiet about it, and getting rid of the fetus on the sly by swallowing some castor oil. No – I will have this baby, she says to herself, digging her toes into the sand. Once it's born, Kongzi will leave me alone, and I'll never have to get pregnant again. Suddenly she sees a vision of herself as a girl, leaning over an enamel basin and splashing icy water onto her face before setting off for school. She remembers the coldness of the water seeping through to her cheekbones.

Smells of fish and duck shit begin to rise from the ground. The ducks in the pen preen their feathers and ruffle their wings. Meili sniffs the stale sweat on her skin and longs for a shower or a bath. She knows that although the town's public bathhouse doubles as a brothel, it has warm pools in which visitors can bathe for just six yuan if they bring their own soap and towel. She hasn't dared go there yet, as she hates the thought of having to undress in front of strangers. The river has been too cold for bathing. But winter is over now. She grits her teeth and steps in up to her ankles. The cold refreshes and invigorates her; her feet transmit forgotten memories to her brain. She feels fully awake, conscious of the beating of her heart and the ticking of each passing second. She wades deeper into the river and feels the coldness dragging her further into her past. She is aware of being, at the same time, both a woman and child: her daughter's mother and her mother's daughter. She remembers the day twenty years ago, during the osman-thus-blossom season, when she accompanied her mother to the dentist to have her molar capped, and realises that she is now as old as her mother was then, and that in another twenty years she'll be as old as her mother is now, and that all that will await her after that will be old age and decrepitude . . . As her thoughts begin to freeze, she glances over her shoulder and sees the ducks force their way out of the pen and wade into the shallow water.

Kongzi rolls out of the shelter and rinses his mouth. Meili walks up to the stove, opens a bag of slops she bought from a restaurant yesterday and ladles some into the bucket of duck feed. A large container ship shrouded in diesel smoke chugs past, blasting its horn. The huge wake it leaves behind surges onto the beach, floods the shelter then recedes, taking Meili's flip-flops with it. Meili goes into the shelter to brush her teeth, but discovers that her toothbrush has been washed away as well.

As usual, during the few minutes before dusk, the wind drops and the river becomes calm. Kongzi is sitting at the bow of their boat, gazing at the ducks and the back of Meili's neck as she stands knee-deep in the river, her skirt hitched up to her waist. In her rippling reflection, her skin is the same colour but her white skirt is slightly darker. Nannan lies in the cabin, gazing at her plastic doll in the red dress and singing a nonsense song she's made up: 'A-da-li-ya, wah wah! . . .' A golden, late-spring haze spreads over the river, making the watery landscape resemble a blurred and muted colour photograph.

By the time Kongzi walks down the beach with the bucket of shredded cabbage for the ducks' last feed, the evening sun is so low in the sky that his silhouette is dragged halfway across the river. With sudden alarm he notices six or seven ducks being swept downstream. He wades into the river, scrambles onto the boat, and tries to shoo them back towards the beach with the long bamboo pole. In the commotion, the boat becomes untethered and it too starts to drift downstream. Kongzi turns on the engine and drives it back to its mooring, while Meili chases after the errant ducks and tosses pebbles at their heads to encourage them to swim back. The ducks shake their wings in a fluster, splashing water into the air.

'Call them back, Kongzi!' Meili shouts.

'"What passes is just like this, never ceasing day or night . . ."' Kongzi yells, quoting a line from the *Analects* as he gazes with excitement at the current. 'Don't worry, Meili, I'll put some food on the beach. That'll bring them back.' He leaps off the boat, making it rock so violently that Nannan is knocked onto her side. Meili strides further into the water, positions herself in front of the ducks and with open arms shoos them back. At last, they turn round and swim to the beach, then they shake their feathers dry and wobble off towards Kongzi's bucket.

An hour later, the river sinks into darkness and the island becomes shrouded in a cold dank mist. The kerosene lamp shines on Kongzi's and Chen's weathered faces.

'Beautifully recited, my friend,' Kongzi says, then swigging some beer stares at Meili's backside as she bends over the stove. 'Now let's hear another one.'

Chen crashed his boat into a ship last week, and it will take a month to repair. After Nannan burnt her foot, he bought her a new pair of flip-flops. 'All right,' he says. 'I'll try "Feelings on a River in Early Winter", by Meng Haoran. Here goes: "Trees shed their leaves, wild geese fly south. / Rivers shiver in the north wind. / My home is far away, at a bend of River Xiang / In the Land of Chu, high above the clouds. / A melancholy vagrant, whose tears have run dry, / I fix my gaze on a solitary boat at the edge of the sky. / Having drifted off course, I long to find my way home. / Before me stretch the flat sea and the endless night." Ah, I remembered every line! You really are a fine tutor. Would you consider teaching my daughters as well?' Chen has a gold tooth which at night always glints in the lamplight.

'Yes, I could give them lessons every morning. They may be black children with no residence permits or legal status, but you must think of their futures. At the very least, they should learn to read and write.'

'How lucky we are to be able to rub shoulders with a scholar of your calibre – a descendant of Confucius, no less! Come, a toast to you, my friend!' Chen's face crinkles into a broad smile. As he munches one of the deep-fried silkworm pupae he's brought, a pungent yeasty smell fills the air around him.

'Teachers are the least respected and most poorly paid members of society,' Kongzi says. 'Chairman Mao called us the "stinking Ninth category". But teaching is my vocation. I don't care about the money. As Confucius said, "A noble man should seek neither a full belly nor a comfortable home."'

'Why you not a doctor, Dad?' asks Nannan, stroking her doll's red dress.

'Because I wanted to be a teacher, and I'm too old to change professions now.'

'Wen's cat died today. You must make it better. When I had big burn, you made my foot better.'

'You're right, Kongzi – our pockets may be empty but our will is strong,' says Chen. 'When our children grow up, they can find jobs in factories that provide free food and lodging. They won't have to live like tramps any more.' Since he crashed his boat, Chen has been going over to the town every day to look for work. Kongzi has been busy as well. This morning he hauled a cargo of asbestos to a Sino-Hong Kong flagstone factory three kilometres away.

The island has suffered many disruptions this week. River police, municipal police and family planning officers have turned up repeatedly to check boat licences, residence permits and birth permits. Two days ago, Bo and Juru and Dai and Yiping packed their bags and left. Kongzi now uses their abandoned shelters as supplementary duck pens.

Meili clears away the bowls and chopsticks and says to the men, 'You stay here and chat. I'll go and sleep in the cabin.'

'The gods haven't favoured us,' Kongzi sighs, watching Meili hitch up her skirt and wade over to the boat, her bottom swaying from side to side. 'I still haven't managed to get her knocked up.'

'I just hope our one will be a boy,' Chen says. His wife Xixi is due to give birth to their third child any day now.

'Meili was born in the birthplace of Goddess Nuwa,' Kongzi says.

'The Yin forces of the area are too strong. Every name has a female connotation: Dark Water River, Riverbrook Town, Pool of the Immortals Mountain. Women from such a place are clearly not meant to produce sons.'

'Without a son, a man can never stand tall,' Chen says. 'The bloody family planning policies have ruined our lives! Back in the village we owned two hundred turtles – they were worth eight thousand yuan – but after our second daughter was born, the officers confiscated the lot.'

Chewing angrily on a pupa, Kongzi says, 'Not even the most evil emperor in China's history would have contemplated developing the economy by massacring unborn children and severing family lines! But today's tyrants murder millions of babies a year without batting an eyelid, and if a baby slips through their net, they cripple its parents with fines and confiscate their property.'

'I'm your baby, Daddy, so why you want another baby?' Nannan says, perching on an old motor cylinder beside him.

'Don't interrupt when the grown-ups are talking,' Kongzi says to her. 'It's time you went to sleep. Go and join Mum on the boat.'

Nannan wraps her arms around Kongzi's neck. 'I eaten so much food, I'm a grown-up too, now. Daddy, why you got hair in your nose?'

Kongzi pulls Nannan onto his lap and gently tugs her ear. 'A grown-up, you say? Then how come you still wet your bed every night?' Since Nannan burned her foot, he has become much more affectionate towards her.

'When you're here, I like you. When you're not here, I like Mummy.' The bottoms of Nannan's long trousers are damp and her bare feet are stone cold.

KEYWORDS: *spouse's return, hairy armpits, water burial, Dragon Mother, corpse fisher, dead fish.*

On a sweltering day, while Kongzi is having a lunchtime nap in the cabin, Meili sees a man on the bank waving his bag and shouting out to them. 'Wake up, Kongzi!' she says. 'I think someone wants to hire our boat.' In the last month, she's sold thirty ducks for two hundred yuan, and Kongzi has made three hundred yuan delivering cargos of watermelons injected with growth chemicals, and batches of last year's mouldy rice which unscrupulous traders milled and waxed so that it could be sold as new.

Meili steers towards the bank. Kongzi's gold-rimmed spectacles fell into the river last week, so she's been driving the boat since then. The man jumps aboard and says, 'I need a ride to Yinluo.' He is tall, with unkempt greying hair, a goatee and tortoiseshell glasses. His white shirt clings to his sweaty back.

'What, there and back in one day?' Meili asks.

'I don't know yet,' the man says, wiping his wet forehead.

'What cargo are you picking up?' Kongzi asks sleepily, drawing back the door curtain. He's crouching down, unaware that his penis is hanging out from the open zip of his shorts.

'I'm not picking up any cargo. I'm looking for my mother. She drowned herself in the river last week. I want to find her body and give her a proper burial.'

'You want us to transport a corpse?' Kongzi says, stepping out onto the deck. 'Never! I'll transport fake goods or contraband goods, but not dead bodies.'

'I know it's an unusual proposition, so I'm prepared to pay you eighty yuan for the day.'

'It's not a question of money,' Kongzi says, softening his tone a little. 'Don't you know it's bad luck to bring a corpse aboard a boat?'

'Yes, yes, I understand,' the man says. 'Let's say ninety yuan, then. All right?' He's now so drenched in sweat, he looks as though he's just emerged from the river.

Kongzi thinks it over for a moment, and says, 'I'd want one hundred yuan. No less. And I'll need to pay the twenty-yuan administrative fee at the inspection post, and the mooring fee at the Yinluo pier.' The truth is, Kongzi never moors at the pier, he always anchors along the banks further down.

'Please, brother, do it for ninety. I'm just a humble schoolteacher. I don't have much money.'

'Let's take him,' Meili says, squatting behind the engine, her bare feet forming sweaty footprints on the deck.

Hearing that the man is a teacher, Kongzi feels unable to refuse. 'All right, ninety it is,' he says. 'Meili, you and Nannan stay on the island and look after the ducks.'

'No, it wouldn't be safe for you to drive the boat without your glasses,' she says. 'Xixi can take care of Nannan and the ducks. Her baby's four months old. She can strap him onto her back now and walk around.'

They sail to the island, leave Nannan and the ducks in Xixi's care, then set off for Yinluo. 'I'm a teacher as well, as it happens,' Kongzi says, crouching down next to the man.

As the boat moves downstream, a cool breeze blows through the hot air and rustles the tarpaulin canopy. Meili stands at the stern, one hand on the steering wheel, the other holding down the back of her cotton dress so that it doesn't fly up in the wind. She wonders why the man's mother chose to drown herself. Back in Nuwa Village, a few women killed themselves by jumping into a well and one or two hanged themselves from trees, but most women committed suicide by drinking pesticides.

'. . . I've been searching the Xi River for ten days, but haven't seen any sign of her,' the man says. 'I was told that near Yinluo there's a stagnant backwater where bodies often wash up.' Meili glances at the man through the corner of her eye. Although his face is grimy and his hair dusty and unkempt, he has a distinguished air about him. He pulls off his round tortoiseshell glasses and mops the sweat from his brow.

'Yinluo's not too far,' Kongzi says, taking the cigarette the man offers him. 'We should get there in two hours.'

The man has relaxed a little. He looks no older than forty. He's wearing sports sandals that have labels printed with foreign letters. His grey shorts are mud-splattered and his white shirt has a frayed collar and ink stains, but together they still look quite stylish.

'Why did your mother drown herself?' Kongzi asks bluntly.

'She was diagnosed with breast cancer. The hospital treatment was going to cost a thousand yuan a day. She knew that we're struggling to find the money for my son's university fees, and she didn't want to drain our resources.'

Kongzi's eyes widen. 'So your son has got into university?'

'Yes, we slaved for two years helping him prepare for the exams. He's the only student in our county who's been offered a place. Such glory he's brought to our ancestors! But the fees have risen to eighteen thousand yuan this year, and my salary is just five thousand. Still, I'm determined to raise the cash. I'm planning to give up teaching and look for a factory job in Shenzhen. When the acceptance letter arrived, I showed it to my mother, and she drowned herself that very afternoon.'

'Did anyone see her jump? Perhaps she's just gone travelling.'

'She left a will and a letter instructing me not to search for her body. She said if we found it we'd have to pay for a cremation, and she'd rather we put all our money towards my son's fees. She left her keys on the kitchen table.'

Upset by the man's story, Meili pushes down the throttle handle to accelerate.

'So she chose to drown herself, rather than hang or gas herself, just to save you the thousand-yuan cremation fee!' Kongzi exclaims. 'The government is shameless, trying to make money from corpses. The poor can't even afford to die these days!'

'I don't care how much it costs. I must find her body and give her a decent burial. If I don't, how will I be able to look my descendants in the eye?' He lowers his bloodshot eyes. The sweat on his face evaporates in the breeze.

'If no one saw her jump, she's technically a missing person,' Kongzi says. 'Why don't you contact the river police and ask them to help you look for her?'

'I've spoken to them. They told me a person must be missing for one month before they can open a case, and she's only been gone for ten days. They won't help. Here, brother, have another cigarette.'

'No, I couldn't. They're a top brand. Must have cost you a fortune.'

'Don't worry. The Education Board gives us two packs a month. It's some shady deal they've cooked up with the tobacco company. They deduct the cost from our salary, whether we smoke them or not. What's your name, brother? Mine is Weiwei.'

'I'm Kong Lingming,' Kongzi says, the wind blowing in his face. 'The problem is, if the river police did agree to follow up the case, they'd probably just send a few messages out to local police stations. They wouldn't dispatch a search party unless you paid them a huge bribe.'

'That's why I've come to search for her myself.' Then he raises his head and looks Kongzi in the eye. 'So, Mr Kong Lingming, I presume from your name that you're a seventy-sixth generation descendant of the great sage. It's an honour to make your acquaintance. We have a Kong in our county too, from the seventy-fifth generation. He's a deputy to the National People's Congress.'

'Yes, I am a descendant – but I'm having to live like a tramp now so that I can continue my illustrious line,' Kongzi says, embarrassed by his lowly circumstances.

Green forested mountains begin to tower on both sides. Meili gazes up at the peaks then down at their reflections plunging into the river. She breathes in the green light and feels her mind clear. There are no villages or towns in sight. She closes her eyes and lets the peace and calm wash over her.

'Why not make a television appeal to see if anyone saw her jump?' Kongzi suggests, trying to keep the conversation going.

'I tried. My brother works for the local TV station. He asked his bosses to air an appeal, but they refused to. They've had to broadcast so many appeals for missing children and women recently, they've decided to stop offering the service. I printed hundreds of notices and stuck them on street corners, but no one's responded. There's no official organisation that can help me. I'm all on my own.' He wipes a tear from his eye.

'Don't get upset. It's not our fault we were born into a dynasty that prevents men performing their filial duty.' Since Kongzi lost his spectacles, he's been wearing a pair of cheap brown sunglasses that make him look like a shifty hawker of fake medicine in a country market. 'I toiled for years teaching in a village school, for the sake of my country, but what did the government do for me in return? I couldn't even feed my family on the meagre salary they paid me.'

'But you've plunged into the sea of commerce now, and become a private entrepreneur. I envy your freedom!' Weiwei rubs his goatee, then brings out from his bag a photograph of his mother which a strong gust almost blows from his hands.

Kongzi takes the photograph and studies it in the shade of the canopy. 'What a lovely lady she looks,' he says. 'You wouldn't guess she was ill.'

Feeling the wind blow the back of her dress towards Weiwei's shoulder, Meili pulls it down and stuffs it between her legs.

'We've entered Fengkai County now,' Weiwei says. 'Look up there. That's Yearning for the Spouse's Return Rock, one of Xi River's eight scenic sites.' He swigs back some lemonade from the bottle Kongzi gave him and points to a leaning stack of rocks on the summit of a green mountain.

'Is it a wife yearning for her husband or a husband yearning for his wife?' Meili asks him, squinting up at it. The engine is chugging so loudly now, she has to shout to be heard.

'A wife yearning for her husband, of course,' Kongzi says, before Weiwei has a chance to reply. 'In the past, the men went travelling and the women always stayed at home.' Meili is annoyed that Kongzi butted in – she wanted to hear Weiwei speak. Kongzi turns to him and says, 'When we fled the village, we never thought that two years later, we'd still be on the run. We imagined the rivers would be safe, but they're almost as heavily policed as the roads. So-called Boat Safety Inspection Posts have popped up all along Xi River. The inspectors couldn't care less how safe your boat is, all they want is your money. If they stop you, they'll confiscate your licence unless you pay fees of two hundred yuan.'

Meili pulls a white T-shirt over her sleeveless dress, and feels more comfortable now that her hairy armpits are concealed. With her free hand she rearranges the sachets of washing powder, magazines and bamboo fans behind her into a neat pile.

'How much did this boat cost you?' Weiwei asks.

'Oh, about ten thousand yuan,' Kongzi lies, wanting to impress him.

'And business is going well?' Weiwei's gaze shifts to Meili who is now clutching the steering wheel with both hands, the wind rippling through her hair.

'The money isn't great. Small boats like this can only take heavy cargo short distances. Most of the time, I deliver fake goods that registered boats are too afraid to touch. And the price of diesel keeps rising. I get through forty yuan of it a day.'

'Have you thought of taking up fishing?' Weiwei says, still looking at Meili. 'You could open a crab and shrimp stall on the banks.'

'The river's become so polluted, there are hardly any fish left. Most of the fishermen round here have abandoned their nets and gone to find jobs in the cities. Ah! What a beautiful stretch of the river this is. It brings to mind that Song Dynasty poem: "Clouds appear to drift beneath the moving boat / The empty water is clear—"'

'"—I gaze up, gaze down, and wonder whether / Beneath the lake's surface, another Heaven exists,"' Weiwei interrupts, completing the quatrain. He looks to the right and points to a mountain peak. 'See that white sculpture at the top? That's the mythical Dragon Mother.'

'She's so beautiful,' Meili gasps. 'But she looks like an angel or a goddess, not a mother.'

'But mothers can be beautiful as well – just look at you!' Weiwei says with a smile. Meili looks away bashfully and blurts out the first thing that enters her mind. 'So, is the Dragon Mother a dragon herself, or a human being who's a mother of dragons?'

'She's a local deity,' Weiwei replies, 'a goddess of rain, mothers and children. The legend goes that as a baby she was put on a wooden tray and cast off by her parents into the Xi River, then found and raised by a fisherman. When she grew up, she was able to control the floods. The people in this area call anyone with supernatural powers a dragon.'

Meili feels sick at the thought of a mother abandoning her baby. She imagines waves rolling over the baby's head and its tiny body sinking to the riverbed. She looks up again at the Dragon Mother's sparkling white figure, and the golden temple and bamboo grove behind it. Tourists appear to be crawling up the narrow path to the summit like an army of wriggling maggots.

As the boat approaches Yinluo, the river widens and divides, with a backwater branching off to the right. The dark water appears stagnant, but plastic bottles and polystyrene boxes are moving sluggishly across its surface. Shacks built from broken doors and plastic sheeting are dotted among the long grass at the far end. The warm evening breeze smells of rot and decay.

'This must be the place I was told about,' Weiwei says, gripping the canopy.

Meili steers to the right and advances with care. The water grows shallower and the engine begins to rumble and spew blue smoke into the air. Kongzi moves to the bow and darts from side to side, prodding his bamboo pole into the riverbed to check the depth. When they reach an expanse of floating rubbish that seems impassable, Meili slows the boat to a crawl. She tries veering to the right but Kongzi shouts out, 'No, we'll never make it to the bank this way,' so she steers in the other direction and, after a while, finds a cleared channel that leads to the shore. A man walks out of one of the shelters and stares at them. Clouds of crows and mosquitoes hover overhead, making the grey sky look dark and soiled.

'Are you a corpse fisher, my friend?' Weiwei shouts to the man as they draw closer. 'I'm looking for my mother.'

'When did she drown?' the man asks, walking to the shore. He's wearing black trousers and a white vest, and is fanning his face with a straw hat.

'Ten days ago,' Weiwei answers, rubbing his goatee anxiously.

'Only three women have washed up here this week. How old was your mother?'

'Sixty-five.'

'Those three are much younger than that. One is naked from the waist down. Her hands and feet are bound with rope and her toenails are painted red.'

'And the other two?' Weiwei asks plaintively.

'The oldest looks no more than forty. Dark blue trousers, purple jacket, bare feet.'

'Purple jacket? Let me see her.'

Meili turns off the engine and Kongzi punts the boat to the shore.

'I must warn you, comrade, it will cost you 150 yuan to look at the corpse, and three thousand if you want me to dredge it out and arrange for a van to deliver it to your home. My fees are the lowest, though. That guy up there will charge you two hundred to look at the corpse. But he's a crook. Unlike me, he can read, so he scans the newspapers' missing persons notices, phones the families and tells them to come here, knowing very well he doesn't have the bodies they're looking for. I'd never do that. I have principles.'

'You must make a fortune!' Kongzi says. 'A hundred and fifty yuan just to look? That's robbery! This boat only cost me three thousand.' Kongzi bites his lip, remembering that he told Weiwei it cost him much more.

'No one gets rich from this trade. Only five or six families a year turn up here looking for dead relatives, and we have to buy all the rope and plastic sacks ourselves. There are four of us fishing corpses, and none of us have made much money. If you don't believe me, go and ask them.'

'Does the woman in the purple jacket have grey hair?' asks Weiwei, scrutinising the man's face.

'A few grey hairs, perhaps. Not many. See, I'm an honest man. If you'd asked Chang, he would've lied to you.'

'All right, let me see her. Where is she?'

'All the bodies are tethered to poles under the floating rubbish. But I can't show you the woman in the purple jacket. She belongs to Chang. We stick to the rules here. He's gone into town today. He'll be back tomorrow.'

Kongzi whispers to Weiwei that they should speak to the other corpse fishers, then in a louder voice asks the man if there's a police station nearby.

'Yes, a station was opened near here a couple of years ago,' he answers. 'The police used to pay us a hundred yuan to pull out the bodies, then would take them away to be cremated. But so many bodies washed up last year, the police couldn't cope. For a while, they'd still come once a week, to photograph the corpses and cut locks of hair. But money is tight now, and they've stopped coming altogether. So we have to rely entirely on people like you for our income.'

Weiwei and Kongzi climb the littered bank towards shelters further up, pinching their noses from the stench.

'Stinks, doesn't it?' the corpse fisher shouts out to them, putting on his straw hat. 'It's not easy living here, I tell you!'

They come to a shelter surrounded by heaps of plastic bottles. A man steps out, holding a can of Coke.

'Hello, my friend,' Weiwei says. 'I'm looking for my mother. She's sixty-five, with grey hair. Have you seen any bodies like that recently? Here, have a smoke.' He hands the man a cigarette and searches his pocket for a lighter.

'I saw an old woman's corpse bobbing on the water yesterday, but it was bloated and decayed.'

Kongzi glances back at the man they just spoke to, annoyed that he made no mention of this body to them.

'How long would it take for a corpse to reach that state?' Kongzi asks.

'I'm not in the business, but I should think three weeks at least, a bit less if crabs have got to it. Old Gui down there keeps his bodies under the rubbish for six months. If no one comes to claim them, he drags them back to the river and lets the current sweep them away. But by then they're unrecognisable.'

'So you don't keep any corpses yourself?' asks Kongzi, stepping back from a cockroach he sees crawling towards his feet.

'No, no! That work would give me nightmares. Every morning, the corpse fishers row out into the floating rubbish to check if any bodies have got trapped beneath it during the night. When they come across a patch that smells particularly bad, or has flies hovering above it, they plunge their hooked poles into it, hoping to pull up a body. I don't have the stomach for that.'

'Do you ever get babies washing up here?' Kongzi asks, his mind turning to Happiness.

'Huh! More dead babies wash up here than dead fish! But no families ever come looking for them, so the body fishers leave them to rot on the bank.'

Kongzi whisks the flies from his face and glances at the shacks above.

'Don't bother asking the other guys,' the man says. 'They'll con you out of all your money. I doubt your mother's here. The bodies I've seen recently have been either much older or younger.'

Kongzi and Weiwei return to the boat. Meili is still standing at the stern, her hand clamped over her mouth. 'The stench is unbearable,' she groans as the men step aboard. The brown water below is littered with white polystyrene, empty cans and dead fish. Weiwei stares down dejectedly. 'Perhaps her body has got caught on an anchor, or under a rock on the riverbed, or perhaps it's been swept further downstream and I'll never find it.'

The river and sky are darkening, but the pale swathe of floating refuse is still glowing faintly. Kongzi retreats into the cabin. Meili follows him inside and says, 'I can't stand the smell any longer, and I'm getting bitten to death by the mosquitoes. Let's get out of here.'

'We should give him a bit more time,' Kongzi replies, lighting a cigarette.

'No, I've had enough. I don't care about the money. This place is a floating graveyard. Who knows how many corpses are bobbing under the rubbish?'

'Be quiet – you'll upset him,' Kongzi whispers, peeping round the door curtain at Weiwei, who's still leaning overboard staring down at the floating debris. 'Do we have any beer left?' Kongzi asks.

'No,' Meili snaps. She wants to scream out in anger, but doesn't dare open her mouth too wide in case the insects swarming around her fly inside.

'Anything to eat?' Kongzi asks tentatively.

'No, nothing!' Meili shouts.

Kongzi goes out onto the deck and pats Weiwei's trembling shoulders. 'Shall we get going, my friend? If we don't leave this wretched place soon, we'll have to spend the night here.'

'Yes, let's sail upstream and find a better place to anchor,' Meili says, joining them outside. 'It's too late to go home now. Don't worry, we won't charge you any extra for the night.'

Weiwei reluctantly nods in agreement. Meili goes to the stern, presses a towel to her mouth and starts the engine. As the boat sets off, the breeze becomes cooler and fresher. But the backwater's stench has infused her skin, and whenever it drifts up to her nose, she gags. They sail upstream in the dying light, and her eyes fill with tears as she wonders whether Happiness's body is still lying on the bed of the Yangtze, or has been swept down to this backwater as well, and is decaying under the floating rubbish along with all the other rotting corpses.

'After our second child was ripped out of Meili's womb and murdered by the authorities, we gave him a water burial in the Yangtze,' Kongzi tells Weiwei, crushing out his cigarette. 'At least I know now that if he'd washed up here, the corpse fishers would have left him alone.'

Weiwei looks at him, his face seized up in horror, then buries his head into his folded arms and weeps like a child.

Meili steers the boat towards a distant mooring place below a cluster of brick shacks. In the deep dusk, the water's surface has become as smooth as skin, tearing open as the bow cuts through it then sealing up again behind the stern.

KEYWORDS: *tortoiseshell glasses, greatest good, wet dress, preserved mustard greens, peace of mind.*

Kongzi ties the boat to a small wooden jetty that is coated in fine cement dust. He looks up and sees a brick shack with a wooden sign that says GOOD FOOD RESTAURANT. A child is squatting down for a shit next to a telegraph pole. In a shed close by, an engine is loudly chugging.

They enter the restaurant. Kongzi studies the menu and orders sweet and sour fish, spicy spare ribs, fried string beans and a bottle of rice wine. On a television in the corner, a woman in a flowery dress is singing, '*Your tenderness bewilders me. My fate is loneliness . . .*' The food is brought to the table. Meili stares at the darkness outside the window, glancing occasionally at Kongzi and Weiwei whose faces soon turn red from the alcohol.

'Don't give in to despair,' Kongzi tells Weiwei. 'Death is merely a turn-ing off of the lights. Come on, have another drink. And you too, Meili.'

Meili raises her glass and looks into Weiwei's bespectacled eyes. She assumes he's abandoned the search, but knows that the thought that his mother's corpse may be lying undiscovered in the river must be torturing him. She notices his filthy collar and wishes she could pull off his shirt and scrub it clean.

Kongzi lifts his eyes to the ceiling and sighs. 'The ancient philoso-pher, Laozi, said: "The greatest good is like water: it gives life to the ten thousand things, but does not strive. It flows in places men reject and so is like the Tao . . ." But this Xi River doesn't give life. It's a flowing cemetery of bodies, pollution and waste . . .'

'The Taoist philosophers were attempting to come up with principles to govern human conduct,' Weiwei replies. 'But who's interested in principles now? When his mother passed away, the Taoist sage, Zhuangzi, beat his drum and laughed. His mother died a natural death, so he could regard it with equanimity. But my mother was driven to her death by a government that has washed its hands of the sick and the poor. I can't help giving in to despair. Since the Tiananmen Massacre, this country has lost its conscience. Money is the only religion.' Weiwei puts a cigarette in his mouth and lights up, but chokes at the first puff.

'Don't smoke if you're not a smoker,' Meili says, taking the cigarette from him. She sucks a puff then keeps it held between her fingers, tapping it against an empty cup when the ash becomes too long.

'You're right,' Kongzi says. 'I never dare discuss such things with my wife, but mark my words: one day the official verdict on Tiananmen will be reversed. My old teacher, Mr Zhou, is convinced of it. A toast, Weiwei: "Friends from afar meet but rarely. Let us raise our glass in joy and drown our sorrows!" Since you didn't find your mother today, we won't charge you anything for this trip. Come on, now. It's not often I get to sit down with a graduate. Let's test our wits. We'll take turns to recite a line of ancient poetry that contains a character connected to water. Whoever slips up must drink a shot.' At the back of the restaurant, two men covered in cement dust are drinking beer. The only light in the room is coming from the single bulb overhead and the glowing television screen. A rusty electric fan on the cashier's desk slowly stirs the air. Mosquitoes and flies flit from the plates of food to one of the six forearms pressed on the table.

'Fine, let's toast the Xi River and give it a go!' Weiwei says. He undoes the top button of his shirt, then, glancing at Meili, quickly does it up again.

'"The white sun sinks behind the mountain as the Yellow River glides towards the sea,"' Kongzi recites, tapping the line's rhythm on the table.

'"A low ray of sun spreads across the water which is emerald along one side, and red along the other,"' Weiwei chants, rubbing the edges of his tortoiseshell glasses.

'I said the line should contain a word with a watery connection, not the word "water" itself. You lose! Drink up!'

'If you insist,' Weiwei sighs, and empties the glass. 'But next time, if I manage to replace "water" with another word, while retaining the sense, you must let me off.'

'All right, I'll agree to that. Ready? "The bright moon rises from the sea; at different edges of the sky, we admire the same view."'

'"I at the head of the Yangtze River, you at the tail, we drink—"' The next word is "water" but Weiwei stops himself just in time and says, 'No, make that "we mourn our loved ones who rest on the river's bed."'

'A fine line,' Kongzi says, the image striking at his heart. He pauses to wipe a tear from his eye, then continues the game. '"The moon follows the river's waves for ten thousand li; in spring, its radiance overflows the banks."'

'"The mountain pass is hard to breach; who feels sorrow for the man who has lost his way?"' Weiwei says, pushing his glasses further up his nose.

'No water connotation!' Kongzi shouts out, banging the table. 'You've lost again!'

'But the character "sorrow" contains the water radical on the left.'

'You need two radicals for it to count, I'm afraid. You've definitely lost, brother. Drink up!'

Once the men empty the last dregs from the bottle, Meili whispers to Kongzi that they should return to the boat to sleep. Kongzi ventures out into the dark to find a toilet. Weiwei settles the bill then returns to the table and says to Meili, 'Are you sure you've had enough to eat?'

'Yes, thank you,' she answers, staring at the fish bones on the plates, wondering, with a shudder, whether the fish they've just eaten once fed on the corpse of Weiwei's mother. More flies gather on the plates and crawl over the leftovers.

'You looked so beautiful when you were driving the boat,' Weiwei says. 'Kongzi is a lucky man.' As she looks up at him, he glances out of the window, too embarrassed to meet her gaze, and they hear a loud, grating rumble outside that sounds like a truck emptying rubble onto a boat. Meili's heart begins to thud. This is the first time that any man apart from Kongzi has told her that she's beautiful. Not knowing what to say, she looks down again and stares at the plates and at Weiwei's watch.

'I've put you both to so much trouble today,' Weiwei says, gripping his empty glass. '"Where will I be when I wake from my drunken sleep? / On the willow banks, in the dawn breeze, under a fading moon." That would work. "Drunken" and "banks" both have watery connotations . . .'

'It's been no trouble at all. So, how many children did your mother have?' Meili wants to tell Weiwei that with his round tortoiseshell glasses he looks just like the university professors who give lectures on television.

'Four boys and one girl. I'm the eldest. Tell me your name again.'

'Meili.'

'As in "Beautiful and Pretty"? How apt.'

'How common, you mean. Every woman in the countryside is called Meili. But my "Mei" is the dawn "Mei". I was born in the morning.'

'Ah, that's different, then. "Beautiful Dawn", or "Beautiful Beginning". Very poetic.'

Meili thinks of her mother, and remembers her lying asleep on a chair while breastfeeding Meili's brother, her milk tricking down his cheek. She wonders whether her grandmother is still well enough to walk about and go out into the garden. 'When our parents are alive, we're young,' she says. 'But as soon as they die, we become old.'

'You're right,' Weiwei says, looking down. 'When our parents are alive, they stand in front of us, blocking our view of death. But once they've gone, we find ourselves at the cliff edge. Whether we jump now or later doesn't make much difference. The next step we take will be the end.'

'Don't be so negative. Perhaps your mother didn't throw herself into the river after all. Perhaps she'll turn up at your home one day. You only have one life: you must be kind to yourself.'

'Yes, we're only here once. We're unlikely to cross paths again.' Weiwei returns his blank gaze to the window. The only sign of the river now is the trail of light from a passing boat. The flies and mosquitoes swarming the night air are only visible once they hit the glass pane.

'You have a long life ahead of you, a son who's off to university . . .' Meili says, glancing at the educational programme being broadcast on the television now. Moths flit around the bulb above. One of them breaks a wing, falls to the table and flutters about in distress.

'Somehow, I'd prefer to find out that she was dead. It's the uncertainty that's so unbearable. I know now that there is no greater torture in life than to have someone you love go missing.' Weiwei spots a mosquito on his arm and slaps it.

'No, you men have no idea. The greatest torture any human being could suffer is to be pregnant with a child and not know which day it might be torn from you; and then, when it is taken from you, to have to watch it being strangled before your eyes. My aborted son often appears to me in my dreams, lying dead in a plastic bag, his face all swollen and purple. If he were alive now, he'd probably call you "Uncle Glasses" . . .' She sinks her face into her hands and weeps.

'You're a good mother, Meili, don't cry,' Weiwei says, handing her a paper napkin. 'My mother had a hard life too. She married at the height of the Land Reform Campaign, when the Party was encouraging the masses to kill rich landowners. The day after her wedding, her father was dragged to the village hall and hanged in public, and my parents were made to watch. My mother told me that as his dead body swung from the ceiling, the peasants whipped it with ropes so fiercely that scraps of his flesh splashed onto her face. I was there too at the time, inside her womb. For the next two years, my parents had to remain "empty-handed".'

'What does that mean?'

'It meant that when they left the house they couldn't take anything with them, no bags or wallets. And in summer, they weren't allowed to wear socks or long trousers. The authorities were afraid they'd conceal weapons on their bodies and try to avenge her father's death. Many of the victims' family members committed suicide during those years. But my mother struggled on, for my sake. I was born three months prematurely. I weighed just three pounds. When I was six she taught me the *Three Character Classic* and the English poetry she learned at her missionary school. For my sake she clung to life, and now for my sake again she has killed herself.' Weiwei takes off his tortoiseshell glasses and rubs his tear-filled eyes.

Meili searches for words of comfort. 'I'm not a good mother,' she says at last. 'To tell you the truth, I've had an IUD fitted. I don't want to have any more children. I want to work hard, make money, and live the kind of life where I can eat my meals at a proper table and wash my clothes in a machine.'

Weiwei looks up. 'That shouldn't be hard to achieve. Times have changed. Any woman can set up her own business now, become her own boss. But not every woman can be as good a mother as you . . .'

'I'd like to take a television correspondence course,' Meili says, glancing back at the professor on the flickering screen. 'I venerate learning, but I'm so uncultured and poorly educated. I only went to school for two years . . . Kongzi doesn't know I've had an IUD fitted. Please don't tell him.'

'Your secret's safe. I'll be leaving tomorrow and will probably never see either of you again.'

'I know you look down on us peasants. Once you've gone, you'll forget all about us.'

'No. I'll never forget you. I'll leave you my address. You and Kongzi would be more than welcome to come and stay with us.' Their eyes meet as they inhale the smell of each other's sweat. 'You really are beautiful,' he says. 'How easy life would be if I had someone like you by my side.' In the dim light, Weiwei's hair looks shinier and less grey. 'You have something caught . . .' He points at her mouth, but before she has a chance to touch it, he reaches over and picks out from between her front teeth a strand of spinach. Meili jumps to her feet and asks Kongzi, who's just walked in, where the toilet is.

'Don't go. It's pitch black out there. Wait until we're back on the boat.' She can smell that he's just vomited. His face is purple and bloated.

'It's so quiet now,' Weiwei says, 'I feel much better after that swim.' Meili watches the water drip down his bare back and hands him a towel. Then she goes into the cabin, slips off her wet dress, dries herself quickly with a sheet and puts on Kongzi's long white vest. 'You can sleep in here with us,' she says, poking her head round the door curtain. 'We'll have to squeeze up, I'm afraid.'

The night is breezeless, but a faint smell of osmanthus seems to be moving through the still air. Meili and Weiwei are now lying on either side of Kongzi, who's quietly snoring. Meili can sense that Weiwei is still awake. When they returned to the boat, Kongzi crashed out in the cabin, and she jumped into the river for a swim, having noticed when they arrived at dusk that the water was clean. Weiwei jumped in after her. It was too dark for her to see the expression on his face; all she could make out in the light from the restaurant was the dark outline of the boat.

'I'm so sorry to have inconvenienced you like this,' Weiwei whispers to her across Kongzi's sleeping body.

'Don't worry. It would have been too dangerous to sail at night. This boat is wooden, and would fall apart if it collided with anything. We'll sleep here and head back to Xijiang in the morning.' Although the smells around her are familiar, the cabin feels strangely different. She can't sleep. Kongzi's snoring is embarrassing her. 'You don't snore, do you?' she asks Weiwei. She wedges a jumper under her pillow to raise her head a little, then flaps her damp sheet in the air so that it falls flat over her body.

'No, I don't snore,' Weiwei whispers. 'But I'm finding it hard to fall asleep. I've never spent the night on a boat before.'

'I couldn't get used to it either, when we first moved onto the boat,' Meili says, her nose touching the back of Kongzi's head. 'But now, unless I'm rocking from side to side, it takes me hours to drop off. Are you hot? Our electric fan's broken, I'm afraid. Here, use this bamboo one. I suppose you town dwellers all have air conditioning on at night.'

'No – not many people can afford to have it installed. And even if they can, they're afraid to use it because the electricity costs so much.'

'Which university did your wife go to?' Feeling her hot skin begin to stick to Kongzi's, she edges back a little, then pulls her squashed right breast out from under her side.

'We went to the same university, but were assigned jobs in different towns. She's the sub-director of a circuit board factory in Dunhuang. Her salary's much higher than mine.'

'You may live apart, but at least you're still married.'

Kongzi has sunk into a deep sleep and is snoring his head off.

'Doesn't feel like we're married. When I phoned her to tell her my mother had killed herself, she didn't offer to come down and see me. She doesn't care about me any more.'

'Marriage is for life. Perhaps you should show her more affection, try to win her round. Persuade her to move back in with you.' Meili is embarrassed by the smell of alcohol on Kongzi's breath. She knows that town people brush their teeth twice a day.

'No, she wouldn't give up her job for me. She didn't want to go to Dunhuang at first, but we needed the money to support our family. Now she's so used to it there she doesn't want to come back.'

'You don't know how important something is until you lose it. You mustn't let her slip away. Even if a woman flies off for a while, she'll always want a nest to return to.' Meili remembers the woman with the crimson lipstick she met on the boat to Sanxia, and suspects that her husband in the countryside had no idea she worked as a hair-salon prostitute.

Suddenly Meili wishes she could put her arms around Weiwei. Her body feels as hot as beans frying in a scorching wok. She picks up a jacket lying beside her and drapes it over Kongzi's chest, letting her hand brush against Weiwei's. Immediately, he grasps hold of it, and she feels the heat inside her explode. His hand then slides over her body, moving slowly, then fast, then slowly again. She curls up and lets him caress her to sleep, as she rocks dreamily back and forth inside the dark cabin . . .

At dawn, Weiwei leaves his address, telephone number and two packs of cigarettes on the bamboo stool beside her, and stands at the stern, his face looking slightly calmer than yesterday.

Meili goes out to join him. 'You should give up your search and go home now,' she says. 'Your mother will be more at peace in the river than she would be buried in the earth.'

'No, I must keep searching until I find her, for my own peace of mind,' he replies, then without saying goodbye, he steps onto the jetty, climbs up the bank and walks away.

Meili grabs a bag of preserved mustard greens from the galley area, runs up the bank after him and tosses it into his hands. 'Soak them in water overnight, then simmer them with beef and tomatoes – the longer the better.'

'I'm a terrible cook,' Weiwei says.

'But you must eat them. I preserved them myself.'

He turns and continues along the path. As she watches his departing figure, her stomach churns as though a mudfish were writhing inside it. Without stopping to think, she chases after him, grabs the tortoise-shell glasses from his face to keep as a memento and runs back to the boat with them.

KEYWORDS: *metallic, marshy beach, handicapped, groping hand, rotten shrimp paste, cross-infection.*

'There's going to be an almighty downpour any minute!' Kongzi says, pointing to the leaden sky above Dexian. Seconds later, the dark clouds crack open and unleash torrential rain. 'The deck's too slippery,' Meili cries out to Kongzi. 'Quick, come into the cabin.' The rain crashes against the bow then streams into the river. Inside the bamboo cage, the ducks shake their wings and hoot.

'Look, the rain's so polluted, it's almost metallic,' Kongzi says. 'The boat will get corroded if we stay any longer. Let's lift anchor and get going to Guai Village. Pass me my straw hat and raincoat.'

'But you won't be able to see a thing through this rain,' Meili says. 'What if we crash into something?' Kongzi transported a cargo of quicklime this morning, and when the rain makes contact with the powder that's fallen into the cracks of the deck, white fumes reeking of rotten eggs rise into the air. Nannan vomited last night and has eaten nothing all day apart from a dry biscuit and a cauliflower floret. She's lying on her back in the cabin, gazing out at the pelting downpour through a gap in the door curtain.

Kongzi wipes the lenses of the metal-rimmed glasses he bought last week, then shoves away from the bank. For hours they sail through heavy rain along a bewildering maze of waterways. Occasionally, Meili calls out: 'Be careful, the water smells muddy here – we're probably too close to the bank. Steer to the right a little.' When they pass beneath a bridge and she hears the engine's rumble echo against the concrete arch, she feels anxious and locked in.

After taking Weiwei to Yinluo, they returned to the sand island to find the river police knocking down their shelter. They grabbed a handful of ducks from the pen, collected Nannan from Xixi, then sailed downstream, picking up and delivering cargos as they went, until they reached the dirty industrial town of Dexian in Western Guangdong Province, where they anchored for the last week. Although Kongzi was able to pick up delivery jobs there, it was not a pleasant place to stay. At night the paper factories would spew into the river foul waste water that smelled of rotten shrimp paste and caused the three of them to cough and gag in their sleep.

On their second day in Dexian, Meili bought a pregnancy test in a dockside pharmacy. After she dipped the test stick into her urine and saw the plus sign appear, she wondered why her IUD hadn't worked. Forgetting that her period was already three weeks late when she met Weiwei, she presumed that his groping hand had dislodged the device, allowing Kongzi to impregnate her during the following days. Weiwei's touch awakened feelings she had never known before. In the week after he left, she no longer pushed Kongzi away when he wanted sex, but instead pulled him close to her and told him to move harder and faster. She suspects that it was on one of those nights, between a moan of pleasure and a sharp intake of breath, that Kongzi's sperm penetrated her egg, and the infant spirit once more descended into her womb.

When she told Kongzi she was pregnant, he said that they must find a safe place to live until the baby is born. He asked around and found out about a village called Guai, thirty kilometres downstream, where the family planning policies are not strictly enforced. But the village is set a kilometre back from the river, so for the last few days, he's been wondering how he'll be able to make a living there.

'Look, that must be Guai Village!' Kongzi says, seeing beyond the dust-covered trees on the left a distant huddle of houses spiked with satellite discs.

'It's larger than I expected,' Meili says. 'Are you sure we'd be safe living there? If this baby's ripped out of me, I won't have another. The village looks depressing. I'd prefer to stay by the water and have the baby on the boat. You did say we'll call this one Waterborn, after all.' She glances at the litter-strewn bank and a dusty stack of cabbages on the field above, and feels a wave of revulsion.

'All right, we'll stay on the boat, but we must find a safe place to settle. Happiness died because we chose the wrong place. We can't make that mistake again.'

From under a blanket, Nannan says sleepily, 'I'm hungry, Daddy. I want some nice food. No more dirty fish.' Last night, Kongzi cooked a fish he'd caught in the polluted river, and he can still taste its foul odour in his mouth. It was Meili's birthday. She spent the whole day sulking in the cabin. Kongzi went into Dexian and bought her plates, pans, an electric heater and a pocket mirror, to replace the ones they had to leave on the sand island, but she didn't show any gratitude. Kongzi complained about the Weiwei trip, moaning that not only did they receive no payment, they lost their home as well. Meili is angry that she allowed Weiwei to fondle her that night, and hates him for taking advantage of her.

An oily film of pollution hovers on the river's surface. Along the bank, the willow's branches bend under the weight of litter while their tips struggle upwards towards the sun. Kongzi drives the boat under another bridge, steers left down a narrow creek and stops below a flight of steps leading to what he thinks must be a path to Guai Village. Dogs, ducks and chickens watch them from the bank. 'I heard the village sells handicapped children to criminal gangs,' Meili says. 'Apparently most of the crippled kids you see begging in train stations around the country come from round here.'

'That's just hearsay,' Kongzi replies. 'See those children up there? They look fine to me . . . So we've made it at last! What a journey it's been. It reminds me of that poem: "Mountain after mountain, river after river, it seems there is no way out. / But beyond a shady willow and a tree in bright blossom, another village finally appears." I'll go up and have a look around.' He fetches the gangplank and slides it onto the lowest concrete step.

'Dad, I wait here for you,' Nannan says, peeking round the door curtain at the unfamiliar surroundings outside.

Rising onto her toes, Meili sees, on the large field above, patches of unharvested crops, two tarpaulin shelters, a duck pen, a coiled black hose lying beside an empty ditch and a storehouse with bricked-up doors and windows. Painted in white on the red walls is a notice that says TO AVOID COMMON GYNAECOLOGICAL COMPLAINTS AND VENEREAL DISEASES, IT IS IMPORTANT TO MAINTAIN GENITAL HYGIENE, WASH PUBIC AREA FREQUENTLY AND CHANGE UNDERWEAR DAILY. TO PREVENT CROSS-INFECTION, REFRAIN FROM SITTING ON TOILET SEATS . . . The reflection of the red walls and the blue sky above them waver on the creek's oily surface. Scraps of white plastic float by like a raft of ducks.

Kongzi soon returns with a fisherman who leads him onto the bridge and says, 'See that marshy beach further down the creek? No one's renting it now. It has a pond where you can keep your ducks.' On a road far behind them, a red car drives slowly past.

Meili sits at the bow and begins to remove dead leaves from a bunch of spinach.

'If I wash the spinach in that water, the spinach get clean but I get very dirty,' Nannan says, pointing to the muddy creek.

'Oh, stop talking nonsense,' Meili says irritably.

Kongzi jumps aboard and drives the boat towards the place the fisherman indicated. The banks here are so darkened by dust and pollution that, compared to them, the fumes billowing from the far-away factories look clean. Sickened by the scenery, Meili stares down at her shoes and reflects on her predicament. To protect what might be Kongzi's precious male heir, she'll have to spend another eight months lying low. When she discovered she was pregnant, she suggested they go straight to Heaven Township, where she knew they'd be safe. But Kongzi said the journey would be too long and arduous, and insisted they find a hiding place closer by. Meili's only hope now is that she'll suffer a miscarriage before the government has a chance to tear the baby out. Inside her wet shoes and socks, her feet feel cold and pinched.

The boat draws up onto the marshy beach of mud, coarse grass and dirty pools. Above it are a large swampy pond enclosed by a bamboo fence, and a small bamboo hut. Kongzi jumps ashore. 'This is a perfect place for us to hide until Waterborn is born!' he says excitedly. 'We'll be safe. We could rear a hundred ducks inside that enclosure, easily. And the creek seems to have life in it. The fisherman back there said the rent is only five hundred yuan a year. Look, it's surrounded on three sides by hills. Ideal feng shui for a home!'

Meili looks up at the dry gravelly hills. Villagers have carved terraces into the slopes. Some are cultivated with corn, but the rest have gone to seed. There are a few banana and papaya trees around the enclosure and some lychee trees behind the hut.

'This isn't a creek,' Meili says. 'It's a waste gutter! "Untamed rivers, barren hills . . ."' She's been short-tempered ever since she took the pregnancy test. She's terrified by the thought that the IUD might still be inside her and that the fetus is now growing around it. As soon as she told Kongzi that she was pregnant, she immediately regretted it. In bouts of anger since then, she has been tempted to take Weiwei's tortoiseshell glasses out from under her pillow and fling them into the river. She knows that when his hand moved over her body that night, it was really his mother that he was searching for, and she wishes she could forget him. But part of her longs to talk to him again about matters that still confuse her. Kongzi never has the patience to listen to all the things she wants to say.

'Dad, a snake in the water – look!' Nannan says, pointing to a submerged stick. 'It's dead. No, it's moving!'

So the three of them set up camp on the marshy beach below Guai Village, and wait anxiously for the birth of the seventy-seventh generation male descendant of Confucius.

KEYWORDS: *flood diversion area, bamboo hut, blood donating, tightly stuffed, yellow foam, severe deformities.*

The public road that winds out of Guai Village leads to Dexian, but only two or three cars drive along it each day. The creek connects the Xi River to factories along the Huai River, but it's too shallow for large boats to navigate. In the afternoon, the sunlight lingers on the marshy beach for a while, then disappears behind a distant mountain that is surrounded by fields of yellow rape. Guai Village is in a flood diversion area. At times of emergency, the sluice gates upstream are raised, and the entire village becomes inundated. When the pollution from the factories is severe, yellow foamy waters flow into the creek, carrying dead chickens and dogs.

Guai villagers used to take water from the swampy pond to irrigate the paddy fields behind. But ten years ago, a villager sold his club-footed son to a criminal gang who made the boy beg on the streets of Anhui Province. In one year, the boy was able to send his parents ten thousand yuan. Envious of their good fortune, other parents in the village have sought to get rich through similar means. They mutilate their babies at birth, twisting or snapping their limbs, knowing that the severer the handicap the more money they will earn, then they sell or rent their maimed children to illegal gangs who bundle them off to beg in Shanghai, Shenzhen and Guangzhou. Within months the parents are able to buy colour televisions, refrigerators, imported cigarettes, electronic alarm clocks and mobile phones. The village's economy is booming from the deformed infant trade, and the mud houses have been replaced with three-storey villas. Eager to claim their share of the wealth, the local government has hiked taxes, and to promote the production of the village's valuable commodity, has turned a blind eye to family planning violations. But just to be safe, Kongzi has bribed the village family planning team five hundred yuan to allow Meili to carry her pregnancy to term. The team's chairman told him that if the baby is a girl and they decide not to keep her, the Welfare Office would take the baby off their hands and pay the 4,000-yuan fine for the illegal birth. It's common knowledge that the Welfare Office sells children in their care to foreigners for a 30,000-yuan profit.

Kongzi, Meili and Nannan have moved into the bamboo hut. A Fujian family who lived here before reared turtles in the pond, and made enough money to pay a human trafficking gang to smuggle them into England. Most of the mud plaster has now dropped from the hut's bamboo walls. At dawn, sunlight breaks through the cracks and falls in splinters on the floor. As Meili gets dressed, she remembers the blue tracksuit with two white stripes running along the sides which she wore to primary school. Her uncle who lives in the county town bought it for her. She was the only girl in the village to own one, and it always made her stand out from the crowd.

The rooster in the bamboo cage pops its head out, yodels loudly at the dawn, then draws it back again. Nannan is on the marshy beach, tossing twigs and old batteries into the creek. As the water splashes up, flies resting on a floating banana peel dart into the air.

'We'll never make much money rearing ducks,' Kongzi sighs, watching Meili drop shredded cabbage leaves into the bucket of slops.

'We've sold the first batch and thirty-three from the second,' Meili says. 'That's not bad. But now that winter's set in and the nights are getting colder, the breeding seems to have slowed down.'

'I spoke to your brother when I phoned your parents yesterday,' Kongzi says. 'He can't lend us any money. If we don't raise four thousand yuan to pay the birth fine by the time the baby arrives, I dread to think what will happen.'

'Feed these slops to the ducks, Nannan!' Meili calls out. Her belly is so large now that she can't see her feet. When the flea bites dotted over her toes itch, she has to rub them against a tree.

'No, that bucket's too heavy,' Nannan says, biting her nails.

Kongzi picks up the bucket, takes it into the duck enclosure and pours the slops into two bowls. The ducks ruffle their wings and jostle their way to the feed, quacking and grunting. Downy white feathers flutter into the morning sunlight.

'I'll look after the ducks today,' Meili says. 'You have a cargo to deliver this afternoon. Don't worry, I'm sure if we work hard, we'll be able to make four thousand in the next two months. And if we don't, we'll just have to run away to Heaven Township.' Meili is wearing Kongzi's blue cotton trousers and a white shirt she's left unbuttoned over her bump.

'You think you can run, with a belly that size? No, we'll stay here until the baby is born. A cousin of mine travelled the country giving blood for two years. He's just returned to the village, apparently, and built himself a four-bedroom brick house.'

'Giving blood too often can be dangerous,' Meili says, sitting on a pile of old fishing nets. The willows along the creek sweep their branches across the water as though trying to catch her long shadow.

'It's no more dangerous than having a piss. Once the bladder becomes empty, there's always more urine to fill it up.'

'So you're going to sell your blood, now? You think you have any left after these mosquitoes and fleas have sucked on you all night?' Meili is terrified of needles, and the thought of giving blood revolts her.

'Blood donating is a great career! It doesn't need any investment – the natural resource is inside one's own body. Why didn't I think about it before?' He pulls off his shirt, turns it inside out, picks off a flea from the sleeve and squeezes it. A drop of blood stains his nails red.

'How can you dream of getting rich, when you know we'll soon have another baby to look after?' Meili takes long, deep breaths. Her belly feels as full and hard as a tightly stuffed pillow.

'I want to swim, Daddy,' Nannan says. She picks up a piece of polystyrene lying next to the kennel and flings it into the water. Her feet are bare and the bottom of her long-sleeved dress is wet and muddy.

'No, the water's too cold,' Meili says. 'Go and scrape the rest of the potatoes, then I can start making breakfast for you.'

'The brick has gone,' Nannan says, stroking a long beetle she's picked up.

'There's another brick poking out of the mud behind you. You can use that, or you can scrape them against the tree instead. If you don't help, your father will make you recite the *Three Character Classic*.'

'Nannan, didn't you hear what your mother said?' Kongzi shouts, seeing Nannan walk into the creek. Since they set up camp here in October, they've felt cold and damp every day. At night, after supper, they either retreat to the boat and huddle around the electric heater, or light the fire pit in the hut and snuggle under blankets with hot-water bottles.

'Get out of the water, Nannan!' Meili yells. 'The yellow foam will give you a rash.' Afraid that the pollution might harm the baby, Meili hasn't dared bathe in the creek yet.

'Why the ducks got no rash, then?' Nannan asks, stepping back onto the beach.

'They have feathers to protect them,' Kongzi replies. He stoops down and pulls out an old cloth shoe from the mud. Behind him is a mound of metal rods, wooden sticks, bamboo poles and greasy ropes covered with flies. A procession of small beetles are crawling towards his feet, searching for food.

'You told me Happiness likes the water,' Nannan says, her fringe dangling over her eyes. She has a plaster on her nose because when Kongzi had to stick one over a cut on his nose yesterday, she insisted on having one as well.

'Happiness is dead – he doesn't care if the water's cold,' Kongzi says.

'You miss him, Daddy?'

'No!' Kongzi replies, his eyes flashing with anger.

'So when I die, you won't miss me either?'

'If you mention Happiness again, I'll kill you!' Kongzi shouts, his face crumpling with fury, veins bulging from his skinny neck.

Nannan purses her lips, goes to Meili and says, 'When I die, I won't ever wake up again.'

'Don't worry,' Meili replies. 'When people die, they can't hear or see anything any more. It's peaceful.'

'Happiness is dead, so is Waterborn going to die, too?' Nannan says, raising her flea-bitten face to Meili.

'Go and scrape the potatoes and we'll talk about this later.' Meili feels anxious. She's afraid the authorities will drag her off to have an abortion. She's afraid the IUD is imbedded in the fetus, and has caused severe deformities. She's also afraid that when Kongzi sees the IUD poking out of the baby's body, he will fly into a violent rage.

Waterborn has settled into a routine. As soon as the rooster cries at dawn, it stretches its legs and wiggles its toes. At noon, it stays still for two hours, then, after supper, it turns somersaults, kicking into her ribs, its tiny elbows and toes poking through her skin. During this pregnancy, Meili's hair and nails have been growing much faster than usual. As she can no longer reach her feet, Kongzi has to clip her toenails for her.

'You remember Kong Qing?' Kongzi says as he watches Meili plait her hair, the sunlight falling on her bulge. She's sitting next to the smoking fire pit inside the hut. Soon she will add more twigs to the fire and start cooking a potato gruel flavoured with pickles and preserved egg.

'No, remind me,' she says. Although she lived in Kong Village for three years, she was more familiar with the actors she saw on television than the confusing array of neighbours who shared the surname Kong.

'He's my second cousin, the ex-artillery soldier. You know, the man who came to our house that night, carrying his aborted son in a plastic basin.'

'Oh yes, Shasha's husband. So what's happened to him?' Meili joins Kongzi outside and sits on a rickety cane chair propped against a wooden box. A swarm of rice skippers fly past, leaving a scent of paddy fields.

'Well, after we left the village, their house was demolished and Kong Qing was sent to prison. Shasha travelled to the county headquarters with her daughters every week to complain to the authorities, but was eventually declared mentally ill. Once you've got that label stuck on you, you might as well be dead. You lose your residence permit, work permit and every other document that proves you exist. No official will listen to your complaints. Kong Qing was released from prison last month, but Shasha has now been locked up in a mental asylum and no one's allowed to visit her. Poor Kong Qing's in despair. His parents are having to look after the daughters now. He told me he wants to come and visit us next week.'

'But how does he know where we are?'

'I phoned Kong Zhaobo, and Kong Qing picked up the phone. He said I should come out of hiding and take command of his battle.'

'What battle?' Meili asks, then seeing Nannan rub a potato very slowly against a tree says, 'That's enough, Nannan. I'll do the rest.' Nannan brings the potatoes over and Meili begins to scrape them swiftly with a shard of glass she picks up from the ground.

'No idea what he's planning. But it turns out we're not far from Kong Village. The road to Dexian continues all the way to Hubei Province. He could reach us by long-distance bus in one day.'

'I don't think it's a good idea for him to come. It seems like most of the Kongs in the village have been arrested or jailed at some point. It would be safer if you kept your distance.' Meili stares out at the ducks on the pond, and at the public road far behind that winds towards the distant hills like a long umbilical cord.

KEYWORDS: *uprising, nits, untamed rivers, financial loss, humble disciple, suicide bombers.*

Meili wakes abruptly in the middle of the night, having rolled onto a cold bicycle pump. She hears the ducks padding about and squawking, as though someone were shooing them out of the enclosure. As she crawls out onto the deck, she sees a long shadow flit across the path and disappear. She leans back into the cabin and shakes Kongzi awake. 'Quick! Get up! Someone's stolen our ducks!'

Kongzi grabs his torch, shines it over the enclosure and sees that the wooden hutch has been smashed open and all the ducks are gone.

'I can hear him shooing them on! Quick! That way!' Meili hurries to the bow and points into the darkness.

Kongzi jumps ashore, grabs a sack and a wooden stick and sets off up the hill, following the man's voice. Ten minutes later he returns dragging a large sack of ducks. He takes out the birds and counts them one by one. 'We're eight short,' he says. 'When the thief saw me, he grabbed two ducks by the neck and bolted off into the hills.' They search the bushes, find another six ducks, then return the birds to the hutch, bolt the enclosure gate and go to check the bamboo hut. The two crates of ducklings and bags of birdfeed are still there, but the radio is gone. Kongzi runs outside and curses the village: 'Evil bastards! The ancients were right: "Barren hills and untamed rivers spawn wicked men!"'

'Be quiet,' Meili says. 'The villagers have let us "dwell beneath their hedge". Don't antagonise them . . . Oh God! It looks like he stole the cash we buried. What if he comes back to murder us? Who would bury our bodies?'

'He can't have found it. I'll dig a little deeper.' Since they set up home here, Kongzi has been stashing their cash in a hole he dug beside the hut. 'Don't be silly. No one will kill us. During his thirteen years in exile, Confucius toured the nine provinces and never once came to harm . . . You're right, the cash has definitely gone.' Kongzi rubs the mud from his hands, tramps back to the boat, sits down at the bow and lights a cigarette. 'We must view this setback as a blessing,' he says, watching Meili climb back onto the boat. 'As the ancients said, "Today's financial loss prevents tomorrow's disaster." Our cash has been stolen so that Waterborn can be granted a safe birth.'

'Touring the country, you say? Hah! We're not tourists, we're fugitives, you idiot. I'm fed up of this vagabond life, Kongzi. You think of yourself as some great philosopher, roaming the country, contemplating the troubles of the world, with me tagging along as your humble disciple. Well, I've had enough, I'm telling you! What if that man was from the family planning team? What if he sends his colleagues down to arrest us?'

'No, he was just a simple village thief. I've told you – the family planning officers here don't care about illegal births. They're happy for the villagers to have as many children as they want, so long as they pay the fines. The more maimed children are sold, the richer everyone gets. No one wants to kill the golden goose. So stop worrying.'

'If we can't return to your village, let's go back to mine. I want to live in a house with a tiled roof. Nannan should be going to school now. This rootless life isn't good for us. Let's sell the boat and go home.' Meili squashes two mosquitoes on her arm then wipes the blood on the cabin's canopy.

'Officers have told your parents to report us to the police if we turn up,' Kongzi says. 'So we've nowhere to return to now.'

'But I'm tired of traipsing behind you,' Meili says, folding an empty plastic bag and placing it under the bamboo mat to use later.

'You're tired of me? But I'm a model husband. I don't play mahjong. The moment I wake up, I make breakfast for us. Didn't you say you wanted to live in Heaven Township? Once the baby's born, we'll sell this batch of ducks and sail south.'

'I still have another month to go. I heard that in Guangxi Province, family planning teams with metal helmets and shields have been storming into villages to carry out forced abortions. A village priest who tried to take away the aborted fetuses and give them a proper burial was beaten up and put in jail.'

'This is Guangdong Province – it's much more relaxed than Guangxi.' Kongzi turns off the torch and lights another cigarette. 'Do you remember, in Kong Village, how we'd hear frogs croak until dawn, just like that poem by Han Yu? But at night this filthy creek is as silent as death.'

'What about the buzzing of the mosquitoes?'

'Huh! Where's the poetry in that? Just now, you used the phrase "dwell beneath their hedge". Do you know which poem that comes from?'

'Stop testing me. Let's go back to sleep. You must go into the village in the morning and track the thief down. He'll probably be roasting the ducks by then, so the smell should lead you to his house.' Meili lies back down on the bamboo mat, turns onto her side and feels the taut skin of her large belly relax. 'Oh God, Kongzi! I just realised we left our tricycle cart on the sand island! How could we have forgotten it?'

'Didn't I tell you? Someone stole it while we took Weiwei up to Yinluo. All I found when we got back was a single wheel chained to the tree . . .'

'"Summer wildfires cannot destroy the grass, / For in spring, soft winds will restore it to life . . ."' Father recites his favourite line of poetry and flicks his cigarette butt into the creek. Then he returns to the cabin, squeezes down next to Mother, drapes his leg over hers and unhooks her bra. 'Bet the mosquitoes haven't got to these two soft dumplings yet.'

'Get your hands off me!'

'What are they for, if not for me to fondle?'

'It must be nearly four o'clock. You'll wake the rooster.'

'Until the baby's born, these belong to me.' Father leans over and moves his lips towards Mother's nipple.

'Those weighing scales take up too much space. Let's throw them away.'

'But I use them to prepare the feed.'

Mother pushes the scales out of the way, then folds her arms over her chest as Father coils around her and buries his face in her hair. 'I warn you, I have nits! Don't bite me . . . Get off! Stop pressing on my belly . . .' Nannan opens her eyes. Mother quickly covers them with her hand and says, 'Close your eyes, Nannan, and go back to sleep!'

Overlapping this scene, the infant spirit sees Father, a few days later, sitting in the cabin, listening to a man say, 'We grew up together, Kongzi. You're a brilliant strategist. Without your help, we'll get nowhere.'

Father puts down his glass and says, 'Kong Qing, you're like a brother to me. I admire you for wanting to stand up for the Chinese people and protect the Kong family line. But the rebellion you're planning is doomed to fail. This country has changed since the Tiananmen Massacre. The people have lost their fighting spirit. Where would you base your stronghold?'

'In Wild Man Mountain. It's easy to defend. Armies with heavy artillery wouldn't be able to climb it.' The two men are cross-legged on the cabin floor, smoking. The kerosene lamp illuminates the blue notebook, ashtray and carton of deep-fried broad beans on the cardboard box between them.

'I admit, if you demanded the repeal of the One Child Policy, every peasant in China would support you. But what would you do next? Overthrow the Communist Party? Challenge the People's Liberation Army? You say you want to take over every family planning office in the country, but you must understand that once you've occupied them, you'll become an easy target. It's a game of chess. You might take their knight, but if they nab your queen in the next move, you're finished.'

'All right, forget about the Fertility Freedom Party, then. Let's form a suicide squad instead! Like those Muslim suicide bombers, we'll storm government offices, detonate ourselves, and take the whole corrupt lot of them with us!' Kong Qing punches his fist onto the bamboo mat. Although this scene took place years ago, his punch still judders down to the base of the boat and sends ripples through the moon's pale reflection.

'I'm not afraid of death,' Father says. 'I'm sure you and I would have the balls to storm every family planning office in China. But we'd just be letting off steam. We wouldn't achieve anything.'

'I want to fight, Kongzi, not only to avenge the abortion of my son, but to ensure the survival of the Kong clan and Chinese family traditions. These are causes for which I'm willing to sacrifice my life. Did you know that in the Cultural Revolution, after the Red Guards smashed the Tomb of Confucius, they dug up the corpses of a seventy-sixth generation descendant, Kong Lingyi, and his wife, and thrashed them with spades? It was a declaration of war against the Chinese nation.'

'I know. They dug up and destroyed two thousand ancestral graves. Corpses were pulled out, stripped and hung from trees. I agree we must avenge our family honour, but not by launching a rebellion. The time isn't right. Historically, popular revolts have erupted in times of hardship. But the Party has allowed people to get rich. Who would want to join the revolution now?'

'What destruction Mao unleashed . . .'

'Yes, but Mao's dead, and faith in Communism is dead. The Party has no ideology to legitimise itself now, so it's bringing back capitalism and Confucianism to fill the void. Go into any bookshop, and you'll see that in official publications Confucius is no longer referred to as "Evil Kong, the Second Son" . . . All right, I'll help draw up a constitution for your Fertility Freedom Party, but I tell you now, I won't join any uprising.' Some of their rice wine has spilt on the mat, filling the cabin with a sweet, heady smell.

'Look at all the people who've signed up: Kong Guo, Scarface, Wang Wu . . . I've got a hundred names already. We'll hold our first party congress soon and elect a chair. I hope you'll accept the position of secretary general.'

'No, count me out. Meili's going to give birth next month – so I'll be doing my part to ensure the survival of the Kong clan! But I have three points to make. First: if you do launch a rebellion, you must be aware that you will receive no international backing. America and the UN have given full support to China's population control policies. Second: if you want to get rid of the One Child Policy, you must get rid of the Communist Party first, and that won't happen without a military coup. Tens of thousands of protests flare up across China every year, and in the end each one is crushed by the army. So, my third point is: bide your time and focus on building a network of contacts. Then, when a national uprising similar to the 1989 protests breaks out, you'll be able to take advantage of the chaos and launch your attack.'

Mother walks out of the bamboo hut, leans against a tree beside the creek and pisses into the water. Noticing the lamp still shining in the cabin, she shouts, 'Kongzi, go to sleep! The sun's almost up.'

KEYWORDS: *chrysalids, crow's nest, motherwort, spindly tree, pelvic inflammatory disease.*

Meili herds the ducks up the muddy path that curls through the lychee grove towards the terraced hill. She wanted them to stay on the lower terrace, but the duck at the front catches a scent and climbs a steep track, and the whole flock soon follows behind, shaking their snow-white tails. There are thirty-two of them. The remaining ten are roosting in the hutch or are too sick to come out. Meili wants them to forage for earthworms and snails while she looks for the water chickweed flowers she likes to add to egg soup.

The July sunlight has softened the earth. Steam is rising from the clumps of willows and eucalyptus trees and bags of rubbish scattered over the fallow field. The heat seeps into Meili's flesh. Inside her belly, the fetus extends its legs and excretes fluids into the amniotic sac. As she crosses the field, her pulse racing and her head dizzy from the heat, she feels as though the ground beneath her feet is supporting her like a strong and dependable man. She sees a peony bush, buries her nose in a pink bloom, and inhales. The subtle, mysterious scent makes her lose her balance. She undoes the lower buttons of her shirt, and, breathing deeply, lowers herself onto the grass. As her pulse returns to a slow, steady pace, a Tang poem drifts into her mind: 'Idly I sit while osmanthus flowers fall. / Tranquil is the spring night on the deserted hill. / The moon rises, startling the mountain birds. / All night they call out from the ravine.' Kongzi once copied this poem for her on bamboo paper in graceful 'grass style' calligraphy, and she put it in the wooden box containing the jade earrings her grandmother gave her . . . For an instant, time seems to lose all meaning. She stares at a pink flower in the grass below and tries to remember its name, then looks at the ducks foraging for food in the irrigation ditches, their necks stretching out and shrinking back again. A drake mounts a female duck and waggles its tail as it ejaculates. She saw that pair mate two days ago. As soon as the egg is laid, she'll have to collect it and place it in the hutch for the duck to incubate. Thinking of the eggs makes Meili's belly tighten. As she rubs her bamboo herding pole, she remembers Kongzi making love to her on their honeymoon in Beijing, while Teacher Zhou was out at work. The bed had a soft, sprung mattress. He shook her about in a sweaty fervour for hours. By the end, she was drenched and listless, and her groin was scorched and inflamed. For the rest of the honeymoon, the burning between her legs made it painful for her to walk. When she stepped onto Tiananmen Square on their last day, it hurt so much that she had to sit down and rest on the concrete paving stones. As soon as Weiwei gripped her hand on the boat, the memory of that pain came back to her. She hates thinking of Weiwei now, and still hasn't taken a look at the tortoiseshell glasses she snatched from him . . . She glances up and sees hanging down from the leaves of a shrub, three grey butterfly chrysalids. She hopes that one day she too will be able to break out of her shell and fly. During these last nine months, she's barely had a moment to think of her own future. Sharp spikes of motherwort prick into her ankles. On the broad Huai River far away, boats are docked below a petrol station and large cargos are being unloaded. One boat has a triangular flag, indicating it can sail on foreign waters. Last week, Kongzi transported cargos of security doors and glass panels. He was paid thirty-five yuan a day, but after the cost of fuel was deducted, he was left with only twenty. He spent two hundred yuan when Kong Qing visited, taking him out for meals at the village restaurant. Meili was excluded from their secret discussions, but from the little she overheard she gathered they're planning to set up a company to provide family planning information. Meili asked Kong Qing whether his wife suffered any after-effects from the forced abortion, and he said she contracted a pelvic inflammatory disease which has left her infertile. He said that women subjected to such abortions often develop this disease, and even if they do manage to conceive later, the babies are either miscarried or born with birth defects. He said the government deliberately chooses to perform forced abortions and IUD insertions in primitive places such as village schools, so that women will contract illnesses that will render them barren. Meili is relieved that although she suffered from cramps and heavy bleeding for a while after her abortion, she didn't develop any serious complications. She runs her hands through the grass, searching for her favourite bitter-tasting wolfberry leaves, and for snails to feed to her ducks. For the first time in months, she feels safe and at peace.

Waterborn, Waterborn, she whispers, looking down at her bulge. Whether you're a boy or a girl, you're my flesh and blood, and I will love and protect you. Although the last thing I wanted was another child, now that you're here, it all seems right. I have everything ready: scissors, antiseptic, muslin sheets, a plastic basin, nappies – the expensive disposable ones. I'll give birth to you on the boat. You may not know this now, but in this country having a child can be a crime. That's why we've had to hide in this wretched place. Your brother Happiness was about the same size as you are now when he was torn from me . . . In the centre of a vast field far below stands a frail, spindly tree that no one would notice were it not for the large crow's nest in its upper branches. Indistinct figures are burning paper offerings on a grave mound in its shade. Meili thinks of her mother and grandmother. When she lived in Nuwa Village, she always longed to leave her family, but now that she's so far from home, she wishes she could be with them. She'd like to comb her mother's hair now, or scratch her back for her. She'd like to carry her frail grandmother into the garden and let her sit in the sun, or find a wheelchair and push her along the banks of Dark Water River or up to the temple on Nuwa Mountain. She forgets how many times she went up there on her grandmother's back, clinging to her neck and bumping up and down as her grandmother struggled up the hundreds of stone stairs and finally stepped over the high threshold of the temple entrance.

Meili sees the ducks waddle downhill and head into a swathe of tall reeds. She pushes herself up onto her feet and chases after them, as fast as she can. At the foot of the hill the ground becomes soft and boggy. Through a gap in the reeds she glimpses a sparkling pond, with a cloud of white termites hovering above it. Termites, Meili whispers. That means a storm is brewing. The ducks at the front of the flock have already jumped into the water. Meili pushes through the reeds and tries to drive them out, but when her herding pole approaches their heads, they dive out of the way. What if I can't get them out, or worse still: what if a farmer breeds fish in this pond? She picks two ducks up by the neck, but the rest of the flock are in the pond now, squawking, diving, splashing. She stands rooted to the ground, paralysed by fear. What if the farmer turns up and demands I pay compensation? The flock drifts towards the centre of the pond, beyond her pole's reach. Waterborn swirls in the amniotic fluid. Meili's belly contracts; she breaks into a sweat. Then the ground beneath her judders, and although the sky above is a brilliant blue, suddenly everything around her goes black. She senses someone staring down at her exposed belly. She wants to sink into the water and hide . . .

KEYWORDS: *hot draught, umbilical cord, fetal grease, windless swamp, jellified residue, red cable.*

The village delivery room is in Sister Mao's house. Her brother is a family planning officer, and for five hundred yuan, which she splits with him, she is willing to deliver unauthorised babies. For a supplementary fee she will also break the baby's limbs, if the parents wish. As soon as the farmer came to the hut yesterday to say that Meili had fainted near his pond, Kongzi rushed to her side and carried her straight here. When she woke in the delivery room, in the early stages of labour, she said she wanted to give birth in the boat, but by then Kongzi had already paid Sister Mao's fee.

Her waters have broken and the contractions are coming faster. As another wave of pain approaches, she passes out and sees Happiness's face hover before her, one eye closed, the other staring at her impassively. She lifts her head and looks at herself lying on the metal table, her hands gripping the sides. From the blood-filled hole below her black pubic hair she notices a small arm reach out. A human life is struggling to emerge. The moment has come. This time, the baby will not be murdered upon arrival, though. She will make sure of that. As soon as it's born, she'll grab hold of it and kick anyone who tries to come near. All she needs to do now is go down on all fours, push as hard as she can, and everything will be fine . . . But like the jellied residue of a fish stew heated in a pan, she liquefies and evaporates, and finds herself drifting up to the ceiling and looking down on her body below. She sees her face contort and turn purple, her teeth bite into her lower lip. At last, she hears a slithery plop and sees a mass

159

of human flesh slipping out from between her legs in a stream of fluid that becomes soiled with pubic hair and dirty tissues . . . Echoing voices slowly drag her back into her body . . . 'A good size. Chubby, even.' The room is stiflingly hot now; the wrinkles on Sister Mao's face are filled with sweat. A whirring electric fan in the corner blows a hot draught into the stuffy air. Sister Mao's assistant, Ying, opens the baby's legs and sighs. 'A girl! What bad luck! That's the second we've had today. Ugh, the placenta smells disgusting . . .'

'Quick! Cut the umbilical cord. And bung those sheets in the washing machine. Don't touch the cloth – there's shit on it. Just flick it into the bin.'

Once her senses have fully returned, Meili opens her eyes and scans the foul-smelling room. During the final stage of labour, Sister Mao pressed a cloth-covered brick against Meili's anus, but the last push was so strong that her shit still sprayed out onto the wall.

'Look, she's opening her eyes,' Ying says, wrapping the baby in a towel and wiping her little red face. 'She still hasn't cried yet, though.'

'Slap her bottom, then!' Sister Mao is the only plump woman in the village. When she looks down, the fat beneath her chin bulges out in thick folds.

Meili watches Ying unwrap the baby, swaddle her in white muslin and mutter into her ear. At last, the baby opens her mouth and lets out a feeble wail. You're alive! Meili says silently. We can go back to Kong Village now – your rightful birthplace! She is certain that she's not dreaming any more: she has given birth. After nine months of living in her womb – no, the government's womb – Waterborn has finally come out into the world, and Meili is now a mother of two.

The delivery room has a dropped ceiling with a round fluorescent light that is as bright as a full moon. The curtain hanging over the door has an image of a red crane flying across a blue sky. A red cable dangling from the ceiling sways in the draught from the fan.

Meili feels limp and sapped of energy. She remembers that when she gave birth to Nannan at home she squeezed the metal bars of her bed frame so hard during the final push that they became twisted together. But the excruciating labour pains she endured just now, the splitting of bones and tearing of flesh as Waterborn's head pushed through her pelvis, have already been forgotten and reabsorbed into her flesh. Immersed in a peaceful numbness, she watches the baby who was once part of her body adapt to her new surroundings. She senses that although the umbilical cord has been severed, an invisible thread still binds her to her daughter. They can never become one again, but neither can they ever be truly apart.

'The arm came out first, the waters broke early, the labour was long and arduous: everything was pointing to a male birth,' Ying sighs. During Meili's labour, she said she was convinced the baby was a boy, and is clearly annoyed to have been proved wrong.

'My daughter!' Meili croaks, gesturing for the baby to be brought to her. She tries to think how she'd feel if the baby had been a boy, but just like her amniotic fluid, her imaginative faculties seem to have slipped out of her. I don't mind what sex the baby is. She's mine, and I'll look after her just as I do Nannan. 'Waterborn,' she whispers, taking hold of the baby, a proud glow spreading across her damp face. Waterborn's hands tremble and her head droops to the side. Her fine hair is caked with creamy white fetal grease.

'Boy or girl, it's still one more pair of hands to help out on the fields,' Sister Mao says. 'The placenta has been fully ejected. Scoop it up, Ying.'

Waterborn struggles floppily up Meili's breast, as though searching for the warm wetness from which she's been expelled. When at last her mouth becomes filled with Meili's engorged nipple, her tiny body twitches with relief. 'Drink my milk, little one. Keep sucking. That's right.' Meili's tear-drenched cheeks flush a deep red.

'Now that the baby's born, you should return to your husband's village,' Sister Mao says. 'I've seen that windless swamp where you've been camping. There are mosquitoes everywhere. It's no place to bring up children.'

'But we haven't a home to return to,' Meili says. 'A family planning squad pulled down our house. Besides, my husband said we can only go home if the baby's a boy.' Meili sees her placenta lying in a plastic bowl on top of the washing machine. Flies swoop down and perch on the surface. Ying coils up the severed umbilical cord and places it beside the bowl.

'So, is it a boy or a girl?' Kongzi bellows, charging into the room, reeking of diesel. His legs and arms are lacerated from the glass panels he delivered last week. This morning he transported boxes of human hair to an illegal soy sauce factory. He's brought four packets of instant noodles with him and a tin of processed ham.

'A girl,' Meili answers, trying to sound offhand as she squeezes her nipple back into Waterborn's mouth.

Kongzi walks over to her, lifts the swaddling cloth and examines the baby for himself. His face scrunches in anger. 'So I paid five hundred yuan for you to give birth to *that*!' he shouts, then storms outside and lights a cigarette. Meili breathes a sigh of relief. The government and her husband are powerless now. Her baby will live. Looking down again, she catches sight of Waterborn's left hand and cries out, 'My God! Sister Mao, come and look! She's got six fingers!'

'Yes, there is one too many,' Sister Mao concurs. 'Let me check her right hand. Fine. And her feet. Normal too, thank goodness. Don't worry. One extra finger isn't a calamity. You know what they say: a sixth finger signifies a sixth talent. But if it bothers you, I can chop it off. No extra cost.'

Meili shudders at the thought, and feels the little finger of her own left hand begin to throb. 'No, no, it's fine,' she blurts.

'But the baby does seem a little slow to me. Take her to the district hospital in a month to have her checked. And keep a record of how much milk she drinks, the colour and frequency of her stools. These days there are so many pesticides on our crops, so much formaldehyde in our homes, it's rare to see a baby born without a brain defect, cleft palate or other deformity. Make sure you regularly clear the duck shit from your enclosure. That sixth finger suggests to me that you caught toxoplasmosis during your pregnancy – it's a disease caused by a parasite that lives in animal dung. A baby I helped deliver last week was born with no nose and no limbs, so you should consider yourself lucky.'

Meili's heartbeat returns to normal and a rosy glow suffuses her face. She can't find the strength to close her legs. Her womb feels like an opened cellar, with hot air wafting in and cold blood streaming out. 'Sister Mao,' she says, 'I've changed my mind. Babies don't remember pain, do they? So can you get it over and done with, please, and chop off the sixth finger now?'

KEYWORDS: *paralysis, water on the brain, fishing net, male chauvinism, good by nature, soft spot.*

The evening sun turns the papaya tree and dead banana trees behind the hut golden green. Moths swirl around the hut's doorway. Kongzi sits on a cracked enamel washbasin, his head in his hands. By his feet, a line of yellow ants are marching across an opened tin of lychees. Since the sluice gates were raised last week, foamy floodwaters have engulfed the creek, risen to the pond and are lapping at the base of the willows a few metres from the hut. Half the ducks have died. Kongzi said the pollution in the floodwater must have killed them, but Meili thinks they were poisoned by the contaminated rice he's been adding to their feed. Each time they swallow a grain, their heads jerk back in discomfort. When Meili steams the rice for supper, it turns yellow and gives off the smell of rotten tree roots.

Nannan is standing barefoot among towering water weeds, singing, 'Four, six, seven, eight. The farmer stands by the gate. Too many ducks to count. For dinner he'll be late . . .' A white fishing net hangs over the boat's bow like a bridal veil. Last week, when Kongzi saw that the flooded creek was teeming with dead fish, he bought the net so that he could scoop them out and sell them in the village. He'd heard that once the poisoned fish are gutted, salted and dried, the chemical taste is barely noticeable.

The stink of pollution and decay in the sweltering August air makes Nannan's eyes water. When Waterborn is unable to latch on to Meili's engorged nipples, she cries herself into a purple frenzy. Kongzi has noticed her eyelids are swollen, her mouth hangs open, and that she has a blood-filled lump on her crown, and suspects she might be mentally handicapped. He couldn't afford the 800-yuan cost of a check-up at the district hospital, but with the help of a contact at the Radiance Hair Company, he was able to bribe one of the hospital's doctors a hundred yuan to visit them at the hut. The doctor was a recent graduate and looked no more than twenty-two. After examining the lump on Waterborn's crown and palpating the soft spot above her forehead, he said, 'Her skull shouldn't be this big. She might have a tumour, or water on the brain. If the head grows any larger, she could suffer paralysis and severe brain damage.'

Ever since then, Kongzi and Meili have been quarrelling over what to do with her. Kongzi wants to sell her, but Meili won't hear of it. He raises the subject again now, and Meili charges out of the hut holding a greasy wok lid in one hand and Waterborn in the other, and shouts, 'Over my dead body! She's my flesh and blood. I'll never let you take her away from me.' Nannan, who's sitting on a plastic crate eating a banana, kicks her legs about, sending the mud on her bare feet flying into the air.

'Just think things through, Meili!' Kongzi says, wiping his wet face on his T-shirt. 'The brain surgery alone would cost thirty thousand yuan. And even if it's successful, she'll still need full-time care for the rest of her life.' He flinches as his tongue touches the two large ulcers on his gums, which cause him so much pain he hasn't dared have a cigarette all day.

'You love Nannan, so there's no reason you can't learn to love Waterborn as well. I'm sick of your male chauvinism. No wonder Confucius wasn't welcomed during his travels – jabbering on about male superiority all the time!' Meili stares out at the heat haze above the pond, and at the large banyan tree on a hill far behind that is blotting out the setting sun. Then she goes to the stove and puts some water on to boil.

'She needs the operation,' Kongzi continues. 'The doctor said she might have a brain tumour.'

Meili wonders if the IUD did indeed become embedded in Waterborn's brain, and is the cause for all the problems. She decides to get Waterborn's head X-rayed, no matter how much it costs.

Kongzi pulls a cigarette from his pocket and sniffs it longingly. 'It's nothing to do with her being a girl. We just don't have the resources to look after her.'

'I don't trust that doctor. We should get a second opinion. If she does have a tumour, we'll have it removed.' Meili has rolled her white vest up to her neck. When she bends over, her bare breasts hang down like two long gourds.

'Huh – women: long hair, small brains,' Kongzi mutters under his breath. He turns to Nannan. 'You haven't recited the *Three Character Classic* for days. Come on, give me the first lines.'

'"People at birth. Good by nature. Mother of Mencius. Chose good home. Son didn't study. Broke loom's shuttle . . ."' Nannan walks towards him, swinging her hips in time with the chant.

'Stop – you missed at least six lines,' Kongzi says, then blows out a long stream of air in a useless attempt to cool himself. The hills surrounding this swampy marsh block off all the wind, so in summer the heat is unbearable.

'Ugh, your mouth farted, Dad,' Nannan says, catching a whiff of Kongzi's rancid breath. She turns and runs off into the reeds to look for grasshoppers and cockroaches to feed to the ducks.

'If Confucius came back to life now and discovered that it's illegal to set up unofficial schools, he'd die of despair.' Kongzi still dreams of returning to teaching. Sweat is streaming down his suntanned neck onto his pale chest. He's built a small porch for the hut out of bamboo and plastic sheeting, and laid plantain leaves on the ground underneath, hoping it would provide a refuge from the heat. At midday, it does offer some shade, but when the sun shines obliquely in the late afternoon it turns into a heat trap.

Waterborn is lying naked between Meili's breasts, panting for breath like a wawa fish freshly scooped from a river. When the sun's rays hit her red swollen eyes, she turns her head and wails. Nannan rushes up and says, 'Stop crying, you naughty girl!' then, just as Kongzi used to do to her, she raises a palm and shouts, 'If you don't shut up, I'll hit you!'

'Waterborn will get heatstroke if we don't cool her down,' Meili says. 'I can't bathe her in that filthy creek. Let's take some towels and sail to the Xi River.'

'You need a permit to sail during a flood. If the river police caught us, we'd get a huge fine.' The truth is, Kongzi sailed along the Xi River all morning without being stopped once. He just doesn't want to have to go out on the boat again. He looks at Meili and says, 'If we don't pay off the 4,000-yuan fine for Waterborn's birth soon, we'll be in deep trouble.'

'But now that she's born, we're safe,' Meili replies. Seeing that the water in the pan hasn't come to the boil yet, she goes to crouch in the shade of a willow and pushes her nipple into Waterborn's mouth. 'The officers are rolling in money – they won't bother trekking down here just to collect our miserable cash.'

'Didn't you hear about that woman called Cui who lives at the edge of the village? When she couldn't pay the illegal birth fine, the officers drowned her six-month-old baby in a pigs' water trough. It's true – I promise.'

'That was years ago. You weren't afraid of the officers when I was pregnant. If you're so terrified of them now, why don't you dig yourself a deep hole under the hut and hide from them?'

'Confucius lay in a deep hole for two thousand years, but the Communists still yanked him out in the end. I tell you, these days, there's nowhere left to hide.'

'You were desperate to have a second child, and now, because she's a girl, you want to get rid of her. Has a dog eaten your conscience?' Meili goes back to the stove, drops some dried pulses into the boiling water and kicks an empty liquor box lying at her feet.

'I don't care what you say – I'm still determined to have a son . . . We must lie low next week. Dexian leaders are coming to inspect the flood zone, and they're bound to bring family planning officials with them.' This morning, the village Party Secretary paid Kongzi thirty yuan to take the tramp who loiters outside the village restaurant downriver and drop him in a neighbouring county. He also asked Kongzi to stay away during the leaders' visit, as he'll need to assure them that there are no illegal migrants in the village.

Nannan comes running up with a can of insect killer, points the nozzle at Kongzi and says, 'Waterborn's my sister! You can't sell her!'

'The ground's burning hot, Nannan, put those on,' Kongzi says, pointing at the two, unmatched flip-flops he found in the floodwater today. The sun starts to sink below the distant mountain and the ducks on the pond begin to squawk.

'See, you *are* able to feel compassion for a daughter!' Meili says with a sarcastic sneer. She pulls off her wet vest and turns off the stove. Then she sits down beneath the porch, squeezes both nipples, and crams the one that produces most milk into Waterborn's mouth. 'Don't touch those filthy flip-flops, Nannan,' she says. 'After I sell the eggs at the market tomorrow, I'll buy you a new pair.'

'If we give Waterborn to the Welfare Office, we'll get four thousand yuan to pay her illegal birth fine,' Kongzi says.

'That's not giving, it's selling! I tell you, Kongzi, if you try to get rid of her, I'll leave you and I'll never come back . . . Look how bad her heat rash has become. You said you'd buy some powder for it in Dexian.' Meili wipes the sweat from Waterborn's face. The blood-filled bulge on her crown is now as large as a shallot, and its purple stain has spread down over her forehead and right eye. In the sunset's rosy light, her skin has turned the colour of a rotten mango. She lifts her tiny hands and rests them on the breast she's sucking.

'We've hardly any money left. If we don't sell her, what will we live on?' Kongzi says, staring with bloodshot eyes at the stubborn flood. He once said that his aim in life was to own a motorbike, a fridge, a rice cooker and a colour television. But now, as he looks at the filthy waters and the new baby, this goal seems like a distant dream.

As the last strip of pale light at the horizon is pressed into the earth, the infant spirit sees Waterborn open her eyes. Father goes into the bamboo hut to light a mosquito coil.

'I'm fed up with this useless junk you keep bringing back, Kongzi,' Mother says, stroking Waterborn's cheek. 'Look: scraps of timber, plastic buckets, broken shoes. This is supposed to be a home, not a rubbish tip. If we were back in the village now, I would have spent the last month confined to my bed, with nutritious food brought to

me on a tray. But since the baby was born, you haven't bothered to make one nice meal for me.'

'You're right. You should be drinking chicken soup to build up your milk supply. I've no money to buy a chicken, but I'll make some duck stew for you instead. Once we give Waterborn away we'll be able to eat whatever we want.'

'Even if I were dying of hunger and my milk had run dry, I wouldn't let you take her from me!' Mother says, squashing a mosquito that's sucking Waterborn's arm. 'Come on. Let's get on the boat and sail to the Xi River for some fresh air. My one-month confinement would end tomorrow. I want to wash myself with clean water and soap.'

'The doctor said she's not mentally handicapped – she just has something inside her brain that needs to be removed,' Father says into the dark.

The light from the lamp inside the hut splays through the bamboo wall onto Mother's face. Smells of soy sauce and spring onion briefly veil the stench of duck shit drifting from the enclosure. At night, everything melts into the darkness and becomes equal: water and earth, father and mother, ducks and disposable nappies. On that night many years ago, Waterborn stares at the black sky, or at her strange birthplace, and with all the strength that her four-week-old life can muster, lets out a piercing cry.

'She needs her nappy changed,' Mother says.

'We've run out of clean water,' Father replies, rubbing an unlit cigarette.

'I want to cuddle Waterborn, like you cuddle Mummy,' Nannan says to Father, skipping about restlessly.

Along the distant public road, a few lights twinkle in the concrete houses while closer by the fluorescent strips of the village restaurant and night stalls shine through the dust raised by passing trucks.

KEYWORDS: *win-win situation, egg lady, amino acids, orphanage, fermented hair, motherwort.*

Naked from the waist up, Meili sits on a concrete brick beneath the porch and stares out at the enclosure. In the midday sun, the pond and the white ducks look blindingly bright. A small bird darting across the creek faints from the heat and falls into the water with a loud splash. The sky and earth seem paralysed by the sun's burning rays.

The dead fish Kongzi scooped from the floodwater and laid out to dry were washed away in a torrential downpour last week. Kongzi and Meili have bought thirty new ducklings and cordoned off a section of the pond to protect them from the adult ducks. With any luck, they'll be able to sell them next month for two hundred yuan. Waterborn is eight weeks old now, and still does nothing all day but eat and sleep. Meili is afraid to put her down for naps inside the hut in case she's attacked by stray dogs, so she carries her around all day wrapped to her chest with a long cloth, as is the custom in Guangdong Province. Now, all she wants is to find a job and start making some good money. There's an agricultural market in a town four kilometres downstream, and she's considering going there to ask if she can hire a stall. The feeling of emptiness in her flat belly is reassuring. If family planning officers were to catch her now and insert an IUD into her or even sterilise her, she wouldn't put up a fight.

The two sisters, Gu and Hua, who rent out this plot to them, turn up after lunch. They drop by once a week to collect rent, buy ducks from Meili and pick fruit from the lychee trees. Gu is tall and thin, and is wearing a conical straw hat. Hua, shorter and stockier, is holding a dainty black parasol.

'Nannan, bring the beer crate over here for the aunties to sit on,' Meili calls out, picking up the paper fan that Kongzi made.

'No need,' says Hua, as she and her sister squeeze into the remaining shade beneath the porch. 'Look how the baby's grown! She must be a good feeder.'

'You don't mind if I don't put on a vest, do you? It's just too hot today.' The sweat streaming down Meili's cleavage has soaked Waterborn's face and the piece of cloth in which she's wrapped.

'Your ducks are selling well in the village. They taste just like the ones I used to eat as a child.' From her smooth pale hands, one can tell that Hua has never worked on the fields.

'We feed them a pure grain diet, and don't let them touch the dead fish that wash up on the beach.' Meili's heart always beats faster when she lies. 'Give the aunties some fizzy orange,' she calls out to Nannan, who's standing naked beside the pond, spraying water onto an ant nest.

'Yes, your baby's a sturdy little thing, but look how her feet curl inwards,' says Gu, sneering under her conical hat. 'I heard your husband say that there might be something wrong with her.'

'Think about your future, Meili,' says Hua. 'Bringing up a handicapped child is expensive, and exhausting too. All that money and effort, and you won't even be able to marry her off in the end!'

Meili crosses her legs, rests a foot on a burnt tin can and pushes her nipple back into Waterborn's mouth. 'What does your husband do, Hua?' she asks.

'He works at the Radiance Hair Factory. I believe your husband's delivered some stock to them.'

'What do they do with the hair?' Meili asks, coiling her own hair into a bun then securing it with a twig.

'If it's long, they make wigs out of it. If it's short, they ferment it.' The two sisters are now sitting down on the beer crate, cooling themselves with the paper fans Nannan has just made.

'Ferment it? To make shampoo?' Meili closes her eyes briefly and imagines sailing upstream to a clean stretch of the Xi River, then jumping in and washing herself with soap. Although according to custom she is allowed to bathe now that her confinement is over, she still wouldn't dare enter the filthy creek. Kongzi brings back bottles of clean river water from his trips, but never enough to wash more than her hands and face.

'See that brand of soy sauce you have there?' says Hua, pointing her fan at the bottle. 'It's made from fermented hair. Hair is amazing stuff: it's full of nutritious protein and amino acids, and it never rots. A corpse's hair can survive thousands of years.'

Waterborn frowns nervously. She has very little hair on her scalp, and small scratches on her eyelids and forehead. Although she's in the shade, she doesn't dare open her eyes. Her damp face glistens like a peeled lychee.

'I've heard that parents in the village mutilate their babies then rent them out to illegal gangs,' Meili blurts, unable to restrain her curiosity.

'Nonsense!' exclaims Hua, the gold wedding ring glinting on her chubby finger. 'Only a couple of families have done that. They may have nice houses now, but no one will speak to them. They've ruined the reputation of the village.'

'She's got your ears, I see,' says Gu, 'and your upward-slanting eyes.'

'Thank goodness the family planning officers are relaxed here, or I would have got into deep trouble,' Meili says.

'They used to be much stricter,' Hua replies. 'When the Fujian couple's third daughter was just three days old, the officers came down here and drowned her in the pond.'

'No!' gasps Meili, her eyes moving to the pond's still surface. The drake is floating in the middle, his beak in the air, while the ducks drift slowly around him with bowed heads.

'No, they didn't drown the baby – they kicked her to death up there,' Gu says, pointing to the terraced hill behind. A dog's black tail darts down a path running between the overgrown fields.

'I heard someone's offered you seven thousand yuan for her already,' Hua whispers to Meili.

'If you wait any longer, the price will go down,' Gu says softly.

'So, you're agents?' Meili asks, staring at the crate lying at the edge of the creek, which she uses as a rubbish bin to keep the flies away from the hut.

'It can't be cheap, rearing ducks. Look, it's not as if you're paying Sister Mao to break her legs. You'll be selling her to an orphanage who will export her to a foreign country where there are no mosquitoes in summer, no flies in winter, and medical care is free. She'll be in Heaven!'

'Your baby's retarded, no doubt about it. So do it for her sake. If not for her sake, then do it for your husband and your elder daughter.'

'But I heard that if orphanages can't get the children adopted, they sell them to child traffickers who break their limbs and force them to beg on the streets,' Meili says testily.

'No, no, that's complete nonsense,' Gu says, flicking a fly away from her bottle of fizzy orange.

'Trust us, egg lady, we wouldn't lie to you,' Hua says. The drake on the pond puffs out his chest and grunts.

'My name is Meili – so don't call me "egg lady"!' Meili says, staring down angrily at the plantain leaves on the ground.

'But that's what we call people who live on boats. Perhaps you northerners use a different term.'

'We're not from the north, and we're not from the south – we're from the very centre, just like this!' Meili says, pointing to her crotch, then laughing triumphantly. The sisters roll their eyes, not knowing where to look. 'Yes, I was born in the birthplace of Nuwa, the goddess of fertility and the founder of the Chinese race. So don't patronise me.'

Gu pulls out a box from her bag. 'Try one of these, my dear. I made them myself. You've only recently finished your confinement. You need to build up your strength.'

Meili takes the box and lifts the lid. 'How pretty! Nannan, come and look! I've never seen sticky rice cakes as green as this before.'

'It's a local speciality,' Hua says. 'We colour glutinous rice with crushed motherwort, then divide it into small balls which we steam then roll in shredded coconut.'

'Would you like to buy today's batch of eggs?' Meili asks, trying to steer the conversation further away from Waterborn. 'I'll sell them to you for three mao each and you can sell them on for five. Pay me later, if you don't have cash on you.'

'All right,' Gu says. 'I'll take some and see how I do. If they don't sell, I'll preserve them in salt and eat them myself. Those bananas up there look ripe. Feel free to chop some off.' Most of the banana trees have died; only two are still producing fruit. A swarm of flies are now circling the sisters, attracted perhaps by the smell of warm rice rising from their clothes. They stand up and get ready to leave.

'You're so clever, you family planning violators – you've realised you can make far more money having babies than you could raising pigs!' Hua says conspiratorially. 'How many more do you plan to have?'

'I'm finished now!' Meili says, getting up and brushing off the coconut shreds that have fallen onto her breasts. 'My husband's desperate for a son, but I refuse to have any more.'

'I only ever wanted one,' says Gu. 'I read in the papers that if a woman eats tadpoles on a regular basis, she'll never get pregnant. So after I had my first child, I scooped some from a pond every week and swallowed them. Fine lot of good it did! I was pregnant again within two months!' Gu laughs loudly, revealing her long yellow teeth.

'But who can afford to have more than one child these days, the way school fees and medical fees keep rising?' Hua says.

'So how many children do you have, Hua?' Meili asks, glancing down at the braised duck simmering on the stove.

'Four. Only two of them are legally registered, though.'

'I've told you, Hua, you must hurry up and buy permits for the other two or they won't be able to go to school,' Gu says.

'If you do decide you want to go ahead with the sale, come and speak to us,' Hua says to Meili. 'Don't go to that guy who runs the scrapyard. He's a nasty crook. If the babies are alive, he sells them to traffickers, and if they're dead he sells them to restaurants.'

'I would never sell my own child,' Meili says, softly rocking Waterborn as she starts to cry again. 'If she does turn out to be mentally handicapped, I won't mind – I'd be happy to look after her for the rest of my life.'

'We just want to help you secure a good future for your daughter, and for your family as well,' Gu says. 'If you sell her, everyone will benefit.'

'Yes, it will be a win-win situation, just like President Jiang Zemin said to the US in the international trade discussions last week,' Hua says. 'Come on now, let's go and choose our eggs.'

When the sisters walk past her, they seem to give off more heat than the scorching pot on the stove.

KEYWORDS: *flea-ridden, magnet, scum, beautification fee, gangsters, Custody and Repatriation Centre.*

Returning to the hut and seeing Nannan sitting alone under the porch and the boat gone, Meili knows at once that Kongzi has gone to give Waterborn away.

'Where's Daddy, Nannan?' she shouts.

'He said he's taking Waterborn on a trip. He said he'll be back very soon, and when he comes back I'll be his only daughter and he'll only love me.'

'The evil bastard! I know what he's done – he's gone to sell her to a Welfare Office! Kongzi, you monster! You force me to get pregnant, then you take my baby from me. You're worse than the Communist Party. I despise you. I never want to set eyes on you again!' Shaking with rage and howling curses, she kicks out at the wok and bowls on the ground, stamps on the peanut oil and mosquito coils she just bought in the village, then turns round and marches away into the fields. The ducks in the pond flap their wings and take flight.

'Mummy, come back, I'm frightened . . .' Nannan cries out, but Meili is so delirious with rage she can't hear her. She strides across the fields all the way to the public road, then stops a passing minibus and jumps aboard. She wants to go as far away as possible. No – she wants to return to Nuwa Village, to her birthplace. She finds a seat at the back, buries her face in her scarf and weeps. May you get struck by lightning, Kongzi! she mutters under her breath. All these years you drone on about benevolence, righteousness, propriety, wisdom, then you go and sell your own daughter! How could I have married such a monster? . . . When she met him at seventeen, she believed marriage was for ever, that the government protects and cares for the people, and that husbands protect and care for their wives. But as soon as she got married, these naive beliefs were shattered. She discovered that women don't own their bodies: their wombs and genitals are battle zones over which their husband and the state fight for control – territories their husbands invade for sexual gratification and to produce male heirs, and which the state probes, monitors, guards and scrapes so as to assert its power and spread fear. These continual intrusions into her body's most intimate parts have made her lose her sense of who she is. All she is certain of is that she is a legal wife and an illegal mother. I'd be better off dead, she mumbles to herself. I should throw myself into the Yangtze and join Happiness on the riverbed. With a jolt, she remembers Nannan and wishes she'd had the presence of mind to bring her with her. She decides to spend the night in whatever town the minibus is taking her to, then to sneak back to the hut in the morning and fetch Nannan.

Only at night, when the minibus pulls into the terminal and she steps off, goes outside and looks at the dark road running downhill, does she begin to feel helpless and alone. On a dimly lit fruit stall, peeled pineapples gleam like freshly plucked ducks. The pavements are littered with the trampled pulp of chewed sugar cane. Sensing that the road leads to the centre of town she follows it down. It stretches on through the darkness, desolate as a barren field. At last, in the distance, she sees neon signs flashing from tall buildings, and begins to walk towards them as though pulled by a magnet.

The road bends and becomes wider and brighter. There are cars and buses now. After crossing two junctions, waiting for the pedestrian lights to turn green, she begins to realise that this is not a town but a city. She must ask someone where the train station is. She'd like to go home now and see her parents. The thought of being fined or arrested doesn't frighten her any more. If there's no train to Nuwa, she'll return to Guai Village in the morning, take Nannan and a few belongings, and set off for Heaven Township, leaving Kongzi to fend for himself. She approaches a small kiosk to ask for directions. When she sees the red telephone on the counter, she has a longing to phone Weiwei and pour her heart out to him, but she doesn't have his number on her. She thinks of phoning Kongzi's parents, but is afraid the line might be bugged, and besides, she's not in the mood to speak to them. Clubfoot has a telephone too now, as well as a laptop computer and satellite TV, but she has forgotten his number. The only other person in Kong Village whose number she can remember is Kong Zhaobo. He's opened a dairy farm that supplies milk to an infant formula company. She phoned him a couple of times in Guai Village, asking if he could give her brother a job.

'Want to use the phone?' the vendor asks, leaning over the counter. 'Domestic calls are four jiao a minute. Dial the area code first. The list's up there.'

'It's a Hubei number,' says Meili, as she dials the last digit. As soon as the ringing tone sounds, she immediately regrets making the call. Kong Zhaobo says hello in his heavy accent.

'It's Meili,' she says, feeling drops of milk start to leak from her full breasts. 'You mustn't tell anyone I phoned.'

'Won't tell a soul, I promise. Where are you?'

'I don't know. I've just got off a bus.'

'What's up?'

'Nothing. I just wanted to hear how things are in the village.'

'Oh, there've been big changes. You know Kong Dufa who took over your husband's teaching post? Slimy bastard. Well, he's village head now. His son graduated from university last summer and has got a job at the County Transport Bureau. You won't believe it: the village has become a tourist destination! Six coachloads of visitors arrive every day. My neighbour has built a side extension and opened a restaurant called the Happy Farmer. And that painter, Old Cao, who created the mosaic mural for you. Well, his son, Cao Niuniu, has done well. He's a successful artist now. Lives in Beijing. He came back to the village a few months ago and bought the Sky Beyond the Sky Hotel and has turned it into a painters' colony. He's got a hundred artists living there, churning out copies of foreign masterpieces that he sells back in Beijing. And you heard that Kong Qing's wife was arrested for complaining about her forced abortion? Yes, she's still locked up in the mental asylum . . . Five of the villagers who were arrested in the riots are still in jail. One poor sod is serving fourteen years. Kong Guo was released last month, thank goodness.'

'What about that sweet, gentle man . . . ?'

'Kong Fanhua? He's all right. He chopped down the huge tree in his yard and sold the timber to pay off his fine. His wife has gone to work in Guangzhou. He still cycles around the village every morning collecting eggs . . . Listen, if you do give birth to a son and earn enough money to pay the fine, don't come back here. Go and live in the county town. The schools are much better there.'

'How's Li Peisong, and his son, Little Fatty?'

'Oh, Little Fatty – he's in a juvenile detention centre. Granny Kong told him off about something, and he ended up beating her to the ground with a stick. Well, it's not surprising he's turned out that way. His parents were left destitute after paying the fine for his birth, and couldn't even afford to send him or his brother to school . . .'

As Meili puts a ten-yuan note on the counter to pay for the call, a man behind her says, 'You're not local, are you? Where are you from?'

'Hubei Province,' she says, counting the change before putting it in her pocket.

'Do you have a temporary residence card for this city?'

'No, I haven't brought any documents with me.'

'Well, you won't be able to get a room in a hotel, then. Come with me. I'll take you somewhere that provides free food and lodging.'

Meili follows the man back to the main road. Growing suspicious, she asks, 'So, how come the food and lodging are free?'

'The city authorities pay for it. They know hotels won't accept flea-ridden peasants like you, and they don't want you sleeping on the streets, spoiling the city's image, so they've built a guest house where you can stay for free.'

'Are you trying to say that no one in the city has fleas?' Meili says indignantly. 'I can't believe that's true.'

They reach a dark doorway. When Meili reads the words CHANGSHA on the sign above it, she turns to run, but the man grabs hold of her and drags her inside.

'This is the fourth one I've brought in today,' he says to a uniformed officer at the front desk. 'So that's 120 yuan you owe me.'

'The child you brought in this afternoon doesn't count. He was ten years old and mute. We couldn't have sold him on, so we let him go.'

'You never told me you don't take children,' he says, fingering the loose threads on his shirt where his top button has been tugged off.

'Well, you'd better read the detention criteria again.'

'This one's a peasant. She has no documents.'

'Let me go, comrade,' Meili says to the officer. 'I'll make my own way to the train station. You won't need to escort me.'

'You think you can escape that easily? We'll only release you if someone pays your bail. Old Wu, give her a body search. When did you arrive in Changsha?' The officer picks up a pen and takes out a registration form.

'About an hour ago.'

'Why did you come here? Where were you planning to stay?'

'I was just passing through, on my way to the train station.'

'Education?'

'Primary school.'

'Where were you travelling from? Take off your belt.'

'I'm not wearing one,' Meili says, slapping Old Wu's hands as he runs them up her legs.

'Put all your cash and valuables on the table, then,' Old Wu says, pointing at her aggressively. 'If you try to hide anything from me, I'll fucking kill you!'

'All I have is the thirty yuan I made from selling eggs this morning. Comrade, can I ask you something?'

'What?' the officer behind the desk says, looking up.

'The sign outside said Custody and Repatriation Centre. So is this a prison? Have I committed a crime?'

'No, it's not a prison.'

'What is it, then?' Meili says, her voice shaking.

'It's a place that houses undesirables like you. We've been ordered to evict 300,000 peasants and vagrants from the city before the National Day celebrations next week, and you've fallen into our net, I'm afraid.' He hands her the registration form, tells her to sign at the bottom, then passes her a sponge filled with red ink, two blank sheets of paper and tells her to sign and fingerprint these as well.

'But there's nothing written on them. What am I signing for?'

'None of your business. Just get on with it.'

Meili does as she's told.

'Now take her to the warehouse!' The officer files away the forms, brushes some orange peel from his desk and takes a sip from his mug of tea.

Meili follows a policewoman into a warehouse in the backyard. The interior is dark and cavernous. A single bulb hangs from the high ceiling. There are no beds, just numbered rectangles painted in yellow on the concrete floor. Meili is taken to number 15. A narrow path between the rectangles leads to a large plastic bucket at the far end for the detainees to use as a toilet.

'Where do we go to make telephone calls, comrade?' Meili asks a girl with glasses who's lying on the rectangle next to hers.

'You'll have to wait until the morning.'

'Where do you come from?' Glancing around her, Meili notices that all the detainees are women. Some are crying, others are eating and chatting, but most are curled up like shrimp on their yellow rectangles.

'Me?' the girl says with a look of unease on her face. 'I'm a graduate. I came to Changsha to find work.'

'Ah, you must be very knowledgeable then. So can you tell me, is this a prison?'

'Look at point number 8 of the notice on the wall: "Voluntarily confess your crimes and expose the crimes of others." So it's obvious they consider us to be criminals.'

'I've only had one baby out of quota,' Meili says. 'Is that enough to get me locked up?'

'It's nothing to do with family planning. You're here because you're a peasant, and peasants aren't allowed in the cities unless they have a temporary urban residence permit. Surely you know that?'

A female correctional officer sticks her head round the door and shouts, 'Shut up and lie down, you scum. The light goes out in five minutes!'

'I beg you, government lady, let me go home,' a voice cries out. 'My son's alone in the flat. What if he walks onto the balcony and falls over the rails?'

'You can't just abduct people in broad daylight and lock them up for no reason,' another woman says. 'You're behaving like gangsters.'

'I'm not a peasant. I was just having a meal in a restaurant after work. Is that against the law now? Please let me go. Look, I have a train ticket to Guangzhou. It's leaving in two hours. My uncle will be waiting at the other end to collect me.' This girl has a fashionable bob and a smart dress and could easily pass for a city dweller were it not for her thick rural accent.

'It's strange that they should arrest you – you don't look like a peasant at all,' Meili says to the graduate, then scans the room again while the light is still on, breathing the unfamiliar, pungent smells of perfume and unwashed bodies. The graduate looks away, her expression blank. 'So, when were you arrested?' Meili asks her.

'Three days ago,' she replies. 'There's no one in this city who can help me. I warn you, if your family or friends don't bail you out, you'll be sent to a labour camp for three months. You must phone someone and ask them to rescue you.'

'No, I'm a family planning fugitive. If any of my relatives turn up here, they'll have to confirm my identity, and I'll be sent back to the village and be forced to pay a huge fine.'

'To think that we're illegal residents in our own country!' the graduate says, sitting up and smoothing her hair back. 'God, what a stench. This place is a cesspit.'

'It's much nicer than the hut I've been living in,' Meili says, scratching a loose flake of paint from her yellow rectangle. 'It doesn't smell nearly as bad as our duck enclosure, and there are fewer mosquitoes here, too. I wouldn't mind staying a few days. But I'm worried about my daughter. My husband just sits down and drinks beer all evening. What will they eat?'

'How old-fashioned you are. Don't worry about them! What about you?'

'Well, as Confucius said: "Men are the sky, women are the earth."'

'Patriarchal nonsense! Just wait until he leaves you for another woman.'

'Only men from the cities behave like that. We peasants are much more traditional. My husband would never leave me.'

'How do you know? There are no certainties in life. I never imagined my boyfriend would leave me and I'd end up having to sell my body.'

'You're a prostitute?' Meili says in disbelief.

'Yes. They arrested me while I was talking to a client in a hotel lobby. Look at point number 10: "Individuals involved in prostitution and whoring will undergo re-education and reform through labour for a period of six months to two years." That's what I'm heading for.'

'But you wear glasses. You're a graduate, for goodness' sake! How did you get into this mess?' The light is turned off. Meili smells a whiff of dirty nylon socks that reminds her of Kongzi. She still hates him for giving Waterborn away, but understands what drove him to it. If she were released now, she'd rush back to the hut and demand that he bring Waterborn home.

'I came to Changsha last year to look for my boyfriend and tell him I was pregnant with his child,' the graduate explains. 'But when I found him, I discovered he was engaged to someone else. I was so distraught I went straight to a backstreet clinic and had an abortion. Love only strikes once – when it dies, you're a walking corpse. After the abortion, I was too ashamed to go home. I ran out of money and needed to find work. I didn't care what I did.'

'How dreadful,' Meili says, trying to find words to console her. Her eyes have become accustomed to the dark, and she can see the small flowers embroidered on the collar of the graduate's blouse.

'These custody centres are just moneymaking rackets,' the graduate says. 'If you can't find anyone to pay your bail, local crooks will pay it for you, at a discounted rate, then sell you for double the price to village police who run labour camps up in the mountains. You're forced to work on the fields for three months for no pay. They call it the "bail trade". The city authorities get the bail money, the crooks make enough to build themselves villas in the countryside, and the village police can retire early on the profits from the labour camps. So everyone's happy.'

'Why's the bail so high?' Meili says, then thinks about the thirty yuan that the police confiscated from her.

'They charge thirty yuan a night. It's more expensive than a hotel! Then there's the urban beautification fee, management fee, meals. If you can't pay the bail, you'll just have to come along with me to the labour camp.'

'How will my husband and daughter cope on their own for all that time?' Meili says, regretting her impetuous decision to storm off.

'If your husband comes to bail you out, he'll have to hand over at least a thousand yuan,' the graduate says, shifting to the side so that Meili can share some of her mat. Then she opens her handbag and takes out a mobile phone.

'Is there really no one in this city you can call?' Meili asks, her eyes drawn to the phone. Until now, she's only ever seen one on the television.

'There's no point calling anyone. This is the second time I've been caught for soliciting. I was allowed to pay my bail the first time, but this time they won't take my money. Prostitutes are only given one chance.'

'My parents could never raise a thousand yuan. They wouldn't even be able to afford the train ticket here. And I don't want to ask my husband to bail me out. I stormed off in a fit of anger. It would be too humiliating to have to beg him to come to fetch me . . . Tell me, what's your name?'

'Wang Suya.'

'I'm Meili. I've never spoken to a university graduate before. Is that a mobile phone you have there?'

'Yes. It cost me four thousand yuan. But the battery only lasts two hours. Have a look if you like.'

Meili takes the phone, presses it to her ear, then rolls it around in her hands. 'Amazing,' she says, giving it back to her. Through the darkness, Meili can see that the woman on her right is doubled up in pain. 'What's the matter with her?' she asks Suya.

'She's had diarrhoea for three days. And the guards have the gall to say she's faking . . .'

Meili leans over and shakes the woman's arm. 'Sister, you should go to hospital and get some medicine.'

'Poor thing,' Suya says. 'The officers beat her up before she'd even had a chance to sign the registration form . . .'

The woman opens her eyes and whispers to Meili, 'You're a mother, aren't you? I can tell you, then. I'm six months pregnant. When I arrived, the officers asked me to give them telephone numbers. I told them my village doesn't have electricity, let alone a phone connection. So they punched me and kicked me in the belly. I think they killed my baby. I can't feel it moving any more.'

'They beat you up just because you couldn't give any numbers?' Meili says, wondering which ones she'd give if they asked. If she could remember Weiwei's number, she'd phone him right now and ask him to rescue her. She doesn't have any numbers for Guai Village, so she wouldn't be able to contact Kongzi, even if she wanted to. The only number she can remember is Kong Zhaobo's, but if she gave it to the police, they'd find out her history and send her back to Kong Village. She's relieved she didn't put her parents' address on the registration form. Closing her eyes, she realises that this is the time she would be giving Waterborn her last feed. Her breasts feel tender, swollen, and as hard as rock. The sweet-smelling milk leaking from her nipples has drenched the front of her shirt. She rolls onto her side and squeezes the milk out onto the concrete floor to relieve the pain.

KEYWORDS: *stone cold, follow the chicken, urban residence permit, white cotton scarf, green breeze, re-education through labour.*

When the bus leaves the Custody and Repatriation Centre's cement-walled compound, Meili has a sense of freedom. She's reminded of the day they took Weiwei down the Xi River, when the wind blew through her hair and sleeveless dress and the hot sun shone on her arms . . . Outside the window, busy crowds jostle along the pavements, past concrete-bordered flower beds crammed with pink and red chrysanthemums. A mother in a short denim skirt pushes a pram past a bridal portrait studio. A young couple in white stand hand in hand waiting for the pedestrian lights to turn green. Sunlight spills onto trees, asphalt roads and parasols shading ice-cream carts, and swirls between passing cars and a department store's revolving glass doors. Everyone looks happy and bright as they shop for this evening's National Day celebrations.

A man at the back of the bus shouts, 'See that tall glass building over there? Our team of workers from Henan built that.'

'And that's the orange crane I operate. Look, my hat's still on the dashboard!'

'I work in that office next to the Starbucks,' says a woman on the seat behind. Then spotting a colleague crossing the street, she bangs on the window and shouts: 'Li Na! It's me! Tell the boss I've been detained!'

'Shut your mouths!' the burly man at the front shouts, jumping to his feet.

'This area's nothing special,' Suya says, noticing the look of wonder on Meili's face. 'See that TV tower? All the grand hotels and office blocks are there. A guest at one of those hotels offered me three thousand yuan to spend the night with him.'

'I don't want to hear about that,' Meili says, feeling uncomfortable. 'This city's so huge. I bet it would take two days just to walk from one end to the other.' She stares at the succession of shop windows, mesmerised by the televisions, leather sofas, denim jackets, high-heeled shoes, brogues, satin slippers . . . 'I'd love to walk down this street. Not to buy anything, just to gaze into the windows.'

'If you did what I do, in one year you'd have enough money to open a beauty salon, just like that one,' Suya says, pointing to a window with a poster of a woman with long blonde hair, lying in a bath filled with bubbles.

'I have a husband, and even if I didn't, I'd still never do what you do.'

'Why did you run away, then, if he's so important to you? Why waste your youth living with a man you don't love?'

Meili stays silent. Last night, she said to Suya, 'I'll never divorce Kongzi. As the saying goes: If you marry a chicken, you must follow the chicken.' Suya laughed and told her she was a fool.

When the bus leaves the city, a green breeze carrying the scent of bamboo and wild grass blows in through the open window. Meili hasn't washed for days, so she turns her face to it and inhales large draughts. The patches of leaked milk on her shirt begin to dry. When travelling by bus, the city and the countryside are only a few minutes apart, but for a peasant the distance always feels insurmountable. Meili is frustrated that although she's not pregnant, she's still considered to be a criminal for daring to enter a city. Her dream of living a modern urban life seems remote and unattainable.

At dusk, the bus reaches a village high in the hills and stops outside a compound of brick buildings. The two wooden signs outside the gate say YANG VILLAGE POLICE STATION and YANG VILLAGE LABOUR CAMP. In the setting sun they seem cast in bronze.

After supper, the village Party Secretary turns up. He spits out a toothpick, scoops some wax from his ear with his finger and says, 'Comrades, welcome to the labour camp. Today is National Day, so we served you a local speciality: hot and numbing chicken. Delicious, wasn't it?' He breaks into a wide grin, but the forty inmates seated around him remain po-faced. 'While you're here you must abide by the rules and work hard. If your families pay the thousand-yuan bail, you can leave at once. If not, you'll be with us for some time –'

'I'm a welder at Compassion Villas construction site,' interrupts a middle-aged man dressed in a grubby suit. 'The foundations are going down this week. How will they manage without me?'

'You should've thought about that before you wandered off-site,' a village policeman says, jabbing his finger at him. 'Now you're here, you'll have to do as you're told.' There are only three genuine policemen in the barn. The four others are local peasants dressed in the cheap uniforms of urban control officers that were probably bought in a local market. If these impostors were to enter a town or city, they would also be detained.

'You will undergo re-education through labour and attend introductory classes in politics and law,' the village Party Secretary continues. 'We hope that you will use your time here well and make a valuable contribution to the modernisation of the village.'

'I don't understand why we've been brought to this camp,' a woman at the back says. 'We were taken to a Custody and Repatriation Centre. So why haven't we been repatriated to our villages?'

'Why is it a crime to leave the countryside to look for work? Which city in China hasn't been built by migrants? Which factory in Guangdong, which Sino-foreign joint venture doesn't rely on migrant workers? Are the authorities going to arrest every one of us?'

'Yes, we migrants are the engines powering China's miraculous economic rise. It said so in the newspapers. Don't any of you know how to read?'

'Foreign capitalists are flooding to China to take advantage of our cheap labour, so why are we branded criminals?'

'I was told we were going to be sent back to our villages, so why have we been brought here to work like slaves?'

'As I said, if your bail's paid, you'll be free to go,' the Party Secretary repeats angrily, slipping back into his regional accent.

'You bought us from crooked middlemen for five hundred yuan each, and now you want our relatives to pay you a thousand to release us? We're being traded like cattle in a market. If it's illegal for us to live in our own country, what do you expect us to do? Smuggle ourselves into Hong Kong? . . .' All the inmates are on their feet now, gesticulating angrily and swearing.

'Enough!' the Party Secretary barks. 'That's it for tonight. Fill out the registration forms, take a handbook, and I'll see you at seven tomorrow morning for the name call . . .'

After five days of hard labour in the fields, Meili gains the respect of her fellow inmates. While most of the women plant sugar cane, she helps the men with the back-breaking job of digging and filling irrigation channels. At dusk, when Suya collapses with exhaustion, she heaves her onto her back and carries her to the barn. Suya desperately wants to escape, but the nearest public road is thirty kilometres away. Two Sichuanese inmates attempted to flee three weeks ago, but as soon as they reached the road they were arrested, and were beaten so violently on their return to the camp that they're still unable to walk.

'That lecherous Instructor Zheng has got his eyes on me,' Suya tells Meili. 'I'm afraid to go out at night here. It gets so dark outside, you can't see a thing.' She and Meili have returned to the barn and are sitting on a tattered quilt, their backs against the wall. The ground is littered with laminate flooring offcuts and the scarves, underwear and broken flip-flops left behind by previous inmates. 'Bloody Communist Party,' Suya continues. 'How dare they lock us up in this dump! Once I've made enough money, I'll go and study abroad, and I'll never come back.' She grabs a scrap of flooring and wedges it behind her aching back, then puts a blanket over her legs.

'I haven't slept in a brick building like this for years, so it doesn't feel like a dump to me,' says Meili. 'If you're afraid of the dark, you should try sleeping on a boat at night. It's not only pitch black, it rocks from side to side. You feel yourself floating in mid-air, with no idea where you might land . . .' Then she rubs the mud from her hands and says, 'So, has Inspector Zheng done anything to you?'

'He took me aside today and said if I spent the night with him, I could leave the camp next week. I'd rather die than let that sleazy bastard put his hands on me. Besides, he's a minor official – he has no authority to release any inmates.'

'When you go to the latrines, I'll go with you, and if he dares come near, I'll sink my teeth into his shoulder!'

'You're so brave. Is there nothing you're afraid of?'

'Yes – the land. As soon as my feet touch firm ground, my heart starts pounding, because suddenly I'm a peasant again, a nobody who the government can arrest at will. I always feel safer on the water.'

'Earth is man, water is woman, as the saying goes,' Suya says. 'Grains of soil are seeds of the masculine spirit; rivers are dark roads to the eternal female.'

Meili combs Suya's hair and braids it into plaits. Since her milk began to dry up, her maternal feelings have grown stronger. She yearns to hold Waterborn and Nannan in her arms, and can't bring herself to contemplate where Waterborn might be now.

'How pretty you are,' Meili says, stroking Suya's face. 'Such large eyes – you could almost be mistaken for a foreigner.'

'To tell you the truth, I belong to the Wei Minority, so I suppose I am a bit foreign. Beauty can make a woman rich, but if she relies solely on her looks to get by, she'll always remain under a man's thumb. I believe that every woman should strive to achieve something. Self-respect can only be gained through hard work.'

'Well, as it happens, I'm not pure Chinese either. My mother told me that my grandfather had light brown hair and a big nose. A rumour has passed down that, after he was born and the umbilical cord was cut, his mother smashed a bowl onto the ground, grabbed a shard and slit her throat with it. Apparently, she'd been raped by a foreign missionary and was terrified her parents would beat her for bringing shame on the family. I've never dared tell anyone that before – not even my husband.'

'You've no need to tell him. Now that I look closely, there is a foreign air about you. You have the wholesome look of a peasant girl, but in your eyes, there's a wildness. They slant upwards in the Chinese phoenix style, but the pupils are so black and shiny they almost look blue. If you educated yourself and read widely, you could become a formidable woman. And with just a little grooming and sprucing up, you'd have men falling at your feet.'

Feeling her cheeks colour, Meili lowers her head and says, 'How can you bear making love to strangers?'

'Don't be so childish, big sister! As far as I'm concerned, I'm simply renting out a part of my body that doesn't even belong to me. I don't make love to them, I just allow them to ejaculate inside me. The only man I'll ever love is my boyfriend. When I've got my life in order, I'll visit him and make him sorry he left me. I'll be his lover until the day I die.'

'Lover? I've only heard that word used in soap operas.' Meili thinks of Kongzi, and feels a pang. He's a talented calligrapher and is good with words. All the villagers used to ask him to choose names for their children. If he didn't have such a reactionary, Confucian outlook on life, he'd be the perfect husband.

'In this cut-throat age, women are on the ascendency, and men are being left floundering at the side,' Suya says. 'But there are still only three roles we women can choose: girlfriend, wife or single woman. Which one will you go for?'

'All I want is to be a good wife and for my family to be happy and safe.' An image of Weiwei's face suddenly appears in Meili's mind. To dispel it, she glances around the barn. A woman is standing at the door, begging to be let out to use the latrines.

'A good wife, you say?' Suya says, smiling. 'Do good wives run away from home? Before I turn thirty, I will have been a lover, a single woman and will have made a lot of money. After that I will get married and be a good wife. So in one lifetime, I will have experienced it all.'

Meili is speechless. She never knew it was possible for a woman to lead such a varied existence. She is twenty-four years old now, but still feels shamefully naive. She wonders whether, if she'd had Weiwei's number on her in Changsha and had given him a call, they would now be lovers. Her stomach churns noisily as it has done repeatedly since she ate the turnip soup they were served at lunch.

A woman in a quilted jerkin walks over and says: 'Can you lend me a sanitary towel, sister? I've run out.'

'Go to the latrines, and if anyone walks in ask them for some toilet paper,' Meili replies.

'I know that woman over there has got her period,' Suya says. 'Ask her.'

'No, her period has finished now. She gave me her last towel this morning. She pulled it out from her knickers. Luckily, there wasn't too much blood on it.'

Suya tucks her blanket tightly around her body. She got so cold out in the fields in her thin cotton skirt and blouse that she bought a long-sleeved vest from an inmate before he was released two days ago, but she still gets cold at night. She opens her handbag and takes out her red journal again.

'What do you write in that journal?' Meili asks.

'Everything that happens to me. One day I'll give it to my boyfriend, and he'll be able to see how much I've suffered. If you don't write things down, the past becomes a blank page. Everything is forgotten. All great people keep records of their lives. Will you promise that if anything happens to me, you'll give the journal to him? I promise that if anything happens to you, I'll tell your husband. I don't know how I'll find that little bamboo hut of yours, but I'll do my best.'

'Don't say such inauspicious things! When we're released, I'll take you to the hut myself, and make you some duck stew.'

'No way! You're not dragging me off to that mosquito-infested swamp! When we're released, you'll come with me. I'll open a shop and you can work behind the counter. We'll learn English at night school together, and when I have a child you can be its nanny.'

'I'm not sure if I could look after someone else's child, but I can definitely work in a shop. I can sell vegetables, baby formula, anything . . .'

'That's settled then! Here, I want to give this English dictionary to you. Every day you must learn a new word. The more knowledge you acquire the more paths open before you.'

'After we're released, I'll take you in my boat to a stretch of the river where the water is crystal clear. When you swim in it, all your troubles will float away.' As she leans back, she catches a smell on Suya's skin which seems to offer her an intimation of her own future.

'No, I don't want to swim in a river. I want to go to a spa. I'll soak for hours in a warm pool of gurgling water, sipping green tea from a porcelain cup. Then I'll have a foot massage and a back rub, I'll go to a salon for a haircut and manicure, then finish the day off with a dinner date at a nice restaurant . . .'

'How much would all that cost?' Meili asks, seeing Suya's eyes start to droop. In Changsha, she stared in wonder at Suya's long manicured fingernails, with the tiny garlands of flowers painted along the sides. But after just two hours of work on the fields, they all snapped off. Meili feels embarrassed that in her entire life she has never once stepped inside a hair salon.

'Who cares how much it costs? Money exists to buy happiness and comfort, and to pay servants to look after you. What other purpose does it serve?'

Meili tries to think of the last time she felt comfortable, pampered or cared for. She often washed Kongzi's feet but he never once washed hers. She had a hot bath once, in the Golden Age Hotel when she was travelling round the county with the Nuwa International Arts Troupe. After soaking in the bath for half an hour, she caught a glimpse of herself in the mirror and saw that she looked like a nymph from a Tang Dynasty painting, rising from a steaming pond. But she doesn't want to think about the past now. All she wants is to be free. She has eighty-six more days left to endure in the camp. Suya said that when they reach the sixtieth day, she'll buy some beer and biscuits to celebrate.

'But even when I'm released, will I ever be free, or be able to take control of my life?' Meili thinks aloud. 'The government aborted my second child, my husband has given away my third. I don't want to live in the countryside, and I'm banned from living in the cities. So where can I go now? What can I do?'

'If you want to be free, you must become resourceful, independent,' Suya replies. 'Divorce Kongzi and marry a man from the city who'll be able to give you an urban residence permit. Or set up your own business and buy the permit yourself, and an apartment too. Go to Shenzhen. It's full of businesswomen driving around in their private cars, negotiating business deals on their mobile phones. If you buy a villa in the city, you'll get three residence permits thrown in. You'll be able to live in peace for the rest of your life.'

Meili understands that the root of all her problems is poverty. If she had money, she wouldn't be afraid of falling pregnant – she could simply pay the fine. One thing is certain, though: she will never divorce Kongzi. However monstrously he's behaved, she still believes that marriage is for life.

'What's happened to the pregnant woman the officers attacked yesterday?' Suya says. 'Do you think she's escaped?' The pregnant woman is a member of the Falun Gong spiritual movement. After responding gruffly to a policeman's command in the sugar-cane field yesterday, the policeman knocked her to the ground and kicked her face until it bled. Meili and Suya begged him to stop, but he said, 'Don't worry, she won't die – the Falun Wheel in her abdomen will save her!'

'Yes, I wonder where she's gone. She wouldn't dare run away with a belly that size, and the guy from Jiangxi has been locked up in the prison hut, so she can't be there.' Meili thinks of the yellow shirt hanging on the washing line outside which no one has dared remove. When the wind blows it flaps like a ragged sail. A rumour has gone around that it belonged to an inmate from Shandong who hung herself in the latrines.

At the name call after supper, Suya is nowhere to be seen. Meili searches the fields, the latrines and the construction site behind, and returns to the barn in floods of tears. Last night, when Meili told her it was her birthday, Suya took off her earrings and gave them to her as a present.

Two sisters, who know how close Meili has become to Suya, walk over and sit down beside her. A man came to their village last month and persuaded them to travel with him to Changsha, promising them jobs in a Sino-foreign pharmaceutical company with monthly wages of a thousand yuan and free food and accommodation. But when they arrived they discovered that he'd sold them to work as hostesses in a nightclub. The next morning, they escaped out of the nightclub's kitchen window and went straight to the police, who put them in handcuffs and bundled them off to the Custody and Repatriation Centre.

An hour or so later, as she lies down listening to the wind rustle through the trees outside, she suddenly remembers Suya mention that prostitutes are sometimes transferred from labour camps to specialist penitentiaries that examine women for sexual diseases. But if she'd been transferred, surely they would have let her take her handbag? Meili quickly reaches for the handbag, pulls out the red journal and hides it under her blanket. The lights are turned off, but Meili is too upset to sleep. She stays awake all night, tossing and turning, only managing to doze off a few minutes before dawn . . .

In her dream, she is swimming towards her womb along a dark channel, pursued by thousands of babies. When she reaches the end, she rubs the walls but is unable to find any entrance. The babies come closer, mouths wide open. With a jolt, she wakes, rolls onto her side and notices that Suya's handbag has gone. She has a vague memory of torchlight flitting across her face a few moments ago and of the sound of receding footsteps. She closes her eyes again, but can't return to sleep. She wonders whether Instructor Zheng has dragged Suya off into the woods. As she rubs the red journal under her blanket, she remembers the day her grandmother took her to a market stall beneath a large tree in the centre of Nuwa Village. Among the earth-coloured felt and the bobbins of black thread, she spotted a white cotton scarf and white hairclip that seemed to her immaculate and other-worldly. From that moment on, white became her favourite colour. She remembers the first white van she saw enter the village, with revolutionary slogans blaring from the speakers on its roof and posters of Chairman Mao and Premier Hua Guofeng stuck to the side windows. Then she remembers, when she was about five years old, watching a man daub onto a village wall the words CARRY OUT THE FOUR MODERNISATIONS; IMPLEMENT THE ONE CHILD POLICY. As soon as he was finished, her friend pushed her against the slogan, staining her clothes with chalky-smelling whitewash. Her grandmother shouted at her and told her to go straight home.

Meili thinks of Waterborn and wonders how she's survived these past two weeks without her milk. She thinks how Nannan always kicks off her blanket in the middle of the night, and if it's not wrapped over her again, her arms and legs become stone cold. She thinks of Kongzi's obsessive desire for a son and feels angry, then consoles herself with the thought that at least he's never stolen anything or slept with a prostitute. He may have watched a few porn films and forced her into some of the lewd positions he picked up from them, but compared to the depraved men Suya described, he's pretty respectable and honourable. If only he was willing to talk to her and listen to her more, everything would be fine.

When the wind outside drops, she hears fresh cement being stirred in the construction site beyond the latrines. The male inmates are building a factory. Next year the camp will receive official permission to accommodate four hundred inmates, and to take advantage of this expansion of free labour, the Party Secretary has decided that the camp should manufacture Christmas crackers for export to Europe and America. Suya told Meili that Christmas is the foreigners' equivalent of Spring Festival and that an old man with a white beard squeezes down your chimney at night with a bag of presents and waits for you to wake up. Meili rubs Suya's red journal again and tries to think of a place where she can keep it safe.

KEYWORDS: *sewage, second wife, handjob, visiting Miss Five, grey cheongsam, dead shrimp.*

As soon as Meili walks out of the tiny lift and is hit by a vulgar smell of cheap perfume, she knows that she's been duped. Her legs start to shake. This morning, a genial-looking woman arrived at the camp, offering the female inmates jobs as hotel cleaners. Meili jumped at the opportunity, and boarded the minibus together with the two sisters. Although she signed a one-year contract, she made up her mind that she'd leave after a few weeks, once she'd earned enough money to buy a ticket to Guai Village.

I'm done for, this time! she says to herself as she moves down the red-carpeted corridor. Glancing over her shoulder she sees the woman's face becoming sterner with each step she takes. 'Stay inside and wait,' the woman says gruffly, ushering them into separate rooms and shutting the doors behind. Meili pities the sisters, who've escaped one brothel only to be sold to another. She decides that if she's forced to sleep with a man, she'll follow him into the room, strangle him and escape. So long as the police don't find her, she'll make her way back to the bamboo hut, even if she has to walk all the way.

The door opens and a dumpy girl in a grey cheongsam tells her it's time to eat. Meili follows her through a windowless bathroom stinking of sewage to a room where her contract has been placed on a round dining table.

'Sit down,' says a man in a sky-blue shirt sitting by the window. His hair is blow-dried and his lips have a purple tinge. 'I'm the boss of this nightclub. I won't ask where you're from or check your documents.

But I paid eight hundred yuan for you, so I must make myself clear. If you work hard and do as we ask, I'll let you go in three months – I'll even pay for your bus ticket home. But if you don't cooperate, if you attempt to escape, well, you'll only have yourself to blame for what might happen. No one knows you're here, and no one will know if you disappear. Do you understand what I'm saying?'

'I signed a contract to be a cleaner. I refuse to do any other work, so you'd better let me go straight away.'

'Your job is to be a hostess, to look after our clients. The men who come here are rolling in money: shake them about a little, and coins will fall into your hands. If you do as you're told, you'll have hot meals and a shower every day. For a peasant like you, it's heaven! We'll teach you all you need to know.'

'I'll clean rooms, wash dishes – anything. I'm not afraid of hard work. But I won't sell my body. I'm a simple woman with no education. I'm not suited to this job.'

'But peasant girls like you are very popular with our clients. They'd love your simple, honest, wholesome look, and would pay good money for you. But I warn you straight away: all tips must be handed over to us. From now on your name is Ah-Fang, and you're twenty years old.'

A girl reeking of cheap musk enters the room. She's wearing high heels and a red skintight cheongsam. She places a bowl of noodle soup in front of Meili and sits down, the long slit in her dress exposing her bare thigh.

'This is Ah-Fang,' the boss says to the girl as he gets up to leave. 'She arrived today. Show her the ropes.'

'How can you dress like that?' Meili says to her as soon as the boss has left. 'What if your parents saw you? You'd bring shame to your village.'

'Who cares – now that I've left that miserable dump, I've no intention of moving back!' says the girl, a look of disdain darting across her young face. 'My name is Xu, by the way. When you've finished your meal, have a shower, then I'll give you a new dress, cut your hair and see you transform from a mother hen into a phoenix!'

'Don't boss me about, little sister – I'm a mother of two,' Meili says, casting a condescending eye over Xu's skinny, adolescent frame.

'Well, I warn you, big sister: if you don't cooperate, you'll be treated worse than Communist martyrs were in Guomindang jails. The boss paid good money for you, so you'll have to repay his debt. I was a bit rebellious myself, when I first arrived. See this wound on my thigh? That's where the boss jabbed a needle into me. He never injures your face or cunt, because those are the parts that bring the money pouring in.'

'Why haven't you tried to run away?' Meili asks, staring down at the bowl of noodles.

'Run away? I'm only here because I ran away from my village. Where could I run to now? Besides, I wouldn't get very far. The boss's brother is head of the Public Security Bureau. He launched a crackdown on prostitution last week. The police raided every nightclub and brothel in the city, but they didn't touch this place. If I did escape, they'd arrest me and bring me straight back.'

'But this is such grubby, shameful work. You're a pretty young girl. How can you bear to let all those filthy men touch you? Don't you care about losing face?'

'What does face matter? All I want is money. And being a nightclub hostess is less tiring than working in a salon, where you have to wash men's hair and massage their bloody feet before you have sex with them.'

'You're quite a girl! Do you have a boyfriend?' Meili stares at Xu's straightened, shoulder-length hair and remembers Suya saying that a straightening treatment in a hair salon can cost a hundred yuan.

'No, I'm single. I'm waiting for a rich guy to make me his "second wife" and buy me a car and a nice apartment. Many Korean businessmen visit this place. If you agree to be their second wives, in two years you'll have enough money to last the rest of your life. Still, I'm doing pretty well already. I make a hundred thousand yuan a year. My parents have built themselves a house with the money I sent back. You're a mother of two, so I don't need to tell you about the sex side of things. All I'll say is that if you don't reach orgasm, you must pant and groan as if you have. And there are some terms you must learn. "Fast food" is no foreplay, straight in and out, and costs a hundred yuan; "playing the flute" is a blow job, and costs fifty; "visiting Miss Five" is a handjob, with some breast fondling thrown in—'

'Shut up! I have a husband, for God's sake.'

'You think your husband is any different from the men who come here? I've seen them all in this place – from municipal government officials to foreign CEOs. I may have a flat chest and an average face, but this month I've slept with two British engineers and three American tourists. All of them have wives and children. These days, a man who remains faithful to his wife is either an idiot or a loser.'

'Hah – you and I live in very different worlds, it seems,' Meili says, remembering Suya telling her that prostitutes have to think of themselves as a commodity, not a human being.

'You think so? Bring your husband here for a night and he will leave you within three days! I'll never make the mistake of getting married.'

'How do your parents imagine you make all this money? Wouldn't they be horrified if they knew?' Xu's pink lipstick and turquoise eyeshadow remind Meili of the foreign women she's seen in magazines.

'My parents are village cadres who have to scrape by on sixty yuan a month. I told them I'm a shop manager. When I went home last Spring Festival and handed them a fat envelope of cash, they beamed with pride.'

'I must leave this place!' Meili looks out of the window and sees on a large billboard across the road, a little girl in a pink dress and leather shoes smiling up at her. Diesel fumes from the cars streaming past far below slide into the room through the metal bars of the open window.

'You want to escape? The boss will hunt you down, drag you back and beat you to death. You won't be able to say I didn't warn you.'

Meili lowers her eyes again, picks up her chopsticks and gulps down the noodle soup.

'You'll see, it's not so bad here,' Xu says with a smile. 'I'll give you a health certificate in case the hygiene inspectors turn up. I promise you, in three months' time, you'll like it here so much, you won't want to leave. The boss is putting you in room 303 tonight. There's no need to be nervous. After your shower, rub some lubricating oil between your legs. When the client walks in, turn off the lights, help him off with his clothes, then slip a condom onto him straight away, before his erection wilts. Most of the men will be drunk, so don't waste time making conversation. If they turn violent, kick the door . . .'

'Shut up, shut up . . .' Meili hisses, staring down at the tiny dead shrimp floating on the dregs of her noodle soup.

KEYWORDS: *heaven on earth, cloud of smoke, source of life, unsheathed pillow, blazing fire.*

Meili creeps down the dark corridor and locks herself in the toilet. All she can see are a bucket, a mop, a mirror, a rusty nail jutting out from the brick wall – nothing that she could use as a weapon. The window is open, but it also has metal bars, so there's no escape. The steel security door is the only way out of this place, but it's double-locked. She has no choice but to return to her room. When she enters, she sees the boss lying on the single bed, a bottle of liquor in one hand and a cigarette in the other. He puffs a cloud of smoke into the air and tells her to shut the door.

'No, it's too hot in here, I'll leave it open,' she says, her voice faltering. She decides that if he touches her, she'll fight him off with all her strength. During the shower she took after lunch, she scrubbed off all the mud and grime from the camp, soaked her lice-infested hair in conditioner and combed out every insect. Then she sat on the bed, pulled Suya's journal out of her bag and read the third page: '. . . He pushed my thighs up and stuck his head between my legs. I told him he wasn't allowed to do that, and tried to wriggle free, but he said: "What's your problem? I'm paying you enough money, aren't I?" I pulled his hair and tried to yank him off, but then he pinned me down and rammed himself inside me without a condom, and pounded and pounded, first one hole and then the other . . .' Meili couldn't bear to read any further. Her skin, which had relaxed in the warmth of the shower, became cold and tense.

After flicking his stub onto the floor, the boss grabs Meili by her shirtsleeve and says, 'Let me taste you before the clients have a go.' Meili lashes out at him and digs her nails into his legs, but he keeps hold of her sleeve with one hand, and tugs her trousers down with the other. She bites his arm. Enraged, he jumps up, grasps her by the hair and flings her onto the bed. 'So, you want me to play rough, huh, you filthy cunt?' he shouts, and whips off his belt, loops it around her neck and secures it tightly to the steel bars of the headrest. Then with a pillowcase that he's ripped off from a pillow, he ties her right hand to the bars as well. Meili kicks her legs about like a drowning dog. Her trousers and knickers have been pulled off. The belt is so tight around her neck, she can hardly breathe. Her heart races; she seizes up with terror. He leans over and strikes her across the face with a force that knocks her out. She raises her left arm and waves it feebly. He opens her legs and forces them up against her chest, then slaps again and again over her shoulders and face. Like a boat that's struck a rock, she feels herself break into pieces and sink. He stuffs the unsheathed pillow into her mouth, spits onto her vagina then shoves his hand inside. 'Mother, mother . . .' her vagina screams in despair, but the noise is muffled by the man's flesh. She's suffocating now; her whole body is shaking. Her chest rises, straining for air. He's jabbing against her womb. Gastric fluids surge into her throat. She wants to open her jaws and howl, 'Mother, help me, help me . . .' Feeling raw and scorched inside, she closes her eyes and shrinks back into herself.

'Hah! You're mine, now,' the boss grunts, leering down at her with a lewd grin. He moves in and out, faster and faster, then turns her over, enters her from behind and gyrates like a wild dog, slapping her hard on one side and then the other. With one final thrust, he shouts, 'Filthy fucking bitch!' and spurts his sperm onto the enflamed walls of her womb. Her head is twisted to the side, pressed against the bars. Now that he's finished with her, he shoves her back down onto the bed. She clamps her legs together as tightly as she can, then huddles into a ball, rubs her stinging neck and gasps for breath.

'You're nice and wet now,' the boss says. 'I have ten more men lined up for you tonight, including a French professor.'

Meili's body goes into spasms of shock. She wishes she could escape to a netherworld where there are no men. She wants her defiled body to enter a furnace and emerge from the other side as ash. I'm sorry, Nannan, she says quietly. The man has beaten me. I'm too weak to take my revenge. All I can do is die, then return as a ghost and drag the bastard down to hell.

The boss switches on the lamp on the bedside table and unbuckles his belt, releasing her head. 'Good thing you're pretty. I can never get a hard-on with the ugly ones. You've got a nice round arse. Work hard here, and in a few years you'll make enough money to set you up for life.' He lights another cigarette and stretches himself out. Meili clambers off the bed, reaches for her trousers and pulls them on.

As she squats on the floor, she has a sense that thousands of insects are crawling beneath her skin and that rancid leftovers have been stuffed into the cavity between her legs. She tears sheets of paper from a toilet roll and tries to wipe herself clean . . . The boss is shorter and thinner than Kongzi. How did he manage to overpower me? It doesn't matter now – I'm already dead. It's time for me to join Happiness . . . She remembers that when her periods first started, her grandmother gave her a small soot-filled cloth bag to put inside her knickers, and said: 'You're a woman now. The place from which the blood flows is the source of life. You must protect it, and not let any man touch it. When you're older you will marry, and that place will bring you new life and happiness.' Meili looks up at the wallpaper and sees her grandmother's face. She's crying out, 'Meili, help me. Fire, a blazing fire! I'm burning, burning . . .'

Mother sees that the man has fallen asleep. She puts on her shoes and pulls out her bag from under the bed. Her eyes glazed and empty, she takes a cigarette lighter from the bedside table and sets light to the bed sheet. Then she picks up a half-finished bottle of liquor and smashes it over the man's head. Within seconds, flames engulf his body. He sits up for a moment and waves his arms about, then flops back down with a thud. Mother retreats into the corridor and watches the bed burst into a ball of fire and the flames leap along the carpet and up the papered walls. Black smoke billows into the

corridor. Coughing and spluttering, Mother returns at last to her senses, falls to her knees and crawls to the steel door. Someone opens it from the outside, peers round then runs away in fright. Mother swings the door open, bolts down the stairwell and runs out onto the road. Flames are pouring out from the third-floor window now, and licking the HEAVEN ON EARTH NIGHTCLUB neon sign. Panicked, half-dressed men and women stagger out of the building, knocking into each other like insects fleeing a fire pit. Everyone is screaming and darting about. Mother detaches herself from the crowd, walks to the billboard on the other side of the road and disappears into the darkness.

KEYWORDS: *convent, white chrysanthemums, purple sandals, red journal, nylon tights, mad dog.*

Mother runs as fast as she can across the city, her intense pains deadened by fear. She races past the flower market, the Chairman Mao statue in front of the government office building, the musical fountain in the main square, she sprints along broad avenues of office towers and roads lined with gated compounds of identical apartment blocks, and finally reaches an empty asphalt road that winds along the banks of a dark river. She keeps going, running, walking, then running again. When she hears a car approach, she crouches behind a tree and waits for it to pass. As the sky begins to lighten, she stops and looks up at some houses on a hill in front of her with lights already shining at the windows . . . Although she has left the city, Meili still feels nervous. She climbs over a low wall into a deserted demolition site. Alone and hidden from view at last, she falls to her knees and breaks into sobs, her whole body convulsed. She wants to go back to the bamboo hut. It may be a tiny and ramshackle hovel, but it's her home, the place where she is both a mother and a wife. The thought of suicide frightens her, and she knows she will need to build up her courage before she can carry out the act. In the meantime, she will try to get a lift to Dexian and make her way back to Guai Village. She hears a truck rumble in the distance, and walks towards the noise, picking her way over the broken ground. Below her feet, maize leaves and burst balloons lie caught between shattered bricks. She can smell a stale, masculine scent in the dawn mist, and after scaling another low wall, she finds herself on the edge of a large landfill site. A light is twinkling in the distance. She starts to walk towards it across the refuse. The truck she heard a few moments ago has dumped a load of garbage from the city onto the ground. Workers are circling it, prodding it with spades, turning it over. Foul vapours fill the air. Meili dodges around heaps of plastic bags the workers have emptied and discarded. A woman spots her and shouts, 'No scavenging! We're in charge of this patch!'

'I'm just looking for a lift,' Meili says. Drawing closer, she sees the woman impale a plastic bag with a hooked pole, shake out the orange peel, sanitary towels and food scraps, then stuff it into a large plastic bucket.

Meili approaches the truck. Another woman notices her and says, 'Are you looking for a scavenging job?'

'What's the daily wage?' Meili asks, trying to sound casual.

'Fifteen yuan, with free lodging and lunch. If you're interested, go up there and speak to Mr Deng.' The woman points to a hill behind them that has flimsy shacks crammed onto the lower slopes and black crows hovering above the peak. The prospect of free food and shelter appeals to Meili. She decides to stay for a few days until she's earned enough money to pay for her journey back to Guai Village.

The workers have built the shacks with wooden boards and plastic sheeting below a village that was torn down to make way for the landfill site. The families live and work inside them, dismantling rubbish they retrieve from the site and sorting it into piles of glass, paper, plastic and metal, which are then taken to be weighed at the warehouse. Battered cassette recorders, motorbikes, sofa cushions and other objects the warehouse rejected lie stacked outside each doorway. Shelters occupied by families with young children are surrounded by broken prams and dirty plastic toys. Washing lines have been strung between the roofs of the shacks. The grey bras and tights flapping from them look pure white compared to the filth below. Along the path, pigs nozzle heaps of refuse, searching for scraps to eat, while ducks wade through waste-water streams, ruffling their wet and grimy feathers. On this hillside, the decaying and the living emit the same morbid stench.

On a bright morning three days later, Meili puts on her canvas gloves, sits down on a tyre and stares at the mass of tattered shoes spread before her. With her experience of gutting fish for a living, she managed to secure the job of dismantling shoes, which allows her to sit while she works. To dismantle boots, she has to slide her knife up the leg, rip it off, pull out the inner sole, extract each nail, smash off the heel, remove the rubber outsole and place the leather or synthetic upper into the correct pile. All leather, whether from shoes, gloves or sofas, is shredded and boiled to produce the protein which is added to counterfeit milk formula. Sports shoes are simpler to take apart, as the soles can be removed with one slit of the knife. When Meili finds a shoe she considers too pretty to destroy, she puts it aside in the hope that its pair might turn up. Yesterday, she thought the miracle had happened when she spotted a purple mid-heel T-strap sandal, identical to the one in her hand, lying on top of the heap. If only it was a right shoe, and not another left, it would be a perfect match.

Liu Di, the woman in the shack next to hers, is in charge of sorting through glass bottles. She gave Meili the plasters that now criss-cross her hands. Liu Di has four out-of-quota children. Right now, the three eldest are jumping about on a pile of plastic bags and the six-month-old baby is sleeping in a fly-encrusted crate, wedged between empty Coca-Cola bottles and ceramic wine flasks.

'Get down, you brats!' Liu Di shouts. She smashes another bottle onto the ground and shards of broken glass fly into the sunlight.

'Be careful, children, he might bite you – agh, I've always been afraid of dogs!' Meili says, pointing to the mangy grey dog that roams the landfill site like a piece of walking rubbish. Three metal springs are hooked to his frayed waistcoat. Since his owner disappeared last year, he's become melancholy and unhinged, and no one dares go near him.

'How come she has yellow hair?' Meili asks, glancing at the baby's blonde head nestled in the crate. She remembers the force with which Waterborn sucked her nipples and feels sick with longing. The baby's head is huge, and her cheeks are so swollen that her features have become squashed together. Her hands and feet look tiny in comparison. The day she was born, her father found a watch on the landfill site and so named her 'Little Watch'.

'Her hair was jet black when she came out of me,' Liu Di laughs.

'But after my milk ran dry, I put her on Three Deers infant formula, and her hair turned yellow overnight.' Liu Di is wearing three pairs of nylon tights to keep her legs warm. She's leaning against the pink vinyl armchair in which she eats her meals and takes afternoon naps.

The pile of leather scraps beside Meili is now high enough to block the wind, but not the stench that wafts up from the landfill site. When her shelter's walls flap, she can glimpse the cold light bouncing from a pile of sky-blue plastic canisters further up the path.

A week passes. The purple bruising around her neck has slowly faded, and she has tried to push memories of the rape out of her mind. But this morning, she was shaken out of her numbed state when she saw, lying on a heap of rubbish, the corpse of a tiny baby. She recoiled in horror, and went to sit under a tree far away. Her longing for Waterborn, and rage against Kongzi for getting rid of her, surged to the surface. She made up her mind to work here for another week then go back to Guai Village, making sure not to be caught on the way. Liu Di's husband told her that the only way to avoid arrest is to dress like a city resident. Meili feels relatively safe on the landfill site. Although all the workers are illegal migrant peasants, no government official would be willing to brave the stench to come and check their documents. Meili can work in peace, and in her free moments, flick through magazines she finds on the site to study how women in the cities dress. Yesterday, she found a designer raincoat with a missing pocket which she's swapped with a fellow worker for an imitation jade bracelet and a compact with a patch of foundation powder remaining and a mirror on the inside lid. She's also come across handbags that were probably binned by thieves after they'd extracted the wallets. Many of them are brand new, and contain keys, combs, condoms, pills, packets of tissues and leather address books.

'It can't be easy bringing up four children, Liu Di,' Meili says, wiping the flies from her mouth. She put on some lipstick this morning which she found in a handbag, and flies have been swarming around her mouth ever since. Liu Di told her that the lipstick is probably flavoured with honey.

'It's just a few more mouths to feed, that's all,' Liu Di replies. 'That beef and bitter gourd they gave us yesterday was delicious, wasn't it?' When the boxed lunches are handed out at noon, Liu Di usually gives hers to her children, but yesterday she couldn't resist gobbling it all up herself. She could never afford to eat meat back in her village, but becoming a family planning fugitive has widened her horizons. She has tasted hamburgers and Coca-Cola. Whenever she finds a bottle of Coke that is not quite empty, she sniffs it, and if it doesn't smell too sour, keeps it aside for her children to drink later.

'I wish I could have a shower and wash this stench from my skin,' Meili sighs. She jabs her knife into the seam of a leather brogue, drags it around the base, pulls off the leather upper and tears out the insole which still bears the imprint of a man's five toes.

'Why didn't you go with us to Sunlight Bathhouse the other day, then? It's only two kilometres away.'

'I didn't want to walk that far – I was afraid police might catch me.' Inside the bag by Meili's feet are four pairs of shoes which she hopes will fit Kongzi and Nannan.

'If you spray some cologne into a bowl of water and wash yourself with it, you'll smell as though you've used soap. But I warn you, the nicer you smell, the more flies you'll attract.' Liu Di always laughs when she finishes speaking. The only time she didn't was when she told Meili that her third baby was killed by family planning officers a few seconds after it was born.

At dusk, when the golden sky fills with fluttering crows and sparrows, the workers finish for the day and climb up the path for some fresh air. At the top of the hill, beyond the demolished village, stand the ruins of an ancient convent that was destroyed in the Cultural Revolution. The villagers built pig pens within the crumbling walls, using its tombstones and broken rafters. From up there, the landfill site resembles a dry lake nestled in a green forest. In a few years' time, when the natural dip in the land has been filled, the local government is planning to cover the site with concrete and build a large sports centre to commemorate the forthcoming Beijing Olympics. On the other side of the ruined convent is a field of white chrysanthemums the site manager is growing for his own profit. As the workers return to their huts, Meili keeps climbing the path that's still covered with old mattresses and tabletops laid down during downpours to prevent it turning into mud. She's wearing the two left purple sandals that she's been practising walking in for three days. Red, orange, yellow, green and blue clothes swing from washing lines tied between floor lamps and exercise machines flanking the path.

At the top of the hill, she sits down on an ancient flagstone of the ruined convent and thinks of Suya, who treated her like an older sister. She has read her journal from beginning to end, skipping the words she didn't understand. There are no addresses inside, so she won't be able to find Suya, or give the journal to her boyfriend as she promised. Even if Suya is still alive now, she's unlikely ever to see her again. But she knows that if she hadn't met Suya, she herself would probably be dead now . . . When I thought about killing myself after the rape, Suya, I knew how angry you would have been. You were raped every day for a year, sometimes twenty times in one night. What were you hoping to gain from that life? Independence? Revenge? I can feel you looking down on me now. The pink clouds above are filled with your eyes. Even without looking up, I can see you . . .

As the autumn wind begins to whistle, Meili opens her throat and sings, 'My dearest sister! Alone you cross the Bridge of Helplessness and step onto the Home-Viewing Pavilion from which the dead may throw a last glance at their families in the living world. Before you drink Old Lady Meng's five-flavoured Broth of Amnesia, turn back and look at me one last time . . .' Feathers of gold light flutter through the rosy clouds like strips of satin, then, seconds later the sky becomes as murky and grey as the field of waste below. **In the darkness at the bottom of the hill, the mad dog struggles out of a pool of mud and starts trudging up the path, the bra and plastic net hooked to the springs on his waist-coat trailing behind him. A glimmer of hope sparkles in his eyes. High above in the ruined convent, Mother's lament pounds against the broken tombstones and crumbles into the sweet, fetid air.**

At dawn a week later, Meili senses that she has finally emerged from her state of shock. Although her body still aches, her mind has cleared.

She knows now that she won't kill herself. She will keep the rape a secret from Kongzi, and will struggle on until she finds happiness. As Suya wrote in her red journal, 'To survive in this world, one must have an expansive state of mind.' She will become strong, and will use the red journal as a beacon to guide her along her path . . . I will become as strong and resilient as you were, Suya, and will carry on living, on your behalf . . .

She slips a sharpened shoe knife into her handbag and prepares herself for the dangerous journey ahead. First, she crouches down beside her basin of water, carefully washes her face and neck, combs her hair into a neat bun and fixes it in place with a silver clip. Then she steps onto a broken mini freezer, looks into the mirror and puts on the same frosty-pink lipstick and blue eyeliner she's seen models wear in magazines. She applies some mascara, but the liquid is so coagulated that her eyelashes become glued together. Realising that she forgot to put on the foundation, she quickly presses a dampened sponge onto the small patch of pale powder in the compact and dabs it over her face, taking care not to smudge the rest of her make-up. Her ears and neck now look far too dark in comparison, but there's no more powder left to lighten them, so her face is left looking like an oval of frost on a brown cowpat. She sighs, and tries to disguise the problem by tying a red scarf around her neck. Inside her gold handbag is a collection of business cards she found on the site, including those of the director of the Provincial Bureau for Industry and Commerce, the section chief of a large tobacco company and the president of the city hospital. These cards will be her protectors. She's memorised the details of five of them, ready to reel off if the police attempt to arrest her. She puts on the long maroon skirt Liu Di gave her, a pair of black, undamaged nylon tights, and the two left purple sandals. She notices an ink stain on her fitted white shirt and blots it out with a piece of chalk. Liu Di walks past, catches sight of her, and jumps back in astonishment. 'My God, you look like a prostitute!' she blurts. 'No, sorry – I mean like a secretary of a CEO. Who would have thought that this dump could produce such a beauty! You could get on any bus you like now. No one would think of checking your documents. Ha! If you had a cigarette dangling between your fingers, you could be a guest at a foreign wedding.'

'I'm going back to Guai Village,' Meili says. Last night she told Liu Di the reason she ran away.

'Good for you! As the saying goes: "However far a hen might stray, she will always return to the coop one day."' Last night, Liu Di revealed to Meili that her husband often beats her up, then let out a stream of curses to release her pent-up anger.

'I'm just worried that my smell will give me away,' Meili says. Although she's grown so accustomed to the stench of the landfill site that she can no longer detect it on her skin, she went to Sunlight Bathhouse with Liu Di yesterday and stood under a shower for an hour. Her clothes, however, have a rotten stench that no amount of washing could remove, so all she can do is douse them with a pungent perfume, which she also plans to spray onto her neck before entering any crowded place.

The mad dog comes to sit at Meili's feet. She wonders what she should do with him. Since he heard her wail the funeral lament on the hill last week, he's trailed her every step, gobbling up whatever scraps she tosses onto the ground. She has already cut off his tattered waistcoat with her shoe knife, and before she leaves today, she wants to give him a good wash and see him emerge from the dirt as spotless as a lotus from a muddy pond.

KEYWORDS: *state crematorium, gates of hell, charred and mangled, earthen jar, merciless beast.*

Meili sees Kongzi's eyes widen in disbelief, redden, then become as vacant as still water. Nannan stays sitting on the bed chewing her fingers, not daring to look up at her.

'Come here, Nannan!' Meili tries to shout, but the words come out as a soft whisper. She sits down beside Nannan and wraps her arms around her.

'You died, Mum,' Nannan says, tears welling in her eyes.

'No, I didn't die.' Meili missed the long-distance bus yesterday, so she had to spend the night in Dexian station, huddled up on a metal bench.

'You're dirty, and you stink,' Nannan says, sniffing Meili's neck. Before she left the landfill site, she took the mad dog to a petrol station and scrubbed him with soap and water. By the time she'd finished, the dog was as white as snow but she was splattered with mud. The dog waited with her by the roadside for hours. After a truck finally pulled up and gave her a lift, he chased after it for as long as he could, then gave up and shrank into a tiny white speck.

Unable to control his anger any longer, Kongzi jumps to his feet, slaps Meili across the ear and shouts, 'So, where the hell have you been these last four weeks? We've all been worried sick. When your grandmother heard you'd gone missing, she had a heart attack and died.'

Meili slumps onto the floor, buries her head in her hands and weeps. 'I was arrested,' she cries out. 'Taken to a Custody and Repatriation Centre. It's a miracle I've made it back.'

'And what are you doing dressing like a prostitute?' Kongzi barks, veins bulging from his neck.

'You merciless beast! I've suffered ten thousand hardships to get here, and this is how you welcome me . . .' The only sparks of light on Meili's drawn face are the tears in her blue-black eye sockets.

'I sent people to check every custody centre in the county, but you weren't there. Your brother's been with us for two weeks, and has gone searching for you every day.' He sits back down on the crate of beer, his temper subsiding a little.

'When did my grandmother die?' Meili asks, wiping snot and lipstick on the bed sheet.

'October the 9th – your birthday,' Kongzi replies, taking out a cigarette.

Meili bursts into tears again. Nannan jumps off the bed, crawls into Meili's arms and starts weeping too. The bamboo hut is shaken about so much that dried mud falls from the walls.

Kongzi goes outside. The last segment of the sun is reflected on the surface of the duck pond. A car moves below the black hills in the distance, leaving a thin trail of light. Through the reeds, he sees Meili's brother returning from the village, and waves to him. They enter the hut together and find Meili lying on the floor like a wounded creature, howling at all the miseries and wrongs inflicted on her, her cries beating through the mud, the swamp and the cold autumn wind.

A few hours later, calm finally descends. The kerosene lamp hanging from the wall lights up the four faces in the hut, leaving everything else in darkness. Meili's brother looks just like her, but his eyebrows arch downwards, giving him a crestfallen air. 'I should leave tomorrow,' he says. 'It wasn't easy getting time off from the mine.' Nannan is lying asleep at the end of the bed. Meili's eyelids are swollen from weeping. She bites into a cob of sweetcorn and chews slowly. When Kongzi turns his face towards the lamp, he looks much older. The tobacco smoke streaming from his mouth makes even the darkness seem sluggish.

'There's a detergent factory downriver, a vinyl factory, a fire retardant foam factory,' Kongzi says to the brother, the reflection of the lamp's flame flickering across his pupils. 'They're all looking for workers. Why not stay here and get a job in one of them? I met a guy the other day who used to be a miner. He told me there was an explosion at his mine last year. The director didn't want news of it to leak out, so he immediately sealed up the mine and refused to let rescue workers winch up the trapped men.'

'Yes, coal mining is treacherous,' Meili says. 'Accidents happen all the time.' Now that she's washed off her make-up, she looks more awake than the two half-inebriated men.

'No, I couldn't live here,' the brother says. 'The smell is too foul. Look at the rashes that have broken out on my skin.' He scratches the red patches on his hands. He's wearing a blue down jacket with a grease-stained collar. His chin and neck are ingrained with coal dust. The conversation dries up. Nannan rolls onto her side, making the hut's bamboo walls creak.

'Dad, I need to wee,' she says, waking up and rubbing her eyes.

'Go and do it by yourself,' Kongzi says.

Meili walks over to her, takes her by the hand and leads her outside. 'Do it by that tree. I'll stand here and watch over you.'

'She wet her bed almost every night while you were away,' Kongzi whispers to Meili. 'The foam mattress stinks of urine.'

Nannan returns, holding up her trousers, and climbs onto Kongzi's lap. 'Go back to bed,' he says impatiently.

'Tell me a "Once upon a time" first. A long one.'

'No, it's too late for that. Go to sleep. If you're good, I'll catch a frog for you in the morning and roast it on the fire.'

'You know I don't eat meat,' Nannan whines, snuggling against his chest. 'Meat is pink. I like pink.'

'Go on, let Mummy put you to bed,' he says.

'No, I don't want Mummy!' Nannan cries. 'Mummy smells bad. I miss my grandma.'

'You were only two and a half when you last saw her. How can you miss her?'

'Grandma gave me peanuts. She had white hair.'

'I thought about you every second I was away, Nannan, but you didn't miss me at all,' Meili says, rubbing her ear, which is still sore from Kongzi's slap.

Nannan wraps her arms around Kongzi's neck and nuzzles her face into his shoulder. 'I like you, Daddy. You're warmer than the sun.' Meili pulls her away, carries her to the bed and tucks a blanket around her. 'I didn't miss you a bit,' Nannan says to her, closing one eye angrily. 'Give me my red-dress doll.'

'What an unlucky year this has been,' Kongzi says, tapping his packet of cigarettes. 'First your grandmother died, and now this week I heard my father's fallen ill . . .'

'I miss home as well,' Meili says. 'I want to go and see my parents. I don't care if the authorities arrest me and bung an IUD inside me.' She remembers glancing out of the window this morning, and seeing grey sunlight fall on a tarpaulin shelter in the middle of an empty field. The desolate scene made her pine for Nuwa Village, her family and her parents' house with the osmanthus tree in the garden.

'The village authorities don't just arrest family planning criminals now,' the brother says, cracking a sunflower seed between his teeth. 'They confiscate their cash, and all the money in their accounts, and put it straight into the pockets of the county officials. There's a farmers' market now, near Nuwa Temple. It attracts many visitors. The authorities have set up an inspection post at the village gates, and everyone who passes through has to show their family planning certificate.'

'I'm not afraid of those officers any more,' says Meili. 'It's the custody centres that terrify me. They round up peasants and kick us out of the cities saying we ruin their image. But not everyone in the cities is rich and well dressed.' Her mind suddenly returns to the pregnant woman who was kicked in the fields of the labour camp for daring to speak back to a policeman.

'Well, I saw a notice up in Guai Village today forbidding landlords from renting their property to family planning criminals, so you won't be safe here either for much longer,' says the brother, cupping his mug of rice wine.

'You're right,' says Kongzi. 'And besides, this isn't a healthy place for a family to live. I don't want Meili to give birth to another handicapped child . . .' He turns his eyes to Meili, who stops cracking the sunflower seed between her teeth and looks straight back at him. As soon as she thinks of Waterborn, her body seizes up with rage. She longs to know where Kongzi took her, but hasn't the courage to ask him. She feels guilty for having run away, and can't help seeing her grandmother's death as some divine punishment for her irresponsible behaviour.

'What about that place, Heaven Township, you were talking about?' the brother asks, then spits onto the floor. 'How long would it take you to sail there?'

'Two, three weeks, at least. And God knows how many inspection posts we'd have to pass through on the way and how many fines we'd be forced to pay.' Kongzi spits a small bone onto the floor and wipes his mouth.

'Where has Grandmother been buried?' Meili asks her brother, looking up at him just like a mouse that's fallen into an earthen jar.

'Don't ask him,' Kongzi says, rubbing some dirt off the back of his hand. 'He's so furious about what happened, he says he wants to blow up the county crematorium. Nuwa authorities have ruled that all corpses must be cremated. So now, after someone dies, the family has to pay the state crematorium two hundred yuan for a hearse, a thousand yuan for the cremation and five hundred yuan for the urn. The authorities want to make as much money as they can from the dead before they allow any funeral to go ahead.'

The brother stares down at his feet. 'Yes, we knew we couldn't afford to get Grandmother cremated, so Dad secretly buried her body in the garden, under the shed where we keep the straw. We tried to keep quiet, so that the neighbours wouldn't hear us, but Mum couldn't stop herself from crying. A neighbour peeked over the wall, saw what we were doing and reported us to the police. All tip-offs are given a hundred-yuan reward now. The next day, officers from the municipal court turned up, searched the garden, found the grave and dug out Grandmother's corpse. They couldn't be bothered to take it to the crematorium, so they doused it in petrol and set fire to it, right in front of us. Then to cap it all, they demanded we pay a fine for illegally burying a body. We didn't have enough cash on us, so they confiscated two of our pigs.'

'Those fascists – have they no conscience?' Mother cries out, then winces in pain as her tongue brushes against the large ulcer that's formed on the inside of her cheek.

'These days, you have to pay the government nine thousand yuan to be born and two thousand yuan to die,' says Father, taking off his glasses and rubbing his tired eyes. 'The gates of hell aren't somewhere far beneath us. They're right here on earth.'

'After the officers left, we wanted to give Grandmother a proper burial. Her body was so charred and mangled by the fire, we couldn't put a white funeral robe on her, so we just laid it over her charred remains, then wrapped her in a big cloth and buried her under the peach tree.' He wipes his eyes, spits onto the floor again, then grinds the saliva into the ground with his shoe.

'What day did they burn her?' Mother asks.

'Three days after she died. October the 12th. I hadn't returned to the coal mine yet.'

Mother feels her hair stand on end. Three days after my birthday? she mutters to herself. That's the day I set fire to the nightclub, and Grandmother's face appeared before me crying: I'm burning, burning . . . After a long pause, she looks up at her brother and says, 'There's a photograph at home of Grandmother when she was twelve, with a flower in her hair, standing in front of the entrance of Nuwa Temple. Make sure it's put in a safe place . . .'

The brother pours himself some tea and changes the subject. 'The Nuwa County authorities are giving tourism a big push,' he tells Father. 'The reservoir near Kong Village is a pleasure lake now, with three barges, a small pier and a ticket office. Cao Niuniu designed it. He's the son of that guy, Old Cao, who did the mural for you, isn't he? Well, Niuniu's a successful painter now. He has a studio in Beijing's 678 Art District. He even has an American girlfriend. He drove down to Kong Village last year in his expensive jeep, followed by TV crews and packs of journalists. He's bought the hotel you both worked in, and has got a hundred young locals to live there and churn out copies of Western masterpieces: *Lunch on the Grass*, *The Last Supper* – or is it *The Naked Lunch*? I forget the names. So, Kong Village is now a famous artists' colony!' The brother's eyes light up.

'So, is Old Cao still living in his son's apartment in Nuwa County?' Father asks.

'I don't know. But I have some other news from your village. The local police uncovered a secret plot to subvert state power. It was all over the *Public Security Evening Post*. The ringleader was a guy called Kong Qing. He had some gall, that man. But he's behind bars now, serving an indefinite sentence. He formed a secret cell of three hundred peasants who called themselves the China Fertility Freedom Party. Every member wore a yellow thread around their left arm. They planned to take over the County Family Planning Commission on National Day, and declare a Fertility Freedom Law which would grant the Chinese people the right to decide how many children they have.'

'Oh, Kong Qing?' says Father, glancing nervously at Meili. 'I don't know him very well. He was an artillery soldier, I think. His wife was given a forced abortion before we left, and she never got over it. Who knows, if we hadn't escaped the village when we did, perhaps I too would have started an uprising.'

KEYWORDS: *dark road, waste channel, semicircle, river dragon, Heaven Township.*

'Are we there yet?' Meili calls out from the bow. She stands up, takes a deep breath and feels the tart, bitter, sour night air slip down her throat like a foul medicinal brew. Yes, this is just the kind of air that could kill sperm, she thinks to herself. 'So, this must be Heaven Township, where no woman need ever worry about falling pregnant!' she says out loud. Afraid that Kongzi might have heard her, she closes her mouth, then inhales deeply through her nose, expels the air through pursed lips and feels the toxins stream into her blood. With a rush of excitement, she gazes out at the ragged river that is leading them to their new home.

'Careful of that wreck!' she shouts. The crumbling frame of a boat lying half-beached among the reeds on the right looks like the skeleton of some mythical river dragon. Above it stand two dilapidated, roofless houses. Kongzi proceeds cautiously downstream, his hand over his mouth to block out the chemical stench. The river narrows sharply. There are recently built tiled villas on both sides now, interspersed with ancient grey houses. A few tall pine trees stab into the night sky like masts of a ship.

'No, this can't be right,' Kongzi says. 'This isn't a river, it's a waste channel. We must ask for directions before we go any further. I'll try to stop over there.' He turns off the engine, crouches down and shines his torch over the bank.

A girl is squatting in the mud, scrubbing clothes on a stone slab. There's a red plastic bucket beside her. A semicircle of river in front of her has been cleared of floating rubbish.

'Is this Heaven Township?' Kongzi shouts out, his torchlight falling on her yellow rubber gloves. She lifts her face and lowers it again. Her gloved hands continue to dunk the clothes in the dark water and rub them against the stone.

'This must be it,' says Meili. 'Look how peaceful it is – almost otherworldly.' She takes the torch from Kongzi, lets the beam wander over the buildings then rest on a whitewashed wall with a blue notice that says: USING THE LATEST TECHNOLOGY, OUR DEVICES MAKE YOUR ENERGY METER TURN BACKWARDS INSTEAD OF FORWARDS.

'Well, I can't moor here, there's too much rubbish in the way,' Kongzi says. He starts the engine again and keeps going, leaning over the side of the boat to check that the hull isn't scraping against the riverbed.

A stone bridge appears ahead, with two boats tethered beside it. At one end of the bridge is a kiosk lit by a naked bulb. Meili sighs with relief. This must be the River of Forgetting, she says to herself, and that is the Bridge of Helplessness. Old Lady Meng is probably waiting beside it with her five-flavoured Broth of Amnesia.

Once they've sailed under the bridge a vast lake spreads out before them. Lights twinkle on buildings reflected around the margins. The water is as tranquil as a womb. As they breathe the sulphurous stench, Meili and Kongzi feel they've been banished from the sky and the earth and have slipped into an underworld city, a peaceful haven where they can safely settle down and put an end to their floating life. Meili's face glows with joy. She coughs into her sleeve and hugs Kongzi's thigh. 'We're in Heaven at last – we've found it!' she cries. 'The only place in China where women can never fall pregnant!' As soon as these words come out, she bites her lip, taken aback by her daring.

'Women can't fall pregnant here?' Kongzi says. 'What nonsense! Let's prove that wrong straight away.' He takes his hands off the steering wheel and places them on her breasts. The boat turns in circles over the still water. But they don't need to drop anchor now. This isn't a river they have to follow upstream or downstream. They've reached the end: a place where Meili hopes she can rest, gather strength and live in peace.

'Get your hands off me,' she says to Kongzi. 'I want to look at the lake. Can you believe how big it is? You could fit every duck in China onto it, and still have room left over.' She and Kongzi have only had intercourse once since she returned to Guai Village last month. She was so anxious at the time, she couldn't feel a thing, and pushed him off her before he was finished.

'A wife's duty is to produce children,' Kongzi says. 'Let's see if I can plant another seed in your womb.' He presses her onto the deck, causing the boat to dip forward at the bow. 'We'll capsize if you're not careful!' Meili says, breaking free and crawling into the cabin. Kongzi follows her inside and pins her onto the deck again. 'Get off me. You'll wake Nannan! It's past midnight. Stop being so rough.'

'You've been pushing me away for weeks. Come on, let me stroke your feet, your stomach, your soft, cushiony . . .' Outside, the black night and the black lake sway back and forth, extending to invisible heights and depths.

'Be kind to me, Kongzi,' Meili says. She relaxes at last, and feels her body float like peach blossom on water. 'All right, go ahead then. Pour your sperm into me. I'm not afraid any more . . .' She sucks the night air deep into her lungs, and a tear falls from her eyes.

The infant spirit watches Mother drift down the narrow river and arrive at Womb Lake, then sees itself swim up the dark road between her legs towards the lake of her womb. It knows that this is where its final incarnation began. A third gestation, a third birth, a third fate.

Later that night, unable to sleep, Mother sits at the bow crunching deep-fried broad beans and stares at the multitude of stars and lights shining in the sky and on the lake, inhaling deep breaths of air and spitting out the odd tough shell. The infant spirit watches itself being carried through the cervix by fumes smelling of burnt plastic, then curl up inside a dirty uterine fold and twitch as metallic waste waters seep into its new home, along with an occasional whiff of turnip soup. Mother is not aware of its arrival yet. In her mind, she is saying: my womb is a fishbowl which these chemicals will smash into pieces. Never again will I have to carry a child inside me. I will be free . . . In the distance, near the bridge they passed a few hours

ago, a heap of old circuit boards and plastic tubing has been set alight. Smoke as black as night billows from the orange flames, making the strips of tarpaulin caught in overhanging branches flap to and fro like dogs locked in combat. The plastic and metal waste shrivels and melts. When it trickles down the banks into the water, red sparks crackle and dance above the dark lake.

KEYWORDS: *shady willows, tiger descending the mountain, god and goddess, electronic waste, seedlings, plastic granules.*

Their new home is across the river from the former residence of a Qing Dynasty scholar. Above its high perimeter walls, they can glimpse ancient trees and yellow-tiled roofs. Kongzi has rented a tiny metal hut on stilts which juts out into a river flowing from the lake. It's sheltered by a willow, has a window from which they can see their boat, and the rent is only thirty yuan a month. Unfortunately, the river itself is as red and rancid as mouldy Oolong tea. After they wash any clothes or vegetables in it, they have to rinse them in tap water.

The river should flow eastwards into the sea, but its passage is almost entirely blocked by the electronic waste and household refuse dumped into it daily. Along the banks are shady willows and ancient courtyard houses which a century ago belonged to prosperous merchants. These quadrangle compounds are built in the traditional style locally known as 'tiger descending the mountain', with rear quarters taller than the front quarters. Now damp and crumbling, most of them have been rented out to migrant workers, while the owners have moved to new residential estates far from the filth of the lake. The willow tree beside the metal hut is two hundred years old. At its foot are statues of a local god and goddess. Nannan is terrified of them because they have no legs. Last week, villagers came here and ceremoniously slaughtered a pig, then placed it before the statues, along with other offerings of fish, chicken and fruit. Large red scented candles were lit, and as the fragrant smoke coiled up into the willow's branches, the villagers knelt down and prayed for good harvests, happiness, a baby son or success in their children's high school exams.

Meili works in a recycling workshop on the ground floor of a house next to the Qing Dynasty scholar's residence. Every day there are new heaps of transformers for her to dismantle and plastic film to melt. Nannan usually accompanies her, and plays hide-and-seek by herself among the baskets of electric cables and copper wires.

In the morning, after Kongzi drops them off on the opposite bank, he sails to a neighbouring town to fetch clean tap water to sell to Heaven's residents. Although he makes only forty yuan a day – which is slightly less than Meili is paid – he enjoys being his own boss and sailing through the backwaters at his leisure. When he returns in the afternoon, his boat loaded with barrels of tap water and a passenger or two he's picked up along the way, he feels happy to be living in Heaven Township, despite its sour, acrid stench.

'So, where are you from, captain?' a migrant worker asks, stepping aboard the boat one morning.

'Hubei Province,' Kongzi replies, starting the engine again and watching a vessel dump a load of televisions and scanners onto the muddy bank upstream. 'We arrived here a few months ago. How about you?'

'Oh, I've been here eight years. See those white villas up there? Our team built them last year in just six months. It's getting harder to find work now, though, what with all the new migrants flooding in.'

Kongzi glances up at the villas that, with their cladding of white tiles, resemble a row of public toilets. They're on a hill high above the lake, near the municipal government building. The concrete road running past them leads to a dilapidated Confucian temple where, in the Guomindang era, locals would make offerings to the great sage and his eighteen disciples. Until recently, Heaven was a sleepy, impoverished lakeside town. During the flood season, the lake would inundate the Ming Dynasty theatre close to its shore, and sometimes the whole town as well. In the 1960s, half the population left, many of them setting off on foot, their belongings on shoulder poles, to scrape a living collecting scrap in Guangzhou. But ten years ago, after the first British ship docked at the nearby Pearl River port of Foshan and unloaded a mountain of electronic waste, Heaven's economy took off. An entrepreneurial family hauled some of the waste back to their home in Heaven Township, took it apart and sold the scrap plastic and metal to a local toy factory. As the mountains of European waste grew in Foshan, other families in the township followed their example, opening workshops on the ground floors of their homes and hiring migrant labourers to help out. Today, the front doors of every house are surrounded not by bales of wheat, but bundles of electric cables, circuit boards and transformers. In just one decade, Heaven has transformed from a quiet backwater into a prosperous, waste-choked town.

'I know I could pick up a job dismantling e-waste, but it's dangerous work,' the man says to Kongzi. 'Extracting lead and silver is the worst. The sulphuric acid you have to use produces fumes that can make men impotent. I much prefer working on a building site.'

'Most of the migrants here seem to be family planning fugitives,' Kongzi says. 'I always see loads of kids scampering outside the factories and workshops.' Despite all he's heard to the contrary, Kongzi is confident that Heaven's pollution won't prevent Meili falling pregnant again.

'Those children are the lucky ones, the survivors. What you don't see are the deformed and handicapped ones that are abandoned by their parents and left to die. I once saw a dead baby with two heads floating in that canal down there.'

'The One Child Policy's responsible for that,' Kongzi says. 'Don't blame the parents – they just want to make sure they'll have a healthy child to look after them in their old age. Why else would anyone abandon their own flesh and blood?' Kongzi looks away, conscious that he's trying to justify to himself his own abandonment of Waterborn. 'So, where do you want me to drop you off?' he asks. In his mind, he pictures Heaven's waterways coursing through the human body: the oesophagus to the north, a large stomach in the centre and a long winding colon to the south. He's now sailed through every polluted one of them. They are fed by clear streams that flow from a distant mountain, on whose summit stand an ancient temple, a bathing house and a convalescent home.

'Drop me at Chen's Nurseries,' the man says. 'I'm going there to buy rice seedlings. A county leader is visiting the township next week, and we need to plant rice on the barren fields along the road that he'll be driven down. It's only a temporary job, but they're paying us fifty yuan a day.'

'But rice only grows in paddy fields. How will you irrigate all that dry land?'

'It's only for show, you fool! We'll plant the seedlings in the fields the night before he arrives, and with any luck they'll stay upright until the next morning. He'll be gone by the afternoon.'

'So you've been here eight years? You must have made a fortune by now.' After only three months in Heaven Township, Kongzi and Meili have saved four thousand yuan. Last week, they sent a thousand yuan to both their families. After he and Meili fled Kong Village, his parents and close neighbours were heavily fined. One neighbour was given a double fine, and when she was unable to pay it, her house was demolished. She took to the road, apparently, and is now begging on the streets of Kashgar.

'These days, for a man to be considered wealthy he must have a nice house, a private car and a mistress on the side,' the man says. 'I'm a long way from that. I have made a lot of money, it's true, but I've spent it all in the hair salons.' He laughs broadly, showing his teeth like a monkey.

Kongzi smiles, and presses the accelerator. On the banks above, migrant workers are raking out red, yellow and green plastic granules over square bamboo mats, like farmers raking rice left out to dry in the sun.

'Good idea of yours to start a water-delivery business,' the man says. 'The tap water in Heaven is disgusting. Someone tried digging a well once to see if he could draw clean water, but it came up as red as Oolong tea. I've heard that the groundwater's polluted with toxic chemicals to a depth of ten metres.'

Kongzi proceeds up a river flanked by telegraph poles and empty fields. Casting a backward glance over the boat's gurgling wake, he sees Heaven reflected in the green waters of Womb Lake, shimmering like a city of carved jade that appears more exquisite and unearthly the further it recedes.

KEYWORDS: *Tang poem, deep-fried sparrows, feng shui, armpit, petals, clamour of wind.*

The infant spirit sees Father perched on a plastic stool, sipping green tea and listening to Nannan chant a Tang poem in her high-pitched voice.

'Terrible!' Father shouts, rolling his eyes in frustration. 'Recite it again, and if you forget one word this time I'll slap your hand!'

'Daddy's so nasty,' Nannan says, turning to Mother.

'You know what they say, Nannan,' Mother replies, '"Hitting means hate, cursing means love."'

Father reaches down to pick some sleep dust from the corner of Nannan's eye, and says: 'All right then, just give me the two last lines.'

'"Who knows how many . . . petals fell?"'

'And the line before that?'

'You only asked for the last two!' Nannan says, stamping her feet.

'But that was one line, not two. Never mind. Just start again from the beginning.' Father is drinking Oolong tea in the Guangdong style. After steeping the leaves briefly in a small earthenware pot, he pours the tea into a thimble-sized porcelain cup and takes tiny sips.

'"Spring Dawn" by Meng Haoran,' Nannan announces, then throws her shoulders back and takes a deep breath. '"Slumbering in spring, I missed the dawn, / Everywhere birds are singing. / Last night in the clamour of wind and rain, / Who knows how many petals fell?"'

'Wonderful!' Mother says, spooning some deep-fried sparrows onto a serving plate. 'Now come and finish your supper.' Meili bought the birds from a stall this evening as the vendor was packing up and selling his produce for half price. When she chopped them up before frying them, she found plastic granules, screws and metal caps inside their stomachs.

The two front stilts of the metal hut are planted in the riverbed, so whenever a boat passes everything sways from side to side and bottles topple off the table. The interior of the hut looks quite homely now. Meili has covered the floor with a white plastic mat which she found on the banks and keeps scrupulously clean, and has papered three walls with magazine pages and stuck a poster of Niagara Falls on the fourth. The only unsightly part of the room is by the door, where the food is cooked and the bags are stored. In the light from the naked bulb hanging from the ceiling, the brightly coloured plastic objects in the room shine out.

Father takes a swig of beer. Feeling a sparrow bone slip from the corner of his mouth, he quickly spits it onto the floor. Mother picks it up with her chopsticks and puts it on the table. 'Where are your manners?' she says. 'We're not eating in the fields now. To think you were once a respected teacher!'

'Stop putting on airs. You want us to behave like people from the towns? Heaven might look urban, but officially it's still categorised as rural.'

'No, it's a development zone,' Mother replies. 'I've seen foreigners walking down its streets. From now on, you must wear shoes whenever you go out. It's so uncivilised to wander around in bare feet.'

Nannan is staring at the television in the corner, watching three children follow a blue alien onto a flying saucer. 'I wish I could get on it too!' she cries, and points her tongue at the screen.

'I haven't had a period since we arrived in Heaven, Kongzi,' Mother says quietly. 'That's almost four months. But I can't be pregnant. I haven't felt sick at all.'

'Four months? You must be pregnant, then. I told you: if I plant enough seeds, one of them is bound to sprout! This time, make sure you give me a male heir. Ah, the vitality of the Kong bloodline is indestructible! I put it down to the feng shui of the Temple of Confucius in Qufu. Think about it: the sage's tomb is in the centre, his sons' tombs to the left, his grandsons' to the right. Exactly as the saying goes: "Surrounded by offspring on either side, in prosperity your descendants will always abide." No wonder there are now three million Kongs scattered around the world.' Smiling proudly, he waves his chopsticks over the dog-eared astrology books stacked beside him.

'What superstitious nonsense! If the feng shui was so good, how come the temple was destroyed by the Red Guards? Besides, you may be a Kong, but you don't exactly abide in prosperity, do you? Hah! If it turns out that I am pregnant, you wouldn't even be able to find a safe place for the child to be born.'

'What are you talking about? Heaven must be the safest place in the whole country! There are eighty thousand migrant workers living here. The family planning officers wouldn't know where to start.'

'Don't get your hopes up too early. I've gone six months without having a period before. Perhaps the chemicals in the water have affected my hormones.'

'How did you get pregnant, Mum?' Nannan asks, turning round to look at her.

'I ate some Kong family seeds and one of them has sprouted inside my tummy.'

'And it will get bigger and bigger until you explode?'

'No, when it reaches the right size it will come out, just like Waterborn did.'

'Well, I won't eat any more sunflower seeds from now on! Daddy, I miss Waterborn. I want to let her play with my dolly.' Nannan picks up the plastic doll in the red dress and cradles it in her arms.

'Waterborn won't be coming back,' Father says, scratching the sole of his foot, his flip-flop dangling from his toes.

'Is it because of me you got rid of her?' Nannan asks.

'It's time for bed now, Nannan. Mummy and Daddy will be going to sleep, too.'

'But you and Daddy always sleep in the boat and leave me here on my own.'

'The bed's too small for the three of us. All right, I'll squeeze in with you tonight, then. Quick, put on your nightdress.' Mother pours some water into a plastic bowl, dunks a flannel into it and says, 'Let me wash your feet, Nannan.'

'When people die, do their brains still have thoughts, Mummy?' Nannan asks, perching on the edge of the bed, her large red flower hairclip drooping over her forehead.

'She hasn't written her diary, yet,' says Father, opening the brown notebook. 'See what she wrote yesterday? She couldn't remember the characters for "car" and "crash" so she wrote them in roman letters.'

Mother takes the diary from him and reads the passage out loud: '"Today, I opened the umbrella and ran down the street. I couldn't see where I was going and I was afraid a car would crash into me. Daddy held my hand and Mummy walked behind me really quickly . . ." Not bad, Nannan. When I was your age I couldn't even write my name, let alone recite the *Three Character Classic*. If you went to school, I'm sure you'd be top of your class.'

'I want to go to school, Mummy.'

'I've told you, we don't have a local residence permit, so you can't. But with Daddy teaching you at home every day, you'll learn much more than you would at any school. Now, lie down, there's a good girl.' Mother strokes Nannan's head, puts a blanket over her and gives her a small sausage to chew on. 'When you've finished eating it, close your eyes.'

'Nannan, you have your whole life ahead of you,' Father says, 'so stop talking about death all the time.'

Fallen willow leaves and polystyrene scraps drift under the metal hut. The infant spirit sinks into the river's blank water and momentarily loses all sense of time . . . 'Even after I've washed, I still stink of burnt plastic,' Mother says, running her fingers through her wet hair, a towel wrapped around her waist. She lifts her arm to smell her skin, exposing the tuft of black hair in her armpit.

'You used the bottle of tap water your workmate gave you, didn't you?' Father says, letting his gaze rest on Mother's bare breasts. 'I've told you: it's no use. All the water in this town smells the same.'

'Well, at least the smell of sulphur puts me to sleep at night.' Mother pulls on a sleeveless nightdress and takes a sip from Kongzi's bottle of beer. Nannan is asleep now, her mouth wide open and her hand still clutching the sausage.

'Come and sleep with me on the boat. We can have a nice roll around.'

'Why do you insist on having sex every night?' Mother says, applying varnish to her toenails. 'Can't you give me a night off?'

'Fine. If you're not in the mood, I'll go to a hair salon. The girls there only charge ten yuan for a full service.'

'You dare! You have me to torment every night – that should be enough for you. And why would you want another woman, anyway? Once we take our trousers off, we're all the same.'

'No, every woman has her own particular scent. And I've always wondered what it would be like to do two women at the same time.'

'What? You listen to me, Kongzi! I let you watch those porn films in the grubby video halls. I let you flip me onto my front, shove my legs in the air and enter me from all angles. But I will never, ever tolerate you sleeping with a prostitute. Try it once, and you'll never see me again . . .'

Another patch of fallen leaves drifts along the moonlit river. Inside the boat's cabin, Father presses Mother onto the bamboo mat, pushes into her and rocks back and forth. The boat gently sways, creating waves that expand in concentric circles then softly break against the black reeds along the banks.

KEYWORDS: *toenails, win-win, rustic wine, red congee, fetus soup, yellow hair, castor oil.*

As soon as Kongzi has sailed off with Nannan, Meili pulls out the red journal. Finding Suya's handwriting much easier to decipher now, she opens a page at random and reads a passage out loud, smoothly and with expression. "'Women should be learned and erudite, able to talk about the sciences and arts with authority and grace. What man could tire of such a woman? . . . Her face may not be the most refined, but there's an air about her that's pleasing both to the mind and the eye. She knows nothing about fashion, but has flair and a sure sense of style. She's subtly intoxicating, like a mellow, rustic wine . . .'" Meili opens a dictionary and looks up a few words she doesn't know: 'erudite', 'mellow', 'intoxicating'. I remember Kongzi complimenting me once on my mellow voice, she says to herself. Intoxicated: inebriated, drunk. Drunk? But my face turns red when I drink alcohol. Is that considered attractive? Meili's heart beats faster. Yes, this is exactly the kind of woman I want to be: unique, independent, worthy of admiration. She imagines herself as a company director, strolling down a corridor in a white tailored suit, a Louis Vuitton handbag swinging from her gold-braceleted hand.

Bloody liars, telling me it's impossible to fall pregnant here! It must have happened that first night we arrived, which means this little Kong is more than four months old now. The thought that the infant spirit has once more descended into her womb terrifies Meili. Now that she thinks about it, she realises she's had to loosen her belt two notches in the last month. She closes her eyes and tries to decide what to do. She wishes she could tear her womb out and throw it away. She's twenty-four years old. She wanted to work hard, make lots of money and enjoy herself while she was still young, but now she'll have to put everything on hold and go back to raising another child. Her scalp tightens. The baby must not be born. She must harden her heart and end the pregnancy at once. And Kongzi must not know a thing.

She puts on her straw hat, buckles her sandals and sprays her neck with the perfume she brought back from the landfill site. Then she leaves the hut, locks the door behind her and walks to the backstreet clinic she passed the other day. The lane is filled with heaps of scrap computers, broken phones and televisions. Men sit bare-chested among the waste, smashing, chopping, sawing and smelting. At the end of the lane she sees outside three front doors, small tables stacked with empty pill boxes – the secret sign of an unauthorised clinic. She chooses a door and enters.

The room is bare, and smells of bitter medicinal brews. No surgical appliances are on display. A middle-aged woman clears away a mahjong set from the desk in front of her and brings out some abortion tablets to show Meili. 'These are called Dynotrex. They're made by a Sino-American company. They cause fetal expulsion within three days. One course costs only 250 yuan. But before you take your first dose, I'll need to take some blood from you in order to confirm your pregnancy and assess your health. Roll up your sleeve.'

'Three days?' Meili says, wincing as the needle enters her arm. 'Is there an operation that can be done instead?'

'Well, since you say you're only four months gone, I could do a simple forceps extraction without having to dilate the cervix.' Once the vial is filled, the woman labels it then picks out a piece of sweetcorn skin from between her two front teeth.

'How much would that cost?' Meili asks.

'Five hundred yuan, including two post-operative uterine suctions. A government hospital would charge 1,500 yuan, plus ninety yuan a day for the bed.'

'What's a uterine suction?' Meili picks up the box of tablets. She suspects that they're counterfeit, but since the words printed on the packet are foreign, she can't be sure.

'It gets rid of anything that wasn't scraped away during the extraction. Don't worry, I know what I'm doing. I used to work in a proper hospital. From your accent, I can tell you're a southerner. What's your name? I'm Dr Wu.'

'Yes, I'm from the south,' Meili lies. 'My name is Lu Fang.'

'You don't look like a salon girl, so you probably haven't heard about the fetus trade. Let me tell you then: a few restaurants round here buy aborted fetuses. If the salon girls discover from the scan that the baby is a girl, they continue the pregnancy until the third trimester, then have a late termination and sell the fetus to a restaurant. They can get three thousand yuan for it, or four thousand if the toenails have hardened. So, if you wait two more months, I'll do the abortion for free, then take a cut of what the restaurant pays you.'

'Are you mad? How could I dream of letting a stranger eat my own flesh and blood?' Meili remembers seeing a painted sign above a restaurant she passed on her way here showing cats, dogs, snakes, anteaters and civets peeping out of a large hotpot, and wonders if there's any creature on this planet that Guangdong people would refuse to eat.

'I understand your disgust, my dear. I'm a woman too, after all. I eat human placenta now and then, but I wouldn't eat anything that has eyes and a nose, especially not a live fetus. Huh, some clinics on this lane have no scruples. If a woman gives birth to a baby girl and says she doesn't want it, the clinic will take it from her and promise to get it adopted, but as soon as the woman's gone, they'll wrap the poor creature in a sheet and sell it to the nearest restaurant. I'd never do that. But we live in the Age of Money. If someone has cash to buy something, someone else will sell it to them. The restaurants simmer the aborted fetuses for six hours in a broth flavoured with ginseng and angelica. Fetus soup is said to build up male strength and sexual prowess. You don't believe me? I assure you, it's a prized delicacy now. It's brought out at the end of banquets to impress important guests.'

'I believe that whether a baby is inside the womb or outside, it has a soul. And if a baby's life is taken without good reason, its soul will return in another incarnation and exact revenge. Those cannibals! Aren't they afraid of retribution?'

'Those rich bastards couldn't care less! As long as fetus soup is on the menu, they'll keep ordering it.' Dr Wu opens the freezer. 'Look, I have a fetus right here, waiting to be sold. But frozen ones don't fetch such high prices.' Meili peers down at the tiny corpse. She has a full head of yellow hair, a deep crease between her eyebrows and an ice-covered nose. 'How come she's blonde?' Meili asks.

'The mother is a prostitute from Guangzhou. The father was an English client of hers. She didn't want to have the abortion in Guangzhou in case the family planning officers fined her, so she came to me for a salt-water termination. She said the English client always refused to wear condoms.'

'Well, I'll try the tablets first. If they don't work I'll consider having a surgical abortion.' As soon as Meili utters the word abortion she feels a need to urinate.

'Does the surgery strike you as too expensive? I can imagine money must be tight. As far as I'm concerned, there's nothing shameful about trying to make a little cash from this situation. The government makes a fortune from the family planning policy. A million fetuses are aborted each year – just think how much money they rake in from that! Shouldn't the common people share some of the wealth, in a win-win sort of way? A rich couple from Guangzhou came here and asked me to help find them a surrogate mother, so I set them up with a girl from Chongqing who works in the salon two doors down, and now she's pregnant with their child. She came for a scan the other day, and I told her it was a girl. The couple promised to pay her twenty thousand yuan if it's a boy, but said that if it's a girl, they'd want her to have an abortion and would only pay her expenses. The Chongqing girl knows that if she has an abortion now, all she'll get is the expenses from the couple and three thousand yuan from a restaurant, so she asked me to put "gender uncertain" on the scan report, and she's going to carry to full term. If the couple really don't want the baby once it's born, she'll sell it to a Welfare Office for five thousand yuan. See what a good head for business she has!'

'But surely your clinic will get closed down if you falsify a scan like that?' Meili says, sensing her swelling womb press against her bladder.

'I have no licence, so I don't need to stick to any rules.' Dr Wu has a pudgy, slightly masculine face and appears to be in her late fifties.

Meili considers visiting the government hospital to see whether any doctors have targets to meet and would be willing to give her an abortion for free, but is afraid that Kongzi would be notified. 'Well, I must go away and think about it,' Meili says, turning to leave.

'We also sell castor oil, by the way,' Dr Wu adds, breaking into a light sweat. 'It helps soften the cervix. It's just thirty yuan a bottle. Only drink two spoonfuls, though. Any more and you'll vomit. Come back tomorrow afternoon for the results of your blood test. If everything's all right, you'll be able to take the first Dynotrex tablet.'

As Meili leaves the clinic, the dark clouds overhead open and release a heavy rain onto the asphalt lane, the heaps of electrical waste and the tarpaulin shelters under which the workers are retreating. Meili thinks of the infant spirit curled up safely in her womb, protected from the storm, while she herself has no safe place to hide. She wonders whether she'll find herself bound to the steel table of an abortion room again. Heaven Township may be the safest place in this country, but it's still under the Party's control, with bright red family planning slogans festooned across every street. The rain streaming down her face feels like tepid broth.

In the evening, unable to contain her impatience, Meili kneels down behind the table and slips a Dynotrex tablet into her mouth and a sanitary towel into her knickers. Then she pours Kongzi a large mug of rice wine, sits next to Nannan and watches her trace over characters in a calligraphy book: mountain, rock, sun, moon. Meili turns the page and says, 'Look, you have to find a friend for each of these characters: woman, mouth, birth, grain, bird, axe, fire, ten, horse, son, wood, sheep, middle. So, see which of them you can pair up.'

'Woman and son make a good pair,' Nannan says. Her eyes drift towards the television set. Meili quickly reaches over and turns it off.

After Kongzi slumps onto the bed in a drunken heap, Meili starts prodding her belly, trying to see if the tablet is taking effect. According to the leaflet, she should experience cramping, bleeding, and within a few hours see 'products of conception appear on the sanitary towel like a lump of red congee'. She is certain she doesn't want the baby. Indeed, her desire not to have any more children was the sole reason she came to this town. She wants to get on with her life, achieve something and become financially independent. Before she reaches thirty, she wants to open her own shop and make enough money to eat out in restaurants, live in a brick house, sleep on a sprung mattress and send Nannan to university. She's a modern woman, and should have the right not only to be a mother, but also to enjoy some of life's pleasures. The weather will be getting hot soon, and the metal hut will become infested with mosquitoes. This is no place to bring a baby into the world. She sits on a plastic stool and sees Nannan hiding beneath the table, playing with a Mickey Mouse ball.

'Get back on your chair and finish writing your diary,' Meili says, her nerves on edge. Remembering suddenly that she brought some electric plugs back from work today, she places them in the wok, adds some river water and lights the stove.

'The ball hit my hand and broke my nail . . .' Nannan mumbles to herself as she draws a picture in her diary.

Might as well stay busy while I wait for the pill to take effect, Meili says to herself, popping some haw flakes into her mouth, hoping that they too will help encourage a miscarriage. The work isn't too difficult. All she has to do is wait for the plugs to melt, then pick out from the black gloop the brass prongs which the workshop manager will sell tomorrow for three yuan a jin. Once Nannan is asleep and her work is finished, she scrubs the wok, pours half the bottle of castor oil into it, fries an egg and swallows it, then mops up the oil with a dry piece of bread. By midnight, she's so tired she can hardly keep her eyes open. She turns on the television and sees the Qing Dynasty Empress Cixi tuck into a lavish banquet, then she picks up Nannan's diary and reads today's entry: 'Mummy told me to brush my teeth. I told her my gums hurt, but she looked at me with angry eyes, so I had to brush them. Red-Dress Doll was very naughty today, but after I gave her one of my angry looks, she sat quietly at my feet and let me flick her head . . .'

KEYWORDS: *gritted teeth, sprung mattress, tiled roof, bathed in glory, abortion, Workers' Day Procession.*

After two tablets failed to bring about a miscarriage, Meili was worried that if she changed her mind and decided to continue with the pregnancy, the drugs might damage the baby's brain, so she didn't dare take any more. When her belly became visibly enlarged, Kongzi was so happy, he stopped playing mahjong with the neighbours in the yard, and instead stays indoors all evening, serving Meili hot meals and cups of tea. Meili feels stifled by his affection, especially now that they've moved into a new home with a soft double bed, and he insists on making love to her every night. Meili endures this nightly torment with gritted teeth, hoping that it might cause a miscarriage. Go on then, she says silently when he enters her. As long as there's a chance the fetus will perish. As Suya wrote in her diary, 'The fleshy channel between a woman's legs doesn't belong to her . . .' But when she feels Kongzi pressing down on her belly and begin to thrust with force, she often pushes him away and grunts, 'Stop it. Get off me. Enough . . .'

'Why do you always push me off just as I'm about to come?' Kongzi says to her tonight. 'You're already knocked up, so what are you afraid of?'

Meili shudders and wipes the sweat from her face as images she knows she can never wipe away return to her mind. She's surprised that Kongzi hasn't noticed the change in her. The truth is, since she was raped she has lost all ability to feel pleasure. When Kongzi is approaching climax, she often looks up at him and says blankly, 'The prenatal handbook said that men shouldn't penetrate too deeply when a woman's pregnant,' then she rolls over and folds her arms over her chest.

'The baby's a girl,' she says to him, staring up at the ceiling. 'I dreamed about her last night.'

Kongzi is lying on his back, dripping with sweat. Now that his penis has left her body, it has shrivelled up like a snail that's lost its shell. 'It can't be a girl!' he says. 'I paid a feng shui expert to examine the dates, and he assured me that it's a boy. I will call him Kong Heaven, and register him later as Kong Detian, the seventy-seventh generation male descendant of Confucius.'

'But when have I had a dream that hasn't proved to be correct?' she says. Kongzi doesn't know that, this morning, she summoned up the courage to visit a government hospital. A doctor in the Department of Gynaecology and Obstetrics told her that a free abortion could be arranged for her straight away. A pregnant woman would pay for the procedure on condition that the abortion certificate was made out in her name so that she could carry her own child to term. Meili paced the corridor. If the fetus turned out to be a boy and Kongzi discovered she'd got rid of it, he'd beat her to death. She'd have to tell him she suffered a miscarriage, but what reason could she give? The wrong dose of pills, too much sex, a fetal abnormality? She was certain the truth would come out in the end. Then she thought now that they're living safely in Heaven, the baby should be given the chance to take a look at the world. She thought how nice it would be for Nannan to have a little brother or sister to play with. Then she thought of Happiness lying on the riverbed, and of Waterborn begging on some street corner in Shenzhen or eating cakes in a house in California, and it occurred to her that the birth of this fourth child might diminish the pain of losing her last two. So, still undecided, she left the hospital and went home.

Kongzi lights a cigarette and stares at Meili's belly. This one-room house has not only a proper bed with a soft, sprung mattress, but also a table, two chairs, a cupboard and an electric fan, and the rent is just two hundred yuan a month. It may be damp, stuffy and infested with mosquitoes, but it's a solid brick structure with a proper tiled roof that shelters them from the elements.

'Get a scan,' Kongzi says. 'If it's a girl, you can have an abortion. My brother and his wife have just had a second daughter, and they won't be trying again for a son, so it's all down to me now to carry on the family line.'

'No, I will not have an abortion,' Meili says, sensing suddenly that she was wrong ever to contemplate the idea. She glances at Nannan, who's lying asleep on the long narrow bed Kongzi made for her with scrap timber, and feels a wave of maternal love. 'Whether it's a girl or a boy, it's here through the will of Heaven,' Meili continues. 'Look at Nannan. Do you wish I'd had her aborted?'

'Listen, there's no need to make up your mind now. Have a scan, then see how you feel.' Kongzi stubs out his cigarette and drops it into a bowl. Meili gets out of the bed, puts on her underwear and looks outside. The concrete yard is softly lit by beams of light from the surrounding windows. The folding stools have been toppled to the ground, and maggots and flies are crawling over watermelon peel in the corner. The three other one-room houses around the yard are also occupied by migrant families. In the evening, the adults take turns to wash themselves and clean vegetables at the outside tap while the children wrestle with each other or play catch. Today an older child threw a toy truck at Nannan which left a deep cut on her forehead. Meili was furious, but since she couldn't hit the culprit, she released her anger by slapping Nannan instead.

'I admit, it's not great timing,' Meili says. 'After four years of aimless travelling, we've finally got our lives in order and moved into a proper brick house. I wanted to open my own shop – I know I could have made a success of it. I hoped that in a few years' time we could buy a car and drive home bathed in glory. But once this child is born, none of that will be possible. I wanted to be a modern woman with a brief-case full of documents and one of those credit cards that you swipe over machines.' Meili is lying down on the bed again, staring at her swollen feet.

'Have you forgotten that we're family planning fugitives? Our residence permits have been annulled. When the whole country becomes linked by computers, every institution will be able to see our criminal records, and no one will issue you with a credit card or a shop licence. So you'd better give up your pipe dream of living a modern life.'

'I'll buy fake licences then. In Hong Kong Road, you can buy any fake document you want: ID cards, birth permits, shop licences, degree certificates.'

'You think I don't dream of achieving something great, of returning home with my head held high? I've always hoped that one day I could open Confucian primary schools in every town and city in China. But no ambition is more important to me than producing a male heir. Once our son is born, we can do whatever we like.'

'Have you lost your mind? Not content with breaking the family planning laws, you now want to spread Confucianism around the country!' Meili glances at Nannan again to check that she's still asleep. 'Fine, I'll have a scan. But whether it's a girl or a boy, it's my flesh and blood and I will give birth to it. I tell you now, though: this one will be my last.' She sits back against the pillow, drapes a nightie over her legs and looks Kongzi in the eye. 'I need to ask you,' she says gravely. 'Where did you take Waterborn? I'm her mother. I have a right to know.'

Kongzi throws his hands in the air. 'Huh! Confucius was right! Of all people, women are the hardest to deal with! You have a "right to know", you say? There you go again: spitting out words you don't understand, like a mouse chewing through a dictionary! All right, I'll tell you. I gave her to the Welfare Office in Dexian. When I went back a week later, they told me a man from Hunan had taken her away.'

'So she's still in China. As soon as the One Child Policy is repealed, you must go to Hunan and bring her back . . .'

Rain splatters on the tiled roof and mosquitoes flutter around the ceiling. The infant spirit watches the echoes from the house shake raindrops from the cobwebs in the yard.

'Congratulations, Kongzi!' Mother says loudly. 'For a few grubby coins, you consigned our baby daughter to a life of begging! You know very well that those child traffickers break children's limbs! You evil bastard! One day you will have to find her. You will have to search for her high and low and bring her back to me.' Mother puts on a black nightdress and takes a red journal from under her pillow.

'Write down the Welfare Office's address and telephone number in here,' Meili says, handing Kongzi the red journal.

'So you think the One Child Policy will be repealed soon? Are you planning to start a revolution with Kong Qing? Well, he's still in prison with three other Kongs from our village. We're lucky we left when we did.'

'What other news is there from the village?' Meili asks, staring at a gecko crawling across the ceiling. A few months ago, Kongzi learned that his sister had married a Pakistani trader she'd met in Tibet, and was so angry he said he'd never speak to her again. He didn't even send any money to her for the wedding. Since then, Meili hasn't dared ask him about his family.

'Kong Wen's been sacked from the village family planning team, apparently, and has returned to Guangzhou to set up her own business. And that spindly woman, the mother of my old pupil Xiang, has contracted a serious illness. Her husband's sold all their possessions to try to pay for the medical treatment. Xiang's dowry wasn't enough to cover the cost.'

'What, Xiang's got married? But she's only twelve years old. No, of course, we've been away so long, she must be sixteen now. Still, that's very young.'

'You were only sixteen when you married me,' Kongzi says proudly.

'Seventeen,' Meili corrects him. She remembers the colour photograph of herself aged sixteen, standing arm in arm with her friends Qiu and Yang in the municipal park. All three had their hair in neat ponytails, and she was wearing a cream-coloured jacket and red headscarf, Qiu a blue jumper and Yang a long yellow coat. Meili hadn't joined the Nuwa International Arts Troupe then, but was already dreaming of being a famous singer. She and her friends had travelled to the county town with a group of Nuwa villagers to take part in the 1 May Workers' Day Procession. In the evening, the three of them wore lipstick for the first time, and went to a karaoke hall with the village Party Secretary. Meili never saw Qiu again after that night – apparently she stayed on in the town and found a job as a backing singer in another karaoke hall. A year later, she returned to Nuwa

Village with ten thousand yuan and bought a house and fifty pigs, but by then Meili had left home and started work at the Sky Beyond the Sky Hotel.

The rain is still falling. It streams over the bowed heads of the birds in the straw nest on the roof, runs down the tiles and gushes over the eaves. Inside the four small houses around the yard, everyone is asleep. The infant spirit watches Mother lying on the bed, her hands resting on her belly, and little Heaven floating in the amniotic fluid inside. For a moment, the silence is broken as Nannan's electronic toy sings out, 'I'm a beautiful angel, a beautiful angel . . .' Then everything goes quiet again until all that can be heard is the sound of falling rain.

KEYWORDS: *dismantle, frightened and sick, bitter-sweet, ultrasound, twins, tenderisers, gel.*

With an envelope of cash in her small backpack, Meili leaves the workshop and on her way home returns to the lane filled with make-shift shelters and rumbling machines where the illegal clinics are located. In her white shirt, low-cut jeans and sandals, she picks her way over piles of scrap computer monitors. Bare-chested men smeared in black ash stare blankly at her breasts, belly and thighs. Beyond a parked truck loaded with broken printers, she sees the street stall her workmate told her about. She walks around the crates of soft drinks and enters the small house behind. The doctor sitting at the desk is wearing a face mask. At first glance, she looks just like Suya. 'Your surname isn't Wang, is it?' Meili asks her, before she's even sat down.

'Yes, it's Wang, spelt with the water radical.'

'You look just like a friend of mine – same large eyes and high forehead. She's from Chengdu in Sichuan. Her surname is Wang, but it's spelt the usual way.'

'I'm from Sichuan too, but from Fengjie, on the Yangtze River.'

'I travelled down there a few years ago. I suppose most of the towns have been demolished by now.' Meili's feet are sweating in her tight sandals.

'Yes, they've all been torn down. We could see the Yangtze from the backyard of our old house. Now we've been relocated to a village high in the mountains. It's in the back of beyond and there's nothing to do . . . So, you've come for an ultrasound? How many months gone are you?'

'About six, I think. But I didn't have any symptoms during the first three months.'

Dr Wang opens a cupboard and brings out a computer, a probe and a tube of gel, then she lifts Meili's shirt, lubricates her belly and slides the probe over it. 'Look, that's the head,' she says, pointing at the image on the computer. 'The eyes. The spine. If there's one dot here, it's a girl. If there are two, it's a boy.'

'How come?' Meili asks, her eyes darting from her taut, slippery belly to the grainy image on the screen.

'Because boys have two testicles, of course! Hah! The baby's laughing!' A pregnant woman walks in through the door. Dr Wang looks over her shoulder and says, 'You'll have to wait a minute, I'm afraid. Sit by the electric fan over there.' Meili glances at the woman's huge bump and muddy shoes then returns her eyes to the screen. 'But it's just a tiny skeleton – are you sure you saw it laugh?' she says to the doctor. She moves her face closer to the screen. 'You're tricking me, aren't you? That's not my baby. It's just an image stored on your computer. I dismantle machines like that every day. When I open the memory cards, all sorts of moving images pop up.'

'But look, when your belly moves, the image moves as well. Are you a complete fool?'

'I may not be well educated, but my husband is a schoolteacher,' Meili says indignantly, wiping her damp face.

'Well, hold the probe and slide it around. See how the image changes?'

'All right,' Meili says, reassured. 'Just tell me if it's a boy or a girl.'

'A girl! No doubt about it. But I can put that it's a boy on the form, if you want. Just don't tell anyone I filled it out.' She turns to the other woman and says, 'If you've decided to have the abortion, I can do it straight away,' then pulls down her face mask and whispers to Meili, 'That woman's expecting twins. She's booked for an induction next week.' Without her face mask, she looks ten years older.

'Are they boys or girls?' Meili asks the woman, sitting up on the bed.

'One of each,' the woman answers proudly. 'Is this your first pregnancy?'

'No, my fourth. And you?'

'My third. I used to have two girls, then I got pregnant with twins as soon as I arrived in Heaven.'

'What happened to the girls?' Meili asks in the condescending tone she reserves for peasants less sophisticated than her.

'The eldest lives with my parents, and Dr Wang helped get the second one adopted. We can't afford to bring up daughters.'

Dr Wang looks down at Meili and says, 'If you don't want your baby, I can arrange for her to be adopted as well. They'll pay you four thousand yuan.'

'How much do I owe you for the scan?' Meili answers, wanting to leave at once. 'Please write that it's a boy on the form.'

On the way home, Meili feels her belly become heavier and the small of her back begin to throb. When I give birth to the baby girl, Kongzi might sell her to a Welfare Office, she says to herself. And if I tell him now that it's a girl, he'll force me to have an abortion. The only safe option is for me to keep quiet and for the baby to stay exactly where it is. She remembers how her belly shuddered when the needle pierced her skin and entered Happiness's skull. She remembers the smile on Happiness's face as he lay dead in the plastic bag below her. She remembers Waterborn staring at a lock of her hair as she suckled at her breast. My womb is your refuge, little Heaven, she whispers softly. As long as I'm alive, I will protect you. As she approaches the front gate, she hears barking and quacking, and knows the neighbour's Labrador must be attacking the duck pen again. Mayflies are hovering outside their front door. A few dead ones are lying on the ground, being devoured by beetles. Kongzi has raised seven ducks. He never lets them out on the river, because except for the plastic rubbish and rotten leaves, there's nothing in the polluted water for them to eat.

'It's a boy,' Meili announces, surprised by her nerve. Her legs tense as she imagines Kongzi flying into a rage when the baby is born and he sees it's a girl.

'A boy!' he cries out with joy. 'Wonderful news! My darling wife, everything is in order now! This is the right time, the right place. Hope is in sight. Tonight, I will cook dinner.' Kongzi grabs the scan results and wraps his arms around Meili. The chemicals in Heaven's rivers have corroded their boat so badly that he's had to abandon his water-delivery business and join Meili dismantling machines, so now, like her, his sweat smells of burnt plastic.

'Well, I won't be doing any more housework from now on,' says Meili, lying down on the bed and stretching out her legs. Feeling the baby's weight press on her main artery, she rolls onto her side, then kicks off her tight sandals and watches Kongzi slice some beef into chunks. 'I'm not hungry, Kongzi. Besides, I shouldn't eat beef. The preservatives and tenderisers aren't good for the baby.'

'This is a country where everyone is poisoning each other. It's a game: whoever dies first, loses. Still, this beef cost me a fortune, so you'd better at least try some.' He pushes his glasses onto his head, drops the chopped beef into a bowl and douses it with soy sauce.

'There are specific foods women should eat each month of their pregnancy. If you cared a little more, you'd find out what they are and give them to me. You were much more thoughtful before we married.' Meili is thinking of the time Kongzi bought her her first packet of sanitary towels. Until then, she'd made do with attaching wads of folded toilet paper to a sanitary belt that used to belong to her mother.

'Daddy, why have you made Mummy's tummy grow bigger again?' Nannan asks. 'Rongrong said it's because you piss into Mummy's bottom every night.'

'What a brat! Don't listen to her. Hurry up and write your diary. If you want to live in a house that has carpets when you grow up and not a dirt floor like this, you must study hard.'

'Mummy, can you give Daddy a baby boy and me a baby girl?'

'Whether it's a boy or a girl, you'll be its big sister – that's all that matters,' Meili says. The loving embrace Kongzi gave her a few moments ago has left her with a bitter-sweet feeling. 'I should be drinking prenatal herbal tonics for my sore back and swollen ankles,' she says in a supplicating tone she hasn't used since she returned from her one-month absence. 'I don't think I'll go to work tomorrow. Buy me some pork kidneys in the morning. I need to build up my strength.'

'Whatever you say, my beautiful wife. I'll look after you. I'll work my back off to make sure you and little Heaven have everything you need.'

Meili senses that the baby has given their family a new future. What miseries we've endured in our quest to find happiness, she thinks to herself. She feels an urge to put her arms around Kongzi and burst into tears. Instead, she stares up at the magazine photograph she stuck to the wall showing a slender woman with glossy blonde hair, a white leather bag slung over her shoulder and large gold earrings sparkling in the shadow of her long neck. Then she looks at the photograph next to it of herself, Kongzi and Nannan standing in front of the Ming Dynasty theatre with Womb Lake in the background. In the room's dim light, her wide grin shines out like a strip of cloud torn from the sky. Through the open front door she can glimpse a small section of the lake, which conjures up memories of their years on the river. Their corroded boat now lies abandoned on a muddy riverbank. She remembers how frightened and sick she felt the first few days they spent aboard, and how, after just one month, she was able to jump into the water with confidence, and even swim around a little. During those years, the boat rocked her from side to side, and Kongzi rocked her back and forth, until her body flowed like the river. If she hadn't been constantly afraid of falling pregnant, she would have been able to relax more and enjoy the pleasures of the floating days and undulating nights, the dizzying, watery limbo between sky and land. She thinks of Weiwei and his hand moving over her body. To help erase him from her mind after he left, she made Kongzi make love to her so often that, for a few days, it was painful for her to walk. But since she escaped from the violent assault and arrived in Heaven, she has cast off her former submissive self, and is now determined to become the independent, modern woman Suya told her she could be. She will learn how to type and use a computer, then she'll enter the complex world of circuit boards where you can find out anything you want and dismantle the entire universe into its constituent parts.

'Stop biting your nails, Nannan, you're a big girl now,' Meili admonishes, then turns to Kongzi, and says, 'After Heaven is born, we must work hard and buy ourselves Foshan residence permits so that our children can go to school and university. Then we can go back to Kong Village and build a house in our children's rightful birthplace. Do you hear that, little Heaven? With your mother looking after you, everything will be fine. **Nannan, sing me a song, will you?'**

'No, I'm hungry,' Nannan says, her face pressed against her open diary.

'Please, sing me the nightingale song I taught you last night . . .'

'All right: *Little Nightingale, in your colourful robe, you come here every spring. We've built a large factory with brand-new machinery, so this spring will be even more lovely* . . . Mum, I want to learn Xinjiang dancing, like Rongrong.'

'Read out what you've put in your diary today.'

'This is all I've written so far: "I was afraid the gecko was poisonous, but I still went over and looked at it. It had yellow eyes, and stripes like a tiger. When it crawled, it looked like it was riding a bicycle very fast, trying to escape a nasty enemy . . ."'

KEYWORDS: *pleasant breeze, open-crotch trousers, plucking feathers, separate ward, life rod, hand-held heaters.*

'I have to drink American ginseng all day, or these fumes give me terrible migraines,' says Meili's workmate Ah-Fei. 'Bitter tea just isn't strong enough to wash all the poisons out of my system.' Ah-Fei is disfigured by vitiligo. She wears a large surgical mask, to protect herself from the fumes and to conceal the unsightly white patches on her face.

Meili started this job three weeks ago. She had to leave her last job because the plastic granulating machines in the yard created such a deafening noise that when she went home in the evening, she couldn't hear a word Nannan or Kongzi were saying. The salary here is only thirty yuan a day, and the fumes make her eyes water, but at least when the front and back doors of the workshop are left open, a pleasant breeze flows through.

At first, Meili sat with the other eight women at the long metal table, heating and dismantling circuit boards, but leaning over her bulge and inhaling the toxic vapours made her sick, so she swapped jobs with a woman called Xiu, who is only five months pregnant. Now she sits on a bamboo stool gutting cables, which requires her to pull a cable from the tangled mound beside her, nail it to the wall, run a sharp knife down the length of its plastic casing and rip out the precious copper wires within.

'Heaven Hospital is the best place to give birth,' Xiu says, pausing to rub her belly. 'They let you go home with your baby after twenty-four hours. At Compassion Hospital, the nurses snatch your baby from you as soon as it's born, put it in a separate ward and feed it on formula for a week. They say it's because breast milk isn't nutritious enough, but the truth is they put the babies on the bottle to earn commission from formula companies.' Xiu always has the most up-to-date information on hospitals and childcare.

'Scams like that are the least of our worries,' Cha Na chips in from the end of the table. 'If the authorities decide to crack down on family planning criminals like us, things will get really ugly.' Cha Na has a daughter, Lulu, who's the same age as Nannan, and a three-month-old baby at home, whom she goes back to feed during the lunch break. She's witty and good-natured, and Meili gets on well with her.

'A woman once told me it's impossible to fall pregnant here,' Meili says. 'None of us seem to have had any problem, though!' She thinks back to the woman with crimson lipstick she met on the boat to Sanxia, and wonders whether or not she should feel grateful to her for telling her about Heaven Township.

'I tell you, Meili, a few more years in this place, and you'll be a barren old hen and your husband will be a limp cock!' Ah-Fei sniggers behind her face mask.

Nannan runs inside with Lulu to drink a glass of water. They've been in the backyard, clambering over a heap of computer carcasses and gutted video machines. In the front yard, workers are breaking open television sets and computer monitors with kitchen cleavers and extracting the circuit boards. The thick glass interiors are shaped like huge light bulbs, with the flattened screen at one end. They are of no use any more, and are placed in a pile in the corner.

'The family planning officers in this town only take bribes – they don't bother enforcing the law,' says Cha Na. 'So we'd be stupid not to take advantage of the situation and have as many children as we want.' Noticing her engorged breasts begin to leak onto her shirt, she turns to the side, pulls them out and squeezes the milk onto the ground.

'My husband never took bribes when he was head of the village family planning team,' says Pang, a middle-aged woman whose wiry black hair is braided in tight plaits. 'Everyone looked up to him. He'd come home at night, open a beer and sing: *Armed with violation notices, through every village we scout. When we find a pregnant woman without a permit, we rip her baby out.'* Pang has poor eyesight, and can often be heard yelping as she burns her fingers on the molten lead.

'The mere mention of family planning officers sends shivers down my spine,' Meili says, feeling Heaven's arms jerk about inside her womb. 'Those bastards have blood on their hands. They'll get their just deserts in the end.' Pang gets on Meili's nerves. Her husband has visited the workshop a few times. Last year he was sacked from the family planning team after fracturing his pelvis in a road accident, and moved to Heaven with Pang and their daughter hoping to pick up some work.

'You're right there, Meili. Pang's husband's certainly got his just deserts in that car crash, didn't he? It knocked the life out of his "life rod"! Ha!'

'You may snigger, Cha Na, but your husband's dick will go limp too, one day, mark my words,' Pang says, then coughs into her sleeve. 'Anyway, I don't miss him sticking his dirty sausage into me every night. Never gave me much pleasure . . .'

'Well, I suppose you can at least get a good night's sleep these days,' Cha Na says, her breasts pressing against the metal table as she reaches for another circuit board.

'You really think her husband's gone limp?' Ah-Fei says with a grin. 'I bet when he goes to a hair salon, his hard-on hits the front door before he does!'

'Mind your language, please, there's a young girl at the table,' Xiu says, pointing at the fifteen-year-old girl with shoulder-length hair, dark skin and large anxious eyes. A few years ago, this girl was playing hide-and-seek under the table, just like Nannan and Lulu are doing now.

Yes, one day all those family planning officers will be punished for their crimes, Meili thinks to herself, staring blankly at the eight women as they shake their hand-held heaters over the circuit boards. The fluorescent light above them shines on their hands, the boards and the blue vapours rising from them. Once the lead solder has melted, the women grip a copper wire, a chip, a capacitor or an electrode with their tweezers, wobble it to loosen the hold, then gently pull it out and place it into one of the thirty tea cups arranged before them. When all the components have been removed, they drop the empty boards into the red plastic buckets on the ground . . . Yes, those doctors and nurses who murdered Happiness will receive their punishment one day, Meili says to herself, kicking an empty cardboard box lying by her feet into the corner.

Old Shao, who's responsible for buying and distribution, has taken off his shirt, exposing his round belly and small flabby breasts. He's squatting in the doorway now, picking up the copper strands that Meili has extracted from the cables. He looks up at her and says, 'If you don't buy a fake birth permit soon, Meili, your baby won't get a residence permit. I've heard you can pick one up in Hong Kong Road for five thousand yuan.' Meili likes Old Shao. She always sits next to him at lunch. He's the only person in the workshop who knows that she is now twelve months pregnant. Six weeks after her initial due date passed, she went for a check-up in a backstreet clinic, and the doctor told her she must have got her dates wrong, and that she should relax and let the baby come out when it's ready. Although Meili was certain that her dates were correct, when she applied for this job, she was worried the boss wouldn't hire her if he knew how long the pregnancy had lasted, so she told him she was only six months gone. Old Shao has worked in electronic waste for years. He knows how many jin of lead each brand of computer contains, and the function of every component on a circuit board. He told Meili that there are over seven hundred different chemicals in most electronic machines, and three hundred of them are harmful to the human body. He's always reminding her to wear her face mask.

'No, you'd be better off paying a snakehead ten thousand yuan to smuggle you to Hong Kong, and give birth there,' Xiu butts in, rubbing her bulge. 'The hospital treatment is free, and the baby would automatically get a Hong Kong residence permit, and as her mother, you could apply for one too.'

'Or you could go to Macao,' Cha Na suggests, tweezing the last component from a board. 'It belongs to China as well now, and costs less to get to than Hong Kong.'

'If I had ten thousand yuan I could pay the illegal birth fine and wouldn't need to leave the country,' Meili says, feeling Heaven turn a somersault and kick her in the bladder. She has got everything ready for the birth: sleepsuits, nappies, socks, bibs, even a longevity locket Kongzi bought in the market, but little Heaven still shows no sign of wanting to come out. She wonders whether she did indeed get the dates wrong, or if the pollution she's been exposed to has delayed the baby's development.

'In Guangzhou, the fine for illegal births has risen to twenty thousand yuan,' Ah-Fei says, pouring herself more American ginseng tea. 'So it won't be long before the fines here rise as well.'

'Prices of everything are shooting up,' says Cha Na. 'Have you seen how much nappies cost these days? I'm going to have to stop buying them and put my baby in open-crotch trousers instead.'

'Go to the market in Confucius Temple Road,' Xiu advises. 'You can buy a top-brand pack of thirty-two nappies for just forty yuan.'

'No, I bought some there once for a friend,' says Pang, waving the blue fumes away from her face. 'They're fake, filled with mouldy rags.'

'Remember the family planning officer who came here last month?' says Ah-Fei, her nostrils flaring above her face mask. 'I bumped into her the other day. She's been promoted to chair of Heaven Township's Women's Association.'

'So they've set up a Women's Association here?' says Old Shao. 'That means Heaven will soon be granted county status. That's all down to the hard work of us migrants.' Old Shao walks along the table emptying the cups of sorted components into baskets which he then takes outside and tips into bamboo crates.

'You mean the woman with the long skinny neck who comes here before public holidays to hand out condoms?' says Ah-Fei. 'She's not too bad. When she asked me when I had my last period, I told her I hadn't had one for months, and she didn't kick up a fuss.'

'Spring Festival's only four weeks away now. Will you be spending it with your family this year, Old Shao? If so, please bring me back some salted pickles.' This woman, Yazhen, is from the same region of Jiangxi Province as Old Shao.

'No, the trains will be packed. I doubt I'd get a ticket. I think I'll just stay here.' Hearing the girls shriek in the backyard he goes to the door and shouts, 'Nannan and Lulu, get off those boxes! If you break them, the boss will blow his top.'

'Own up, Old Shao, you've got a mistress here, haven't you?' Yazhen says, raising an eyebrow. 'It's always the same: when men leave home, they forget all about their wives.'

'And if they do live at home, they just come back for dinner, then run off to sauna houses and nightclubs,' says Ah-Fei.

'Aagh!' Pang yelps, burning her fingers again.

A worker shuffles into the room, takes the empty circuit boards into the yard and dunks them into basins of sulphuric acid to retrieve any remaining scraps of gold. Immediately, acrid vapours drift into the workshop causing everyone's eyes and throat to burn. As dusk approaches, all the machines and bamboo baskets of sorted components are dragged back into the workshop and stacked up into tall piles. Meili sorts the red, white, blue, black, green and grey plastic casings at her feet into separate hemp sacks, then goes to help Old Shao label some white boxes.

At this time every evening, in the final minutes before they clock off, the women at the metal table stop chatting and concentrate on their work, their hands darting back and forth, tweezing out tiny square, circular, two-pronged, three-pronged components as though they were plucking feathers from a duck. Through the haze of blue fumes, the hot circuit boards in their hands look like miniature demolition sites.

KEYWORDS: *security door, murder, difficult time, ovary, fully dilated, psychological block.*

'Kongzi, I think my belly's contracting! My God, I'm bleeding! Quick, take me to Dr Tao's clinic.' Meili holds her bloodstained hand up to the light then climbs out of the bed. The clinic is in a village a few kilometres away. Xiu gave birth to her baby son there and recommended it to her. Meili visited it two months ago, by which time Heaven had been inside her belly for a year and a half. Dr Tao examined her and said that she only looked about eight months pregnant, and that the fetus probably needed more time in the womb. Since then, she's suffered occasional cramps, but this is the first time that Heaven has shown any sign of wanting to emerge.

'All right, let's go!' Kongzi says, raising his head sleepily from the pillow. While surfing the Web in an internet cafe late last night, he was delighted to learn that the China Institute of Confucian Studies held a conference in Beijing recently to celebrate its sixth anniversary. He has learned to type, and plans to post an article online recommending that study of the Confucian-inspired Qing Dynasty text, *Standards for being a Good Pupil and Child*, be reintroduced into the school curriculum.

The sky is still dark. Kongzi opens the front door. The air outside is slightly cooler and tastes poisonous.

'We'll have to leave Nannan here,' Meili says. 'Take five hundred yuan from my handbag. Look, my belly's going tight again.'

'Today is August the 18th. The date Chairman Mao addressed a million Red Guards in Tiananmen Square. How could little Heaven choose such a rotten day to be born?'

'Stop blabbering. Is there enough diesel in your water-delivery van?' Meili leans against the wall waiting for a contraction to subside, then she pulls on a short-sleeved dress and picks up the plastic bag she's prepared for the birth. A few months ago, Kongzi removed the outboard motor from their crumbling boat and sold it for eighty yuan, and with a further eight hundred yuan he'd saved, bought a small van, which is in fact a rusty wreck that he found lying in the back of a car-repair workshop. It has no bonnet, bumpers or windscreen. When he drives it through town, it resembles the tattered coat of a homeless beggar, with its oil pipes, exhaust pipes and electric cables fluttering behind it in the wind.

The infant spirit watches Father, in the darkness before dawn four years ago, drive through narrow lanes, with a cigarette in his mouth and goggles over his eyes. Mother is sitting beside him groaning with pain. As her temperature soars, she unbuttons her shirt, while in her womb, which is hotter still, the fetus writhes. Father's cigarette smoke pours into Mother's lungs and bloodstream, then flows through the umbilical cord into the fetus's brain. At last they arrive at the clinic. Father jumps out and bangs on Dr Tao's steel security door. 'Who's there?' a voice eventually replies. 'Don't you know how to use a doorbell?'

Mother lies on the doctor's bed, hunched up in pain as the contractions become more intense. When the cervix is fully dilated, the fetus descends but its head becomes stuck between Mother's pelvis. 'I can see its hair!' Dr Tao exclaims. 'One more push and it will be out . . .' Mother grits her teeth and pushes with all her strength. The fetus thrashes about, and its neck becomes so constricted that for a few seconds no oxygen reaches its brain. 'Oh, the pain . . .' Mother screams. Fighting for its life, the fetus grips Mother's pelvic bone and propels itself back into the womb. Dr Tao shines a torch into Mother's vagina and sees a tiny petal-like hand hanging out of the cervix. He reaches in and grabs hold of it, but as he tries to yank it out, he hears a small bone in the arm snap. 'Bring me forceps and cotton wool, Qin!' he shouts to his assistant. 'Hurry!'

Mother's legs are shaking uncontrollably. Trying to distract herself from the pain, she bites into her lower lip until it bleeds.

'Relax, don't tense up,' Dr Tao tells her.

'I can't!' Mother shouts, her whole body juddering. 'I keep remembering my baby son kicking his legs about after he was pulled from me, then seconds later seeing the doctors strangle him to death. I can't get those images out of my mind.'

'I'm here to help deliver your child, not murder it. Come on, start pushing again, or I'll have to call your husband in.'

'No, it's bad luck for husbands to see their wives giving birth,' Mother says, her head swaying from side to side as another wave of contractions creeps up.

'In foreign countries, men stay with their wives during childbirth to offer support and comfort,' Qin says, pressing Mother's legs down onto the bed.

'Well, we're not fucking foreigners!' Mother yells. 'Come out, little Heaven! Don't be afraid. No one's going to kill you, I promise . . .'

The infant spirit watches the fetus curl up with fright. When it was expelled from Mother's ovary and rolled down the fallopian tube at the beginning of this third incarnation, it was aware of the two previous times it had made this journey. It remembered Mother screaming: 'Don't come out into this world, my child! Return to me in another incarnation. Murderers! Animals! . . .' Then, when it reached the womb and was penetrated by Father's sperm, memories from its former lives returned with greater clarity. It recalled Father's anger on discovering that Waterborn was a girl, and it grew fearful of its own birth. As its senses developed, it became more aware of its surroundings. It cringed when Mother sighed with disappointment after being told she was pregnant with another girl, and squirmed when the bitter pollutants flowed through Mother's blood. It realised it would have to choose between the poisons of the womb and the hostility of the outside world. The fetus isn't sure what lies outside, but is certain now, after taking a brief look, that this isn't its rightful birthplace. The date tree that was blessed in Nuwa Cave when it was a sapling isn't growing in the yard. It decides that it must stay inside Mother's womb, like a fish in a glass bowl, and wait for her to carry it back to Kong Village.

Mother howls out again, her legs splayed open like a forked tree.

'Don't let me return as a woman in my next life! I'd rather be a dog or a rat than suffer this pain again!'

'You've had two doses of oxytocin, but the baby still won't budge,' Dr Tao says, tugging the fetus's foot with his forceps, struggling without success to pull it out. 'I've never seen a Chinese fetus resist so much. Are you sure it doesn't have foreign blood?' Giving up at last, he releases the foot and watches it slip back into the womb. 'If I'd pulled any harder, its spine would have broken.'

'Foreign blood?' Meili shouts. 'How insulting! I'm a descendant of Goddess Nuwa. My baby's one hundred per cent Chinese! . . . Let me squat on the floor and try pushing again.' Mother turns onto her side and eases herself off the bed.

'It's no use,' says Dr Tao. 'I've delivered hundreds of babies, but this one clearly has a psychological block: it just doesn't want to come out. There's nothing more I can do. I won't take any payment. You must go to a government hospital at once and ask for a surgical delivery.'

'You think I'd let someone put a knife to my belly? Never! Fetch me some more towels.' Mother is squatting with her back against the bed, looking as though she's trying to shit, but however hard she pushes, nothing is coming out.

'I promise you, I couldn't have pulled any harder,' Dr Tao says, perching on a stool to catch his breath. 'That fetus has unworldly strength!'

'Of course it's strong!' Mother says, mopping the sweat from her face. 'It's been inside me for twenty months!'

'Twenty months now, is it? When it does finally come out, it'll be able to jump off the bed and scamper around the room . . .'

The contractions slowly abate, the cervix closes up, and the womb becomes still. Mother topples to the floor in exhaustion. The breeze blowing from the air-conditioning unit smells of old blood and deep-fried fish.

'Still not out yet?' Father says, walking in with a carton of orange juice.

'The fetus has embedded itself into your wife's flesh. I couldn't extract it.'

'When I came to see you two months ago you said the fetus was only eight months old,' Mother says. 'How can I believe anything you say?'

'Listen, I've had enough!' Dr Tao says. 'I don't want your money. Just go and get a surgeon to take it out for you.'

'So that he can then strangle it to death?' Mother cries. 'Never!'

Seeing Father about to light up, Dr Tao shakes his head. 'Sorry, this room is air-conditioned. No smoking allowed.'

Father drops the cigarette back into his pocket and says, 'I know a bit about Taoist astrology, Dr Tao. Perhaps we should pay a priest to choose an auspicious day for the birth.'

'Don't waste time with that nonsense,' the doctor replies. 'Just listen to my advice: take her to a proper hospital straight away and pay for a Caesarean.'

'All right, all right,' Father says. 'Let's go home and fetch some more cash, Meili.'

'No, I refuse to have my belly cut open. You know how I hate the sight of knives and blood . . .' Meili is resolute. She's terrified not only that the doctors will murder the baby, but that Kongzi will explode with rage when, after spending a fortune on a Caesarean, he discovers that the baby is a girl. Since the baby's determined not to come out, Meili decides that she should have another ultrasound to confirm its sex. Perhaps it will turn out to be a boy, after all. How could that woman tell that the fetus was a girl from the blurred and grainy image on the screen? She will allow little Heaven to stay inside her for as long as it wants, and they'll get through this difficult time together. If Kongzi or the government try to force her to do otherwise, she'll resist them with every fibre of her body.

KEYWORDS: *respected scholar, red and pink balloons, maternity dress, looking for whores, hammer and sickle, candlelight.*

'Let me see if you've got everything you need,' Kongzi says, opening Nannan's satchel and checking that it contains the Year One textbooks, her pencil case and a ruler. She is eight today, and tomorrow he'll take her for her first day at an illegal school for children of migrant workers. It's housed in an aluminium warehouse on the southern edge of town, and the fees are reasonable. As a descendant of Confucius, Kongzi is annoyed that he didn't think of opening a school like this himself.

After breakfast, he listens to Nannan read out the first chapter of the literacy textbook. He's recently taken up a temporary, part-time post at Red Flag Primary – a government school next to the Confucius Temple – covering for a Chinese-literature teacher who's gone on maternity leave. He and Nannan are sitting at a small table in the yard, the sunlight shining on their faces. The landlord now uses the three other houses as storerooms for his broken televisions, so the compound is much more peaceful. Kongzi's delivery van has broken down and now stands in the corner covered with rusty metal sheets and bicycle frames. The ducks waddle out of the pen and peck at the noodles Meili is scattering on the ground.

Nannan reads out the words as she follows Kongzi's moving finger. '"The red flag flaps in the wind. The hammer and sickle in the centre represents the Chinese Communist Party: eternally leading the people forward . . ."'

'"Question One: What is the name of the flag? . . ."' Kongzi says, lowering his voice to an authoritative pitch. Although he only teaches three afternoons a week, he is delighted to have returned to his true calling. As soon as he wakes up, he puts on his dark grey suit and polishes his glasses, whether he's working that day or not.

The Sunday broadcast booms through the town from distant loud-speakers: 'As part of our ongoing campaign to improve the implemen-tation of national population control policies, Director Jie Ailing, Deputy Chair of the Provincial Family Planning Association, will visit Heaven Township today to carry out a thorough investigation of . . .'

'Did you hear that, Kongzi?' Meili says, looking in the mirror attached to the front door as she applies her lipstick. 'Does that mean we'll have to lie low today?' She's wearing her favourite cream coat and a white maternity dress she paid a seamstress to copy from a photo in a fashion magazine.

'No, don't worry,' Kongzi says. 'Director Jie won't have a chance to inspect anything. Heaven officials will whizz him around town on a quick sightseeing tour, then take him out to lunch and get him drunk.'

'Dad, when the family planning has finished, will we be able to go home?' Nannan asks.

'The Family Planning Policy is a protracted war waged against women and children,' Kongzi replies. 'No one knows how long it will last. That's why your little brother is still inside Mummy's tummy. He's too afraid to come out.'

'Why didn't I get family planned?'

'You were our first child, so your birth was legal. When you're older you'll be able to apply for a residence permit and go to university.'

'Mummy has a residence permit, so how come she was arrested when she went to that big city?'

'Because she has a rural permit, not an urban one, and she didn't have any money on her.'

'Do we have money now?'

'Some. Not much. When we have a bit more, we'll be free. We'll be able to go to whichever city we like.'

'I don't want to go to university. I want to make money for you and Mummy.'

'Nannan, remember that saying I taught you: "Children who don't read books don't know what treasures they contain. If they knew how precious these treasures were, they'd stay up all night, reading by candlelight." The meaning is simple: if you study hard, you'll get rich.'

'But, Dad, you studied hard, so why aren't you rich?'

'Because I've had to concentrate on making sure you have a little brother. Once he's born, I'll make lots of money for us, I promise.'

'Why doesn't Grandpa give you money?'

'You mean my father? He doesn't have much money now. But before the Communists came to power, his father – my grandfather that is – was very wealthy. He was a rich landowner and respected scholar. Everyone in the village looked up to him. In 1951, when Mao told peasants to attack counter-revolutionary forces, every landowner in Nuwa County was buried alive, but no one touched my grandfather. He was arrested ten years later, though, and died in prison.'

'What happened to his wife?'

'You're too young to hear about all this, Nannan. All I can tell you is she died a few years later, in the Cultural Revolution.'

'What about your mother's parents – what happened to them?' For the last week, Nannan has refused to eat breakfast. She hasn't touched the fried eggs and soya bean milk Meili gave her, and is just nibbling on a coconut bun left over from yesterday.

'They died years ago. Enough questions! Back to your work. Let's have a look at Lesson Five. The title is "What a good idea!"'

Nannan turns to the page and starts reading: '"One day, when Chairman Mao was seven years old, he and his friends went into the mountains to let their cattle graze on fresh pastures. The question was: how could they keep an eye on the animals, collect firewood and pick wild fruit, all at the same time? Mao had a good idea. He divided his friends into three teams and told the first team to look after the cattle, the second team to chop wood, and the third team to pick fruit—"'

'Fine, class over,' Meili interrupts. 'Nannan, you're coming with me today.' She ties a scarf around Nannan's neck and heads off to work.

'Don't forget to kill the rat in the toilet, Dad,' Nannan shouts to Kongzi as they walk out of the gate.

When they've left, Kongzi wonders again how much he'll be able to get for his broken van. Three hundred yuan at the most, he thinks. The owner of the car-repair workshop is coming to buy it back this morning. Once it's sold, Kongzi will open a new bank account. Since they arrived in Heaven, they've been stashing all their earnings under their bed, apart from the small sums they send back to their parents or spend on food and rent. They've saved sixteen thousand yuan already. If they bought shares with the money, they could make a fortune. Kongzi visited an underground gambling house the other day. It charges no entrance free, provides a free lunch at noon, and if your money runs out, it will lend you more. He spent all day there and lost eighty yuan. Today, he'll try his luck again. If the gods look favourably on him, perhaps he'll have a big win, and will be able to open his own Confucius school. The Confucius Temple would be an ideal location. When he's saved enough money, he'll discuss the matter with the local Education Department and request official authorisation. Yes, he'll go gambling again today. Even if he loses a few hundred yuan, Meili will never find out. In preparation for Nannan's birthday meal tonight, he inflates some red and pink balloons and hangs them outside the front door. Meili said she'd buy a cream-filled birthday cake on her way home this evening. Before he has time to finish his cup of tea, the owner of the car-repair shop pulls up outside the compound and honks his horn.

At noon, Kongzi arrives at the entrance of the underground gambling house with three hundred yuan in his pocket, but as soon as he steps inside, four men huddled around the card table jump onto their stools, pull guns from their pockets and shout: 'Freeze!' Kongzi and the other gamblers in the room are handcuffed, bundled into a van and driven to the local police station, where they're dragged to the backyard, searched and cross-questioned one by one. The first three men to be dealt with only went to the gambling house for a free lunch, and have no money on them. After a fierce kicking, they're released, and are left to crawl out onto the street, bruised and covered in dust.

Kongzi is the last to be seen. He fills out a form and empties his pockets. 'I'd only just stepped through the door,' he says angrily. 'I didn't go there to gamble. You had no right to arrest me!'

'What were you doing with all this cash, then – looking for whores?' a young officer says mockingly, picking up the wad of notes and counting them.

'Give that money back to me, you fucking gangsters! I didn't commit any crime.'

A bald man standing behind him kicks him in the shins. 'You dare swear at us, in this place?' he shouts. Kongzi falls to the ground, then quickly jumps up, but just as he's about to swing his fist at the bald man's face, another officer kicks him down again. The bald man pulls out an electric baton and smashes it onto Kongzi's head. As Kongzi attempts to rise to his feet, the bald man grabs him by the hair and rams his knee into his jaw.

'Come and hit me again, you motherfuckers, if you think you have the balls!' Kongzi cries out after falling flat on his back.

'Shut your mouth, you filthy vagrant!' the young officer shouts, and kicks Kongzi's mouth until it bleeds. Kongzi spews out another stream of abuse. The three officers crouch down, pin back his arms and legs, then the bald man leans over and shoves the electric baton into Kongzi's mouth. 'After this, you'll never be able to swear at us again!' he says, and flicks on the switch.

Just as Meili is placing Nannan's birthday cake onto a plate after returning home from work, the landlord runs into the compound and tells her that he's heard Kongzi has been arrested. She leaves Nannan in his care, rushes to the police station and finds Kongzi lying semi-conscious in the waiting room. While she pays the thousand-yuan fine before taking him off to hospital, the sergeant behind the desk tells her that Kongzi confessed to sleeping with a hair-salon prostitute. 'You think we beat him up for no reason?' he says. 'No, he attacked us and we fought back in self-defence. He's lucky we're letting him go. But when he wakes up, tell him this: next time we find him in a gambling house, he'll get ten years behind bars.'

When Kongzi returns from hospital two weeks later, the electrical burns on his lips and tongue have almost healed, but he's still unable to speak. This episode has cost them a total of eleven thousand yuan. Meili had to take time off work to look after him in hospital, and

Nannan had to stay with Lulu. The events have upset her greatly. She went missing yesterday. Meili searched for her for several hours, and found her at last standing all alone on a riverbank.

Although Kongzi is on the mend, Meili is on the verge of a breakdown. The morning of Kongzi's birthday, she takes out the 'Fishing Boat Lullaby' CD she gave him when they were living on the sand island, and attacks it with the kitchen cleaver. She tolerated him watching porn movies, but the thought of him sleeping with a hair-salon prostitute is too much for her to bear. She deplores the police's brutality but loathes Kongzi's degenerate behaviour even more. The village teacher she once worshipped has become a man who fills her with disgust. She looks down at him now and spits: 'What were those sayings you kept rattling off? "Cultivate yourself and bring order to your family, and the nation will be at peace . . ." and "The gentleman embraces virtue and the sanctions of the law . . ." Huh! You foul hypocrite!' She stares into his eyes and asks him if he did indeed sleep with a prostitute, and he looks back at her and calmly shakes his head. She knows it's possible that the sergeant was lying when he told her about the confession, but suspects that he wasn't. When Kongzi first returned from hospital, the sight of his gruesomely swollen face aroused her pity, but as soon as he was able to take his first sip of milk, she felt like grabbing her shoe-cutting knife and plunging it into his neck.

As evening falls, Mother continues to curse Father, tears streaming down her face. 'You spineless rat! You heartless, brainless bastard! Drinking, gambling, sleeping with prostitutes! Where did you get all the energy? Did you really think that there would be no consequences?' Father opens his eyes feebly then closes them, unable to respond . . . 'Filthy sod! Not satisfied with eating from the family wok, you have to scoff from the dirty saucepans as well! Womb Lake is just out there! I wish you'd fling yourself into it and drown . . . Kong the Second Son, indeed! Remember what they used to sing about Confucius? *Kong the Second Son was an evil man. He spouted righteousness from his mouth, while concealing ruses in his heart.* **How right they were!' Mother dances around the room, singing the Cultural Revolution song, her hands cupping her swollen belly. Nannan**

peeps out from under her blanket. Father stays still, his eyes tightly closed. Several hours later, the lights are finally switched off. In the darkness outside, the wind sways the strings of dried chillies and shrivelled red and pink balloons hanging from the front door, then races out through the gates, lifts chewed sugar-cane pulp from the pavements and swirls along the riverbank, tossing scraps of tarpaulin into the river.

KEYWORDS: *dirges, black coffin, wild ghost, gold-rimmed glasses, lotus pond, funeral objects, mandarin ducks.*

After she finishes work for the day, Meili decides to go to the market to buy chicken blood and chives for tonight's dumplings. Spring Festival is only a few days away, but she still hasn't prepared a decorative table display. She's bought New Year sticky rice buns and some dates to make the traditional 'give birth to a noble son' cakes. Little Heaven has now been inside her for two years. It thoughtfully keeps itself tightly curled up, so her bulge is much less noticeable. When Kongzi's mouth was injured, Meili began having long conversations with the infant spirit instead, and this has continued even now that Kongzi is able to speak again.

On her way to the market, she strolls down Magnificent Street. The sparkling jewels and designer clothes in the shop windows and the bright hoardings overhead divert attention from the peasants selling oranges on grubby carpets, and the oily smells of grilled mutton wafting from the street stalls. Between the Cloudy Mountain Printers and the Friendship Hotel is a winding lane Meili went down last week to check out a noodle shop that was up for rent. The shop itself was all right, but she was put off by the clinic for sexually transmitted diseases next door, and its large notice that said WE SPECIALISE IN SKIN COMPLAINTS. Since Kongzi's arrest and hospital treatment ate up most of their savings, Meili has wanted more than ever to give up work and open her own shop. Knowing that it's a short cut to the market, she turns into the lane and immediately hears funeral wailing, then sees a large white mourning tent erected further down. A lead runs from the window of a house to a bulb on the tent's roof. The wailing is coming from a cassette player. She thinks at once of her grandmother and feels her eyes fill up. Without hesitating, she strides into the tent and introduces herself to an old man in white mourning dress who's standing beside an open coffin. 'I can sing funeral laments,' she says to him, glancing down at the corpse. It's a woman in a white robe. She looks about fifty and has a big smile on her face. Roasted heads of a chicken and a duck have been placed on her chest. There are eight banquet tables of guests, all dressed in white. Plates are clattering, everyone is chatting noisily. 'Fill your glasses,' someone shouts. 'Drink! Drink!'

'What do you charge per hour?' says a middle-aged man standing in front of a large photograph of the deceased. Meili assumes that he's the husband.

'Two hundred yuan,' she replies, sweeping her gaze over the bright interior.

The husband goes to fetch his father-in-law who asks her in a thick southern accent, 'Can you sing "The Memorial Altar" and "Soul Rising from the Coffin" sutras?' He has white hair and is holding a walking stick with a dragon-head handle.

'Yes, I can sing dirges for fathers, husbands, mothers – the whole repertoire. How many children did your daughter have? If you tell me some interesting events from her life, I can weave them into the lament.'

'Our family's from Chaozhou,' he answers. 'We don't understand your northern dialect, so sing what you like. Improvise as you go along.' He coughs loudly into his hand. A woman walks up and leads him back to one of the tables.

'The funeral band we hired has been delayed and won't be here until ten,' the husband says. 'So, yes, you're welcome to sing for a couple of hours. I'll fetch you a microphone.' As he walks off again, Meili suddenly regrets offering to sing, but knows it's too late to back out now. Although she watched her grandmother perform at funerals, she has never sung at one herself.

Meili takes off her jacket and drapes a white funeral cloak over her shoulders, and remembering the white turban her grandmother used to wear, ties a large napkin around her head. She steps nervously onto the dais, takes a deep breath and sings into the microphone: '*My dearest mother, what grief we feel! You've left this world before you've had a chance to savour one moment of joy . . .*' Real tears begin to run down her face. She closes her eyes and listens to her high-pitched lament pour out of the loudspeakers, pound the walls of the tent and flow into the lane outside. She feels herself drown in the deafening noise . . . '*Sparrows search for their mothers under the eaves of roofs. Pheasants search for their mothers in bramble bushes. Carps search for their mothers among river weeds. But where can I go to search for you? . . .*' When she comes to the end of 'Yearning for My Departed Mother on the Twelfth Lunar Month', she sits down on a stool, wipes the tears from her face and looks out at the guests seated before her. Some are still wolfing down their food, shoulders hunched over their plates, some are deep in conversation, but most are looking up, staring straight back at her. She has no idea what these southerners made of her performance. She's never sung with such intense grief before. Feeling another wave of sadness take over her, she sinks her head into her hands. Someone taps her shoulder and gives her a bottle of mineral water. She takes it without looking up, but feels too weak to open it. She thinks of how Kongzi, the only person she thought she could rely on, sold her baby daughter, and has very probably slept with a prostitute. She thinks of how the nightclub boss pinned her to a single bed and raped her, and how the government pinned her to a steel table and murdered her newborn son. Unable to control herself, she kneels beside the black coffin and weeps: '*Beloved husband, five hundred years ago, our marriage was predestined in Heaven. In this lifetime we met at last and became as inseparable as two mandarin ducks. But now you've released your hand from mine and returned to the Western Paradise. Who will feed the geese and chicken in our backyard? . . .* I hope that evil bastard burned to death in the fire . . .' Harrowing images flash through her mind. She weeps about her grandmother's corpse being dug up and burned, about Happiness lying on a riverbed, about Waterborn's unknown fate, and about her fear of giving birth to Heaven and of Heaven's fear of being born. Moaning and sobbing, she cries herself into a stupor.

'Take a break,' the husband says, handing her a plate of rice and fish. 'Have something to eat.'

'Thank you,' she replies, her snot dripping onto the floor. She looks at the deep-fried fish, but has no appetite to eat it. Through the tent's open door she sees windows light up in the dark lane, and whispers to the infant spirit: It's time to leave. Your daddy and sister will be getting hungry. I'll make a soup for them with the turnip and squid Cha Na gave me. She glances down at the fish again and whispers: All right, little Heaven, I'll have some, just for you. Then she picks up the fish with her chopsticks, takes a bite, and studies the paper funeral objects displayed below the portrait of the deceased: miniature cars, fridges, houses and wads of American dollars – all the things that she herself hopes to acquire one day. As she looks down at the discarded chopstick wrappers and cigarette butts on the floor, she senses someone's gaze fall on her. She turns round and sees a tall bespectacled young man in a black suit and tie.

'How beautifully you sang!' he says. 'I wish I could have recorded you.'

'That wasn't singing, it was just wailing!' Meili replies. She looks down at the coffin and imagines the woman inside listening to their conversation. She saw many corpses at the funerals her grandmother took her to, so isn't afraid of them.

'Well, how beautifully you wailed, then! Where did you study?' The young man's hair smells freshly blow-dried. Meili has become familiar with the smell of scorched hair and lacquer. She visits the hairdresser once a month now for a wash and blow-dry, and walks out looking like a film star.

'The songs were passed down through my family,' Meili says, then shudders at the thought that her grandmother is now as motionless and lifeless as the woman in the coffin.

'You sound like that Hong Kong singer, Anita Mui. I'm very happy to meet you. My name is Zhang Tang. Just call me Tang.'

'Anita Mui is a superstar! How can you compare me to her?' Meili turns her head away to swallow the remaining food in her mouth.

'She was my aunt,' Tang says, pointing to the corpse. 'She died of pancreatic cancer. I'm sure the pollution was to blame.'

Meili wipes her mouth with a napkin. 'Your accent isn't strong. Where are you from?'

'I grew up here, but went to university in Europe. I graduated last year.' When he closes his mouth his two front teeth protrude over his lower lip.

'Europe? I've dismantled lots of computers and phones from there. Is it a nice country?'

'It's not a country, it's a continent! France, Italy, Germany – they're all part of Europe. I was studying in England.'

'Well, those countries must be much better than China. They dump their rubbish on us, and we treat it like treasure. How lucky you were to go there. Why on earth did you come back?'

'I love this place. When I was a child, it was idyllic. There was a beautiful lotus pond near the harbour and every house had a clean well. My friends and I would go to Womb Lake after school and fish for carp and shrimp.'

'I live right by the lake. It's squalid. The rivers are so polluted that just six months after we arrived, our boat rotted away.' Meili doesn't want to continue the conversation. She steps off the dais and pretends to read the messages on the flower wreaths.

'I'd like to give you an Anita Mui CD,' Tang says, following her.

'Don't bother. I'm twenty-six now – too old to think of being a pop star.' She puts her plate on the ground and, trying to get rid of him, says: 'Could you move away a little? I think I should sing a last song.'

'I can't,' Tang says, pushing his gold-rimmed glasses further up his nose. 'It's my turn to stay by the coffin.'

The husband walks over and hands her a paper cup of tea. Wanting to make an escape, Meili gulps it down in one and says, 'Boss, my throat is sore. I don't think I can perform any more laments.'

A few minutes later she strolls out of the tent, whispering to the infant spirit, I bet you're even more afraid to come out after hearing Mummy wailing like that! She thinks of how the dead woman will be given a proper burial tomorrow so that her soul can rest in peace until its next incarnation. Nobody wailed when her grandmother died and her mangled remains entered the earth, so her spirit is doomed to wander for eternity as a rootless wild ghost. Meili puts the cash she was paid into her pocket and examines the business card Tang gave her before she left. As they were saying goodbye, he told her that his sister-in-law is looking for a nanny, and asked if she'd be interested in the job. She thinks of Nannan, and hopes she's home by now. For the last few days, she's gone to the train station after school to collect discarded ticket stubs which Kongzi then sells to business travellers who claim the cost back on expenses.

Mother loses herself in the lampless winding lane. She passes a tricycle covered in a yellow cloth which in the faint light from a window above looks like a dusty cream cake. At last she sees a bright street ahead, and quickens her pace. In the distance, she hears a pop ballad lilt from the mourning tent: *'Has anyone told you they love you or shed tears over the poems you wrote? . . .'* **After crossing the street, she takes two lefts then a right, and comes to the lotus pond near the harbour. The plastic rubbish heaped around its edge emits a cold, deathly light. She walks down towards the lake and follows the stone path that leads straight to their gate.**

When she opens the front door, she sees Kongzi stuffing clothes into a bag, and asks him where he's going.

'My father died,' Kongzi says, quietly enough for Nannan not to hear him.

'When?'

'Three months ago, on his birthday.'

'Was it an illness or an accident?'

'He drank some fake wine and it perforated his stomach.'

'But if you go back to the village, the police will fling you in jail. My brother said that they have evidence you took part in the riots. Your family have always begged you not to go home. They didn't contact you when he died, did they? They were probably afraid you'd want to attend the funeral. Anyway, he's been buried for months, so what's the point of going back?' She puts her arm around him and takes him to sit down on the bed. Her heart softens. 'Don't be too hard on yourself, Kongzi. I know you would have liked to have attended his funeral, but I'm sure your father wouldn't have wanted you to put yourself in danger.' She rests her head on his shoulder. This is the first time they've touched since his arrest.

Kongzi punches his chest and wails like a strangled cat: 'What an unfilial wretch I am! I should be garrotted, stabbed ten thousand times . . .' Nannan runs out into the yard and sits in a corner with her eyes closed.

'After my grandmother died, my mother fell ill and had to have an operation, but I didn't go back to see her,' Meili says, stroking his back. 'Don't leave tonight. It would be too hot-headed. See how you feel in the morning.'

'Enough,' Kongzi says, putting his hands over his ears.

'Well, you sit here quietly and I'll get supper ready.' She wipes the table and sets out plates of marinated peanuts, deep-fried shrimp and mini tomatoes. 'So who told you he died?' she asks. 'Who arranged the funeral?' She tries to picture Kongzi's father, but all she sees in her mind's eye is the dead woman in the black coffin.

'I phoned home to ask if they'd received the ham and dried fish I sent them for Spring Festival, and my mother told me the news. There was a proper ceremony. The County Party Secretary sent a wreath, and a Communist Party flag was draped over the coffin.'

'What an honour! Aren't you proud?' Meili rubs the cash in her pocket, and thinks what an odd coincidence it is that just after singing at a stranger's funeral she hears of a death in her own family. She resolves never to sing at a funeral again.

'He was a twelfth-level cadre, so of course he was entitled to have a Party flag over his coffin.' Kongzi takes a sip from the mug of warm wine Meili gives him, then swallows the rest in one gulp. Nannan runs back into the room with Lulu, who's come round to see her. Unlike Nannan, whose eyes slant elegantly upwards, Lulu has large goldfish eyes.

'Go out and play, girls,' Meili says, noticing tears drip down Kongzi's face. She gives the girls two date biscuits and says, 'Off you go now!'

'But I'm tired,' Nannan says, pursing her lips. She's wearing her red flower hairclip, blue jeans and a red jumper covered with stickers of cartoon characters.

'Can you take Nannan back to your place, Lulu?' Meili says. 'Tell your mother I'll fetch her in an hour.'

KEYWORDS: *tumour, bedraggled alchemists, heart as soft as tofu, electronic messages, refurbished, second-hand.*

Hearing loud wailing, Meili leaves the kitchen, goes up to little Hong's bedroom on the second floor and picks her up out of the cot. 'Don't cry, little one, here's your milk,' she says. She pushes the bottle's teat into Hong's mouth and watches her stomach rise and fall in time with the sucking noises, and drops of milk run down her chin and neck. Meili can tell genuine imported milk powder from the fake domestic products simply by squeezing the bag. While running her market stall in Xijiang, she learned that imported powder is soft, but fake powder is hard and granular and tastes so bad that babies will only drink it if strawberry flavouring is added. She's been working as a nanny for Tang's sister-in-law, Jun, since Jun gave birth to Hong seven months ago. She often fantasises that Hong is little Heaven, who's still stubbornly planted in her womb. Hong's fine black hair has grown so long that it now falls below her eyes. When it's brushed back into a ponytail, the white marks from the chickenpox she contracted last month are visible on her forehead. Beside the cot are a nappy-changing table and a chest of drawers piled with soft toys – teddy bears, puppies, monkeys, elephants – which make the bare room seem full of life.

'Don't let her finish the bottle, Meili,' Jun shouts up from the first-floor sitting room where she's playing a game of mahjong. 'I want her to finish off with some of my milk.'

Meili doesn't like the sitting room. The beige fake leather sofas and blue tiled walls dazzle her eyes, and the Hong Kong soap operas blaring from the television and constant clatter of mahjong grate on her nerves. Tang's family bought this three-storey Western-style villa four years ago. Most of the Heaven residents who've made money from electronic waste live in houses like this. The ground floors are used as workshops or storerooms, the first and second floors for the living areas, and the flat roofs for drying clothes and sitting out in the summer. Meili hands Jun the baby to breastfeed, then stands at the kitchen sink washing bottles and bibs, listening to Tang speak to his brother about England. 'And they've even stopped building new motorways, just so children can play safely in the fields . . .' he says, glancing at little Hong as she latches onto Jun's breast.

'They put children before the country's economic development? No wonder they're an empire in decline.' Tang's brother slides a mahjong piece forward and expels a stream of tobacco smoke through the corner of his mouth. He has the same buck teeth as Tang.

'Human life is more important to them than money. Heaven is so choked with waste these days that even if you're rich, you have no quality of life.'

'How can you say that?' the brother replies. 'You live in this beautiful villa, dine on fresh seafood every day, sleep on an imported sprung mattress and you can hop over the border to Hong Kong or Macao whenever you like. What more could you want?'

'Yes, if China's economy hadn't developed so fast, you wouldn't have been able to study abroad,' Jun chimes in. 'Down, naughty dog!' she shouts to the black lapdog that's coming up the stairs. Since Hong was born, the dog has been banished from the sitting room and has to live among the crates of cables on the ground floor.

'May this fish bring us abundance!' Meili says, walking out of the kitchen with steamed carp she has prepared in the Cantonese style. The fragrance of ginger, spring onion and sesame oil briefly masks the odours of sulphur drifting up from the workshop downstairs.

She sits between Tang and his brother. After Jun finishes nursing Hong, she serves Tang's mother a chunk of suckling pig and switches on a soap opera called *The Qing Dynasty God of Medicine*. An ancient courtyard residence is on fire, and men with long pigtails are rushing about in panic, shouting commands in Beijing accents. Tang's father comes in and joins them at the table. He doesn't like mahjong, so spends most of his time with the workers downstairs or tending his plants on the flat roof.

Meili takes little Hong from Jun and studies the dishes she's brought to the table. The pigs' trotters braised in bitter gourd and the garlic-fried aubergines look fine, but when she sticks a chopstick into the carp she sees flecks of blood near the bones and wishes she'd given it two more minutes.

'Thank you, Meili,' Tang exclaims. 'What a feast!' He fell in love with her as soon as he heard her sing at the funeral, and now that she's working for his family, he's continually finding excuses to spend time with her or give her a small tip. When Hong has her afternoon naps, he teaches her to type and guides her through the internet, helping her explore her areas of interest. Meili likes to watch clips of fashion shows and pop concerts. The first time she saw a Madonna video, she abandoned her dreams of becoming a singer for good. 'What a star!' she sighed, gazing at her cavort around the stage in a golden bodice. Every morning, Tang puts on a surgical face mask and goes jogging around the lake. He told Meili that in England, he used to jog every day in the forest near his university campus. When he gets back, Meili gives him a bowl of fish slice congee, a bread roll or a custard tart. He's not fussy about what he eats.

Meili appreciates the kindness he shows her, especially when his mother or Jun scold her for not cleaning the bottles properly or for overcooking the rice. On those occasions, Tang will always look up from his computer, ask Meili to pour him another cup of tea, then whisper in her ear that his mother has a mouth as sharp as a knife but a heart as soft as tofu. His words reassure her, but she doesn't want him to grow too fond of her. She's afraid of men, and of losing control. But when she hears him sitting at his desk talking to female friends on the phone, she feels sad, and wonders if she'd feel the same if she heard Kongzi speak to other women in a similar tone.

After clearing away the dinner and washing the dishes, Meili goes to the second floor to say goodbye to Tang. He points at his computer screen and says, 'Look, this student has written an article about pollution in Heaven Township: "Using 19th-Century Techniques to Dismantle 21st-Century Waste". See here, it says: "Migrants toil like bedraggled alchemists in family workshops, washing circuit boards in sulphuric acid to salvage tiny granules of gold." And look at this picture: "Female workers strip plastic casings from electric cables with their bare hands, their only tools a fold-up table and a rusty nail . . ."'

'That woman there . . .' Meili gasps, 'it's me!'

'My God, you're right! I recognise that flowery shirt. Let me enlarge the photo. Yes, no question about it. It's you!'

'My face is filthy. How embarrassing! Close it at once!' Meili puts her hands over the screen. 'Must have been that student from Guangzhou University who came to our workshop last year. He walked straight in, squatted down beside me and started snapping away without asking my permission.'

'I'm going to download the photo. How amazing! My little village songstress has entered the world wide web . . . Look at this article I found on a British website. It says: "The *Emma Maersk*, the largest container ship in the world, sailed from China to the United Kingdom to deliver 45,000 tonnes of Chinese-manufactured Christmas toys, then returned to southern China a few weeks later loaded with UK electronic waste . . . Heaven Township is now the largest e-waste dump in the world. As much as 70% of the world's toxic e-waste is shipped to this area of southern China, where it is processed in makeshift workshops by migrant labourers who are paid just $1.50 a day . . ."'

'Will everyone in the world be able to see that photograph of me?'

'Yes, once it's online it can't be removed. This is the age of the internet.'

'So, if I sang on the computer, the whole world would be able to hear me?'

'Yes, you can upload anything you want onto the net . . . Look – this is the most important part: "88% of Heaven residents suffer from skin, respiratory, neurological or digestive diseases. Levels of lead poisoning and leukaemia among children are six times higher than the national average. In just ten years, Heaven Township, once a collection of sleepy rice villages, has become a digital-waste hell, a toxic graveyard of the world's electronic refuse. The air is thick with dioxin-laden ash; the soil saturated with lead, mercury and tin; the rivers and groundwater are so polluted that drinking water has to be trucked in from neighbouring counties . . ."' Tang peeps over his glasses to check Meili's reaction.

'I'd hate to contract a skin disease,' she says. 'If you know computers are so dangerous, why do you sit in front of one all day?'

'They're only dangerous when you take them apart . . . Look here: "High levels of infertility have been detected among women who have resided in Heaven Township for over three years."'

'Lucky them! No illness can match the pain of childbirth.'

'Meili, you're not pregnant, are you?' Tang asks tentatively. 'Forgive me for asking.'

'Are you saying I look fat?' Meili has become accustomed to this question over the last two and a half years.

'No, no – not fat. It's just that your belly looks a little bloated, that's all. I was worried you might have developed a tumour, or something, from working with all that toxic waste.'

'You're right, I probably have cancer of the womb. I should rip my uterus out and give it back to the state.' She turns to leave, but Tang grabs her hand and pulls her back.

'I don't think you look fat,' he says. 'I promise you. I'm just . . . so fond of you, that's all. I can't help saying what's on my mind.'

'I'd better rinse the bottles again before I go,' Meili says, trying to pull her hand free. He often attempts to plant a kiss on her cheek before she leaves, telling her that this is what foreigners do, but she always backs away. She strokes her belly and says to herself, Yes – little Heaven is a tumour growing in my flesh. If anyone asks me if I'm pregnant, I'll tell them I have a tumour. I have the right to have one, and I have the right to be too poor to have it removed . . .

'How long have you been married?' he asks, still clutching her hand.

'Ten years,' she says, her cheeks reddening. 'We had the wedding in the village, then honeymooned in Beijing,' she blurts, wanting him to know that she's visited the capital. Since Kongzi was arrested for gambling, she no longer feels proud to be his wife. And since she returned to him after her escape from the brothel, she has felt that the old Meili died somewhere out on the road. She wants to be a strong, adventurous woman who doesn't rely on a man for her happiness. She is comfortable treating Tang as a friend or a younger brother, but if he asked to be her lover or husband, she'd cut all ties with him. As Suya wrote in her red journal, 'Love is the beginning of all pain.'

'So, what did you think of Beijing?' Tang asks, stroking the desk now that Meili has tugged her hand free.

'The Forbidden Palace was so huge it terrified me – only emperors would dare live in such a place . . .' Meili says, then dries up. She isn't used to being asked her opinions. 'I went into a supermarket to buy a drink. There was a mountain of lemonade bottles on display but when I tried to pay for one the checkout girl said no one could buy any until Workers' Day . . .'

'Look at these photographs I took in England. This is my lecture hall. This is the university garden when it snowed.'

'Was one of those your girlfriend?' Meili asks nervously, standing behind his chair.

'She's Spanish – a great dancer! And the other girl's from France. I travelled to Switzerland with them.'

'Huh – I don't want to hear about that,' Meili says disapprovingly. The photograph shows Tang sitting between two foreign girls, his arms around their shoulders and a big grin on his face. On the table in front of them are glasses of wine and a large birthday cake.

'This is a protest march in Paris . . . St Peter's Square in Rome.'

'Let me see if any of the countries you visited have population-control policies,' Meili says, leaning over to type a few keywords into the search box.

'I know that England certainly doesn't. Pregnant women are treated with respect there. They have specially allocated seats on buses and trains, and can give birth in hospital free of charge. The government even pays parents a weekly allowance to cover the cost of milk powder and nappies.'

'You're lying to me! How could such a wonderful place exist?'

'I'm not lying. Lots of pregnant women smuggle themselves out of

China to give birth in Europe or Hong Kong. If you plan to have another baby, you should do the same. Now that China has entered the WTO, foreign countries are much more welcoming to Chinese visitors.'

'You'll have to teach me English first,' says Meili, then remembering how Suya said men should be used but not loved, she kneels down and looks up at him with a smile. 'You mustn't say I'm stupid, though. I only went to school for three years.'

Tang puts his arm around her. 'You're not stupid. You're just pure and wholesome and . . . Listen, I wanted to ask you: will you let me take you out for dinner at the China Pavilion Restaurant tomorrow evening?'

'What for? No, no . . .'

'It's your birthday. Have you forgotten?' He strokes her hair and looks lovingly into her eyes. 'You must have more belief in yourself and value your talents. In England, the first thing our professor told us was that we should find the confidence to surpass him . . .'

'Are you still here, Meili?' Jun calls out from the landing. 'Then you can change Hong's nappy before you leave.'

Tang pulls a face and whispers: 'Better do as she asks.' When his buck teeth show, he reminds her of the pet rabbit she had as a child.

It's dark outside now. The fluorescent strip on the sitting-room ceiling and the blue light from the mute television in the corner make the room feel cold and stiff. **The infant spirit sees Mother change the nappy of the screaming baby, put it to sleep in a cot, and move downstairs. On the ground floor, workers are dismantling and smelting. The smell of burnt Bakelite follows Mother out into the garden that is fenced with corrugated iron and barbed wire. She opens the steel security gate and closes it behind her. In a shop window at the end of the dark street she sees a seascape painting framed in bright strip lights above a bowl of pink plastic tulips. Smiling down at her belly, she whispers, Still don't want to come out? Well, he's noticed you, little tumour. Look at those nice jeans in the window. If it weren't for you, I could fit into them . . . Mother puts one hand on her hip and throws the other in the air, mimicking the pose of the mannequin in the window . . . Back in the house,**

Father is filling out forms while Nannan is writing essays in exercise books, wearing a blue dress with a panda badge pinned to the front. 'Did you know you can explore the whole world on the internet?' Mother says as she walks in. 'We must buy a computer. They're so much more interesting than televisions.'

'You can barely read – what use would a computer be to you?' Father says. 'Just stick to dismantling them.'

'I can type words using Roman script. Once I learn all twenty-six letters, I'll be able to go online by myself and travel the world. We'll be able to send our relatives electronic messages and photographs which they'll receive in seconds. I dismantled computers for two years, but I've only just understood what they're used for . . .' Mother sees Father smear green tea and ink over the exercise books Nannan has written in, and sandpaper the corners of the forms. The floor is strewn with pencils and balls of cotton wool. 'What's going on here?' she asks.

'Inspectors are visiting Red Flag Primary next week. We have two hundred pupils, but to get a larger government subsidy we need to tell them we have two hundred and fifty. So I'm having to fabricate fifty students. Help me fill some exercise books. If they're all in Nannan's handwriting, it'll look suspicious.'

'I've finished twelve literacy homework books,' Nannan says. 'Daddy said he'd buy me some candyfloss as a reward.'

'You can do Year 3 homework, Nannan?' Mother says. 'Clever girl!'

'She knows more characters than you do now, and she can write out each of the three hundred Tang poems from memory. She will be a worthy descendant of Confucius!'

'Daddy, Confucius was an evil man. I wish we didn't share his surname.'

'Who told you he was evil?' Father says. 'Confucius was a great sage. You should feel proud to have him as an ancestor.'

'If he was so great, why don't they mention him in our textbooks? Lulu keeps singing "Down with Kong the Second Son!" but I pretend not to hear her.'

'I assure you, Nannan: Confucius was a great philosopher and teacher. He taught us to respect learning, honour our parents and care for our young, and lead a virtuous life, even in times of turmoil. He said that people should obey their leaders, but only so long as their leaders rule with compassion. For two thousand years, his words formed the bedrock of Chinese culture. The Communist Party may have cursed him, vilified him, dug up his grave, but his ideas live on. You're almost nine years old now, Nannan. You must study hard and build up the knowledge that will help you carve a path through this difficult world. Tell me how that saying goes?' Father puts down the forged exercise book he's holding and stares into Nannan's eyes.

'"Children who don't read books, don't know the treasures they contain. If they knew . . ." blah, blah, blah.'

'That's right. But listen to me, Nannan. The tide is changing. Confucius's name is being mentioned in the newspapers. One day he'll be rehabilitated, and those evil cadres who spat on his corpse thirty years ago will light incense sticks in his temple and beg forgiveness.'

'Don't talk to your classmates about any of this, Nannan,' Mother says. 'Your school may not teach you about Confucius, but it will teach you Tang poetry, so I'm sure you'll rise to the top of the class. Remember: learning is a joy, not a burden.' Mother turns on the electric fan and takes off her dress. 'Kongzi, I want to open my own shop. I only need twenty thousand yuan to get started.'

'I'm too busy to talk about that now,' Father says. 'Fill up this homework book for me. Use your left hand. No, come to think of it, you write like a child with your right hand so just stick to that.'

'I want to open a baby shop that sells milk powder, toys, cots,' Mother says dreamily. 'When mothers see me stand at the counter with my pregnant bulge, they'll come flocking in. Or I could sell refurbished computers. This town has mountains of scrap components but no one's thought of reassembling them to make functioning machines. I'm sure we could earn more money assembling computers than these workshops do taking them apart. We could sell them to people in the countryside. The market for cheap second-hand computers there must be enormous.'

Nannan completes an exercise book then starts writing on the first page of another, her long hair dangling over the desk.

Meili walks barefoot over the white vinyl mat. A large black spider crawls behind her. Kongzi has become very close to Nannan, she says to herself. Perhaps by the time the baby's born, he'll come round to the idea of having another daughter and everything will be fine. I'll find a nanny for little Heaven, set up my own business, then return to Nuwa County and open a chain of second-hand computer shops.

Three hours later, Kongzi is still crouched on the floor, scribbling in the exercise books. Meili has nodded off on the chair, her ink-stained hands resting on her belly. In her dream she sees her future self galloping up a hill, her hair and the grass blowing in the wind. When she reaches the top she takes flight. From a heap of computers below the infant spirit shouts out to her, 'Keep flying, keep flying. You're crossing the border. If the soldiers see you, they'll gun you down . . .'

KEYWORDS: *clam dance, zero protein, sticky rice, banana tree, steel tower, rainbow.*

When Meili opens the door in the morning, she has to drag the children's bicycles and baby-walkers onto the pavement before she can make her way to the counter. This shop may be small and cramped, but it has given her a foothold in society. With a look of calm contentment, she plugs her mobile phone into the charger and gazes out of the window. The shop belongs to Tang's family. She pays them two hundred yuan a month in rent, and buys the stock herself. In her spare moments, she surfs the internet on the computer Tang has lent her. He's taught her to breach the firewall and access the BBC Chinese-language website, so she now knows that Chinese illegal immigrants in America can earn more in one year than their families back home earn in a lifetime. She has also researched the local component trade and worked out the cost of reassembling a computer. Tang has told her she has a good business brain.

It was Hong's first birthday yesterday. Meili phones Tang and asks how the party went. She was sacked from her job as nanny because while she was changing Hong's nappy on the ironing board, Hong burned her hand on a hot iron. Jun was furious, and banned Meili from ever setting foot in the house again. Meili still feels terrible about the accident. A couple of days ago, she chose the most expensive baby-walker from her shop and asked Tang to give it to Hong for her birthday.

'Your present's a great success!' Tang tells her down the phone. 'Hong's walking around the sitting room with it. She loves the music and flashing lights.'

'Make sure she doesn't push it anywhere near the stairs. And remind Jun to tidy all the electric cables away. At twelve months, babies start chewing everything in sight.'

'No chance of Hong doing that. She has a dummy stuffed in her mouth all day.'

'Really? I may sell dummies in the shop, but don't let Hong use one – they make babies' teeth stick out.' Meili bites her lip, afraid that the buck-toothed Tang might have taken offence.

'I need to answer some emails,' Tang says. 'I'll pop by at lunchtime.'

'To collect the rent? But it's not due until Monday . . . Well, if you're coming, you can fix the electricity meter for me – it keeps tripping. Fine. See you later.' Meili puts the phone down and goes online. Last month she searched the name Wang Suya, and it produced 4 million results. Adding the keyword 'university' returned 6,500 results. Remembering that Suya studied English and was from Chengdu, she narrowed the results down to twelve and managed to send each of these Wang Suyas a letter. Although she still hasn't found the Suya she's looking for, she has struck up online friendships with two of the Suyas who replied. She's also visited chat rooms where other women like her lament the babies they've lost through forced abortions. The babies' ghosts haunt the conversations, making the website feel like a graveyard. The women are planning to set up a virtual memorial garden to give the aborted fetuses a safe resting place. Meili has learned that 13 million abortions are performed in China each year, an average of 35,000 per day.

Through the side window she sees a troupe of dragon dancers appear at the end of the lane. Processions are a common sight in Heaven Township, not only on Workers' Day or National Day, but before weddings or the openings of new businesses. Behind the dragon, four men are holding aloft a statue of the Dark Emperor, the black-bearded Taoist deity. Meili visited a Taoist temple with Tang, and prayed to the Dark Emperor to protect the baby in her womb. When she told Tang that she's pregnant and that the baby refuses to come out, he said he'd take her to a temple in Foshan where she can pray to a huge statue of the Golden Flower Mother, the goddess of fertility and childbirth.

He said that all the Golden Flower Mother statues in the temples in Heaven Township are replicas of the one in Foshan. Meili sees the procession stop at the intersection beneath a ragged red banner that says THE IMPORT OF ELECTRONIC WASTE IS ILLEGAL, and a young couple step out from the crowd to perform the 'clam dance'. The man dressed as the fisherman has a wicker basket tied to his waist and is swaying his hips and clapping his hands in the air. The woman playing the clam fairy is moving her arms, opening and closing the shells attached to her back. When the fisherman reaches out to catch her, she snaps her shells shut, trapping his hands. He keeps trying, and she keeps snapping, but each time they touch, she grows fonder of him and tightens her grip, until by the end he can't prise his hands free. Meili thinks of the video clip Tang downloaded from a foreign website of a woman being penetrated by two men. She turned away as soon as he showed it to her, but the images have stuck in her mind. Whenever she passes a marital-aids shop now, she casts a brief glance at the products in the window. She has started to wear prettier clothes, and has had her hair cut in a fashionable shoulder-length bob.

Although Meili has kept Tang at arm's length, he is still besotted with her, and the knowledge that she's pregnant hasn't put him off. He even lent her ten thousand yuan to settle the unpaid bills for her mother's operation. She doesn't know when she'll be able to repay him. She makes three thousand yuan a month from her shop. But the cyst that was removed during her mother's operation was found to be cancerous, and if the disease returns, there will be endless medical bills to pay. Her father and brother have exhausted their savings and have sold the pig they were hoping to eat at Spring Festival. She can imagine the wretched scene at her parents' house now, with no money to heat the brick bed, or buy New Year posters or her mother's favourite five-spiced sunflower seeds. Tang has become her protector and benefactor. She's grateful for his help, but is still careful not to cross any lines. She suspects her emotions are blunted. Kongzi still burrows his way inside her every night, but as soon as he's finished, she washes all traces of him from her body and returns to how she was. She knows she won't leave him. He assured her that he never slept with a prostitute, and having no proof, she's given him the benefit of the doubt. As long as both sides remain faithful, she believes that marriage should last for ever. She knows this is a stupid belief. It seems as childish to her as the infant spirit who's now smiling inanely at the toddler playing with a bamboo snake in the doorway. But at the same time, she is aware of deeper longings. She wants to be as independent and confident as Suya, as enterprising as Tang. She knows that a simple peasant woman like her has no right to an independent existence, but she understands that money can widen one's choices in life, so is determined to earn as much as she can. Without money, no marriage or family is secure. She feels that, for years, her true self has been lying buried in the depths with Happiness, but that since meeting Tang, it has begun to rise to the surface again. She wants to dismantle the Meili that has been damaged by men and the state, and reassemble it, like a refurbished computer that may not be as sophisticated as the latest model, but is at least stronger than it was before. She will struggle on and, as Suya advised, use her past suffering as an impetus to achieve happiness.

After the procession has passed, Kongzi phones to say that his sister and her Pakistani husband have had a son. 'They've taken their little black baby to Kong Village to spend Spring Festival with my mother. What a loss of face for the Kong clan!'

'Oh, you have such a feudal mentality!' Meili replies. 'Who cares what colour the baby is? The black dolls in my shop sell just as well as the white ones. And besides, the Kong family could do with some new blood. After two thousand years, they still haven't produced an offspring of Confucius's calibre.'

'We'll talk when we get back,' Kongzi says, slamming the phone down. Since Meili told him that her mother has been forcefully fitted with an IUD, he becomes short-tempered whenever babies or childbirth are mentioned. Meili is also upset that both their mothers have had IUDs shoved inside them as a result of their quest for another child, so she puts up with his outbursts. She knows the importance Kongzi places on his responsibilities as a son to his mother. Whenever they made dumplings at home, he'd always serve his mother a bowl first. Now that his brother has moved back to the village following the death of their father, she knows Kongzi is racked with guilt that he's not there too, looking after her.

A young man suddenly storms into the shop and says, 'We're from the Bureau of Industry and Commerce. Open all the bags of milk powder in that crate!' He looks barely out of high school. There are four officers behind him wearing hats emblazoned with gold badges. A large truck is parked outside.

Meili notices that one of the officers is a woman who visited the shop last week, and quickly slips a one-hundred-yuan note into her palm.

'I can't take it,' the woman whispers, glancing behind her. 'Someone's reported you, and we've been told to search your stock and confiscate any counterfeit goods.'

'This brand's definitely fake,' the young man says, pulling a bag from the crate. 'There was a big report about it last week: it contains zero protein. And these ones? Let's see: "Milk Powder for Primary School Children", "Calcium-Enriched Milk Formula" – yes, they're fake too.' His eyes flit between the list in his hand and the bags he pulls from the crate.

'No, that brand's not fake,' Meili protests. 'The government awarded it a gold prize last year. I research my products very carefully, I assure you.'

'Drag the crates outside,' says a middle-aged officer standing in the doorway.

'I bought them from a legitimate wholesale company,' Meili says. 'How was I to know that they're fake?' The truth is, she is fully aware that everything in her shop is counterfeit. If she bought genuine products, her costs would quadruple and she'd make no profit.

'If you had a child of your own, you'd never dream of feeding it fake formula,' the young man says. 'They provide no nourishment at all.'

'I do have a child, and if I could afford it, I certainly would give her this. The women who buy my formula are migrant workers, many of whom have several children, so they get through a lot of it, but not one of them has ever come back to complain.'

'Real formula is a creamy colour, but look, this stuff is white,' the young man says, opening a bag and pouring the powder onto his hand. 'This is just ground rice and instant chrysanthemum tea powder, with some melamine added to ensure it passes the protein tests. Melamine – that's the plastic that kitchen cupboards are made of. If a baby were to drink this powder, it would develop kidney stones and die.'

'We'll fine you and confiscate your goods,' the middle-aged officer says. 'Count yourself lucky. If you dare sell fake products again we'll revoke your licence.'

Meili's heart sinks as she watches the eleven crates of milk powder being dragged out of her shop and loaded onto the van. That's a thousand yuan lost for ever.

One of the officers notices Meili's round belly and says to his colleague, 'This place really is a heaven for family planning fugitives!' in a local dialect he mistakenly presumes Meili doesn't understand.

Passers-by gather outside the shop and mutter among themselves: 'We can't trust anything we eat these days! Tofu fermented in sewage, soy sauce made from human hair, mushrooms bleached with chlorine, and now fake baby formula! Whatever next? . . . Apparently, after just three days on that powder, babies lose weight and develop "big head disease". . . I heard that thirteen babies have died already from kidney stones . . . Those evil peasants who make this stuff – have they no conscience? . . .'

Meili looks down, aghast, at the 5,000-yuan fine the officers handed to her. She considers phoning Kongzi, but is afraid he'll blow his top, so she phones Tang instead and asks him to come over straight away.

'I want to throw myself in the lake,' she sobs as Tang walks in.

'This fake milk powder has been in the news a lot recently. The government announced that there would be a national crackdown. Hundreds of infants have developed swollen heads, apparently, and a few have already died. One manufacturer raised the protein levels in the powder by adding ground leather from old shoes and boots. Can you believe it?'

'Why didn't you warn me?' Meili says, feeling stupid and incompetent.

'I had no idea you sold fake goods.'

'But everything in Heaven is fake! Those Clarks shoes you're wearing are as fake as the baby Nike trainers on that shelf. That teddy bear with the Made in France label, that American dummy, that Hong Kong baby-walker, even the President Clinton autobiography I've put in the front window – they're all pirated, copied, fake, made in Shenzhen . . . I have a sack of foreign designer labels which I can stick on any product I want. If I didn't sell fake goods, how could the government expect me to pay all the fees they charge? Just take a look at these!' She opens a drawer stuffed with bills. 'Urban infrastructure improvement fee, private leaseholders' public security administration fee, migrant worker integration fee, public security joint defence fee, children's products company administrative fee, fire prevention fee—'

'All right, I understand,' Tang says. 'Come on, let me invite you to lunch. It'll help you take your mind off things.'

The Hunan restaurant he takes her to is a five-minute walk away. By noon the place is packed, and filled with the noise of clanking crockery, loud television and animated chatter. Meili takes a small bite of the taro croquette she ordered, then carefully dabs her mouth with her napkin to stop her lipstick staining the food.

'I have something important to tell you, Meili,' he says. 'I want to set up a business selling second-hand computer components. Would you be my general manager? The salary will be low to start with, but I'll give you a percentage of the profits and shares in the company.'

'Yes, I'd love to! But what about my shop, and your family's business?'

'You can find someone to run the shop for you. And I've had enough of working for my family. I need to strike out on my own, be my own boss. I've researched the computer trade. Dealers from Beijing are already travelling down here to buy used components. There's a big demand for CD drives and motherboards from repair shops up there. An old classmate of mine has set up a similar company in Guangzhou. We can start by supplying him first, then gradually expand nationwide.'

'Have you thought of selling second-hand televisions as well? I bought one for two hundred yuan the other day. It's been cleaned and repaired, and works perfectly. A similar model would cost five thousand yuan new. If you sell cheap products like that to the poor, you could make a fortune. After all, most people in this country are peasants.'

'We can think about that later. But first let's come up with a name. How about Fangfang Electronics? No, that doesn't work well in English.'

'What about your English name, "Hugo"? In Chinese it sounds like "Virtuous Accomplishment". Isn't that good?'

'Yes, Hugo Electronics it is then . . . Oh yes, I spoke to the headmaster of Red Flag Primary. He said he couldn't allow Nannan to attend even if you bribed him. The county guidelines insist that all pupils have local residence permits. So she'll just have to stay at that migrant school, I'm afraid.'

'Well, she's lucky to have a place there. It only takes fifty students but there are tens of thousands of migrant children in Heaven. And just think how many millions of other migrant children there are in this country who are being denied an education. It's a national disgrace.'

'Wait until I'm a member of the People's Congress, and I'll sort it out,' Tang says, pouring himself some more tea.

'You've studied abroad. You should go into education, not politics.' As Meili bites into a chunk of the roast duck, Heaven kicks her stomach so hard that she almost blacks out. Mummy got into big trouble today, little one, she says under her breath. So be kind, and keep still . . .

'I'll go to the Bureau of Industry and Commerce this afternoon and see if I can get your fine reduced,' Tang says. 'The shop licence is in my name, after all. But don't worry – however much it is, I'll pay it.'

Meili smiles gratefully. 'But it was my fault. I can't let you—'

'Ah, you look so pretty when you smile! You can thank me with a kiss.' Tang closes his eyes and offers his cheek to her. Not wanting to bend over her belly, she gets up, walks round to him and places a kiss on his forehead. 'You're a good woman,' he says, taking her hand. 'If you get divorced, I'll be the first in line to—'

'And you're a good man, Tang. Whoever does marry you will be a lucky woman. Perhaps you and I will get married in our next life.' She pulls her hand away, returns to her seat and thinks how wonderful it would be to start her life again from scratch.

Tang picks up a piece of steamed pork with his chopsticks and places it in Meili's mouth.

'Do you know who gave me a second life?' Meili says.

'Me?' Tang replies, his buck teeth glinting.

'Well, of course, I wouldn't be where I am today if it weren't for you. So, let's say you gave me a third life. But the person who gave me my second life was a graduate called Suya who I met in a Custody and Repatriation Centre. I was with her for only two weeks, but she changed the way I look at the world. She was unlike anyone I'd met before. Even the way she moved and held herself set her apart. Through her, I began to understand the qualities that distinguish one person from another.'

'So what happened to her?'

'We were transferred to a labour camp, and she disappeared just before I left. I sneaked her journal out with me and have kept it with me ever since. But I've no idea where she is now, or even if she's still alive.'

'Those custody centres are a scandal. The police trawl the cities rounding up peasants, slam them in detention, then sell them to village officials who force them to work on farms for no pay. It's a modern-day slave trade . . . So, where was Suya from?'

'Chengdu. But I don't have her address. I feel as though my old self died in the camp and now Suya is living my life. I was never brave, strong or clever. I'm terrified that if something bad happens, I'll fall apart, like I almost did in the shop just now, and return to who I was. I'd like to go to Chengdu and try to track Suya's parents down. If they tell me she's dead, at least it will give me peace of mind. But if they've had no news from her . . .' Meili thinks of Weiwei searching the Xi River for his mother, and realises she hasn't thought about him for a long time. She looks up and scans the faces of the other diners in the restaurant.

'Who are you looking for?' Tang asks.

'I was just thinking about someone. A man I met. His mother was ill, and she drowned herself so that he wouldn't be burdened with her medical fees and could send his son to university. He travelled up and down the river for weeks, searching for her. I don't know if he ever found her.'

'People usually commit suicide to escape pain. But the pain doesn't go. It's just passed on to the relatives they leave behind.'

When Meili returns home an hour later, Kongzi is busy correcting homework. She takes a deep breath and says, 'An inspection team swooped into the shop today and confiscated my goods,' then waits for him to explode. But he remains silent, takes a last drag from his cigarette and flicks the stub onto the floor. Meili squats down, picks it up and drops it in the bin.

'My eyelid keeps twitching,' she says, flopping onto the bed in an exhausted heap. In the corner, the television is buzzing and white snowflakes are flashing across the screen. The room still smells of the five-spiced tofu they ate for supper yesterday. 'It's my right eye. I forget, is that supposed to be a good or bad omen?' Heaven presses against her spine, cutting off the oxygen to her brain. She feels faint, and rolls onto her side, then reminds herself that Tang will pay her fine, saving her from financial ruin, and sighs with relief.

'If a man's right eye twitches, it's a good omen; if a woman's right eye twitches, it's the reverse,' Kongzi says blankly. He has cut a cardboard box in half and is lining up Nannan's textbooks inside, their spines facing outwards. 'So, what did they take?'

'All the milk powder. A thousand yuan's worth.' She waits again for an angry outburst. A few days ago when he saw a photograph online of the Temple of Confucius in Qufu being ransacked during the Cultural Revolution, he kicked their bookcase onto the ground, incensed that this humiliating episode in the Kong family history is now available for the whole world to see. Meili looks down at the cups, toothbrushes and socks soaking in an enamel basin, then at his books stacked up in the corner near the shattered bookcase. On the table, next to Nannan's satchel, three green caterpillars are crawling about in a paper cup.

But tonight, Kongzi doesn't explode. He goes into the yard, sits down on a chair and pulls out a bottle of beer from under the pile of plates beneath the gas stove. Since his mouth was electrocuted by the police, his ulcers have become so chronic that he's almost given up smoking and can only eat small amounts of food.

'Mum, I'm hungry,' Nannan whines, crawling sleepily onto Meili's lap.

'I've got some delicious steamed pork with sticky rice and hot-sour noodles for you.'

'But I only want fish and chocolate.'

Meili pulls the table over to the bed, opens the cartons she brought back from the restaurant, empties the contents into two bowls and calls out to Kongzi. 'Come inside and eat . . . Are you still sulking about your sister's baby? Don't worry, his name won't be entered in the Kong Family Register. And anyway, she can't be the only Kong in China who's had a child with a foreigner. You should learn to move with the times.'

'Mum, how come your baby still hasn't come out?' Nannan asks, swaying from side to side as she tucks into the food.

'Perhaps it's afraid it will be as unlucky as Happiness was, and be strangled before it takes its first breath.'

'When I grow up I want to live in a country that doesn't kill babies.'

'Well, if I make enough money, you can go and study abroad when you're eighteen,' Meili says. 'Look, even your little green caterpillars know they need to find the right place to live. When we're all tucked up in bed, they'll climb out of the cup, crawl over to that nice bush out there, weave themselves into chrysalids, then ten days later they'll turn into butterflies and fly away.'

'If I lie down on this bed long enough, will I turn into a boy?' Nannan asks.

'It's not so bad being a girl. When you grow up you can wear earrings like mine, and necklaces and nice long dresses.'

'Mum, Daddy said that after Heaven is born we can go home. You'll have a son and a daughter, and everyone will be happy.'

'But we don't have a home to go back to,' Meili says. 'That's the price we had to pay to bring Heaven into the world.' Meili feels a sudden sense of pride that for three years, her belly has given Heaven a safe refuge. She wants to blurt out that Heaven is a girl, but stops herself. During the day, she pushes Heaven to the side so that it hugs her hips, making her bump much less visible.

After Nannan falls asleep, Meili pours herself a glass of beer and lies down on the bed. A man on the television sings, '*Let the moonlight bring you peace, let the sunlight bring you joy . . .*' and is then abruptly interrupted by an advert for Wahaha children's sausages. She switches off the television, lies in the dark, and suddenly sees an image of Weiwei's tortoiseshell glasses. That encounter happened years ago. How come her thoughts still return to it? All he did was stroke her in the dark. She remembers the sudden downpour that fell that night as they lay in the cabin, and the sound of the rain battering against the canopy, then forming a swishing pool above her that crashed onto the stern when the boat rocked to the side. But she knows that memory can't be right. The canopy always leaked, so if it had been raining, water would have dripped down the rusty pipes of the cabin's frame and seeped across the wooden deck all the way to her thighs . . . In her dream, she sees a banana tree tilt under the weight of its heavy fruit. She runs towards it and dissolves into a swarm of butterflies. She enters a desert cave, climbs up a sand dune and hears a voice whisper, 'You've returned to your place of birth . . .' Then she raises her head and sees herself looming above like a steel tower, her iron legs planted firmly in the ground and her vagina arching through the blue sky like a rainbow.

KEYWORDS: *deep well, foreign blood, index finger, telephone booth, pink blossom, tiger and dragon, paper women.*

As Meili is about to kick off her high-heeled shoes after returning home from a long day at the shop, Cha Na rushes in and says: 'I've just heard that Kongzi's lying blind drunk outside the Beautiful Foot Massage Parlour. You'd better go and rescue him. Nannan can spend the night with us.' Meili grabs an umbrella and heads for Hong Kong Street where, sure enough, Kongzi is lying conked out in the rain below the massage parlour's entrance, his head resting on the front step. His drenched clothes seem to be weighing him down, because though he's not a heavy man, Meili is unable to lift him onto her back. She tries dragging him along the pavement, but his bare feet become bloody as they scrape against the concrete. The girls in the massage parlour stare mockingly at her through the window. Summoning all her energy, she grabs his hands, swings them over her shoulders and with a flick of her hips manages to shift him up onto her back. Like a farmer carrying a pig to market, she lugs him to the end of the street and hails a taxi home. It's her birthday today. Tang wanted to invite her to a French restaurant in Foshan, but she persuaded him to take her for a simple dim sum lunch in Heaven instead. She knew Kongzi would forget that it's her birthday, so she'd planned to tell him she wasn't up to cooking supper, and suggest that they go to a Cantonese restaurant called Lured by the Fragrance, You Dismount your Horse. She thought she'd be brave and order dog hotpot, and 'tiger and dragon fight to the death', a local speciality of fried cat and snake meat which is believed to help rebalance the body's yin and yang.

Back in the house, the room fills with a sickening stench as she removes his vomit-soaked clothes. When she pulls off his trousers, she sees his shrivelled penis is sheathed in a condom. She freezes in horror and her scalp tightens. Her first impulse is to chop off the penis or set fire to it. She screams and pounds his head and chest until his cries become an echo of her own.

Kongzi pushes her off, sits up and sees the condom lying on the ground. Sperm has escaped and formed a yellow stain on the white mat. Meili grabs her shoe-cutting knife and, as her mind returns to the nightclub boss who raped her, she shouts: 'You depraved bastard! You ugly, festering lowlife! If you have any balls left, show them to me, come on, pull them out and let me chop them off!' She raises the knife high in the air then swings it down straight onto her left hand, severing her entire index finger. Her blood splashes onto the mat near the pool of sperm. She drops the knife, flings the door open and rushes blindly out into the rain.

For an hour she walks round the lake in utter despair. Then, feeling that the sky is falling on her head and the earth crumbling beneath her feet, she makes up her mind to go to an empty graveyard and hang herself from a tree. I'll never trust Kongzi again. The fraud! Going to work in a suit and tie, pretending to be a man of virtue . . . She sees a telephone booth and steps inside to shelter herself from the rain. The bloodied stump of her index finger hurts so much she's tempted to chop off the whole hand. Listening to the rain smashing onto the plastic roof, she picks up the receiver and considers phoning Weiwei, or Tang, but every man seems tainted to her now. She puts the receiver to her ear and imagines Suya picking up on the other end. Do you hear the rain here in Heaven Township, Suya? It's pelting down. You celebrated my birthday with me, and the next day you vanished into thin air. You too were attacked and defiled. But I set fire to the man who raped me, to avenge that crime, and all the crimes that other men committed against you. You were right – this is no country for women. It's pointless forgiving men and expecting them to change. They never do. They're filthy scum, every one of them. Where are you now? Can I come and stay with you? I've nowhere left to go . . . Noticing a figure standing outside waiting to use the phone, she puts down the receiver and leaves, concealing her left hand in the crook of her right arm. The rain washes the blood from her wound. What hope is there left? she mutters as she wanders down the deserted street. She feels she's been born into the wrong time and the wrong place, and is descending into a spiral of misery where the only escape is death.

By the time she reaches the graveyard, the rain has stopped. Through tear-filled eyes, she stares at the rows of granite tombstones and the funeral offerings arranged below them: oranges, apples, sodden cardboard cars and paper women labelled MISTRESS in black ink that has blurred in the rain. She presses the bony stump of her finger and a sharp jolt of pain races straight to her heart, then blood begins to pour from it again like water from a tap. She rips off her sleeve and wraps it tightly around the wound to stem the flow . . . My life is dripping away from me. This is where I will say goodbye to the world . . . When she married Kongzi she persuaded herself that although he might not be rich, he was descended from an educated and illustrious family, and that together they could lead a contented life. She never asked for much. She agreed to abandon their village and live as vagrants in order to give him the male heir he yearned for. But over the years, his obsessive desire for a son has blinded and warped him, and he sees her now only as a creature of reproduction. She'd hoped that once little Heaven was born, she could return to Kong Village, open a shop, look after her mother and live in peace. But this hope has vanished. Yes, she should walk straight to the end of her life and step over the edge . . .

Glancing down at her feet, she sees an imitation wedding certificate with a magazine snapshot of the beautiful film star Gong Li pasted next to a photograph of a wizened old man. Didn't Kongzi once say that when he reaches the netherworld, he too would like to marry Gong Li? Perhaps in that faraway land, all dreams really can be fulfilled. This isn't the burial place she'd imagined for herself, but what does it matter? In the end, we must all return to the earth, and one patch of soil is no different from another. She remembers, aged seventeen, sitting in a black car on the way to her wedding, her face caked in thick, itchy make-up. Attached to the roof were gifts of folded bedcovers and a warm, musty-smelling basket of ducklings. Kongzi turned to her and said, 'Once we're married, you'll belong to me, and I'll be making all the decisions in the family. Don't even think of spreading your pink blossom over the garden walls.' He put his hand on hers and she felt sick with shyness. As a child, she loved to hear her grandmother tell her the story of the cowherd and the celestial weaver girl, who crossed the Milky Way once a year on a bridge of magpies just to spend one night together, and she hoped that one day she would experience a love as passionate as theirs. Meili walks to a tree and leans against it. She has no idea what it's called. It has leaves as large as her hands and smooth, snake-like branches. All she needs to do now is pull her belt off and strap her neck to a branch . . . Although Tang and Weiwei showed her affection, she has never been unfaithful to Kongzi. To save him distress, she never told him about the rape, and avenged the crime herself. Glancing at her feet, she sees a fat-bellied frog crawling through the grass and feels an urge to stamp on it. Her left hand has gone numb. Blood is dripping from the wound onto the wet, corpse-filled earth. She regrets that her efforts to help Kongzi preserve his family line prevented her fulfilling her duties towards her parents. For years, she's denied herself luxuries, scrimping and saving so that they can send money home, but most of it goes to Kongzi's family. She knows her mother would never contemplate drowning herself, as Weiwei's mother did. She remembers how her mother hugged her with trembling arms the day her friend jumped into a deep well with her four-year-old daughter strapped to her back after finding out that her husband had slept with another woman. Am I afraid of death? Meili wonders, reminding herself that in a few minutes' time she'll be hanging from the tree. No, I'm not afraid. I shake with terror at the sight of a family planning officer, but when I look death in the eye, I feel perfectly calm. She pulls off her leather belt. Perhaps she really does have foreign blood in her veins. She remembers hearing how her great-grandmother slashed her wrist after giving birth to a fair-haired child, and wonders whether a tendency for suicide runs in her family . . . Her brother has been slaving down the mines seven days a week, leaving her father to look after the fields on the weekends, but between them they still can't afford to pay for the imported drugs that have been prescribed to her mother to keep her cancer at bay. Her brother was considered to be the clever one, and Meili had to leave primary school early so that her parents could afford to send him to high school. But he failed his exams and never made it to university, so their sacrifices were in vain . . . If she dies in this graveyard, where will she be reincarnated next? All she knows is that if she does hang herself, she'll never see her parents or Nannan again, and little Heaven will die as well . . . My baby is still growing inside me. I can't let it die. I should at least wait until it's safely born before I end my own life. Oh, this is all Kongzi's fault! Why should I have to condemn myself to another reincarnation because of his sordid infidelity? Her muddled mind begins to clear. Yes, he's the one who should be hanging himself from a tree, not me.

On a weed-covered grave below, two mice stare up at her, reminding her of the two children she has lost. If she gives birth to Heaven, she will leave Kongzi, save enough money to pay the family planning fine, then move back to Nuwa Village with her two daughters. But if she wants to make enough money to have a comfortable life, she must never fall pregnant again, and the best way of ensuring that is for Heaven to curl up tight and stay where it is. She must become an independent woman, a person who not only has a body, but also a mind capable of thought. She shouldn't have to punish herself for her husband's crimes. She can sense that there is a woman asleep inside her who is slowly coming to life. She stands up and wraps her arms around herself . . . Yes, Kongzi can go to hell! I'm twenty-eight today. My best years are still ahead of me. I'll struggle on and make my way back to my place of birth, like the sturgeon that swim up the Yangtze. I won't let you die, Heaven. Whatever the future holds, we will withstand it together . . .

Meili staggers out of the graveyard. The long road stretching through the darkness before her shimmers like a river of shattered ice.

KEYWORDS: *wild grasses, urinal, escalator, complex characters, fast food, worm-like, missing girl.*

Four months later, Meili, now with only nine fingers, is still living with Kongzi, but they've moved to a place further away from the hair salons of Hong Kong Road. Misfortunes always seem to come in pairs. The day Meili was hospitalised for blood poisoning when her unhealed stump became infected, she heard that her brother had got into a fight with the coal mine director over unpaid wages and had been arrested and sentenced to two years of reform through labour. Her family has sunk to rock bottom. Her mother's cancer has returned and her father has had to give up his job in the mine to look after her. Meili is now her family's only lifeline.

Meanwhile, Kongzi's temporary position at Red Flag Primary has come to an end, and he's taken up a permanent post as deputy head of the migrant school Nannan attends. In the evening, he puts on his glasses with an even greater air of authority as he sets about correcting homework. A few hours before he made his fateful visit to the Beautiful Foot Massage Parlour, he went online and read a telegram the Red Guards sent to Chairman Mao after they'd destroyed the Temple of Confucius. They told their leader that they had burned ten thousand ancient books, smashed six thousand engraved stone tablets and a thousand gravestones, and toppled the statue of 'Kong the Second Son – that so-called Teacher of Ten Thousand Generations', so that the radiance of Mao Zedong Thought could shine over the temple grounds once more. Kongzi told Meili that the telegram threw him into such a frenzied rage that he swallowed a full bottle of rice wine, and he has no memory of what happened next, or how he ended up lying on the steps of the massage parlour. The girls in the parlour told Meili that he asked for a 'fast food' service. When they'd finished, he said he didn't have any money on him, so they had no choice but to throw him onto the street. Meili had concealed a hammer in her jacket, and was planning to smash the parlour up, but when she saw the girls in the back room lying asleep on camp beds, she felt sorry for them and changed her mind. She imagined all the days Suya spent on a bed in a similar, sour-smelling room, being treated like a human urinal as one nameless man after another pulled down his trousers and emptied himself into her.

She's had little time to think about her injured hand. When she returned home from the graveyard, she picked up her severed finger and wrapped it in a cloth, telling Kongzi, 'I'll keep it until we go home, then bury it in my parents' garden where I too will be buried one day. A body must enter its grave complete, after all.' After the turn of the year, her spirits lifted, and she felt that at last her run of misery had come to an end. The sight of Kongzi consumed by his work, reading and marking late into the night, has allowed her to recapture the pride she used to feel as the schoolteacher's wife in Kong Village. Although the migrant school is as illegal as the children who attend it, and his salary is miserable, Nannan is now able to study there free of charge. Their lives are back on track. Meili has asked Cha Na to run her children's shop, and has started work as general manager for Hugo Electronics. She no longer allows Tang to hold her hand. While she was in hospital, he visited her every day and warned Kongzi that if he ever dared sleep with a prostitute again, he'd have him arrested. He lent Meili a laptop so that she could surf the internet from her hospital bed, and when he appointed her general manager, he not only gave her half the shares in the company, he set up its bank account in her name. She knows that she can't give him anything in return other than friendship and support.

Tang has rented an office in a smart block near a components warehouse in the centre of town. Since Meili first stepped on the escalator that leads to the first-floor office, her joy has been tinged with anxiety. She is not afraid that the company won't make money. The success of her children's shop has convinced her that her business instincts are good. She has helped to create a website which has attracted great interest from traders in the north, and has researched the latest developments in electronic machinery. Last month, she happened to hear that computers made in China will soon be installed with CD drives that can record as well as play, so she immediately slashed the price of their soon-to-be-defunct drives and managed to get rid of them in one day. Her anxiety stems from insecurity over her peasant background. She often feels like a scruffy partridge that has wheedled its way into a modern chicken pen. She has bought herself many clothes, but is never sure which ones to wear. (Fortunately, when she's in the office, little Heaven curls up so tightly that her belly shrinks to half its size.) She is self-conscious about her appearance, and also her lack of culture. When Tang showed her his extensive collection of CDs and foreign novels, she felt like an ignorant child, and was determined to fill some of the huge gaps in her knowledge. She's bought pirated discs of Beethoven, Puccini, Gershwin and Miles Davis which she listens to through earphones late at night, and is reading her way through translated editions of *Les Misérables*, *A Christmas Carol*, *Light in August* and *A Brief History of Time* which were selling for half price at a government-run bookstore. She feels that there's so much to discover, she has no right to remain ignorant. Every day she tries to increase her vocabulary, but when she comes across text on the internet from Hong Kong or Taiwan which is written in complex characters, she still has to ask her colleagues for help. When everyone has left the office at the end of the day, she remains at her desk flicking through journals and magazines and talking quietly to little Heaven. Since Kongzi begged for forgiveness and vowed on bended knees never to visit a massage parlour again, she has felt that it's now safe for Heaven to be born. She knows Kongzi will be disappointed to discover the baby is a girl, but is confident that as he's in such disgrace, he wouldn't dare attempt to give the baby away. She's told Heaven that it can come out as soon as it wants. Everything is ready.

Their new home is directly opposite the illegal migrant school. It's an ugly tin shack, but at least it's watertight and windproof. In the yard outside is a barren durian tree whose bare branches are hung with damp laundry and bags of washing powder. Nannan found a dusty felt flower on the road the other day and has stuck it on the end of a branch. If it were an osmanthus tree, Meili would almost feel she were back in her parents' house. She has discovered from the red journal that osmanthus was also Suya's favourite flower. The shack and school are surrounded on three sides by abandoned fields fenced with the redundant glass interiors of dismantled televisions. Ten years ago, before the farmers turned to the e-waste business, these were well-irrigated rice fields, but apart from a few scattered plots cultivated with celery or taro, they are now overgrown with wild grasses and morning glories. Heaven Township can be seen to the north, its squat houses dwarfed by ancient trees. The air smells mostly of manure and grass, and the chemical odours are much less pronounced.

The migrant school is in a fertiliser warehouse at the other end of Meili's washing line. The rent is cheap, as the area is low-lying and liable to flood. Last year in the rainy season, waters from Womb Lake flowed through here towards the sea, laden with timber and burnt plastic. Meili hopes that after one more year of hard work, they can move to an apartment in the centre of town, bring her parents to live with them and pay for her mother to be treated in Heaven Hospital. Her cancer has spread, and the rural hospitals are unable to perform the complicated operation she needs. The warehouse is only just large enough to seat the school's fifty pupils. If government inspectors turn up, the children escape through the back door and hide in the fields. During the nationwide clampdown on illegal schools last year, the teachers put the students on a rented bus and drove them into the countryside, giving lessons as they went.

At eight in the morning, the children stroll into the warehouse singing a Hong Kong pop song: '*Neither fragrant like a flower, nor tall like a tree, I'm just a blade of grass that people walk past. Nobody knows it's me . . .*' Meili drops her mobile phone into her bag, looks into the mirror hanging from the durian tree, applies a coat of lipstick, then steps into her kitten-heeled shoes and heads off to work up the road that runs along the river. It's Spring Festival next week, and before the holiday starts, she wants to sell off the company's excess stock of transistors, inductors and resistors. A small factory in Hubei has become an important client. The manager is one of the Wang Suyas with whom she formed an online friendship. This woman always sends cash payment before consignments are dispatched, and has even promised to travel down to Heaven with her five-year-old daughter to pay Meili a visit.

Through the morning mist rising from the river, Meili sees a Bureau of Industry and Commerce van parked further ahead. She turns on her heels, goes to a nearby kiosk and tries to phone the headmaster of the migrant school, Mr Sun, but he's teaching an elementary maths class and has switched off his mobile phone. She phones Kongzi, but he's asleep, so she pulls off her shoes, returns to the school as swiftly as she can and tells Mr Sun to take the children out into the fields and hide them in the irrigation channels. As the children file out, she pushes the school bags, exercise books and lunch boxes into a corner and covers them with a black sheet. Then she goes into the yard and rakes out a pile of plastic granules so that the inspectors assume this is an e-waste warehouse. When Kongzi wakes up, she tells him to join the children in the fields.

Mr Sun reappears in a flustered state. 'Can you take the morning off work today and help us out, Meili? I've ordered a bus. Go to the intersection and flag it down. Here's the driver's business card.'

When Kongzi ushers the children onto the clean bus, he wishes he'd had time to put on his usual suit and tie. The children glance at his mud-splattered shorts and dirty flip-flops, and smirk. He's due to teach a maths class and two literacy classes this morning, but he has no textbooks with him, nor do most of the children.

'Keep going,' Meili tells the driver, pointing the way with her left hand, which she quickly hides in her pocket, embarrassed by the missing finger. 'Just stick to the quiet roads.' Then she looks over her shoulder at the children, saying, 'How about I teach you a song?' The children cheer and clap. 'All right. This one's called "Waking from a Dream". It's the theme tune for a new TV series you might have seen: *I remember you describing Heaven to me, drawing the outline of a house with your finger . . .*' Her phone rings. She presses the answer button. 'Yes, I'm the general manager,' she says. 'Fine. I'll send my assistant to inspect the goods at midday. And remember, we want hard box packaging . . .'

The bus drives on through a string of quiet villages. Poplars, willows and telegraph poles slice through the view outside the window. When a fresh breeze blows into the bus, Meili knows they've left Heaven Township behind. The bus stops at the edge of the next village. Apart from two figures in the distance and the aerials swaying on the roofs, everything is still. A pale blue banner proclaiming NEW TRENDS IN MARRIAGE AND PROCREATION SPREAD THROUGH THE NATION; FLOWERS OF JOY BLOOM IN EVERY HOUSEHOLD hangs from one end of the village to the other. The long empty road makes Meili nervous. She tells the driver to carry on and stop at the crossroads so that if the police turn up, they'll be able to escape.

Kongzi stands at the front of the bus, opens a textbook he's borrowed from a child and says, 'Turn to Lesson 18, please, and let's read out the story at the bottom of the page. Altogether now: "The Raincoat. Late one night, Premier Zhou Enlai was working feverishly by candlelight when suddenly there was a clap of thunder and a heavy rain began to fall. He immediately ordered his maid to take a raincoat to the man guarding the gate. The maid draped the coat over the guard's shoulders and said: 'Premier Zhou asked me to give this to you, and to remind you that one must never stand under a tree during a thunderstorm.' The guard was so moved by the premier's thoughtfulness that he didn't know what to say."' Kongzi returns the textbook to the child and says, 'Right children, make a list of the new vocabulary.'

Two hours later, the bus turns round and heads back to the school. Meili kneels on her seat and says, 'Don't worry, students. We should be back soon, so you won't miss lunch.' Smells of nitric acid from a workshop outside flow in through the open window.

'Auntie Meili, how come you still haven't given birth to your baby?' asks a boy at the front who has a worm-like bogey dangling from his nose. 'Nannan told me it's been inside you for four years.' A yellow-clawed eagle is embroidered on the front pocket of his red coat.

'I'm waiting for the baby to become legal, so that it can get a residence permit,' she says, thinking on her feet. 'Otherwise it will be like you lot, and won't be allowed to attend a proper school.' She's wearing jeans, a red-and-white-striped shirt and gold earrings today. If she had glasses on, she'd look like a teacher of a government primary school.

Lulu is sitting next to Nannan. She raises her unblinking goldfish eyes to Meili and says, 'My dad told me my residence permit is fake. Does that mean I won't be able to go to university in Beijing?'

'What's the point of us studying, Teacher Kong, if none of us will be allowed to go to university?' says a chubby boy with hair neatly parted down the middle.

'I want to be a judge when I grow up, and sentence all the family planning officials to death,' says a small boy at the back wearing a blue jacket with a broken zip.

'Don't worry, students,' Kongzi says. 'Mr Sun has applied for authorisation from the Education Department, so with any luck, our migrant school will soon be legal.'

'Teacher Kong, did Confucius get into as much trouble as us when he set up his own schools?' asks a girl with a ponytail, her small eyes darting behind her overgrown fringe.

'Back then, Confucius was an unofficial teacher, just like me,' Kongzi says with a smile, 'but he wasn't treated like a criminal. Anyone could set up their own school. Things may be very different now, but we mustn't lose heart. Every child deserves an education, whether they're recognised by the state or not. We must assert our rights, or this country will never change.'

'Yes, students, our paths are made as we tread them,' Meili says, rising to her feet. 'We must have the courage to strike out on our own and challenge injustices. On the internet, more and more people are daring to voice criticisms of the One Child Policy. The government is launching campaigns telling young couples that girls are as good as boys – that shows they're aware of the millions of baby girls that have been killed because of their evil policies.'

A girl in a black-and-white-checked jacket gets up and says, 'Teacher Meili, I miss my mummy. She works in Zhuhai. After I speak to her on the phone, my grades always go down.'

'Teacher, why are we peasants?' asks a girl in an orange jacket with a white collar.

'Because we were born in the countryside,' Meili replies. 'And if we're born there, our fate is sealed: the authorities deny us free education, housing, medical care and all the other privileges city dwellers enjoy, and through the household registration system and family planning laws they bind us for ever to the land. But we mustn't despair, students. There are 900 million of us. We make up two-thirds of China's population. We can't be kept down for ever. Look how many millions of peasants have already dared to ignore the laws and move to the cities. We're on the move and no one can stop us. I've heard the police no longer bar peasants from boarding trains to the cities. Soon, pregnant women will be able to walk through the streets without fear of being dragged off for an abortion, and peasants will be able to move to any place they wish. The cages that have imprisoned us for so long will topple to the ground, and we will all be treated as legal citizens.'

'Please, Teacher, what is the countryside like?' asks a boy with a flat nose and thin, sparse hair. He is the youngest child in the school, and the only one who was born in Heaven Township.

'Look, that's the countryside,' the boy next to him says, pointing his dirty finger at the window.

'Do those farmers have residence permits?' asks the flat-nosed boy.

'Probably,' says an older girl behind him. 'It's just us kids born without permission who aren't allowed to have residence permits – we can't even get rural ones.'

A police car overtakes them and screeches to a halt, blocking the road ahead. Two officers step out and climb onto the bus. 'Who's the teacher here?'

'I am,' Meili says, confident that she'll be able to handle the conversation better than Kongzi.

'SARS has broken out in this county,' says one of the officers, whisking a fly from his face. 'Didn't you receive the notification?'

'No,' Meili says, then remembers reading about the disease on the internet. 'Oh, you mean the acute respiratory disease? Yes, of course we were informed. We were told not to go into school, so we've taken the children out on a trip.'

'A strict curfew has been imposed. The instructions were clear.

Return to your school immediately. A team from the World Health Organisation is touring China to make sure we're in a fit state to host the Olympics. If they find out we've got SARS here, it will be a disaster, so no one must wear a face mask.'

'Fine, thank you, officers, we'll let everyone else at Red Flag Primary know,' Meili calls out to them as they return to their car.

'Auntie Meili, I need to go to the toilet,' a little boy says, frowning in discomfort.

The boys at the back laugh. 'He's always asking to go to the toilet in class, Miss! He never stops drinking – that's why. He's always thirsty.'

'Says if he doesn't keep drinking water, he'll die!'

'Be quiet! OK, get out and go behind that tree.' It occurs to Meili that the toilet pit behind the school hasn't been scooped out for months. Back in the village, excrement from the pits was removed regularly, dried and used as fuel, but in Heaven it all goes to waste.

'Why won't the government let us go to their schools?' Nannan asks as the bus sets off again. She's wearing a pink jumper and has her hair scraped back in a tight ponytail. When Kongzi took her to Red Flag Primary on his last day there, she took one look at the orderly rows of desks and bright posters in the classrooms and said she wished she could stay there for the rest of her life.

'After the Education Department grants us authorisation, our school will be just like their ones,' Kongzi replies. 'We'll get ourselves a tall flagpole, a big entrance lobby, flushing toilets and a canteen. Hey, have you at the back finished writing out the vocab?'

'I thought you wanted us to do the sums,' says the naughtiest boy in the class. Kongzi found him smoking in the toilet pit yesterday and gave him a sharp kick in the shins.

'No, I told you to copy the new words from Lesson 17. Rivulet, ocean . . .'

'We'll be back in time for lunch, I promise,' Meili tells a child. 'There'll be rice, vegetables and a soup.' She reaches into her pocket and answers her phone: 'Hi, Cha Na . . . Yes, those Disney DVDs have been selling well. You'd better order some more.'

'Turn over your sheets of paper, everyone,' Kongzi says. 'I'll read out some keywords from the text. Write them down then copy them out ten times. Ready? Illuminate. Green meadows. Serene. Verdant . . .'

Meili stares at the picture of the little girl in pigtails on the cover of the textbook she's holding, then looks outside and sees a large photograph of a missing girl stuck to the side of a passing van. On the van's boot is a notice with a telephone number and the message IF YOU FIND OUR DAUGHTER, WE WILL GIVE YOU ALL OUR SAVINGS AND BELONGINGS. Meili feels a stab of sympathy, and instantly thinks of Waterborn.

'I've seen lots of notices like that recently,' says Kongzi, watching the van speed off into the distance. 'I read in the papers that 200,000 children go missing in China every year, and that very few are ever found.' The eucalyptus trees along both sides of the road bask in the midday sun. The pale green leaves at the top look as soft as babies' hands. Kongzi turns round and shouts: 'Dong Ping! How dare you throw that carton out of the window!'

'But I picked it up outside,' the boy in the blue tracksuit says, kicking his legs about, 'so it belongs out there.'

'Oh, just stay still,' Kongzi says impatiently. 'If Confucius were here, he'd slap your hands with a wooden ruler.'

Boys in the seat behind get up and cheer. 'Hit him, Teacher!' one of them shouts. 'Here, you can use this ping-pong bat!'

'Use my hat!'

'No, whack him with my trainers!'

Meili puts her phone away and says, 'Quieten down. Now, listen, children. Spring Festival is coming up. If your parents haven't decided what to give you yet, tell them to visit my shop. It's called Fangfang Toy Emporium. It's packed with wonderful toys and games. If they bring one of these business cards I'm handing out to you, they'll get a 20 per cent discount . . .'

At the southern outskirts of town, the bus picks up speed and hurtles past lines of shacks with aluminium rain barrels glinting on the tin roofs.

KEYWORDS: *Ming Dynasty theatre, face shape, toffee apple, swaddled, jewel-encrusted, sensitive.*

At the end of the dancing policemen act, Nannan weaves her way back through the crowd of spectators with three bottles of Coca-Cola, and reaches her seat just as the curtains rise again. The instrumental prelude of a Cantonese opera begins to pour from the large loud-speakers flanking the stage. Meili, Kongzi and Nannan are sitting at the back. A group of scruffy workers who've wandered out from their nearby dormitory house in shorts and flip-flops are standing behind them, smoking. Local officials are seated on the front rows, dressed in freshly pressed trousers and short-sleeved shirts. 'We're in the birthplace of Cantonese opera,' Kongzi shouts over the din. 'This theatre is even older than the Confucius Temple and the Town God Temple. It's the perfect place to watch *The Seventh Fairy Delivers her Son to Earth!*'

'Is the opera based on the weaver girl and the cowherd story?' Meili asks, putting her arm around Nannan. She cracks a sunflower seed between her teeth and spits the shell onto her bulge. 'Here,' she says, offering some seeds to Nannan.

'You know I don't like them,' Nannan says, pushing them away.

'But these ones are freshly roasted, just try one – they're delicious,' Meili says, wishing Nannan would overcome her irrational dislike of seeds. The drums are so loud now, she has to raise her voice to be heard.

'Yes, the Seventh Fairy is the weaver girl, the seventh daughter of the Jade Emperor and the Mother of the West. When she fell pregnant with the cowherd's child, her mother was furious and commanded her to return to Heaven. Now that it's born, she has to hand it over to the father.'

Gongs, violins, drums and guitars all sound out at once, drawing the audience's attention to the brightly lit stage, where two men with hoses are filling the air with white smoke in preparation of the fairy's descent to earth.

'Look, there she is!' Nannan cries out, jumping to her feet. A canvas backdrop is lowered, revealing the green landscape of terraced tea plantations beneath a clear blue sky. The sea of heads, hats and paper fans below wave about in anticipation.

A woman in a jewel-encrusted headdress and a long red robe wafts down from the sky with a baby in her arm, singing: '*The Seventh Fairy cradles her swaddled baby son, and looks down at the Nine Regions and weeps, her tears flowing like a river . . .*'

'This is boring,' Nannan moans. 'I much preferred the moon-dancing policemen just now.' This free show has been staged by the Foshan Song and Dance Troupe and the Shenxian County Cantonese Opera Company to celebrate 1 August Army Day. Meili, Kongzi and Nannan arrived at the theatre at five o'clock to make sure they'd get seats.

'Shut up!' Kongzi says, tapping Nannan's leg.

'*My darling son is too young to know the meaning of grief, to know how my heart breaks at the thought of leaving him . . .*' the fairy sings. The cowherd walks onto the stage wearing a headdress decorated with pompoms and tassels, a thick-belted tunic and padded boots. To a melancholy strain from the violins, he twirls around the fairy and takes her in his arms.

'Feel how fast my heart is beating, Kongzi,' Meili says, pressing his hand against her chest. The sunflower seeds on her belly scatter to the floor. 'The baby reminds me of Waterborn. She was no bigger than that when you sold her. I was still producing milk six months after she was gone. My body was yearning for her to come back.'

Kongzi pulls his hand away and takes a swig of Coca-Cola. Nannan sees a classmate in the crowd and waves to her. The sweltering, muggy air smells of cigarette smoke, sweat and sulphur. The open-air Ming

Dynasty theatre is on the north shore of Womb Lake. Its ornate stage resembles the entrance to the Confucius Temple, with a golden roof supported by large red pillars. Lights pointing at the upturned eaves illuminate strange carved beasts glaring at the audience with mouths agape.

'*Forget your sorrow for a moment,*' the cowherd sings to the fairy. '*Let me wipe the hot tears from your face, and hold my son in my arms.*' He takes the baby from the fairy and, gazing down at him, dances about the stage, the drums beating in time with his rhythmic steps.

'That baby's not real,' Nannan says, brushing a mosquito off her arm. 'See, it's not moving at all.'

'*I am a celestial being and you a mere mortal,*' the fairy sings. '*Our love defies the Laws of Heaven. For giving you a male heir, I have been berated and humiliated . . .*' As the fairy bursts into tears on the stage, in the unlit darkness at the back of the theatre, Meili weeps as well. Although she can remain on the earth, she has to live like an escaped convict, searching in vain for a place where she can legally give birth to her child. At least no one has tried to harm the fairy's son. As soon as her own son was born, he was killed and condemned to another reincarnation.

When Meili returns her tear-filled eyes to the stage, suddenly the fairy looks identical to her, and the cowherd to Kongzi.

'*What miseries you've had to endure to produce a child for me!*' the cowherd sings.

'*I have no regrets,*' the fairy sings back to him. '*The hundred days we spent together could vanquish a lifetime of sadness.*'

'*Yes, for one hundred days, we were as happy as two fish in a lake. And now, as I hold my son in my arms, my sorrows melt away . . .*'

'*My dear love, we're not fated to remain together. Now that I have delivered our son to you, I must return to the Celestial Palace. I in the sky and you on the earth, with the Milky Way between us: it won't be easy to meet again . . .*'

Meili pats her belly and whispers, Don't worry, little Heaven, I'll make sure that this incarnation will be successful. The family planning laws won't last much longer. Just wait patiently in my womb a few more years until it's legal for you to come out. And when that time comes, if you still refuse to budge, I'll dig into my tummy button and pull you out with my bare hands! On the stage, the heartbroken fairy circles the cowherd, tossing her head back and flicking her long sleeves in despair. Meili strokes Nannan's ponytail, and feels her tears slowly dry up.

'Why were you crying, Mum?' Nannan asks. 'That baby won't die. I understand Cantonese. The daddy said he'd look after him.'

'I was just thinking about Waterborn,' Meili says, wiping her eyes carefully, trying not to smudge her eyeliner.

'If I died and came back as a boy, you and Daddy would be so happy! I hate myself. I hate being a girl . . .'

'Stop muttering and look at the opera,' Kongzi says impatiently. Nannan leans over Meili and taps her empty Coca-Cola bottle on his head.

'*How sad that you must leave us!*' the cowherd cries. He is stifling in his thick costume, and sweat flies from his face whenever he moves his head. '*My love for you is like a river. Not even the sharpest sword can sever its flow. Farewell, sweet fairy . . .*'

'*My heart is dying, but we mustn't cry. Goodbye, husband, goodbye, child . . .*' Meili watches the fairy step onto a cloud and rise into the blue sky, and feels a part of herself rise to the heavens with her.

By the time they squeeze their way out of the departing crowd, Meili's dress is drenched in sweat. Halfway home, Kongzi takes her hand and says, 'Let's go to a restaurant. My treat.'

'Your treat?' Meili says, taken aback. 'OK then, follow me.' She decides to take them to the Hunan restaurant Tang introduced her to. She loves its homely atmosphere and rich, spicy food.

After Kongzi pours himself a glass of beer, Nannan challenges him to an arm wrestle. She grasps his fist and forces it onto the table. Kongzi retaliates, slamming hers down with greater force. 'Calm down, Kongzi,' Meili says, 'and serve out this steamed pork.'

'I thought you'd given up meat,' Kongzi says.

'I had, but I think I should eat some for the baby's sake. The pickles and raw vegetables I've been living on this week can't have provided much nutrition.' Meili downloaded a vegetarian diet drawn up by a Taiwanese nutritionist, hoping it would help her lose weight.

'I don't like meat, either, Mum,' Nannan whines. 'I want a toffee apple.'

'Why didn't we ever take a photograph of Waterborn?' Meili asks Kongzi. 'Who did she look like?'

'She had my face shape and your features,' Kongzi says. He fumbles in his pockets for his cigarettes, then remembers he's given up, and wraps his hands around his glass of beer instead.

'No, Waterborn was my sister, so she must have looked like me,' says Nannan. 'I remember when you came back after giving her away, Daddy. You said: "Don't be sad, Nannan. From now on, I'll only love you."'

'Nonsense, don't lie: I'd never say such a thing!'

'I heard you say it countless times!' Meili retorts. 'Kongzi, there's something I've never told you before: Waterborn was born with a sixth finger on her left hand. Sister Mao chopped it off in the delivery room.'

'So that's why her hand was bandaged!' Kongzi says. 'You told me Sister Mao accidentally cut her with the forceps.'

'Dad, why did you call me Nannan? It sounds like "boy-boy". My classmates said you chose the name because you wished you'd had a son.'

'No, what I've always wanted is a son and a daughter: one of each.'

'Don't lie to me. You two are always arguing about wanting a son. Now I'm older I understand. It's because of me that those family planning officers killed Happiness and that you gave Waterborn away. The government only allows parents to have one child living with them.'

'That may be the rule, Nannan,' Kongzi says. 'But still, your mother and I are doing our best to make sure you have a little sibling to keep you company once we're gone.'

'If you wanted me to have a sibling, why did you sell Waterborn?' A fly darts off Nannan's hand and settles on the table.

'Don't touch the fly – it's filthy!' Meili says to Kongzi, as he's about to swat it, then she turns to Nannan and says: 'Your father, he – he just wasn't thinking straight that day. He and I are working hard, saving up money so that you can go to university when you're older. Kongzi, I'm still hungry. Order a yellow croaker steamed with salted vegetables.'

'No, you're saving up money to buy little Heaven a residence permit,' Nannan says.

'Yes, that too,' Kongzi says. 'We want our family to have a bright future, Nannan. That's why we came here: to make money and give you a better life . . . A yellow croaker, please, waitress, and . . . mm, let's see, a "chicken of the immortals" as well.' Kongzi closes the menu and pushes it to the centre of the table.

'No, you came here to escape the family planning officers. All my classmates' parents are on the run from them. I understand everything now. If it weren't for me, you wouldn't have left the village. If I hadn't been born, Happiness would be alive today. I hate myself.' Nannan stands up and leaves the table.

'*Mere mortal that I am, I can't join you in the sky. The Heavens weep in sympathy, but are powerless to end my thousand autumns of longing . . .*' Kongzi warbles, then thanks the waitress as she puts another dish onto the table.

'Stop singing, Kongzi,' Meili says. 'Listen, Nannan is growing up. Her body's starting to develop, and she's become very sensitive. We must be careful what we say in front of her. You must stop making her recite the *Three Character Classic* and *Standards for Being a Good Pupil and Child*. You're putting too much pressure on her.' She rests her elbows on the table and rubs her throbbing temples. Last night she took Tang and six members of their staff to the Princess Karaoke Bar to celebrate his birthday, and she had far too much to drink.

'I read Nannan's diary,' Kongzi confesses. 'She wrote that she doesn't have a home to go back to and that she's like a stream flowing to nowhere.'

'The other day she asked me what "despair" means. I said it's when you feel there's no hope.'

'Don't talk to her about matters you don't understand. The Confucian Doctrine of the Mean says that we should neither cling to life nor throw it away, and should avoid extreme emotions of joy and despair. We should learn to be happy with our lot.'

'You just want an easy life. Where's your ambition gone? When my brother's released from the labour camp, I'm going to ask him to come and work for my company.' Meili looks down at her left hand and rubs the shiny scar tissue on the stump of her index finger. The nails of the four remaining fingers are painted with sparkling red varnish.

Kongzi picks up a slice of pork smothered in sticky rice. 'But your brother has no skills. What would he do?'

'I didn't have any skills either, but I still managed to help set up a company and become general manager, didn't I?'

'Yes, but you and he have different personalities,' Kongzi says, pouring himself some more beer. The restaurant is only half full. On the next table a man wearing a wig and a smart grey suit is serving himself and his elegant guest some vintage Five Grain Liquor.

'Did Nannan go to the toilet?' Meili says. 'This toffee apple should be eaten hot.' She looks up at the laminated menu of Hunanese food on the wall: CHILLI-STUFFED PEPPERS, HOT-SOUR DOG MEAT, CRISPY DUCK IN SESAME SAUCE . . . then stares at the goldfish swimming about in a dirty fish tank on the counter, next to a ceramic fortune cat that is continually raising and lowering its left paw.

'How I'd love to eat one of my grandmother's sticky rice cakes right now,' Mother says, gazing into her pocket mirror as she retouches her lipstick, 'or one of those deep-fried sesame twirls she used to make . . . I wasn't always this confident. All those years you made me travel across the country with you, barefoot and pregnant, my personality was crushed. It's only here, in this electronic dump of a town, that I've finally gained a sense of direction. Once Heaven is born, I want to open a chain of shops across the country, then buy ourselves a Foshan apartment and resident permits so that Nannan can go to a government middle school. My parents have no income now. They hired someone to help out on the fields, but the price of fertilisers and seeds has risen so much that they didn't make any profit. The five thousand yuan I sent them this year kept them afloat, but it wasn't enough to cover all my mother's medical bills. Who knows how much more treatment she'll need?'

When they have both eaten their fill, the conversation peters out.

Father cleans his teeth with a toothpick while Mother checks the messages on her phone. The infant spirit watches the fetus shift position inside Mother's womb. Nannan still hasn't returned to the table.

'Where has Nannan gone to?' Mother says. She and Father look over their shoulders at the dark doorway.

'Look, she's over there, by the lake, under the willows . . .' Father says.

'Stop kicking me, little one — a family planning officer might see you!' Mother says, rubbing her belly.

'Don't speak to the fetus like that — you'll frighten it to death,' Father says, wiping his glasses with a paper napkin.

'Fetus? The baby's four and a half years old. By the time it comes out it will be able to recite the *Analects* to you.'

KEYWORDS: *Spring Festival, ghostly figures, firecrackers, Sacred Father of the Sky, stone baby, yellow mud.*

Seeing Meili struggle to stuff dumplings with her maimed hand, Kongzi puts down his chopsticks and offers to take over. The table is already laden with dishes of sliced pork tongue, braised trotters, stir-fried chilli prawns and drunken chicken.

'I wish we still kept ducks, but the Heaven rivers are just too polluted,' Meili says. 'Those birds you reared in our last place tasted foul. Do you remember how wonderful it was back on the sand island when we could eat roast duck every day?'

'Yes, it doesn't feel right not being able to kill our own bird at Spring Festival.'

'Don't say the word "kill" on the eve of Chinese New Year. It'll bring us bad luck. Here, have some of this Five Grain Liquor my assistant gave me. Let's hurry up with these dumplings, or the food will get cold. Nannan, turn down the television and join us at the table.'

'What about that sweet garlic you pickled?' Kongzi says. 'I'd love to try some.'

The room is clouded with cigarette and incense smoke. On a side table, three fat incense sticks are propped up in a bowl of rice, in front of three small paper tombstones on which Kongzi has inscribed the names of his father and his father's parents. Around the bowl are offerings of cigarettes, boiled sweets and king prawns. Nannan ignores Meili and stays on her small bed, smiling and frowning at the televised Spring Festival Gala. She's wearing the red nylon jacket and white scarf Meili bought her yesterday. Nannan had wanted a purple jacket but Meili managed to persuade her, after a heated argument, that red suited her better. On the studio stage, a Han Chinese woman is belting out a love song while girls in Tibetan and Uighur costumes dance around her in a circle. Nannan is only eleven years old, but this morning she got her first period. Meili was sitting in the yard plucking hairs from the pigs' trotters when Nannan rushed out from the toilet pit with blood running down her leg. Meili presumed she'd cut herself, but when she removed her stained skirt and underwear, she discovered she was menstruating. She placed plastic bags and towels over her bed and made her lie down. She told her not to worry, that this is what happens to every girl when they become a woman. But it was no use. Nannan was inconsolable. She burst into tears and said she didn't want to be a woman, and that she hated Meili for making her a girl. Kongzi went out to sweep the yard, came back to make Nannan a cup of brown-sugar tea and then went out again to buy her a hot-water bottle. Before the television gala started this evening, she burst into tears again, saying she wished little Heaven would come out so that she could go away and die. Afraid that Nannan might do something rash, Kongzi has decided to stay in all night. Every couple of hours, Meili gives her a glass of water and a fresh sanitary towel.

Meili looks at the dumplings Kongzi has made. Each one is long and thin, just like him.

'Oh yes, I haven't told you yet,' he says. 'I bumped into the manager of the Hunan restaurant the other day, and we fell into conversation. When I told him my name, he said a guy went to his restaurant some time ago, asking for us. A tall guy, well spoken, with round glasses. Do you think it could have been Weiwei – you know, that man who lost his mother?'

'When did this happen?' Meili asks, her heart pounding, certain that it was her who Weiwei wanted to see.

'Two years ago, just after Spring Festival.'

That was around the time my shop was ransacked by the inspectors, Meili thinks to herself as she drops the stuffed dumplings into a pot of boiling water. And when I had lunch at the Hunan restaurant with

Tang that day, I saw a man who looked just like Weiwei. No wonder my eye kept twitching.

'Daddy, what is happiness?' Nannan asks, after watching a man in a white suit sing 'Your happiness is my joy . . .'

'Happiness is when you forget yourself,' Meili says, watching the dumplings bob to the surface of the boiling water, holding a slotted spoon in mid-air.

'Happiness, my daughter, is you coming back from school with a good mark. It's the nation at peace, our family united.'

'Here, come and have your dumplings, Nannan,' Meili says, spooning some onto a plate for her. 'And I'll pour out some vinegar for you to dip them in.'

'I hate dumplings. Mum, I want to go home.' Nannan leans back against the small headrest. Beside her pillow is an opened packet of rice cakes.

'But this is your home, and your bed,' Kongzi says, pointing to the large collection of dolls lying by her feet. Cha Na has given Nannan almost every doll that's sold in the shop, but Nannan's favourite is still the plastic doll with the red dress that Kongzi gave her many years ago, even though it's old and dirty, and the red paint on its mouth has chipped. To her great sadness, however, she hasn't seen it since they moved into this tin shack.

'No, what I mean is I want to go back to Kong Village,' Nannan says. 'This place doesn't feel like home. I miss Grandma.' On her crumb-strewn quilt is a copy of the school textbook, *Cultivating a Moral Character and Forging a Successful Life*, and a spiral-bound songbook. Since the beginning of winter, Nannan has become moody and withdrawn. In a lunch break last week, she pushed Lulu onto the ground, and since then none of the children in her class will play with her.

'You were only two when we left – how can you miss her?' Meili says, as she and Kongzi stare at the television screen and tuck into the hot dumplings.

'Besides, your home is wherever your parents are, so right now, this is your home,' Kongzi says. He takes a sip of Five Grain Liquor and smiles contentedly. As well as being deputy head of the migrant school, he's also been given a two-year contract to work as a supply teacher at Red Flag Primary, thanks to Tang putting in a word for him with the Education Department.

'I can't remember what Grandma looks like but you told me she was always nice to me,' Nannan says. 'Why didn't you bring any photographs of her, or of our old house? I want to phone Grandma and Grandpa and wish them Happy New Year.'

Nannan still hasn't been told that Kongzi's father has died. As soon as she mentions him, the contented smile vanishes from his face.

Noticing his distress, Meili turns to Nannan and says, 'If you miss them, go and prostrate yourself before the altar over there.'

'Prostrating is feudalistic,' Nannan replies.

On hearing this, Kongzi jumps up from his seat and grabs Nannan by her collar. Meili pushes him away and puts her arms around her, saying, 'She's only eleven! You can't expect her to understand about filial piety!' Kongzi flings his chopsticks on the floor to release his anger, then turns up the volume of the television. A woman in a green police uniform is singing: *'You angel in a white coat, when I came into this world, yours was the first face I saw. You picked me up in your soft hands and wrapped me in a blanket. With this song, I give you my thanks . . .'* On the street outside, a string of firecrackers explodes.

Nannan snuggles into Meili's embrace and says, 'Can I have some Coca-Cola, Mum?'

'You shouldn't drink cold fluids in your condition.'

'But I want some.'

'All right. Kongzi, fetch her a bottle from the fridge.' They've had the fridge for only two days, but it's already packed with food. Meili's placed her severed index finger on the bottom shelf and Kongzi has hidden their cash in the freezer compartment.

'There's not so much blood coming out now, is there?' Meili whispers to Nannan. 'Tomorrow there'll be even less.'

'You said this will happen to me every month from now on. Well, I don't want to go to school any more. How come it hasn't happened to the other girls in my class?'

'I'm sure it has, they just haven't told you. Before I fell pregnant, I had them too every month, but I could still carry on as usual and wear pretty dresses and nice shoes. You'll see, it's no big deal, I promise . . .' Meili looks down and sees that Nannan has fallen asleep on her shoulder.

'I'm completely stuffed,' Meili says, as the Spring Festival Gala draws to an end. She rests her maimed hand on her belly and feels Heaven's heart thud below her skin.

'Me too,' Kongzi says, taking off his glasses. During the traditional comedy double act a few minutes ago, he roared with laughter. After a long silence he says: 'At Spring Festival people go to the temples to give offerings to the Jade Emperor, the Bodhisattva of Mercy and the God of Prosperity, but no one thinks of giving offerings to Confucius.'

'It won't be long now. I read on the internet that the government said that Confucian thought still has a lot to teach us. They're even publishing books explaining how we can use his philosophy in our daily lives.'

'That was just for the Olympic bid. The Party wanted to give the impression that China still has a strong traditional culture, even though thirty years ago it ripped Confucianism to shreds and replaced it with the foreign creed of Marxism-Leninism.'

'Who cares what the Party's motives are? Confucius is officially back in favour, so perhaps little Heaven will be less afraid to come out now . . . You must stop buying Nannan sweets all the time. She already has two rotten molars. Poor girl. It is strange she's started menstruating so young. I didn't have my first period until I was fourteen.'

'It must be the chemicals in the water.'

'Let's leave her to sleep and go for a walk.' Meili tucks a quilt around Nannan then changes into her favourite pale blue jeans. She saw a picture on the internet the other day of a woman in stonewashed jeans and a white shirt knotted at the waist, and liked it so much she used it as the background for her computer screen . . . Won't you come out, little one? she whispers, glancing down at her bulge. Tomorrow, you'll have been inside me for five years. Give your poor mother a break.

Since the migrant school broke up for the Spring Festival holiday, everything has quietened down. In the moonlight, the concrete yard, durian tree and aluminium warehouse appear as scratched and blurred as an old black-and-white photograph. Along the road that follows the river, ghostly figures drift through the darkness with lanterns swinging from their hands. Light from a street stall reveals a woman carrying vegetables on a shoulder pole and a man wearing a large baby's head made out of papier mâché. Fireworks explode in the sky, and the outline of distant buildings becomes briefly visible. When Kongzi and Meili reach the end of the road, they follow the crowds to the bustling forecourt of the Town God Temple. Pink and red paper lanterns hang down from the surrounding trees and the temple's pointed eaves. Food stalls decorated with festive red banners are selling steamed buns, sesame rolls and peach-shaped rice cakes. The stalls nearer the entrance sell imitation paper money and bundles of incense sticks.

'Are those two supposed to be married?' Meili asks, pointing at the painting on the entrance door of a beautiful girl and a white-bearded old man.

Kongzi has no idea who those two deities are supposed to be. He takes Meili's hand and leads her inside, saying, 'Let's light some incense and ask Sacred Father of the Sky to grant us good fortune in the new year.'

'Our accountant comes to this temple every day after work. She said she's going to pray to the God of Wealth on the fourth day of Spring Festival, the Golden Flower Mother on the sixth, then she'll visit the Shrine of the King of Medicine and the Temple of Lady Wang. She never stops . . .'

The temple's interior is brightly lit with candles, and thick smoke is rising from an incense column that is taller than Meili. People rush past, carrying roasted swine heads, fried fish and deep-fried chickens to place on the altars of their chosen deities.

Kongzi points to the small statue of the Golden Flower Mother, who is flanked by the God of Grain and the God of Landowners, and says, 'Look, there she is. The Goddess of Fertility and Childbirth. You should pray to her, and beg for a safe delivery.'

327

'Little Heaven is afraid of coming out into this hell – there's nothing the goddess can do about it,' Meili says, crossing her arms protectively over her belly. 'It's too crowded in here. All those firecrackers going off outside frighten me. What if this place caught fire? Let's go home. We can come back in the morning.'

'Don't say the word "hell" on New Year's Day!' Kongzi says angrily.

'Well, I'm leaving – are you coming with me or not?' Meili says, her heart racing as images of the burning nightclub flash through her mind.

'Firecrackers can't cause fires. Listen, we've come all this way, we might as well light some incense while we're here.' Then looking up and seeing the terror in Meili's eyes, he changes his mind. 'All right, all right, let's go then.' They turn round and head for the door, two downcast figures pushing their way through the excited crowd.

Later that night, Meili is woken by another thunderous burst of fire-crackers. She wishes she could seal the window and door to keep the noise out. Without peace and quiet, her thoughts cannot rise to the surface. During these past nine years, the only chances she's had for quiet reflection have been when she's woken in the middle of the night. At such moments, she's able to think quietly about her born and still unborn children, and about all the various Meilis: the woman, the mother, the young girl who loved to laugh and sing, the labour camp inmate, the escapee, the businesswoman. She lay awake like this, her mind deep in thought, on the terrible summer night when she felt herself sink to the riverbed with Happiness's corpse; the autumn nights after Waterborn was taken from her; those muggy nights after Weiwei left and his tortoiseshell glasses lay under her pillow; and this winter night on which she's learned that Weiwei came all the way to Heaven to look for her. Although the first day of the new year has not yet dawned, she already senses that the past has been brushed away and the new is being ushered in. She knows that if Kongzi is unfaithful to her one more time, she will leave him and make a new life for herself with Tang. To be fair, as far as she knows, Kongzi has only strayed once, and that was only after they arrived in Heaven. Compared to the many men they've come across during their travels – powerful cadres who are always surrounded by attractive young women, scruffy peasants who sleep with hair-salon girls several times a week – he's relatively upright and loyal. Still, when she's with him, she is never more than a pregnant wife. With Tang, she is a complete person. Over these nine years, she has transformed herself from a shy peasant girl to a strong capable woman. She could never return to those muddle-headed days when Kongzi would boss her about imperiously and she'd obey without question. She thinks of the child that has lived inside her now for five years, untroubled by thoughts of what to eat or drink or fears of what the future might hold. She doesn't dare contemplate what calamities might have befallen her had they not found refuge in Heaven Township, how many times her belly might have been carved open. The Communist Party has no humanity. For them, killing a baby is no different from swatting a fly. She doesn't know when Heaven will finally decide to emerge, but when it does, she will gently lower the drawbridge of her castle and let it travel down her dark road into this hell . . . Yes, it's time you came out and tested your mettle, little one, she says silently. I can't protect you for ever. But don't worry, I won't force you out before you're ready. My womb may have been assaulted and abused, but it's still intact, and allows us to coexist with a certain grace. She smiles to herself, proud of being both a woman and a mother: two identities seamlessly fused into one body. Tomorrow she will sign up for prenatal yoga classes with a teacher trained in Hong Kong. She's heard the exercises help soften the pelvic bones, making childbirth no more painful than laying an egg. She will also go to Foshan to prostrate before the huge Golden Flower Mother statue, and ask her to protect little Heaven and grant it a safe birth. She knows that once the infant spirit leaves her womb, she and Heaven will have to end their symbiotic existence. She understands as well that although life is a long and arduous trek, with sufficient effort, a degree of comfort can be achieved at the end. Little Heaven will come into the world as an illegal outcast who has no right to an education or a job. Meili will try to earn as much money as she can to create a small path to happiness for this unauthorised child, even though she is still uncertain in which direction happiness lies.

In the darkness, she sees Weiwei walk towards her. She goes up to him and says, I can't leave Kongzi. We have raised a daughter together, we share the same bed and the same pillow. I can't abandon this path. And besides, you are not in my heart . . . After daring to imagine this scene, she feels her cheeks grow hot and a sense of calm descend on her. She gives Kongzi a prod and whispers, 'Wake up! It's nearly six. It's unlucky not to watch the sun rise on the first day of the new year.'

'Yes, pour me another one,' Kongzi mumbles under his breath, then rolls over and falls back to sleep. Meili gazes at the Kongzi who ten years ago she worshipped and admired, and feels a pang of regret. The past seems to her as drained of colour as wilting lotuses on the bottom of a dry lake.

'Let's open that bottle of French claret my client sent me,' she says, getting out of bed and slipping into her flip-flops. The jubilant crowds, fireworks and singers in red dresses flashing across the silent television screen fill the dark room with festive light.

'I dreamed of our son just now,' says Kongzi. 'He looked just like me when I was a child. He was standing on a street corner, flicking marbles into a hoop, like I used to do. What fun I had as a kid. I'd come home at the end of the day beaming with pride, my pockets stuffed with the *Romance of the Three Kingdoms* cards I'd won playing snap with my friends. I wonder where I put my card collection. I'm sure Heaven would like to play with them when he's older.'

'Huh! Little Heaven won't be interested in those cards. You'll have to buy him a computer game, or an electronic doll, if he's a girl.' Meili occasionally raises the possibility that Heaven might be a girl, to test Kongzi's reaction.

'If you let Heaven stay inside you any longer, he might very well change into a girl. Or he might calcify like that stone baby – the one I read about in the papers, that a ninety-year-old woman gave birth to after carrying him in her belly for sixty years.' Kongzi takes a sip of the French claret and frowns. 'Ugh! So sickly sweet. Chinese liquor has much more of a kick to it.'

'I haven't tried to stop Heaven from coming out. She's probably afraid to leave the womb because she knows you don't want a daughter. If she is a girl, you must promise to be kind to her.'

Kongzi remains silent. Relieved by his subdued reaction, Meili continues. 'Someone from my family should go to Nuwa Cave tomorrow to pray for a speedy delivery. I wish I could give my parents a call. My brother's due to be released from the camp this month. And I'd like to make sure they received the money I sent last month. I transferred it to my uncle's account – the one who lives in the county town. When I phoned him last month he promised me he'd give it to my father.' From this phone call, Meili found out that after her brother was jailed, her father travelled to the county town to complain about the miscarriage of justice. When the authorities refused to listen to him, he stood outside the County Party Committee Hall singing the 'Internationale', with a big placard around his neck that said FREE MY SON. Within ten minutes, the police arrived, and he was bundled into their van and locked up for a week. She pictures her parents' home, the three-room house with the tiled roof and the osmanthus tree in the garden, and remembers how her grandmother would sit with her beneath the tree, brushing her hair and telling her stories of Goddess Nuwa, the deity with the face of a woman and the body of a snake who created the world and humankind. She told her that near Nuwa Mountain is a magic lake that can catch the moon's reflection, and that at the beginning of time, this lake pulled Nuwa down from Heaven. After months of walking around the lake by herself, Nuwa felt lonely, so she sat on the shore, scooped up clods of yellow mud, moulded them into human beings and gave them life. After a while, she became frustrated by her slow progress, so she pressed a rope down into a pool of mud then flicked it from side to side, and when the flecks of mud fell onto the ground they were transformed into a mass of people.

'Turn up the volume,' Father says, 'they're talking about share prices. I bought some stocks in Shenzhen TV the other day . . .'

Mother holds the remote control and stares blankly at the screen. A spiral of incense smoke rises to the ceiling and escapes into the night through a hole in the roof. The infant spirit leaves the house and slips off towards Womb Lake, continuing its journey back in time.

KEYWORDS: *red dust, white uniforms, Golden Flower Mother, Guinness World Record, red envelope, missing person's case.*

After a sudden downpour, a procession escorting the Town God Temple's statue of Golden Flower Mother advances along the wet street. Large crowds pack the pavements. For a moment, all Meili and Nannan can see is a loudspeaker attached to a moving van, from which a high-pitched voice is singing: '*China has entered a new age. The nation is secure and the people live in peace. Dreams harboured for a hundred years are coming true. Happiness will be ours for ever . . .*' Behind the van comes a group of workers in red baseball hats, holding a cloth banner that says HEAVEN TOWNSHIP PLASTIC GRANULATION WORKSHOP VALUES EDUCATION AND DONATES GENEROUSLY TO LOCAL SCHOOLS. Meili scans the faces and sees Pang, her wiry plaits sticking out from under her hat, and Ah-Fei, who's wearing thick make-up to conceal her vitiligo. She waves to them as they pass; they smile and wave back. Meili wonders how Old Shao is doing. Cha Na told her that he contracted pneumonia and has returned to his village in Jiangxi. Drummers appear, followed by schoolgirls in white uniforms, twirling spears and swords. Three boys march on either side, holding placards advertising a supplier of second-hand military electronic components. The humid air dampens the thud of the drums. Meili looks down and sees Nannan gaze admiringly at the schoolgirls' white dresses, white socks and white shoes.

'I wish I could follow them and see them dance,' says Nannan. She's wearing a yellow long-sleeved T-shirt over a red blouse, and jeans tucked into gumboots. The downpour has washed most of the smell of burnt plastic from the air, leaving only a faint tang of sulphur. Meili watches women dance past in low-rise jeans and white shirts, exposing their navels as they raise their arms in the air.

'It's too crowded now,' Meili says, tugging Nannan back from the street. 'Let's have some dim sum, then I'll take you to Foshan to see the largest Golden Flower Mother statue in the county.' She's heard that Golden Flower Mother's powers are at their height today, and that all requests made to her will be fulfilled. She's already withdrawn five hundred yuan from the cash machine to give as an offering. She and Nannan retreat into the entrance of a clothes boutique behind. The aluminium roll-up door suspended above bulges in the middle like the belly of a pregnant woman. Meili has agreed to have dim sum with Tang today, and to prevent him making any advances, she's bringing Nannan along, even though she knows that the infant spirit inside her belly is her best protector. For the last six months, not even Kongzi has dared touch her.

They have to wait half an hour before the statue of the Golden Flower Mother finally appears. She's inside a small wooden pavilion, carried on poles by four men in black mandarin hats and embroidered silk suits. Red powder has been rubbed onto her cheeks, and a plastic baby boy has been placed in her arms. She looks much more alive than she did last night in the Town God Temple. A few stragglers trail behind, smoking cigarettes and stopping now and then for a chat. Then dancing lions appear, jumping to the beat of more loud drums. The spectators on the pavements stare at them blankly as though they were watching a television show.

Tang has chosen a table at the back of the restaurant. Meili's heart races as she makes her way towards him. She smiles stiffly and grips Nannan by the hand.

'*Kung hei fat choi*, Tang!' she says, unbuttoning a tailored white down jacket she bought recently to replace the thick, cumbersome one she's had since she left Kong Village.

'So you speak Cantonese now!' Tang says with a smile. 'This town certainly has changed you!' His hair is wet and his face flushed with excitement.

'Sorry we're late. The streets are packed. The e-waste company I used to work for made its workers parade through the streets with banners bragging that it supports education. What a joke! All its workers are illegal migrants. If the company's so public-minded, why doesn't it start by demanding the legalisation of migrant schools?'

'Trying to change government policies is a waste of time. All we can do is find ways to work around them. Look, both you and I are registered as peasants, but I managed to study abroad and you're now a general manager. So we haven't done too badly, have we?'

'You used to go on about wanting to campaign for a cleaner environment, better education and health care, an end to corrupt bureaucracy, but it looks like this town has changed you as well.' Although Nannan is present, Meili is still on guard, and is trying to keep the conversation polite and formal.

Tang orders a few dishes then asks Nannan what she'd like, but Nannan just shrugs her shoulders and sticks her thumb in her mouth. 'A custard tart should be enough for her,' Meili says. She wants to check her lipstick, but is too embarrassed to take out her pocket mirror.

'I've ordered your favourites, Meili: fish slice congee and taro croquettes,' Tang says. 'You're looking more and more like your mother these days, Nannan. You have the same beautiful phoenix eyes.'

Meili is self-conscious about the unsightly brown pregnancy patches on her face and her swollen ankles, and feels that Tang's constant flattery is undeserved. But it pleases her, nonetheless, and is one of the reasons she still likes to flick through glossy fashion magazines.

'A local businessman was planning to let off a one-kilometre string of firecrackers today, hoping he'd break a Guinness World Record,' Tang says, 'but he had to call it off because of the rain.'

'That must have cost him a fortune to make!' Meili says, glancing at the lipstick imprint on her white cup.

'He owns three e-waste companies, and makes a million yuan a year,' Tang says. 'So, tell me, how is your husband liking his new post at Red Flag Primary?'

'Very much. He's so grateful to you for helping him get it. He would've joined us today, but he's meeting the headmaster to ask if he can persuade the local authorities to let him restore the Confucius Temple.'

'To think he's the seventy-sixth generation descendant of the great sage! Well, he's not let his ancestor down! The Education Department was very impressed when I told them he was a direct descendant – that's why they gave him the two-year contract. Yes, it would be great if the Confucius Temple were brought back to life. In the Cultural Revolution it was used as the headquarters of the Municipal Road Department, but since then it's fallen into ruin.'

'Which god do you believe in, Tang?' Meili asks, noticing a picture of the God of Longevity above a potted bamboo tree by the doorway.

'None of the gods you see in the temples, that's for sure. I used to believe in another kind of god, but less so since I've returned to China.'

'I want to visit the Golden Flower Mother statue in Foshan and ask her whether she thinks I should give birth.'

'The baby's been inside you for five years now, hasn't it? It's time you let it come out. You've already broken the Guinness World Record for the longest pregnancy!'

'No, there's a ninety-year-old woman in this province who was pregnant for sixty years. Anyway, it's not as if I haven't tried to give birth to my child. I went into labour and pushed as hard as I could, but she simply refused to come out.' It's always a relief to Meili when she's able to refer to Heaven as a girl.

'I've heard that a strict new director has been assigned to the County Family Planning Association, so Heaven Township might not be a safe refuge for pregnant women for much longer.'

'As long as I stay near that filthy lake, I should be fine. Officers don't like having to trudge through all the rubbish down there, and even when they do come, I always manage to send them packing. Did you realise that the lake is the same shape as the womb of an eight-month-pregnant woman? To think that I moved to Heaven so that I wouldn't have any more babies! I was assured the air here kills human sperm. But the first night I arrived, I got myself knocked up!'

'Ha! You make me laugh! You're so fresh and natural.'

'Coarse and uneducated, that's what you mean!' It suddenly occurs to Meili that although she can now buy almost anything she wants, her new wealth has given her no meaningful satisfaction. During the years they were too poor to eat out at restaurants, she, Kongzi and Nannan were much closer. They appreciated each other's company more and had time to savour the simple pleasures their meagre income allowed.

'No, you're strong, invulnerable. You haven't allowed any of the ordeals you've suffered to dent your spirit.'

'Well, I've had to develop a thick skin. Can you imagine the looks I've got, walking around town with this belly for five years? Family planning officers stop me in the street and tell me my bulge is bad for the town's image and that I should hurry up and give birth. But I tell them that little Heaven is living in my womb, eating my food. She's no burden to the state. She has a right to stay inside me as long as she likes. I told them that as soon as the government repeals the One Child Policy, I'll give birth to her. As soon as it promises that every child born in China will be given full legal citizenship, I'll tug her out with my own hands, if I have to.'

'You should be more careful. Haven't you read that in other parts of this county, women are dragged off the streets and given forced abortions? It happens every day.'

'I know. It happened to me too, once. The doctors injected poisons into my fetus hoping to kill it, but when he came out, he was still alive, so they strangled him to death right in front of me.'

'That's not an abortion,' Tang says, his face turning pale. 'That's cold-blooded murder! I had no idea you'd experienced such a terrible thing.' He rubs his chin and casts a concerned glance at Nannan.

'So, you see, until this government decides to stop killing children, Heaven is safer staying where she is. As her mother, all I can do is provide her with a warm home. Unless someone comes to demolish it and force her out, she can stay inside as long as she likes. She and I will just take each day as it comes.' She sprinkles some white pepper onto her congee and swallows a small spoonful.

'You're like the heroine of a Victorian novel, rebelling against oppressive convention in the pursuit of happiness! Yes, you have that air of stubborn defiance. Have you read Charlotte Brontë?'

Meili shakes her head, blushing at her ignorance. 'No, I haven't read that book. But do lend it to me, if you have a copy.'

Knowing she was coming out to lunch today, she had her white shirt washed at the New China Hotel, whose laundry is sent to Foshan and returns smelling not of burnt plastic but of roses and osmanthus. Despite her apprehension, she'd been looking forward to this meal, but now she wishes she could grab Nannan's hand and leave.

Instead, she serves Nannan some deep-fried squid and says, 'When I get to the office tomorrow, I'd like to go through last year's accounts and cross off all the bad creditors from our client list. What do you think?'

'Let's not talk about tomorrow. So, tell me, how did you see in the new year?'

'We just ate dumplings and watched the televised gala. Spring Festival was so much more fun when I was a child. At the crack of dawn, we'd walk round the village visiting our neighbours and they'd fill our pockets with boiled sweets.' She remembers tying a brand-new scarf around her head before setting off one new year's morning. The inky smell of the stiff cotton swirled around her all day.

'Have you taken any festive photographs with the digital camera I gave you for Christmas?' Tang asks.

'Not yet. I want the first photograph I take with it to be of little Heaven.' Meili notices Nannan drawing faces on her fingers with a ballpoint pen, and nudges her to stop.

'The camera will be out of date by then! Now we've entered the digital age, electronic products will become obsolete within months. Everyone wants to upgrade to larger screens, bigger hard drives, more memory, so e-waste is growing at an alarming rate. Did you know that Heaven received five times more e-waste this year than it did in the last three?' Seeing Meili's eyes begin to glaze over, he draws a red envelope from his pocket and hands it to Nannan. 'This is my New Year gift to you,' he says. 'There's some Lucky Money inside!'

Nannan opens the envelope. 'Wow! A hundred yuan! Cool! Lulu's mother only gave me one yuan. Thank you, Uncle Tang. Can I buy a plane ticket with it?'

337

Meili is embarrassed that she's only put ten yuan in the red envelope for little Hong, so she excuses herself, sneaks off to the toilet and replaces it with a hundred-yuan note.

As Tang answers his phone on their way out of the restaurant, Meili takes the opportunity to say a brief goodbye, then hails a tricycle rickshaw which agrees to take them to Foshan for forty yuan. 'What's the point of going to see the Golden Flower Mother statue?' Nannan says grumpily. 'You think she can phone your baby and tell it to come out?' Some of the faces on her fingers are crying, some are laughing.

'Oh, shut up, and stop grumbling.' During the last few months, Meili has tried to be tolerant of Nannan's bad moods, but occasionally her patience snaps.

'Mum, can you put a red spot here between my eyebrows,' Nannan says as they approach the centre of Foshan half an hour later. 'It's called a "Lucky Dot". I read it can protect you from demons.'

'Wait a second, we're here now. Let's get off!' Meili takes out her lipstick as she climbs off the rickshaw, but just as she's about to dab some between Nannan's eyebrows, a large crowd pushes them forward, so she quickly drops the lipstick back into her bag.

They pass a line of food stalls with greasy mutton skewers smoking on charcoal braziers and semi-raw pigs' trotters simmering in woks, then enter the large temple and are hit by clouds of incense smoke. Meili sits down, and nearly retches from the oily stench and feels Heaven's stomach turn as well.

'Mum, is it true that Heaven won't come out unless I disappear?' Nannan asks, as Meili rises to her feet.

'No, no, what made you think that?' she answers, looking distractedly at the visitors jostling past.

'You said you're afraid of giving birth to Heaven because you've already got me.'

'No, it has nothing to do with you,' Meili replies, taking Nannan's hand and following the crowd into the main hall. When they reach the Golden Buddha, Meili prostrates before it like everyone else, but forgets what she should be praying for. On her left, she hears a young man pray for success in his university entrance exams, and on her right a taxi driver pray for a prolonged rainy season that will bring him more customers. Her mind clearing at last, she clasps her hands together, looks up at the Buddha and prays that her mother's cancer will be cured, that her brother will be released safely from the labour camp, and that Waterborn is not begging on a street corner but is being looked after by a nice family who give her good meals three times a day . . . The loud murmur of voices around her makes her lose her train of thought. She gets up, takes Nannan's hand and goes to look for the statue of the Golden Flower Mother.

'I don't want to see the statue,' Nannan moans. 'It's too crowded in here.'

'Wait for me over there, then,' Meili says, 'and don't go wandering off this time.' As Nannan heads to the entrance, Meili proceeds to the less crowded area at the back where the huge Golden Flower Mother statue stands. She lights an incense stick, goes down onto her knees, and performs repeated prostrations, turning to the side when she reaches the ground so as not to squash her belly. Then she sits down with legs crossed, takes a deep breath, and looks up at the Golden Flower Mother's scratched and childlike face. For a moment, she thinks she sees the painted mouth curl into a smile. Then she blacks out and sees a young girl walking down a dusty path on a sunny day, a hemp sack of autumn leaves swung over her shoulder. She can hear the girl laugh, but can't see her mouth moving. The girl has just crossed a dense forest, and her face is as scratched as the rosy cheeks of the Golden Flower Mother statue . . . Suddenly the stump of Meili's left index finger begins to throb like a sightless eye searching for light. Little Heaven stretches out and rams its head into Meili's lungs, then turns in a circle and punches her navel. After taking a few minutes to compose her thoughts, Meili addresses the statue, saying, 'Golden Flower Mother, your powerful eyes have seen the Five Lakes and Four Seas. I am a simple woman from Nuwa County, and am pregnant for the fourth time. Although the government doesn't want my child to be born, and my child doesn't want to be born either, as her mother, I think I should give birth to her, for a mother must not only conceive children, but also release them into the world and watch them grow.

So I entreat you, Golden Flower Mother, tell me how this will end? What does the future hold for me? Good fortune or calamity?'

The Golden Flower Mother statue looks down impassively and says: 'Praise be to Amitabha, Buddha of Infinite Light. Life is a sea of suffering – but turn your head and there is the shore. In time, you will cross the sea, transcend the cycle of birth and death, and reach the other side. But before then, you must deliver the child within you and allow it to accumulate its own karma.'

'Oh, Mother, I am an outcast. Wherever I go, people tell me this isn't my home. If I give birth to my child in a place where I don't belong, will she be destined to a life of misfortune?'

'You have journeyed through the red dust of illusion, and through suffering have achieved profound wisdom. But your sorrows cannot compare to mine: I have never known the happiness of marriage, the joy of motherhood. At fourteen years old I was snatched from my parents and declared the Goddess of Childbirth. After that, no man dared come near me. At the age of forty, still alone and unloved, I threw myself into Womb Lake and drowned. My bones are still lying on its muddy bed.'

'I never knew you drowned yourself! So you really have seen through the red dust! I thought about killing myself too, a few years ago, but realised that if I went ahead with it, I'd be killing my unborn child as well. But, Sacred Mother, things aren't so bad for you, surely? You must have amassed great karma through your work in this temple, helping bring new life into the world. And look at all the delicious offerings you've been given: chicken, wine, sesame oil, rice—'

'No, my life hasn't improved since I died. Don't be fooled by my sumptuous robes and ornate flower headdress. Since the foundation of the Communist Dynasty, I've been persecuted mercilessly. When Emperor Mao advocated later marriages and fewer children, I was dragged from the altar and locked in a storeroom, deprived of daylight. Then Emperor Deng brought in his One Child Policy, and my temple was converted into a grain depot. Now, two decades later, it's been demolished to make way for the Heaven Township Stock Exchange.'

'Well, at least you're in a nice place now.'

'You think it's nice having to squeeze myself into this dark corner, cheek by jowl with all the other gods, and rely on the offerings of strangers? I was only brought here on condition that I consent to be an ambassador for the wretched family planning policies. Have you read the slogan they've hung above my head, threatening women with forced sterilisations and abortions? What a wicked disgrace! For thousands of years I was the Goddess of Fertility and Childbirth, but this depraved dynasty has turned me into the Goddess of Fewer Births. Before long I'll be the Goddess of Abortions! I tell you, death is much worse than life.'

'Cheer up, Sacred Mother. You've been fortunate enough to experience the dual realms of life and death. Your blessings have protected countless expectant mothers and granted their babies safe births.' Sensing Heaven begin to writhe and kick again, Meili straightens her back to give it more room to move.

'Yes, I've tried to comfort myself with that thought. Although I've never been loved by a man, I've watched baby girls being born into the world, grow into women and then prostrate themselves before me, asking me to grant their own babies a safe birth. Seeing the joy that each new life brings to a family consoles my sad heart, but can't fill the void of having no children of my own.'

'Being a mother in this country isn't easy, Sacred Goddess. If you returned to the world and fell pregnant, you'd soon start thinking you were better off dead.'

'Mortals may feel no shame slaughtering innocent life, but if they force us gods to endorse their barbaric acts, what will become of the world? Praise be to Amitabha, Buddha of Infinite Light. I have said enough. It's time for you to go.'

Just as Meili is about to get up and leave, she pauses and says to the statue, 'Just one more thing, Sacred Mother. Six months after we fled our village, my second baby, Happiness, was murdered by family planning officers. But the baby's spirit has followed me ever since, and has reincarnated a second and now a third time. It's a peculiar spirit that seems to have no gender or fixed identity. Sometimes it seems to be lodged inside the fetus in my belly, sometimes it seems to be looking down at me from above. Sometimes I feel it's looking back at me from a future realm, as though my present is its past. And on some occasions, I've felt that it exists in a completely separate realm that somehow overlaps with ours. But when I try to put these feelings into words, my mind spins and time seems to go into reverse. This third reincarnation has been the strangest. I should confess to you now: the baby has been inside me for five years. I've read of a woman whose pregnancy lasted sixty years, but when she finally gave birth, the baby was dead and as hard as stone. I can't bear to think that I'll never hold this child in my arms. Please help me, Sacred Mother.'

'The infant spirit will follow you until it achieves successful reincarnation. If it can't reincarnate before you die, it will return to your place of birth upon your death and reunite with your soul. Remember, the universe is in perpetual flux, changing constantly from yin to yang and from yang to yin, from being into non-being, then back again. If, through the cycle of deaths and reincarnations, you accept the flux and do not oppose it, eventually you will achieve a state of perfect peace and happiness . . .'

A crowd of pregnant women has gathered behind Meili, waiting to light their incense sticks before the Golden Flower Mother statue. Wiping tears from her eyes, Meili rises to her feet and kicks her numb legs about until the feeling returns. She pushes her way through the crowd, but when she reaches the entrance, there is no sign of Nannan. She remembers that Nannan has one hundred yuan on her, and presumes she's gone to buy something to eat. She walks out onto the front steps and scans the food stalls below.

Her mobile phone beeps. Tang has sent her a text: Through your beautiful dark eyes I saw straight into your heart. A smile hovers around her mouth. The thought that her physical appearance is appreciated lightens her mood. From her fake Louis Vuitton handbag she takes out her pocket mirror and retouches her lipstick. The red looks too garish in the daylight, so she presses a handkerchief to her lips to soften the effect. Against the lipstick, her teeth gleam like ivory. Her eyes are still red from crying. She wishes she'd brought her kohl with her and could draw a dark line along the lashes ending in an upward flick . . . The Golden Flower Mother has never experienced love or affection, Meili thinks to herself. I too have endured many hardships, but at least I have a husband and a daughter. Happiness is within reach. Now that Golden Flower Mother has bestowed her blessing, I will ask Kongzi to consult his almanac and select an auspicious date for Heaven's birth. Do you hear that, little one? Next time I come to this temple, I'll bring a jacket for the pretend baby in Golden Flower Mother's arms, and she'll make sure that you're born quickly and safely and that our family will at last be complete.

Wondering whether Nannan has gone to the toilet, Meili goes back into the temple to look for one. On her way, she sees a canister of fortune sticks, and leans down, selects two and tosses them onto the ground. They both land painted side up. Knowing this augurs bad luck, she picks up the sticks and throws them down again. This time they both land the other side up: calamity. Beginning to panic, she goes back to the entrance to look for Nannan. As she studies the faces of every girl in sight, she is suddenly hit by the horrifying thought that Nannan may have been abducted. With a sick feeling of dread in her stomach, she widens her scrutiny to include a man's leather jacket, a boy's woollen jumper, a woman's cropped hair and large earrings. Spotting a red collar peeking out over an orange sweater, she shouts, 'Nannan! Where are you going? Nannan!' The girl turns round, but it isn't her.

She phones Kongzi and tells him to leave his meeting and come at once, then she goes to scour the surrounding streets. After the heavy rainfall, the whole of Foshan appears to have turned dark green. Beneath a line of distant trees, motorbikes in waterproof covers stand parked like forest creatures waiting in ambush. Again she returns to search the temple, then comes out once more and sweeps through the crowded streets, her head darting from left to right like a mother eagle in anxious flight. She questions every hawker outside the temple, asking each one if they've seen a girl of Nannan's description, but they all say no.

Kongzi and Tang turn up and help with the search, but by duskfall there's still no sign of her. At last, they decide to report her disappearance to the police. When they leave the station an hour later, Meili is in despair. She staggers down the steps, her tear-soaked hair hanging over her face, with Kongzi and Tang supporting her on either side. Clenching her maimed left hand, she turns to Kongzi and says, 'Think, think – which other friends might she have gone to?'

'Her only friend now is Lulu. I've phoned Cha Na six times, but she says they haven't seen Nannan all day.'

'The police refuse to help us,' Meili moans. 'What if she got onto a long-distance bus? Three buses leave Foshan every hour.'

'But she hasn't any money to buy a ticket,' Kongzi says, loosening his tie.

'She was given a hundred yuan today for Spring Festival. Oh God, I must sit down . . .' Her belly tight and aching, she places a hand on the concrete step and gently lowers herself onto it. The coconut tree on the other side of the road stabs the upper air like a green umbrella.

'I'll phone my mother tomorrow to see if she's made her way there,' Kongzi says, sitting down beside her and struggling to stay calm.

'Does Nannan know her address?' Tang asks.

'Yes, she's posted four letters to her. I made her address the envelopes herself. Last week she sent her a copy of the photograph I took of her class in front of the Ming theatre.'

'Well, let's check the long-distance bus station, then,' Tang says. 'Did you read about the child-trafficking gang that was busted in Guangzhou last week? The men hung around train stations, tricked young girls into boarding their vans, then sold them to brothels in neighbouring cities.'

'The police said they won't open a case on Nannan until she's been missing for a month,' Kongzi says, his anger rising again. 'But by that time, she might have been carted off to a nightclub a thousand kilometres away, or sold as a wife to a peasant in some mountainous backwater. Well, I'm not budging from here. I'll stay on these steps until the police agree to help find her.'

Tang's phone rings. 'Thanks for returning my call, Director Wu,' he says. 'Yes, it's my friend's daughter . . . Eleven years old . . . We've just spoken to them – I'm outside the station right now. I asked if we could see Sergeant Zhang, but they wouldn't let us. I know he's a good friend of your brother's, so I was wondering if you could give him a call and persuade him to open a missing person's case and send out a search party . . . Wonderful. Thank you so much.' Tang hangs up and says, 'That's promising! Sergeant Zhang is second in command at that station. I'll go and get us something to drink. You two wait here.'

'I'll wait here, but Kongzi – you go to the bus station,' Meili says, placing her mobile phone on her lap, yearning for it to ring with news. She still can't accept that Nannan has disappeared, that this is really happening to her. Apart from her four-week absence, she and Nannan have never spent a day apart . . . If I lose Nannan, it will be like losing an arm, she says to herself. No, it will be worse than that, much worse. *If I lose her, I will die.* As this thought sinks in, she almost passes out, then her head begins to throb as she remembers the sound of Nannan wailing as a baby. When Nannan was three months old, she cried inconsolably for two days. Meili couldn't work out what the problem was. At last, her neighbour Fang came round, checked Nannan's ears, mouth and bottom, then lifted the folds of her neck and discovered that they'd become raw and infected from drops of breast milk that had collected inside.

Tang returns with bottles of Coca-Cola, but Meili doesn't want any. She remembers her father giving her a bottle for Spring Festival one year, and not wanting to be so selfish as to drink it all herself, she fed half of it to Nannan in small spoonfuls. Nannan was only five months old at the time, and ended up with severe diarrhoea.

'Go on, have a sip,' says Tang, kneeling down beside her. 'Don't cry, Meili. I'm sure Nannan's just wandered off to play by herself and will turn up at home this evening. I have noticed that the papers have been full of stories about missing children recently, though. Last week, I read that the police stopped a coach travelling from Guangxi Province and discovered twenty-eight baby girls in the boot, tied up in black plastic bags. They were all under three months old. The police suspected they were going to be sold to restaurants in Foshan. One of the poor babies had suffocated to death.'

'Nannan is eleven years old – no restaurant would want to make soup out of her. It's far more likely that she's been abducted and sold to a brothel. Will you search all the nightclubs round here? She wouldn't dare take a bus to another city. Since I was caught in Wuhan, she's known how dangerous it is for peasants to enter cities and large towns.'

'Yes, it is dangerous. Did you read about that young migrant called Sun Zhigang? He had a college education, a respectable job. He was stopped by the police on the streets of Guangzhou, taken to a Custody and Repatriation Centre for not having the right documents, and ended up being beaten to death. It's all over the internet.'

'She's too young to be locked up in a custody centre. Oh God, why is it that as soon as we leave the polluted backwaters, something terrible happens? Are we migrants forbidden to breathe clean air?' She stares across the road at the long red wall and the blue sky above that appear to be pressed against each other as uncomfortably as two lovers who've fallen out of love.

KEYWORDS: *murky water, skeleton, crumbling balcony, Womb Lake, CD drive, fountain, faintly visible.*

On the afternoon of the fifth day of Nannan's disappearance, Kongzi waits at Heaven Township Long-Distance Bus Station to check the last bus from Guangzhou, then sets off for Womb Lake down a rubbish-strewn path lined with willows, his long thin shadow trailing behind him. When someone approaches, he runs up to them, lifts a photograph of Nannan and says, 'Comrade, have you seen this girl? She was wearing an orange jumper with a red collar. Her hair was in a ponytail, and she had a red Lucky Dot here, between her eyebrows . . .' When he senses they're not registering what he's saying, he repeats his words louder and more insistently. But the elderly residents he approaches don't understand his accent. Most of the migrant workers shake their heads, and tell him that dozens of children go missing in Heaven each month, and he should give up hope of finding her. Before returning home, Kongzi always walks round the lake, as he's afraid that Happiness's ghost might have dragged Nannan into it. Last night he did see a girl standing in the water, but when he ran towards her she disappeared. He remembers how, aged about ten months old, Nannan used to like hiding in a cardboard box in her bedroom, and as soon as he found her, she'd burst into peals of laughter and crawl away at top speed. On the first night they spent on the boat, she ran to the edge of the deck, stepped into thin air and plunged into the river. If he hadn't heard the splash, she would have drowned. By the time he shone his torch on the water, all he could see was a small tuft of her hair. A year later, when she was leaning overboard shaking water from

347

her hair, she fell into the river again, but this time was able to grab hold of the side of the boat and clamber back onto the deck all by herself.

Kongzi leaves the path and walks towards the lake over a stretch of broken printers. The sky is not yet black. On the left is a Qing Dynasty stone house with carved lintels and eaves, whose front half has toppled into the lake. Migrants occupying the back half have hung their laundry out to dry on the crumbling balcony. On a small stone jetty that juts out from the house, ducks are pecking at leftover scraps. The dark red water below smells of dung and rotten fish. Kongzi stares at the ducks and thinks of the birds he used to keep in the cage on the side of their boat. The rooster that each dawn would shake the dew from its wings, peer at the river and let out a piercing yodel became chicken stew the night of Nannan's third birthday. Its meat tasted of fresh sweetcorn. But the ducks that feed on Heaven's chemical waste taste of sulphur, and their stomachs are filled with plastic screws and nylon string. To his right is a swathe of rubbish which the lake's tide has pushed up into a mound. As he begins to climb, his eyes fall on the wooden skeleton of an overturned boat. He goes over, squats down, rubs the soft wood and thinks about their old boat. In the early days, he had no idea how to look after it. The first two times it leaked, he had to pay a fellow boatman to mend the cracks. Then, in spring, when the sun was warm but the river still cold, he decided to buy some tung oil and try to seal the exposed wood himself. While he lacquered the decks, Nannan kept him company, lacquering her doll, her shoes and her pillow. He gets up and examines the vessel more closely. My God, he whispers. This is our boat, Meili! You don't believe me? Look. Ten steps from bow to stern. The length of our boat exactly. If I dig through this timber, I'm sure I'll find the cabin in which we slept and raised our child. Now that Nannan has gone, the government won't dare charge us any fines. Let's leave Heaven Township and sail home. Phone your mother and tell her we'll be there soon . . .

When he finally reaches the shore, he stares out at the lake's maroon surface and says, Nannan, your daddy loves you. If you come back, I promise I'll never get angry with you again or make you recite Tang poems or the *Analects*. Then glancing down he sees, to his amazement, Nannan's plastic doll, its blue eyes staring up at him through the murky water, its flesh-coloured limbs only faintly visible beneath.

Don't pick it up, he hears Meili say to him. It's not Nannan's doll. Her one had a red dress.

The chemicals in the water would have dissolved the dress long ago.

But, don't you remember – she lost the doll when we moved into the shack, not out here by the lake.

It could have fallen into a channel and been swept down by the current. The rivers flowing out of the lake are choked with refuse, so it's not surprising that it should end up floating by the shore.

You sound like a professional corpse fisher! Listen, Kongzi. That doll is called a Barbie Doll. My shop sells hundreds of them. There are probably more Barbie Dolls in this world than there are real people. You can find them scattered over every rubbish dump in this town. It's filthy. Just leave it where it is.

Kongzi reaches into the water and fishes out the doll by its leg. When he sees that the red paint on its mouth is unchipped, he flings the doll onto the mound behind.

After he returns to the path, a girl who looks about three years older than Nannan calls out, 'Would you like to buy a CD drive? We've got Sony and Samsung.' She's standing at the end of a road that leads to the market. Kongzi knows that round the corner is a shop that sells sugar cane, dried tangerine peel and ground ginger.

He walks up to her, takes the leaflet she offers him, then passes her the photograph of Nannan and says, 'Have you seen this girl? She has a large burn scar on her left foot.'

'No, I haven't seen her, but I have a dress like that.' The last light of the sun is reflected in her dark eyes. The small shed behind her is surrounded by stacks of computer drives.

'Have you worn it recently?' asks Kongzi, remembering someone telling him he'd seen Nannan near the lake a couple of days ago. He catches a chemical smell as sweet as osmanthus drifting from the trees or from the crushed components on the ground. His mind turns to

Meili, who for the first four days after Nannan's disappearance wandered through Foshan holding a missing-person placard. When she returned to the shack in the evening, she'd slump onto the bed and chant: 'She has two rotten molars and a burn scar on her left foot . . . She likes milk and sweets . . . When I took her to the baby clinic for her first jabs, she soiled her trousers and I had to wash her in the fountain outside . . . When she was learning to walk, she'd struggle up onto her feet hugging her big toy rabbit, take three steps, then topple to the ground, still holding her toy tightly in her arms . . .' But last night, Meili didn't return home.

He wonders what he will do after he phones his parents again tomorrow and is told once more that Nannan hasn't turned up. A shiver runs down his spine. She hasn't gone back to Kong Village, she hasn't drowned herself in the lake, so she must have been kidnapped and sold to a peasant in the mountains. He often reads about the police rescuing abducted women who've been sold to men in the remote countryside. But Nannan is only eleven – too young to be anyone's wife. She must have been sold into the sex trade, then. The papers often report on police efforts to crack prostitution rings. Yesterday he read about three teachers who pimped their pupils to corrupt officials, personally escorting the teenage girls to the officials' private homes.

As always after the sun sinks out of view, the sky becomes bathed in reflected light, the lake turns gold and the town shimmers like burnished glass. When they lived in the metal hut on stilts, Nannan would come to this part of the lake, wade in up to her knees and fling things in the water. She flung Kongzi's straw hat in here, a thermos mug she'd burnt her lips on, a satchel with a broken strap, a pair of shoes that pinched her toes and a battery-operated car that wouldn't stop beeping. She threw almost everything she disliked into the water, as she felt the water was connected to her unhappy past.

Kongzi turns back and heads for their shack on the outskirts, which since Nannan's disappearance feels to him more like a coffin than a home. He feels that he has nothing left now but the wounds on his body. He wishes he could dig a knife into his hand, so that for a moment he could forget his torment. As he walks along, he can remember carrying Nannan to her cot when she was a baby, the sound of her breathing contentedly into his neck, the feeling of her saliva dampening the collar of his shirt. He'd hold her close to his chest, patting her softly on the back until he was certain she was asleep, but as soon as he leaned over the cot to put her down, she'd pat his back with her little hand to let him know she was still awake. He remembers how, when they were living on the boat, Nannan would often shake him awake in the middle of the night and shout, 'Stop making that horrible noise!' and he'd quickly roll onto his side because Meili had told him he snores like a pig when he's on his back. What haunts Kongzi most of all is Nannan's unfulfilled yearning for Kong Village. He'd presumed that since she was only two when they left, she'd soon forget it. But nine years later, she still had vivid memories not only of his mother, but of the date tree in the yard and the snow that fell in winter. She said the snowflakes were black when they fell from the sky but turned white when they settled on the ground. He'd given her his word that they'd return to the village as soon as Heaven was born. Some memories can't be blown away: they force their way back, flying against the wind, and hover stubbornly around the mind. But all his memories feel empty now. If Nannan doesn't return, not even little Heaven will be able to fill the void she's left. He feels guilty about selling Waterborn, and the pain it caused the family. Meili was so distraught, she ran away from home, and Nannan cried for weeks afterwards, begging him to bring Waterborn back. This is his punishment. For giving away a child he didn't want, he has lost the child he loves. Why do people who leave their native soil always suffer a miserable fate?

Kongzi's phone rings.

'I've found Meili,' Tang tells him. For the last five days, Tang has searched every Custody and Repatriation Centre in the province, and has posted missing-person notices on hundreds of websites. When Meili didn't come home last night, Kongzi asked Tang to look for her as well.

'Take her back to our shack,' Kongzi replies. 'I'm on my way there myself. It's too dark to see anything now . . .'

The news wakens Kongzi from his daze. At least Meili has been found. Yesterday, she said she couldn't bear to stay inside their shack another second because she could feel Nannan's breath flowing from every object in the room. On the phone just now, Tang said he was going to take Meili to hospital as she seemed disturbed and confused. He'd found her sitting on a pavement, smashing a rock against the locked entrance of a sauna house. He said she was in such a bad way that if she passed Nannan in the street now, she probably wouldn't recognise her.

As he proceeds through the dark, Kongzi flares his nostrils like a dog, trying desperately to sniff out the scent of his daughter from the confusion of toxic vapours. The smell he remembers most vividly is the musky scent of Nannan's neck. Unlike the acrid chemical stench of Heaven's air, this scent was earthy and natural and made him think of the soil, the seeds and the water that lie beneath the thick layers of electronic waste.

In the sombre dark before dawn, Kongzi holds his torch in one hand and supports Meili with the other as they walk to the far edge of town along a channel choked with waste. This used to be a free-flowing river. The tethering posts once used by ferry boats can still be seen along the banks. The stone path is thickly littered with discarded rubbish. A few green fronds poke out from between smashed printer cartridges and scraps of burnt fibreglass, signalling the arrival of spring. Last night, Meili said she must give birth on a boat because if Heaven were to be born on the land it would share the same sad fate as Happiness. Before they left, she placed a pair of scissors inside the plastic bag that contains baby clothes, towels and muslin cloths and the digital camera she's been saving for this day.

'If we go any further we'll reach the sea,' Kongzi says. The large sack swung over his shoulder is stuffed with pillows, blankets and plastic sheets. A passage he read from Nannan's diary last night flashes into his mind: 'Daddy slept with a prostitute. I pulled the quilt over my head and cried. After Mummy ran off in a temper, Daddy gave me ten yuan and told me to go and buy him some cigarettes. The horrible beast! I can never love him again . . .'

'No, the sea's still far away, beyond that distant line of trees,' Meili says. 'But look down there, Kongzi! It's our boat! It must be. I can hear the ducks quacking. I can even smell their rotten eggs.' The truth is, Meili can't see the sea. The sky is still too dark, and besides, the unfinished buildings in the mid-distance block out most of the view.

Rejected scrap from the workshops of Heaven is brought to this stretch of the river and incinerated on the banks, as it's considered far enough away from the township's residential area. The camphor and coconut trees along the side of the path are coated in a black ash, and emit a smell that reminds Kongzi of burnt gunpowder. He looks down at the wreck Meili is pointing to, and remembers coming across their boat somewhere else, but can't remember where.

'Are you sure you've gone into labour?' he asks.

'Yes, my belly is definitely tightening,' Meili replies. 'Very soon, we'll be able to meet little Heaven. Let's go down and climb onto our boat. It may not be sturdy enough to take us out to sea, but at least it can shelter me while I give birth to our child. The boat is on the water, and the water is moving. No family planning officers would dare come to this wretched place. I will give birth to Heaven, for the sake of our lost Happiness. Weiwei couldn't find his mother. We can't find Nannan. This is what fate has decreed. But after one child disappears, another will arrive. Oh, Golden Flower Mother, I haven't exceeded my quota. My only child will be a legal citizen, and will be granted a residence permit when we return home. So I beg you, make sure that it arrives safely into the world today.'

Kongzi helps Meili descend the garbage-strewn bank and tells her to sit down while he gets the boat ready. The wreck is half in the water and half out, its bow resting on water reeds and a heap of mobile-phone batteries. The planks wobble and creak as he steps aboard. He climbs carefully into the cabin, spreads the plastic sheets over the deck and lays out the pillows and blankets. Then he treads onto a pile of crushed transformers on the bank, pulls a tarpaulin off a mound of ash and wedges it under the bow to stabilise the deck. 'It's ready now,' he says. Meili steps aboard and crawls into the cabin. She pulls off her trousers, lies down on the blankets, places a pillow between her thighs and stares out at the dark blue sky. 'When it gets a little lighter, I'll be able to see straight up into Heaven,' she says with a smile. 'Will you shift the boat round a little, Kongzi, so that the baby will come out facing north, towards its rightful place of birth? All that's missing now is the date tree in the yard.'

'The stern is rotten. If I try to move it, the whole boat will fall apart.' Kongzi's face is perspiring heavily and his legs are caked in mud and ash. He closes his eyes and sees another page from Nannan's diary: 'I have felt happiness a few times, but it has always been tinged with sadness. My parents think I'm just a naughty child. I don't think much of myself either. Mum hates me. I hate Dad – I wish I wasn't his daughter . . .'

'Do you remember the first day we spent on this boat?' Meili says, kicking off her sandals and brushing the flies from her face.

'Yes, you felt so seasick that night, you vomited all over yourself, and Nannan vomited in her sleep.'

'The first time I stepped aboard, I fell flat on my back.' Meili rubs the rotting plank beneath her and remembers Nannan kneeling down in the cabin and using the stern deck as a table on which to draw pictures or write stories. 'That night, you said that now that we had our own boat, I could give birth to a whole brood of little Kongs. Well, it's time for this one to be born. I drank two bottles of castor oil yesterday to induce labour, so whether Heaven wants to or not, it's coming out today. Look, my belly's contracting again.'

'I didn't ask for a brood. All I wanted was for you to be able to give birth safely to little Happiness.' Kongzi tramples over broken memory cards to remove some rotten planks from the stern. The floating detritus covering the river is perfectly still. Only a few small patches of water are visible.

'The contractions are getting stronger. Can you find something to wedge under my back?' Meili turns onto her side and moves her legs about, trying to find a comfortable position. The two metal rings of the scissor handles poke out from the plastic bag beside her. 'I can feel the head pressing against my cervix. I must start pushing.' Remembering the yoga she learned in the prenatal classes, she breathes deeply into the base of her lungs and exhales softly through pursed lips. Sweat seeps from her skin. She unbuttons her white shirt, gets onto her hands and knees and lets out a strange gravelly moan: '*Oh, Mother, Mother . . .*' Kongzi has never heard such a noise before. It sounds like a funeral lament flowing out from the depths of her womb.

'Oh, Mother, Mother . . . *Silkworms that produce silk in spring die before summer arrives. A candle's flame extinguishes when the wick shrivels to ash. Pear blossoms are washed to the ground by rain, and form rivers of tears. Oh, Mother, you have moved into the darkness and left me in the light. Death lies between us. You stand on the Bridge of Helplessness and stare out into the emptiness beyond . . .*'

'Why are you singing a funeral song? Aren't there any birth songs you could sing?' Kongzi says. He sits down on a dusty patch of grass further up the bank and takes out his phone to check the time.

'The songs give me strength,' Meili shouts, panting loudly. '*Oh, Mother . . . !*' Her rippling howl makes the wreck, the water and the riverbed shake. '*You toiled so hard, caring for your children, with never a thought for yourself.* . . . Happiness, Waterborn, Heaven: you can come out now! Don't be afraid. I will protect you, and make sure none of you go missing. Once you're born, we can all sail home. Help me push, Kongzi. Let's get all these little Kongs out of me. *Oh, Mother, you have vanished now, never to return. How I wish I could follow you into the Dark Realm, and care for you as a dutiful daughter should . . .*'

Kongzi crouches outside the cabin and stares at the black hole between Meili's legs. Flies crawling over her pale thighs kick their hind legs and take flight.

'Keep your voice down,' Kongzi says, 'someone might hear you.' He has left his glasses in the shack, so his vision is blurred. He turns and squints at the mounds of rubbish behind him, unwilling to return his gaze to the black hole that for ten years gave him so much pleasure.

'Don't worry, Kongzi. All the discarded machines around here are foreign. They can't understand what I'm saying.' Meili's sweat has soaked her hair and her shirt. A faint scent of diesel moves through the air, reminding her of their years on the boat, and of the rape and fire she never dared tell Kongzi about . . . '*Mother, you tread the path towards the Yellow Springs. Whose shoulder can I cry on now? . . . How could you leave me alone? Hold my hand again, I beg you . . .*' Tears stream down Meili's face. As another wave of pain comes over her, she tugs at her hair with her right hand and shoves her maimed left hand into her vagina. Immediately, the stump of her index finger sends images to her brain, giving her an interior view of the mysterious dark channel that she has never visited before. She moves her hand deeper inside and sees on the wet and creased walls the marks left by male intrusions. She spots the fungal infections and Confucian quotes left by Kongzi, the fingerprints of the nightclub boss, Weiwei's departing silhouette, and various clots of her thoughts and memories. Then the stump sees Tang, which puzzles Meili as he's never entered this place. The only moment of intimacy they shared was when she took him and some colleagues to the Princess Karaoke Bar to celebrate his birthday, and he persuaded her, after much pleading, to sing some funeral laments and Anita Mui songs. If little Heaven hadn't kicked her so hard, she would have gone on singing for hours, not from a sense of gratitude, but because of the intense joy it gave her. She'd experienced moments of happiness before: on the honeymoon train journey to Beijing, for example, when she lay on the upper bunk chewing preserved plums and marvelled at the unfamiliar landscape unfolding outside, or when Nannan waddled across the yard as a toddler bringing her a bamboo stool to sit on, or when Waterborn lay asleep in her arms and she watched her mouth spread into an angelic dimpled smile as breast milk dripped onto her cheeks. Meili laughed with joy on every one of these occasions, but not with the same abandon as she did in the Princess Karaoke Bar. That night, after their colleagues had left, she held Tang's hand, closed her eyes and sang about times past and future with such a sense of release that she lost herself. When she woke up later, Tang was fast asleep with his head on her lap.

Her hand continues up through this fleshy corridor that is owned and governed by men, and approaches the entrance of the Communist Party's residence. It occurs to her that, nine years ago, she would never have dared bang on this state-owned gate. She feels brave enough to bang on it now, but doesn't know if she dares enter. Trespassing government property is a crime. She pauses to think things through. Only the Party can decide which child can be born and which child must die, but as long as she pays the necessary fine, little Heaven will be allowed to live. The Party will have its money, and she will have her child. Surely that is just the kind of win-win situation that Premier Jiang Zemin has been advocating? With her legs parted like splayed duck wings, she wipes the flies from her wet face and says, 'No one is here to register the birth, so we must take our fate into our own hands, Kongzi!' Without waiting for him to reply, she pounds on the fleshy gate. 'Mummy has come to collect you, my child.' With the four fingers of her hand she pushes through the cervix, pierces the amniotic sac, gropes around and finds a foot. 'One life departs and another arrives! You're coming out now. Enough prevarication! There's nothing to be afraid of . . .' Meili pulls and pulls but the baby refuses to budge. Bursting into tears of frustration, she cries, 'Please, help me out, little one. I've done as much as I can.' She rips off her white shirt and shouts, 'Kongzi, take off my bra! I'm sweltering.' Then she pushes one more time and collapses in agony, her splayed legs shaking.

'If it won't come out, let me phone 999 and pay for you to have a Caesarean,' Kongzi says. 'The police will certify that Nannan has gone missing, so Heaven will be our only child, and his birth will be legal.' He looks down nervously at the black mounds of burnt plastic by his feet, then stares at the bulbous interiors of televisions discarded on the opposite bank.

'Shut up, Kongzi! The police were clear: missing isn't the same as dead. We'll have to wait ten years before we can apply for a death certificate. That bag! Open it. Take the string and tie back my hair. Oh God, the pain is unbearable! Don't grasp my flesh so tightly, little one . . .'

As she pushes again with all her strength, her contorted face turns scarlet and milk spurts from her nipples. The crumbling wreck rocks from side to side. With her eyes squeezed shut, she wails: '*Darling child, I call out to you from my sleep . . . Dearest Mother, I repeat your name, and kneel before you filled with remorse . . .*' The lament fills every part of her body then bursts into the air. A rancid, yeasty smell starts to escape from her. After another intense push, blood drips out from her vagina onto the damp deck, forming blossom-like stains, then gushes out with greater force. 'Little Heaven, come down to earth now,' Meili cries. 'Mummy's waiting for you . . .' She thrusts her left hand inside again, grabs hold of a leg and, with one final tug, rips the child from her womb and lets it flop down onto the deck.

Desperate for a first glimpse of her child, she cranes her neck down between her legs and sees it lying in a pool of blood, its body as green and shiny as an apple, its eyes and mouth wide open. Kongzi steps aboard again and hurriedly opens its legs. He hears another plank crack underfoot. 'My God, you shook this boat about so much, it's falling apart,' he says. He lifts the umbilical cord still connecting Meili to their child. 'Look how long it is! Where shall I cut it?' Meili points to a place in the middle. He takes the scissors from the bag, severs the cord and ties a tight knot.

'My hands and feet are numb,' Meili says, the colour draining from her face. 'Everything is going black. Can you see me? I'm standing at the wheel now, the wind blowing through my dress and through the clouds in the sky . . . Tear off some toilet paper, Kongzi, and wipe me clean. I'm sorry that our child is a girl. But how sweet she smells. Just like osmanthus.'

'But Heaven's a little boy, can't you see? The pain must have disturbed your mind. Anyway, we knew years ago from the scan that he was a boy. Look, feel here, between his legs. You think he could have changed sex in the womb? Poor child, I don't think he realises he's born yet.' Kongzi leans down and picks his son up in his arms. 'So, my life has not been in vain. We have produced a seventy-seventh generation male descendant of Confucius. I give my solemn pledge that I will earn enough money to ensure he has a birth certificate inscribed with the name Kong Heaven.'

'But why is he so green?' Meili says. 'He looks like one of those green aliens in the computer games . . . Ah, look over there, Kongzi! What a beautiful dawn! White infant spirits are falling from the sky, like beans scattered by Goddess Nuwa, but as soon as they touch the earth they vanish.'

'White beans – do you mean snowflakes? Your mind's playing tricks on you. It can't be snowing. Today is March the 9th, the first day of spring. Yes, I can see the sun is about to come up.'

Water begins to lap over Meili's legs. Her white toes rise above the surface like lotuses on a green lake. 'He still hasn't cried yet,' she says. 'Carry him up onto the field so that the sun can shine on his face.'

Meili isn't smiling any more. The wreck has completely disintegrated, and she's lying in the water, her long black hair extending behind her like a boat. Slowly, her body sinks below the surface, and her hair sinks too and wriggles about her face like a shoal of fish.

As Mother's body descends towards the riverbed, the infant spirit breaks free and begins to retrace its long journey backwards through three incarnations, travelling upstream along the many rivers and waterways towards its final place of rest.

Holding his child close to his chest, Kongzi climbs the bank and heads out into a grey expanse of waste that seems to stretch to the horizon. He treads across corroded circuit boards that poke up from the ground like excavated tiles, across graphic cards stripped of their memory chips, and over the copper and silver shells of mobile phones. He crunches over Intel microchips and bullet-shaped audio connectors, then, his legs shaking from exhaustion, he struggles up a hill of stripped scanner motherboards and lifts the motionless child up to the first light of dawn.